Fiona Harris and Mike McLeish are a talented husband-and-wife writing and performing team. They have carved out impressive and unique careers in the arts, both as individuals and as a creative duo.

Fiona has written and co-written fifteen books, for both children and adults. Her extensive work in prime-time TV includes sketch comedy shows like *Flipside, Skithouse* and *Comedy Inc.*, as well as marquee television dramas like *The Beautiful Lie, Tangle* and *Offspring*.

Mike has worked in mainstage musicals – including *Keating! The Musical, Shane Warne the Musical, Georgy Girl: The Seekers Musical* and *Beautiful: The Carole King Musical* – and television, in shows such as *Utopia, Mustangs, Wentworth* and *The Time of Our Lives*.

In 2019, Mike and Fiona released their internationally award-winning comedy web series *The Drop Off*, which to date has won a dozen international 'Best Web Series' awards. Channel 9 screened a telemovie version of the show in 2021.

THE
PICK-UP

FIONA HARRIS &
MIKE McLEISH

echo

PUBLISHING

An imprint of Bonnier Books UK
Level 45, World Square,
680 George Street
Sydney NSW 2000
www.echopublishing.com.au

Bonnier Books UK
4th Floor, Victoria House,
Bloomsbury Square
London WC1B 4DA
www.bonnierbooks.co.uk

Echo Publishing acknowledges the traditional custodians of Country
throughout Australia. We recognise their continuing connection to land,
sea and waters. We pay our respects to Elders past and present.

This is a work of fiction. Names, characters, businesses, places, events,
locales and incidents are either the products of the author's imagination
or used in a fictitious manner. Any resemblance to actual persons,
living or dead, actual events is purely coincidental.

First published 2021
This edition published 2024

Printed and bound in Australia by Pegasus Media and Logistics

The paper in this book is FSC® certified.
FSC® promotes environmentally responsible,
socially beneficial and economically viable
management of the world's forests.

Page design and typesetting by Shaun Jury
Cover design and illustration: Design by Committee

A catalogue entry for this book is available from the
National Library of Australia

ISBN: 9781760688028 (paperback)
ISBN: 9781760687090 (ebook)

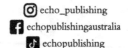

echo_publishing
echopublishingaustralia
echopublishing

*For Miranda, whose endless support and love for us
and the arts has galvanised our creative resolve
over and over and over again. We love you.*

'Wait, what?'

'I said, they're gone!'

'They can't be *gone*. Where would they go?' Megan looked panicked. 'Maybe they're just hiding somewhere?'

'The girls have searched the whole camp.' My voice sounded shaky. 'They ... are ... gone.'

I was trying desperately to stay on point, but another part of my brain was still reeling over my second shock of the night.

'Shit!' All the colour drained out of Sam's face as he ran his hands through his hair.

Megan took a step forward. 'Are you sure? They're probably just ...'

'I told you!' I roared. 'Are you listening to me, or are you still too wrapped up in ...?'

'Hey, hey, come on, guys,' Dave said, stepping forward. 'We're not going to get anywhere by attacking each other.'

'Shut up, Dave!' I snapped. 'You don't know what I saw when —'

'Don't!' Megan glared at me before her face crumpled. 'Jesus, this is all my fault.'

'It's *our* fault!' I hissed. 'I'm to blame, too!'

'Come on!' Sam stood up. 'We have to find them.'

Dave nodded, then looked back at me. 'And we have to tell the others,' he said.

A strange feeling of calm washed over me. 'No. We're not telling anyone. Not yet.'

Chapter One
Lizzie

Seven weeks earlier...

'Who's that?'

'She's familiar,' Sam said, handing us our coffees.

'She's babelicious,' Megan added.

I agreed with both sentiments. In fact, the first time I laid eyes on Rania Jalali, I thought that Meghan Markle had mistaken our school for a crisis centre.

We all stared at the gorgeous woman creating a stir at Baytree Primary on this warm February morning. Excited Grade Six girls (and some equally excited parents) zeroed in on the mystery woman, acting like ... well, like paparazzi with Meghan Markle.

Huge sunglasses covered the upper half of her face, but even so, it was clear that this woman was exquisitely beautiful. The kind of beautiful you don't expect to see in real life, let alone a school playground. Her burnt-orange wrap dress highlighted toned legs and slim brown arms, and long, freshly tonged dark hair bounced around her shoulders. A tiny boy, with equally thick dark hair and dressed in the Baytree uniform of navy-blue shorts and light-blue polo top, hid behind her impossibly long legs. He was staring at a phone and seemed oblivious to the hysteria caused by his mother's presence.

'Maybe she's one of those YouTubers who talks to kids

about following your influencer dreams,' Sam suggested, joining us on the bench.

'Maybe.' Megan's smooth brow creased. 'But Penny didn't mention anything. I would've put it in the newsletter.'

Sam and I shared a look. Ever since her official coronation as 'Best School Mum and Community Member', my best friend Megan prided herself on being across *everything* that happened at Baytree Primary. Prior to that, she wouldn't have been able to pick her son's teacher out of a line-up.

But Megan Wylie had won the admiration and respect of the entire community after masterminding the school Christmas concert two years ago. Since then, her involvement with Baytree Primary had significantly increased. She was now in charge of compiling the weekly newsletter (rebranded *The Baytree Buzz*) and was on the committee for the Grade Five/Six Camp, which she would also be attending. Sam and I found this gobsmacking for two reasons:

1. Oscar was in Grade Four, so Megan had no parental obligation to be involved.
2. Megan wasn't the camping type. Her idea of roughing it was staying in a three-star hotel.

There were few things I could think of that would be worse than spending three days with forty pre-pubescent children who didn't belong to me, but Megan seemed excited by the prospect.

'Hey, did you see?'

Dave's voice was even more manic than usual. The forty-something dad was jogging on the spot at the end of our bench, like a man in desperate need of a loo. Dave

Podanski was a scruffy-faced Robin Gibb lookalike, who usually wore an ensemble of skinny jeans, maroon Converse and some kind of geek-branded T-shirt. Today's shirt was emblazoned with a large mathematical pi symbol. He always wore a goofy grin on his bearded face, but this morning's had an unnerving intensity, and his eyes were wide behind his Buddy Holly frames. It was difficult to tell if he was excited, horrified or having an aneurysm.

'You mean Miss Hotness over there?' I nodded at the woman now posing for selfies with a succession of girls and their mums. 'Did she recently marry a prince?'

'You don't know her?' He sounded as though we were all looking at Oprah.

Megan raised a hand to shield her eyes from the bright morning sun. 'No idea, but I'd kill for her sunnies. Oscar rushed me out the door for band practice and I left mine at home.'

'Here.' Sam offered his bright blue-and-green-framed polarised sunglasses.

Megan recoiled. 'Yeah, nah, I'm good.'

'Rude.' Sam scowled and put them back on.

Baytree's queen of style wouldn't be seen dead in Sam's daggy dad sunglasses. Megan was one of those infuriating women who always looked amazing, even if she was wearing something as basic as a T-shirt and leggings. Although, now it appeared as if she could lose her throne to the sleek new mum on the block.

'Wow.' Dave looked at us each in turn. 'I can't believe you don't know who she ...'

'Dave!' I cried. 'Just put us out of our misery!'

'That is Rania Jalali!' Dave held out his hands, like a priest reciting the prayers of the faithful.

A noisy game of four square going on nearby became more audible in the long pause that followed this announcement.

'Who?'

Dave shook his head. 'Rania Jalali!'

'Saying it twice doesn't help.' Sam scratched at his stubble in frustration. 'Actor? Singer? Influencer?'

'Rania! From *The Rebound*!' Dave held his Astonished Man pose – shoulders up, arms out, eyes bulging, mouth agape – for at least three seconds. 'How can you not know this?'

Megan screwed up her face. 'The *reality TV* show?'

'Thank you!' Dave released the tension in his body with grand relief.

I'd never watched *The Rebound* but had overheard many conversations about it at work. Even if you hated those types of shows where women degrade themselves for the attention of a muscly dude who made millions selling protein supplements to bullied kids, you'd have to have been living under a rock not to have heard of the TV juggernaut Aussies loved to hate. My hospital co-workers had spent weeks dissecting the personalities of the unfortunate contestants, as each one was humiliated in cruelly creative ways. They'd speculate about who would sleep with whom, or who was the biggest bitch-slash-bastard. From what I could glean, the premise of *The Rebound* was something along the lines of: recently single, attractive Aussies (with rock-bottom self- esteem) looking for – you guessed it – a rebound. Classy. I mostly tuned out when these discussions started up, but I did recall often hearing the name Rania.

Even my fourteen-year-old daughter had got caught up in the tawdry frenzy when it first aired last November.

'Please, Mum?' Zara begged at dinner one night. '*Everyone* is watching it!'

'I'm not.' I'd then proceeded to point one by one at her siblings around the table. 'Archie's not ... neither is Stella, and Max definitely isn't watching it, so ...'

'You know what I mean!' Zara hadn't appreciated my hilarious pedantry. '*Everyone* in Year Eight is watching it!'

'Well,' I waved my fork in the air, as though gesturing towards Zara's invisible classmates, '*everyone* in Year Eight can look forward to rewarding careers stacking supermarket shelves.'

For a moment, it seemed as if Zara was considering flipping the table, but instead settled for her signature eye roll. That was the last time *The Rebound* was mentioned in the Barrett household.

'Some of the guys at work watched it,' Sam said. 'Apparently, the "hot Pakistani chick" was everyone's fave.'

'Aren't men great?' Megan asked derisively.

'So, what's she doing here?' I watched as a small collection of dads started sidling their way into Rania's orbit. 'Shouldn't she and her new life partner be walking the red carpet at the opening of an envelope somewhere?'

'They broke up,' Dave said, bereft. 'A week after the last episode aired.'

'Aw, mate, you okay?' Sam said. 'Did the reality stars shatter your dreams when they consciously uncoupled?'

Sam's wife, Bridget, had left him for another man two years ago, significantly diminishing his romantic streak. These days, he was living his best life on Tinder and having lots of sex. Lots. We could always tell when Sam had got lucky the night before because he'd take an unnaturally long breath the moment he sat on our bench at drop-off. This was our cue to ask how the date went, which we always did. Megan and I were happy for Sam and his sexcapades. He deserved it after putting up with Bridget for so long.

'Rania has a five-year-old son.' Dave sat down, eager to fill us in. 'He must be starting here.'

'Gotta say, wouldn't have picked you for a reality fan, Dave,' I told him.

As a self-confessed uber geek, comic-book aficionado and talented graphic novelist, Dave was the unlikeliest viewer of reality-TV trash.

'Oh, Keshini *loves* it,' Dave said, slapping his hands on his thighs. 'I wasn't into it at first, but it sucked me in. I mean, if you start breaking it down, there are some great archetypal characters there.'

'You do realise these are actual human beings with actual feelings, don't you, Dave?' Megan snapped.

Oblivious to the warning tone in Megan's voice, Dave continued, 'Well yeah, of course, but these shows have been around long enough for people to know what they're signing up for.'

I had to agree with him there. Had people learned nothing from the litany of fallen and faded reality TV stars over the years?

Rania was still smiling and posing, but her gigantic sunglasses made it hard to tell if she was genuinely loving the attention or simply going through the motions. Either way, I suddenly resented this D-grade celebrity's intrusion. Megan wasn't the only parent who had unearthed her community spirit at Baytree Primary. Everyone contributed more these days, including me. The most recent working bee had broken all records for attendance (a meagre record to break, in fairness) and Megan, Sam and I were now the official organisers of the annual junior school Christmas concert. Last year, the kids performed Hans Christian Andersen's *The Little Match Girl* (not a dry eye in the house), and this year Megan and the drama teacher, Miss Mitchell, were planning an ambitious production of Leo Tolstoy's *Papa Panov's Special Christmas*. If anyone could pull it off, it was my bestie. Christmas was still a while away, so Sam and I had told Megan she wasn't even allowed to say the word 'concert' until term three.

There'd been a fair shifting of sands in my personal life over the last couple of years, too, including the fact that I now had two kids in secondary school. This was something I still found difficult to wrap my head around. There had been the whole private-versus-public discussion with every friend, co-worker and family member during Zara and Archie's last year of primary school. Greg and I couldn't afford private school, so two years ago we'd sent our twins off to Baytree Secondary, and hadn't regretted it for a moment.

Sam slung his charcoal Crumpler over his head and stood up. 'Gotta go.'

Megan frowned. 'I thought you started at ten?'

It was still weird to see Sam in his new work get-up. Up until a few months ago, he'd lived in jeans and a hoodie, but now that he was a respectable working man, a shirt (ironed), slacks and sensible shoes was the new look. He had a job in the next suburb over selling food- processing equipment. He didn't exactly love it, but he didn't hate it, either.

'Who could ask for anything more?' he'd said.

With his updated wardrobe, brown/grey stubble, short, dark hair and rosy cheeks (probably from all the sex), Sam was happier, healthier and more handsome. He'd had a 'glow up' as my teenagers would say. Amazing what ridding yourself of a toxic wife could do for a man's libido and complexion.

'He wants me in at nine-thirty from now on,' Sam said. 'Early bird catches the mega-boring sales data and all that.'

'I'll walk with you!' Dave jumped up. 'Maybe I can sneak a selfie with Rania.'

'Please don't,' Sam groaned as he turned towards the gate.

Up until a year ago, Dave had only hung around on the periphery of our trio, but three had slowly become four and Dave was now one of us. He and Sam had even started an acoustic duo that played at last year's Mum's Night. They still didn't have an official name, although Megan and I had suggested many. Our top three were The Dad Jokes, The Baytree Bangers and Nana Nap, but the duo had chosen to ignore our inspired ideas and remained nameless. Actually, Remain Nameless was a pretty good name too, come to think of it.

'Yeah, okay,' Dave said, trotting after Sam like an obedient puppy. 'Probably best if I wait to get her alone.'

'Wow, that doesn't sound creepy at all.' Megan stood up, too. 'I have to talk to Penny about the newsletter. Bloody Nicola wants two full pages spruiking her Therapy Kitchen Hamper business.' Nicola McGinty was a school mum with a PhD in passive aggression.

'Okay, see ya tomorrow.'

'Not this arvo?'

'Nah, working.' I made a work-dread face. 'Aunty Carmen's doing pick-up.'

'Well, let me know if you need me to get them any other days this week,' Megan said. 'Us single mums gotta help each other out!'

Single mums. Ouch.

Chapter Two
Megan

'There's always one, Meggsy!'

Megan slid a blueberry muffin across the counter towards her mother. 'Did Susie apologise afterwards?'

'Lord no!' Ellie handed Megan a ten-dollar note. 'Why the hell should she? Harriet *was* being a pain in the arse.'

A few Applewood residents at a nearby table murmured their agreement.

'I mean, honestly!' Ellie raised her voice for the eavesdroppers. 'No one wanted to sing "Morning Has Broken". It was aquarobics, not a bloody morning mass!'

One of the eavesdropping women guffawed, almost losing her false pearly whites in her cup of tea. Ellie Wylie smiled, triumphant. Megan's mum was renowned for her comedic skills at Applewood Retirement Village. Her morning visits to The Cozy Corner café counter regularly turned into an impromptu stand-up set. Tiny and slim, with a grey pixie cut, her bright little face and green eyes had always reminded Megan of an elf from one of her Enid Blyton books when she was younger.

After six months of working in the café, Megan had become used to Ellie and her friends' gossiping. Ellie loved regaling her daughter with the most recent goings-on in the village, which usually involved the bossy octogenarian Harriet Firth. Megan couldn't figure out if everyone genuinely disliked Harriet, or if they just latched onto the most trivial of incidents so they had something to talk about each morning. Megan suspected the latter.

'Well, Harriet was in here this morning looking pretty miserable,' Megan said, ringing up Ellie's muffin and herbal tea. 'So, it might be nice for you and the girls to check on her.'

Ellie's smug expression vanished. Despite appearances, Megan's mum was kind-hearted.

'The silly old chook,' Ellie said. 'We'll ask her to sit with us at bingo.' She picked up her morning tea and hurried over to her friends, Lucy, Carol and Helen, who were all eagerly awaiting the gossip from that morning's aquarobics.

Megan smiled and turned back to the half-empty cake-display cabinet. Yang would need to start baking larger batches of the chocolate-and-raspberry brownies. They were a hit and had been selling out before midday. She took a pen and notepad out of her jeans pocket to jot it down, then added a few more notes to herself:

Timber frame for blackboard.
Charcoal pot-plant holders.
Devil's ivy.
Pendant lights?

That last one would take some convincing, but Megan was confident Yang would go for the plants and timber-frame idea. She was determined to give The Cozy Corner a facelift before she moved on to greener professional pastures.

With its white walls, stackable plastic chairs, white square tables and a single motel-style painting of a nondescript rural landscape on the wall, the café was crying out for a makeover. The only exotic feature in it was a five-foot-high bronze statue of a silverback gorilla guarding the door. The residents had dubbed him Magilla – named after an ancient cartoon character Megan had never heard of – and patted his head for luck every time they walked through the door. Despite her misgivings that Magilla wasn't exactly Buddha's belly, Megan had soon found herself following suit.

Help me find a real job, Magilla, she wished every morning as she touched his cold, bronzed head. Unfortunately, she had no idea what a 'real job' might look like for a 37-year-old woman with no experience in anything besides running an online kids' fashion business. All Megan knew was that she wasn't destined to spend twenty hours a week in a job where her biggest daily dilemma was mediating senior citizens' petty disputes and running out of brownies.

She'd had a few start-up ideas since selling Chill, including a digital art gallery and an online lookbook to encourage kids to build their own sense of style, but none of them lit a fire under her. If she was going to put her heart and soul into a career, the passion had to be there. Megan still had a decent chunk of money in the bank from the sale of her business, so she could afford to take her time. Working in the café and volunteering at Baytree Primary kept her busy in the meantime, and she was looking forward to the Year Five/Six camp at the end of term one. Megan had missed out on her own primary school camp because of a Kmart-catalogue gig that was booked for the same week. She hadn't been too fussed about missing a few days in the not-so-great outdoors. Also, her fee of three hundred bucks had felt like a million dollars to an eleven-year-old.

When Megan first told her boyfriend, Eddie, last year that she'd signed up for Baytree's camp, there was a long silence, and she thought maybe the line had dropped out.

'Eddie? You there?'

'Yeah …' Eddie had said finally. 'Um … isn't Oscar in Grade Four next year?'

'Yes, but the school needed volunteers,' Megan had explained. 'And I know the Five/Six kids well from running the concerts.'

'Right.'

Megan had felt a prickle of annoyance, hearing the obvious disapproval in his tone. So what if she wanted to go on a school camp? She'd never been to Kinglake and it was supposed to be a stunning part of the world. Megan knew Eddie considered the work she did for Baytree trivial, but not everyone wanted to spend their life travelling the world convincing companies to implement environmentally friendly business solutions. Sure, Eddie's job sounded noble as hell, but it also seemed pretty boring. Some people, like Megan, enjoyed being part of a school community and serving sandwiches to seniors while they figured out their true purpose.

The stopgap café job had its perks, too. After five years with only a laptop for company, Megan enjoyed her chats with the residents. In fact, she'd recently decided that old people were her favourite kind of humans.

Even Megan's ex-husband, Bryce, approved of her new gig. He ran motivational courses called Dream It Real, so he was all for Megan 'manifesting her journey'.

'Adam and I are thrilled for you!' Bryce had been almost manic in his enthusiasm.

'Because I got a hospitality job in a retirement village?'

'Yes! It's all part of the rediscovery process! I mean, who would have thought, huh?'

Indeed.

'This is true self-examination and a natural step in your reinvention,' Bryce had continued. 'It's something we should all be brave enough to do.'

According to Bryce, everything from stepping outside your front door to doing number twos in a public toilet was 'brave'. To be fair, Bryce had earned the right to throw the b-word around, considering he'd left his wife for a man. Megan might've hated him for it at the time, but she couldn't deny that it had taken some balls.

'*Ming!*'

Yang's sharp voice cut through the café, making half the customers spill their tea. Megan turned to find her boss scowling at her from the other end of the counter, two full grocery bags in her arms.

'What's this shit?' Yang said, gesturing towards the speaker in the corner of the ceiling.

The customers chuckled and one regular, Daisy, cupped her hand around her mouth and crowed, 'Ummmaaaahhhhhhhhh!'

Megan put a hand on her hip and stared defiantly back at her boss. 'This "shit" is Sarah Blackwood. And everyone loves it, don't they?' She swept her eyes across the café with an expression that clearly told her customers they better agree.

Loud murmurs of 'Yes, Megs!', 'Oh, it's lovely!' and 'I'm going to buy the record!' echoed around the room.

'Arse lickers!' Yang flicked her hand at them and stormed into the kitchen as the room erupted into chortles and snorts of delight. Megan smiled and curtsied her gratitude to the oldies, who clearly enjoyed these fiery exchanges.

They all knew that, despite her impressive grouchiness, Yang Liu was a good woman who loved her customers. And the feeling was entirely mutual. Megan's boss was all bark and no bite. She would snap at the oldies if they dripped on her floor or complained that the 'curried-egg sandwiches were nicer last week', but Megan had also seen Yang rub the wrinkly hands of worried residents more times than she could count.

Six months ago, when Ellie had first dragged Megan into The Cozy Corner and announced to Yang that she'd found the perfect person to fill the advertised 'Café Assistant' position, the small woman wasn't convinced.

'You got any experience, Yao Ming?' Yang had asked, narrowing her eyes. Her accent was the perfect blend of quickfire, nasal Chinese, and ocker, nasal Aussie.

'No, but I'm a fast learner,' Megan had said, matching Yang's assertive tone. 'And who is Yao Ming when they're at home?'

'Only the best basketballer in the world,' Yang cried. 'And a giraffe, like you.'

Megan had taken an instant liking to the petite, blunt woman. Yang reminded her of Lizzie but seemed to care even less what people thought of her.

'I'll look him up,' Megan said.

'I'll give you a one-week trial,' Yang snapped, 'but only because Ellie Jelly is your mum.'

'Ellie Jelly?'

Ellie beamed proudly.

'Because nobody's ready for Ellie's Jelly,' Yang said, as if it should have been blatantly obvious.

Megan was liking Yang more every second. 'You a Beyoncé fan?' she asked.

'No,' Yang said firmly. 'I like Destiny's Child. Beyoncé's been swallowed by her own bum.' She pointed out the window at a bunch of wet-haired women in rubber crocs walking towards the café. 'You can start by serving these old farts.'

'Um, okay. Is the register …?'

But Yang had already disappeared into the kitchen, muttering about old farts dripping all over her floor.

'I'll show you, Meggsy!' Ellie said excitedly. 'I've done it *many* times!'

And so began Megan's new career, under the guidance of a surly boss, who only occasionally drip-fed her information about her life. Over the past six months, all Megan had learned about Yang was that she was a teenager when she and her family migrated to Australia in the sixties, had never married or had children, had a cat called Moshi (whose photo was blu-tacked above the coffee machine) and was part of a Chinese Community Group.

Megan could hear Yang now banging around the kitchen as she unpacked groceries, and decided not to suggest the pendant lights until her boss was in a better mood.

'Morning, love!'

'HEY, MAGGIE,' Megan shouted. 'HOW ARE YOU TODAY?'

Maggie was one of Megan's favourite customers, and at ninety-three was almost completely deaf.

'Very good, thank you, darling girl!' Maggie leaned over to pat Megan's hand. 'I'm going to be naughty today and have one of those delicious-looking meringues.'

'Why not?' Megan said, picking up the tongs. 'TREAT YOURSELF!'

Maggie reached into the small powder-blue handbag

17

that seemed to permanently hang off her left arm and took out a pink furry clip purse. 'Have you got any plans tonight, sweetheart?'

'Eddie and I are having dinner at our favourite restaurant,' Megan said.

'What's that, love?'

'DINNER WITH EDDIE!'

'Oh, lovely!' Maggie smiled. 'I hope to meet your special fella one of these days.'

'He's away a lot for work,' Megan said loudly.

'Oh, that's right, he's very important, isn't he?'

'Yep!' Megan deliberately lowered her voice. 'And I'm going to ask him to move in with me tonight.'

After two years, Megan felt ready to commit to the relationship. Eddie had dropped a few hints about them moving in together, but she had chosen to ignore them. Recently, however, her feelings had changed. Eddie had been away more and more for work and she missed him. As a strategic advisor for a big environmental company, Eddie regularly travelled to Fiji, Vanuatu and other Pacific Island paradise spots. Megan always imagined him lying by a pool and drinking cocktails the entire time.

'Not quite,' Eddie said when Megan shared this work-life fantasy with him one day. 'More like sitting in stale-smelling conference rooms drinking terrible coffee all week.'

One night during the summer holidays, Megan was over at Lizzie's when she first decided she would ask Eddie to move in. Sitting on her friend's back deck, drinking gin and tonics and watching Greg and Sam chatting at the BBQ, she had a sudden longing for Eddie to be there, too. Lizzie and Sam hardly knew her boyfriend. Living together could be the first step towards the kind of unbreakable bond Lizzie and Greg shared. Maybe this time next year there'd even be an extra kid running around the backyard?

★★★

'Are you serious?'

'I'm so sorry, Megs.'

They had just finished a delicious meal of sashimi and tempura at their favourite Japanese restaurant in town. Megan had been just about to pop the big 'Want to move in together?' question, when Eddie had dropped a bombshell of his own.

He wanted to end it.

'But ... I don't understand ...'

Megan's eyes were bone-dry, but her heart was thumping. How had the night gone so wrong so quickly? A night that was supposed to end with amazing sex back at her place – their place! Noisy, passionate, pulling-off-each-other's-clothes-in-the-hallway sex because Oscar was at his dad's tonight.

'Come on, Megs,' Eddie said gently. 'We hardly see each other anymore, and I'm just not sure ...'

He stopped, but Megan immediately understood. He no longer loved her.

She stared across the table at the face she knew so well. The left cheek mole, the tiny pockmark beside his right eyebrow, deep blue eyes and that impossibly thick mop of shaggy brown hair. She'd always loved running her hands through his hair.

The busy restaurant hummed and buzzed around them, and Megan prayed her voice wouldn't wobble. 'You don't love me.'

Eddie pressed his eyes shut with his hands and took a

deep breath, and Megan had a strange sensation that she was sitting across from a stranger. She wondered exactly when he'd decided to leave her. She was such an idiot. If she'd been paying attention, she would have seen that the signs had been there for a while now. Ironically, it was Megan who had encouraged Eddie to take the promotion last year that meant he'd be away a lot more.

Eddie opened his eyes and looked at her. 'We want different things, Megs.'

'Like what?'

'I don't want to be a dad!'

Megan had never heard Eddie raise his voice in public. He sounded panicked.

He pressed his palms down into thin air, as if keeping something at bay. 'Oscar's great, but I didn't sign up for him. I signed up for you, but ...' He stopped again, his face full of sorrow and ... something else.

Megan felt a chill. 'Who is she?'

'Megs, this isn't —'

'*Please* don't lie.'

Eddie lowered his eyes and began picking at the label of his Asahi bottle. 'She works with me. We just ... she's a senior projects manager and so we ... connect on a lot of levels.'

'You mean she can talk about something other than school fundraisers and eightieth birthday parties?' Megan said sharply. 'Wow. I had no idea my boyfriend was a superficial corporate arsehole.'

'Come on, Megs, it's not like that.'

'I think it's exactly like that.' Megan's gut twisted and her hands started to tremble. She had to get out of this room. Now. But she didn't know if she could trust her legs.

'We've been travelling together a lot over the past few months and —'

'Stop.' She stood up, gripping the back of her chair for support and praying her knees wouldn't give way.

'Megs, please, sit down.'

But Megan turned and walked straight out of the busy restaurant without looking back, eager to get home to a place that was still only hers.

Chapter Three
Sam

To: jack_woz_here@hotmail.com
From: samhatfieldchef@bigpond.com
Subject: Wasn't Christmas Yesterday?

Hey dickhead,

I had to look twice at my phone this morning when it rudely informed me that today was the first day of February. Have you fully recovered from your Xmas Meat-A-Thon? I've never known a human to be able to consume so many different types of animal.

So, let me give you a brief update since our last correspondence, before Christmas and the heady days of summer swallowed us whole.

Bridget is still my ex-wife. She contributes very little to us financially because of her fancy divorce lawyers but continues to lavish the kids with expensive everythings when she has them every other weekend. Our air conditioning is broken, but God forbid she'd want to help her kids be cool in the house they actually live in the vast majority of the time. Even with this new job, I still need her money and it kills me. She loves it when I ask for money, because she knows full well it kills me, so I really try to avoid it. Maybe if I knuckle down and work my way up the food-processing-equipment sales ladder, I'll eventually become a food-processing-equipment mogul and be able to pay for my own air con to get fixed with my food-processing-equipment billions. A guy can dream.

The job is okay, actually. It's easy and the money is very helpful. The woman who works opposite me used to be a singer. She got this job as a stopgap until her music career took off. But she's been there nine years now and seems genuinely content. Told me she bought a flat in Northcote last year and is getting the bathroom retiled this week. I'd like to be able to consider the option of retiling. That'd be nice.

Mum is still tut-tutting and shaking her head mournfully every time I see her, two years after the divorce. She's always had good stamina, my mother. Her last salvo of delight included blaming me (again) for my failed marriage. I reminded her that Bridget cheated on me, and that I chose to leave her. Her response was to raise her eyebrows and point out that the kids still don't have a mother as a direct result of my 'choices'. Yes, she did the quotation-mark thing with her fingers. I couldn't be bothered telling her that the kids barely had a mother in the first place.

Lola is being a stone-cold bitch, lately. Last night she told me to 'Sard off!' The only way I had the slightest inkling of what the hell that meant was the venom with which she said the words. I know she's eleven and apparently it's the age and all that, but it's bugging me. I think the divorce hit her harder than I realised, and I didn't notice, which makes me feel like shit. I made the mistake of mentioning it to Bridg after her last weekend with the kids. She just scrunched up her face and said, 'Oh Jesus, Sam, she's fine.'

When we got home that night, Lola was out of the car, in the house and slamming her bedroom door before I'd barely pulled the handbrake. I looked at Tyler in the rear-view mirror. He was just nodding slightly with his eyes wide and had this weird smile on his face. It was a perfect GIF-reaction face. I asked him what he reckoned. He said, 'She's more like Mum after we've been with Mum.'

Sheesh.

I asked if he'd had a good time at his mum's and his GIF face barely changed; nodding, eyes wide. 'Yeah. I played Red Dead Redemption in my room till I fell asleep.'

Sheesh.

Lola will be fine. She's still my beautiful, kooky girl and I love her, but yeah, I'm a bit worried. Lizzie said she enrolled Stella in acting classes when she was in a bit of a slump last year, and it really helped. I'm gonna ask her about that. Even if it's not Lola's cup of tea, it'll get her out of my face for a couple of hours.

I got a WhatsApp message from Sasha. She's in Marrakesh. That's in Morocco, dickhead. Which is in North Africa (I had to look that last bit up). To be honest, I don't think I'd have the cojones to travel to Africa on my own. She's a fearless nutjob. She sent the most amazing photo of her on a balcony overlooking this huge market and everything looked orange and red and chaotic and beautiful. I'm happy she's having a good time and that she wants to tell me about it. It's probably the most civilised break-up I've ever had. Not that I have an extensive list of ex-lovers to compare it to.

I'm glad we're still friends. But if she keeps sending me gloating selfies from spectacular locations, I may have to rethink that.

Here are the stats for this week:

- Three dates.
- Two sexual experiences.
- One Bunny Boiler.

Fortunately, I didn't have a sexual experience with the Bunny Boiler, even though I've always had a thing for Glenn Close. But this BB in no way resembled GC. She had more of a Kathy-Bates-in-*Misery*-meets-80s-Molly-Ringwald thing going on. On her Tinder profile, she'd managed to expertly amplify the Molly vibes and somehow digitally erase any hint of *Misery*, but quite the reverse was true in person. The only remnants of Ringwald were Molly's most pouty, entitled silver-screen moments. You with me? Good.

This particular lady chose an Ethiopian restaurant in Footscray for our date. I'd heard of the place and was bang up for an African feast. (Sasha can galivant around actual Africa all she likes!) Alana – *Misery* Molly's real name – was there when I arrived. I was ten minutes early, as I tend to be, and was immediately ill at ease. Not only had she arrived *très* early, she was already eating. A lot. She wasn't a big woman, but she was eating like Ethiopian cuisine was about to be banned by Border Force.

I flashed my friendliest smile and she looked at me and nodded like I was getting in the way of her speed eating. She managed to swallow her mouthful while telling me to 'Sit, sit, sit!' It felt like a job interview.

Hot.

Alana then produced a piece of paper that I noticed had a bulleted list of questions on it.

Question 1: Why did you get divorced?

Question 2: Are either of your kids gay?

Question 3: Can you control your orgasms? (Hindsight answer: Yes, but only if you talk about my kids' sexuality while we're doing it.)

Question 4: Can you cook?

When I revealed my dark past as a chef, she paused, wiped some flatbread into what looked like a very tasty eggplant dip and pushed the whole lot into her mouth.

At this point, I managed to get the attention of one of the wait staff. A tall African queen snaked through a few tables and arrived at my side, notepad in hand (I still appreciate a restaurant that processes orders the old-fashioned way. I hate watching wait staff swirling their finger in front of a touch screen like they're at a self-checkout). The queen had a striking, slender nose and eyebrows that would make Penelope Cruz jealous. I couldn't help but wonder whether she might be on Tinder. She smiled (this woman was truly stunning) and asked a perfect, one-word question: 'Drink?'

A tiny click-roll of the r was the final straw. All I could think was, *Why aren't I sitting opposite you, African queen? Why? WHY?!*

I asked for an Ethiopian beer, and the queen produced a bottle of Hakim Stout.

I raised my glass and offered Alana a weak, 'Cheers.'

She didn't smile, but picked up her glass of fizzy, non-alcoholic something and took three good gulps. I matched her with my Ethiopian stout. Alana placed her drink back on the table and asked if I drank a lot. I saw an opportunity and confessed to being a heavy drinker. I've actually gotten a lot better with my drinking in the last year, but I laid it on thick in the hope that admitting alcoholism might provide an escape.

That backfired, dickhead. Alana veritably lit up. Turns out she's an alcoholic, too and doesn't see why people think it's such a big deal. I asked why she was drinking a non-alcoholic fizzy thing. She reached into her handbag and, not at all discreetly, revealed the top of a vodka bottle. Okay, then. Owning up to being a booze hound had quadrupled my appeal to Alana.

Flash forward and I'm five stouts to the wind, when Alana leaned across the table and started talking dirty. With her mouth full. I didn't catch the first thing she said, so I innocently leaned in and asked her to repeat herself.

'I'm going to bite into your cock like a bratwurst.'

Those were her exact words. I sobered up remarkably quickly. It felt like I'd been smacked on the forehead. Or bitten on the cock.

The next two minutes were a flurry of apologies and stumbling over chairs and flinging too much money on the table and waving a final frantic goodbye to Halima, the African queen, and literally running from the restaurant. I caught a final glimpse of Alana as I closed the door behind me. She was still chewing, but at the same time staring at me like De Niro at the end of *Cape Fear*.

So, there you go, dickhead. There's my gift to you on this humid Monday night. I'll give you the intimate details of the sexual experiences another time.

I can never eat a bratwurst again.

Hope you're doing okay, mate. Make sure you write back with all the news from your redneck backwater.

S x

27

To: codenamedave@gmail.com
From: samhatfieldchef@bigpond.com
Subject: Kenny Goals

Hey Dave,

We still on for rehearsal this week? You said you might have to shift it. If you're all good let me know. Also – assuming we go ahead – may I once again request that you tune your guitar before you arrive? I think you tuning up at my place is damaging the kids' mental health. Thanks in advance.

I thought we could brush up on some of the songs we played at the school Mum's Night last year. Although everyone's lasting memory will undoubtedly be Susie C jumping into full splits at the end of *Footloose*, we had a few compliments on our set. Good Lord, those women definitely know how to let loose. I think Higgsy still regrets putting his hand up to man the bar.

Anyway, for us it was definitely an improvement on the bush dance. The only song we need to hold on to from that set is 'The Gambler'. Always handy to keep a bit of Kenny in your back pocket.

Let me know if Wednesday's a goer.

Cheers, Sam

To: samhatfieldchef@bigpond.com
From: codenamedave@gmail.com
Subject: Kenny Goals

Hola Bro!

YES! OMG the Mum's Night was craycray to the extreme LMFAO. Being the only three dudes at a LADIES NIGHT is dangerous stuff. Higgsy LOLOLOLOLOLOL! PUMPED for the Night Market gig. Baytree LOVES us! Do we know if there's gonna be a STAGE yet??? I've been thinking A LOT about our band name. I got my list down to a top twenty (a couple of my big faves were ACOUSTICOPHANY and THE ACOUSTICATS), but then I had a mega BRAINWAVE! I was totes overthinking the whole thing. Check it! We should go fully simple vibes and just call ourselves SAM & DAVE. Or DAVE & SAM. I've said both ways out loud HEAPS over the last few days and I like the sound of Sam & Dave better. Or maybe samanddave all lowercase, like radiohead. Or sam'n'dave. Whaddayathink????

stay craycray, dave

To: codenamedave@gmail.com
From: samhatfieldchef@bigpond.com
Subject: Kenny Goals

You're a genius. We should actually become a legit soul duo and write songs with titles like 'Soul Man' and 'Hold On I'm Coming', or – I dunno – 'Gimme Some Lovin'.

You good for Wednesday?

Sam (of Sam & Dave fame)

To: samhatfieldchef@bigpond.com
From: codenamedave@gmail.com
Subject: Kenny Goals

OMFG I love those song titles!!! So is that a BOOM HELLA YASSSSS to our new name???

To: codenamedave@gmail.com
From: samhatfieldchef@bigpond.com
Subject: Kenny Goals

Sure.

Maybe do a quick google first just to double-check it's not taken.

Are. You. Good. For. Wednesday. Night?

To: samhatfieldchef@bigpond.com
From: codenamedave@gmail.com
Subject: Kenny Goals

DEVO!! It's taken!!! What are the chances amiright???

This Sam & Dave duo WERE A SOUL DUO! OMG my brain hurts.

Weds is sweet as, braaaahhhhh.

To: codenamedave@gmail.com
From: samhatfieldchef@bigpond.com
Subject: Kenny Goals

Ah well. Back to the drawing board.

Maybe in the meantime we could call ourselves Sonny and Cher. Or Hall & Oates.

Just spitballing.

See you Wednesday 6 p.m. at mine. With your already tuned guitar.

Sam

To: samhatfieldchef@bigpond.com
From: codenamedave@gmail.com
Subject: Kenny Goals

??
??????????????

Chapter Four
Lizzie

I arrived home from my shift around eleven o'clock to find Aunty Carmen wide awake and watching *The Walking Dead*.

'My little cat, you look like you've just escaped from the Vatos gang!' she cried as I walked into the lounge room.

'Thanks,' I said, leaning down to plant a kiss on her soft cheek.

I assumed the Vatos gang was a *Walking Dead* reference – and meant that I looked like shit – but I was too shattered to ask or care. While I may have resembled a survivor from a post-apocalyptic zombie world, my seventy-year-old aunt looked as fresh as a daisy, despite the late hour. Aunty Carmen was a night owl, which was why she was on babysitting duty tonight and not my father. He was usually snoring in front of whatever A-League match was playing on the tele by 8.30 p.m.

I flopped onto our grey modular couch and let out a long groan. 'Ohhhh, that's better. My feet are throbbing.'

Aunty Carmen frowned at me from across the room, then nodded, as if answering a question only she'd heard. 'Hot chocolate,' she said.

'No, I'm fine really, don't ...'

'Shush!' Aunty Carmen hoisted herself upright. 'I'm making you a hot chocolate!'

I didn't have the energy to argue. Especially not with a

woman who'd rather force-feed her adult niece an entire tin of Milo than listen to anything she had to say.

As Aunty Carmen successfully achieved the vertical position, she began shuffling towards the kitchen. 'Bloody stiff knees!'

Her knees may have been stiff, but my aunty still moved well, and was in better physical shape than a lot of women half her age – forty-plus years spent working in our family restaurant had kept her body and mind fit and nimble – and took pride in her appearance. Tonight, she was wearing bright pink lipstick and a chunky blue necklace, and was resplendent in an iridescent-green shift dress, light-blue leggings and white sandshoes. Her short, spiky blonde hair was wrapped in a yellow-and-blue tie-dyed scarf. Carmen Abela was a kaleidoscope of colours, textures and fabrics, like a Pixar character making a guest appearance on *Ru Paul's Drag Race*.

'How were the kids?' I asked, leaning forward to pull off my (less impressive) scuffed white runners.

'Angels!'

I doubted that. But if anyone besides Greg or I could keep my kids in line, it was Aunty Carmen. She was definitely more lenient with her great-nephews and great-nieces than she'd ever been with us, but she could still put the fear of God into any one of my four children with a single look.

Aunty Carmen began to reel off the afternoon's 'Barrett Children Highlights Package' from the kitchen as she poured milk into a saucepan.

'Zara told me she's going to be stage master for the school play, Archie put all his fairytale cards in piles, Stella made me ask her teacher if she can bring her iPad to camp and the teacher says, "Absolutely not," and Max spilt a tin of Milo on the couch and broke your "Yummy Mummy" mug with his soccer ball.'

Noticing my horrified expression, she quickly added, 'But I made him pick up all the pieces and vacuum.'

Just listening to this litany of accidents, activities and updates was exhausting, but I wasn't at all surprised by Stella's sneaky request to take her device on camp. My eleven-year-old was obsessed with checking topbroadwaynews. net and theukstage.co every day. She was already having palpitations about not being able to stay up to date with the latest news on her favourite musicals for three whole days. I did enjoy hearing Archie's Dungeons & Dragons cards described as 'fairytale cards', and that Zara was 'stage master', but not that my favourite coffee mug was in pieces in the bin.

'Did you take the devices off them before …?'

'Yes, Dragon Lady!' Aunty Carmen wagged the milk carton at me. 'I took the screens away before bedtime!'

'You would've been just as strict about screens!'

'Probably worse.'

'No "probably" about it.' I reached under my scrubs to unclip my bra and snaked the strap through my sleeve. Bliss.

'Lizzie, you working too much!' Aunty Carmen shouted from the kitchen. 'Can't you ask for less shifts?'

It wasn't the first time I'd heard this from a family member of late.

'We need the money.'

It was as simple as that. Yes, I was tired. More tired than usual. And yes, I felt guilty about missing out on after-school antics, and not being there to tuck my kids in every night. But there was just no other option.

'Maybe if you let your father and I ...'

'No,' I said firmly. 'We'll be fine.'

'Pah!' Aunty Carmen violently shooed her hands at me, almost knocking over the tin of cocoa. 'You're so bloody stubborn, like your father!'

'Rubbish. You know I inherited all my best qualities from you.'

Her mouth turned down the same way Max's did when I told him he couldn't have a second serve of ice-cream. 'This is true.' She shrugged.

She poured the hot milk into a mug, and a delicious chocolatey scent wafted into my nostrils.

'Ohhh that smells *so* good! Thank you. Exactly what I need after three babies in ten hours.'

'You with Aileen or the new girl tonight?' Aunty Carmen said, handing me the mug.

'Both.'

I blew gently on the hot liquid and tiny chocolate waves lapped at the rim of the mug. When I was a kid, I'd always see how hard I could blow on my hot chocolate without making it spill. It didn't always end well. Aunty Carmen sat on the couch beside me, lifted my right foot up onto her lap and began to massage my aching arches. I didn't protest. Apart from her many other talents, the woman was a naturally gifted masseuse.

'Is the new girl still annoying?'

'She's all right.'

The new girl, Kate, started at the hospital a couple of months ago, and at twenty-three years old, she knew it all. In her first week, she interrupted as Aileen was guiding her through a breach birth to say that she knew all about the hospital's 'more traditional practices'. Aileen told

Kate to, 'Keep your fecking knowledge to yourself.'

My best friend and co-worker of almost twenty years had never been one to mince words. Her soft Tralee accent and small stature fooled most people into thinking she was a gentle Irish soul, but Aileen could reduce the hardest of men to a puddle of fear with a few sharp words.

When she discovered Kate sitting in the break room one morning, scrolling through Instagram instead of measuring a belly, she went full Irish banshee on the poor girl.

Kate's know-it-all behaviour had abated somewhat since then and she'd kept a low profile around us. Until she overheard me telling Aileen that, 'Rania someone off that rebound show' had caused a hullabaloo at school that morning.

'*Rania Jalali*?!' Kate's delighted face popped around the corner of the midwife station, where Aileen and I were grabbing a quick cuppa between patients. '*Rania Jalali* was at your school?!'

'I thought you were taking Mrs Landon's blood pressure?'

'I did, it's fine,' Kate said, waving her hand, then turning back to me. 'Rania is my spirit animal! Oh my God, did she mention Saunagate?'

Kate's usually pale cheeks were flushed red with excitement.

'I didn't talk to her. And our kids are in different grades, so I probably never will.'

'Oh, that sucks!' Kate was devo. 'She, like, *totally* broke my heart with her story about her ex,' she continued. 'Do you know that he left her with a toddler to run off with some skank he met on Tinder? I mean, *what* a bastard!'

Of course, Aileen and I googled Rania Jalali the moment Kate disappeared from view, scrolling through dozens of tabloid stories, and even finding a current-affair-style video of a camera crew confronting Rania's ex-husband in a café. After suitably provoking him with questions like, 'Do you feel guilty about ditching your wife and young son?' they eventually got the reaction they'd been hoping for when the stubbled, blond-haired man in his twenties knocked the camera to the ground and shouted, 'Fuck off!'

Kate was right about Rania being the show's favourite. The nation had seemingly taken the beautiful young Pakistani-Australian to its heart. She had even managed to leave the show with her self-respect intact, hand in hand with her 'perfect match'. Aileen and I eventually came to the conclusion that we were right about the show being yet another example of a crumbling civilisation and agreed it would be best if I never mentioned Rania's name around Kate again.

'She's just young,' I told Aunty Carmen as she rubbed my aching feet. 'We were all annoying at that age.'

Aunty Carmen snorted. 'You certainly were.'

I knew she was referring to my runaway-bride stunt in my early twenties but chose ignore it.

'At least I've got tomorrow night off,' I said, changing the subject, 'even though Stella has acting class and Zara has rehearsals. The house is a lot quieter these days with all of them off doing their own things.'

'You should be grateful,' Aunty Carmen said. 'The quiet is the best part of your kids getting older.'

She knew what she was talking about, having raised my three brothers and me. Mum passed away when I was four and Aunty Carmen moved in to help Dad raise us and run the family restaurant. Didn't hesitate. Just gave up her job at a Williamstown clothing boutique and reorganised her entire life in a matter of days. Now, here she was, decades later, stepping in again to help me.

Working and living with a man as ornery as my father for so long must have been intolerable at times. No one would have blamed her for running back to the rocky coves of Malta a long time ago. But Aunty Carmen was still here and still, miraculously, on speaking terms with my dad. Everyone in the family knew she adored her big brother. The fact that she frequently referred to him as 'the ungrateful old bastard' was neither here nor there. I loved my three brothers, but there was no way I'd last five minutes under the same roof as them, let alone forty years.

Aunty Carmen patted my foot then placed it back on the cushion. 'Okay, *ftit qattus*, I'm gonna head back over the bridge.'

I stood to give her a hug. 'Thank you.'

'You take it easy, okay?' she said, hugging me back before heading for the door. 'There is enough on your dish right now.'

She was right, I thought, closing the door behind her. My 'dish' had been full for a while now, and the last twelve months had been tough. The building industry took a hit last year and Greg lost some big contracts. Also, it seemed like every appliance in the house – from the fridge and the washing machine, to the toaster and the vacuum cleaner – had all decided to pack it in within hours of their warranties expiring. Then our car died and we were presented with a three-thousand-dollar bill to fix it, which put us back with our mortgage repayments. So, when Greg received an offer at the end of last year for a six-month contract in Sydney, we were in no position for him to decline. We examined it from every angle and decided that six months apart was worth it to get our finances on track. Initially, we thought Greg could fly back every weekend, but soon realised that the expense defeated the purpose of taking the job in the first place.

'Short-term pain, long-term gain,' Greg had said.

Three weeks ago, the six of us had headed off to Tullamarine airport in our second-hand, newly repaired Toyota Kluger to wave off our husband and father, knowing we wouldn't see him again until Zara and Archie's birthday party in early March. Saying goodbye was hard on the kids and it broke my heart to see them lining up to hug their dad. When it was Max's turn, he'd clung to Greg like a limpet, wrapping his skinny little legs around his middle, and burying his tear-soaked face in Greg's thick neck.

'I'm gonna miss you, Dad.'

'I'm gonna miss you, too, mate. But I'll be back before you know it.' Greg gently unwound Max's legs from his waist, popped him on the ground and took Max's chin in his big, calloused hand.

'You'll be so busy with school and soccer and helping your mum that you won't even notice I'm gone!'

'I will,' Max sniffed, wiping his nose on his sleeve.

Although he was struggling, Greg was trying to keep it together for the kids.

Zara and Archie stayed calm as they hugged and kissed their dad goodbye, but I saw them discreetly dabbing at their eyes when Greg turned to Stella. My poor sensitive middle child had been crying all morning. She was Daddy's girl, always had been, and couldn't fathom the idea of Greg being away for a few days, let alone six months.

'What if you never come back?' she sobbed, her arms around his neck. 'What if you like it better up there?'

I'd wondered the same.

After hugging and consoling his children for a bit longer, Greg turned to me. It was the moment I'd been dreading for months, but I knew I couldn't break down and wrap my own legs around his waist in front of the kids. Greg pulled me to him and nuzzled my neck.

'Are we doing the right thing, buddy?' he whispered. 'Because I don't know.'

It took every ounce of strength I possessed to not shout, 'You're right! Come on, let's go home! Dad's not going anywhere!'

Instead, I ruffled his soft, sandy hair the way I have a million times over the past seventeen years. 'It's six months, buddy,' I whispered. 'We can do this. Short-term pain, long-term gain. Remember?'

'I love you.'

'Love you too.'

The ride home had been fun. All five of us sniffed and snotted our way down the freeway, and by the time we got home we were ready for a lie-down and a *Harry Potter* movie marathon.

These last three weeks hadn't gone by as fast as I'd expected them to and I was starting to wonder again if we'd done the right thing. Greg was miserable, too. He liked the guys he was working with, apart from his boss who was a 'complete tool', but hated going back to an empty apartment every night.

'I was watching *Adventure Time* on my phone last night,' he'd told me last week, 'just so I could feel like Max was with me. And this morning I listened to Billie Eilish in the shower. Dark times.'

As I climbed into bed, I remembered that I'd meant to

ask Archie to draw some *Adventure Time* pictures for Greg to stick up on his wall. I'd ask him tomorrow. Right now, I just wanted to send Greg my nightly goodnight text, then sleep.

I dug my phone out of the bottom of my bag and saw a missed call from Megan. Whatever it was could wait until tomorrow.

I opened a new message to Greg and typed:

Night-night. FaceTime tomorrow? Miss you. Love you. Xxx

I turned off my phone, knowing my husband wouldn't reply until his alarm trilled at 5 a.m.

Falling back onto the pillow, I stretched my hand out across the space where Greg's body usually lay. Through our entire marriage, Greg and I hadn't been apart for longer than a night or two, and lately I'd been thinking about the comments Sam used to make about Bridget's constant absence in the lead-up to their separation.

'You can rationalise it all you want,' he'd said, 'but nothing can challenge the tyranny of distance.'

Greg and I aren't Sam and Bridget, I told myself. Not by a stretch. But the distance was starting to feel oppressive. Also, I wasn't sure I could pull off this working-single-mum-of-four-kids thing. I'd always prided myself on my multi-tasking, but this was next level. I was tired all the time and had a twenty-four-seven headache. And it was only month one of six.

Every day I chanted the 'short-term pain, long-term gain' mantra, but the next few months were unfurling before me like a road rushing towards a horizon I could barely see.

Chapter Five
Megan

It had been two weeks since Eddie had ended their relationship over soggy daifukus and Asahi beers, but Megan's heart still felt raw. Those first few days afterwards, she'd just felt empty. Like someone had scooped out her insides.

As expected, Lizzie was an amazing support and friend. She'd returned Megan's call at seven o'clock the morning after the break-up. As soon as she heard Megan sob, 'Eddie dumped me,' down the phone, Lizzie had hung up and arrived at Megan's house in record time.

'What is it about me that makes men want to sleep with other people?' she'd wailed to Lizzie on her doorstep. 'Bastard!'

'Arsehole,' Lizzie said, hugging her friend. 'What did you tell Oscar?'

'Nothing yet.' Megan sniffed into Lizzie's shoulder. 'He stayed at Bryce's last night.'

'Listen to me,' Lizzie said in her best stern-midwife tone. 'You and Oscar come straight to my house after school, okay? The girls are out tonight, so I'll order pizza and we'll send the boys to their rooms with their devices. They'll think it's Christmas. Then you and I can talk and drink wine. Deal?'

'It's fine, we can —'

'Deal?'

'Okay, thank you.'

Megan felt bad about dumping her misery on Lizzie, especially when her best friend was dealing with the daily dramas of looking after four children, but she also knew that even if Lizzie was juggling ten children and three full-time jobs, she'd still be there for her.

'Arsehole,' Lizzie muttered again.

'Bastard,' Megan croaked.

Over the next two weeks, whenever Lizzie wasn't working night shifts, Megan and Oscar ate dinner at the Barretts'.

'Why are Megan and Oscar here again?' she overheard Archie ask Lizzie one night when they were washing the dishes. 'Are they homeless?'

'No, but you will be if you don't rinse that plate properly.'

Megan was blessed to have Lizzie. Sam too. When she'd first told him what had happened, he couldn't comprehend it.

'Wait, *he* broke up with *you*?'

When Megan had confirmed that was indeed the case, Sam had labelled Eddie 'an idiot of the highest order'. He'd gone on to say that Megan was one of the best women in the known universe and she should be the first human to meet extra-terrestrials when they inevitably made contact.

'Even though,' he'd said, 'the aliens would soon be disappointed when they saw the rest of us.'

Sam's platitudes may have been slightly over the top, but Megan still appreciated them.

Ellie was furious, too. 'What a lousy, good-for-nothing little shit-faced ...'

'Calm down, Mum,' Megan said. 'And please don't tell anyone here, okay? I don't need everyone asking if I'm okay every time they order an Earl Grey.'

They were sitting in Ellie's sunroom, and Megan's mother had spent the past five minutes pacing back and forth, ranting about Eddie's iniquities. Megan had known this would be Ellie's reaction, which was why she hadn't told her in a public space.

'I hope he gets Dengue fever,' Ellie growled. 'In his dick.'

That made Megan laugh for the first time since Eddie broke her heart.

When Oscar had asked, 'Is Eddie coming over this weekend?' Megan had faked a coughing fit and run from the room. Once she'd composed herself enough, she had sat down with her son and explained that she and Eddie weren't seeing each other anymore, so he wouldn't be coming around this – or any – weekend.

'But I like Eddie.'

'I liked Eddie, too, but he's really busy with work and we hardly get to see each other, so it's just easier this way.'

He's also a lying, cheating arsewipe, darling, she thought, watching Oscar's disappointed expression.

Oscar was upset, but after talking about it for a bit longer, he seemed to accept that these things happened with grown-ups sometimes and went back to constructing his Lego City Monster Truck. Thankfully, Eddie hadn't even come close to becoming the male role model Megan had hoped he'd be for her son.

Bryce's reaction was as predictable as ever.

'You have to respect his truth, Megs,' he'd said, placing a well-meaning hand on her arm.

'His cheating truth?'

'Exactly,' Bryce had responded, entirely unsarcastically.

And as for Eddie? Megan hadn't heard boo from him,

which was fine. There was no need for him to make contact since there was nothing of Eddie's in her entire house. With the benefit of hindsight, that felt telling. To think that she'd been fantasising about having a baby with this man! A man who hadn't kept so much as a toothbrush or razor in her bathroom cupboard in their two years together. But Megan couldn't be imagining his commitment to her, at least in the beginning. He told her he loved her. He'd made her believe that he loved her. And whenever he returned from a trip, he told her how much he'd missed her and how lonely he was without her. All lies, since he'd actually been shagging his very interesting, not boring, senior projects manager.

Megan sat in the schoolyard now, watching Max and Oscar play four square with their mates, and the thought of Eddie's affair made her stomach turn just as it had at least fifty times a day over the past fortnight. As Megan experienced the familiar jolt of pain surge through her chest, she wondered if he gave her any thought at all? Or if the other woman had filled that space in his thoughts before Megan even knew she existed.

'Hello?'

'Sorry, what?'

Sam grinned down at her. 'I said, good morning. We've been waving at you like lunatics for the past ten seconds. You were staring straight at us.'

'Oh, hi.' Megan forced a smile. 'Sorry, thinking about camp stuff.'

Lizzie handed Megan her coffee and shot her a sympathetic look, definitely not buying the excuse. Megan made a decision not to be a misery guts this morning. She was going to give her mates a bit of the ol' Megan Wylie spirit instead of being her usual sad-sack self.

'Hey,' she said brightly, 'do either of you know anything about consolidating photo libraries?'

'I don't even know what you just said.'

'A bit,' Sam said. 'Why?'

'I've got over fifty thousand digital photos and loads of photo libraries on multiple hard drives,' Megan said. 'Last night I found twelve duplicates of a photo I took of a shopping list in 2016.'

'I can take a look tonight,' Sam said.

'Really?'

'I'll be at your place anyway, so might as well.'

When Megan had first signed up for the evening classes, Sam had offered to babysit, and she had been extremely grateful. She hated having to ask Bryce for favours. It also meant that Oscar got some quality hang-out time with Sam's son, Tyler. As an only child, it was a treat for Oscar, and slightly lessened her guilt for not providing her son with a sibling.

'Thanks!'

'Hey yeah, tonight's your first kids' writing class!' Lizzie said, tapping Megan's thigh. 'Exciting!'

'Nerve-racking,' Megan said.

'Nah, you'll be awesome. Liane Moriarty better watch herself!'

Sam frowned. 'Does she write kids' books?'

Just the thought of walking into that classroom tonight made Megan shudder. She was actually terrified. 'Can you bring a couple of valium tonight, too, Sam.'

'I'm all out. But happy to roll a joint,' he replied.

'With Oscar in the house?'

'I can teach the little fella to roll a three-paper.' Sam grinned.

Lizzie waved a hand in Sam's direction. 'And the Babysitter of the Year Award goes to …'

'Since when are you a computer nerd?' Megan asked Sam. 'I thought that was Dave's wheelhouse.'

'Hey, I may be a two-finger typist,' Sam said, holding up both pointer fingers. 'But I'm pretty handy with tech stuff.'

'It's a bit of a dog's breakfast,' Megan said with a grimace.

'Nothing could shock me after seeing Dave's man cave,' Sam said. 'It's like *Mr Robot* in there.'

'So, no hot date tonight, then, Sammy?' Lizzie teased.

'I'm over Tinder,' Sam said. 'I should create an app called Fuck Buddy. Just tell it like it is.'

A few kids shooting hoops nearby turned and stared.

Lizzie snorted. 'Good one, potty mouth.'

'Look out,' Megan said, nodding towards the red-brick school building.

Sam and Lizzie followed Megan's eyeline to see Rania Jalali walking around the side of the building, with a posse of three excited school mums in tow.

'Excellent!' Sam grinned. 'I love the smell of fawning on a Wednesday morning.'

'Nice.' Lizzie turned to Megan. 'How is it possible you didn't know who Rania was when you spend half your life on social media?'

Megan baulked. It was true she was an avid Insta user, but the implication that she'd follow a vacuous millennial whose only mission in life was to be famous was insulting.

'I don't follow *her*!' Megan cried. 'And I don't watch reality TV.'

'All right, relax.'

One of Rania's mummy minions pointed at their bench and Rania began heading in their direction.

'The lady approacheth,' Sam announced with suitable pomp.

'She does not-teth,' Lizzie said.

Sam turned to Lizzie. 'She's looking at you!'

Megan had to agree. It did indeed look like Rania was smiling at Lizzie.

'What? Why?'

Sam forced a frozen smile onto his face. 'Act natural!'

'Oh, for fuck's sake!' Megan rolled her eyes. 'She's not the bloody queen. She's a —'

'Shut up!' Sam hissed.

'Hello!' Rania Jalali was standing in front of them in all her shiny, famous glory. The morning sun appeared to form a shimmering halo of light around her perfect physique, which today was clad in a white spaghetti-strapped summer dress and her trademark sunglasses sat atop her head, leaving large brown eyes on full display.

Megan took in the goddess before her, and for the first time in her life felt like a frumpy middle-aged mum.

'Hi,' Megan said, noting her unintentionally curt tone of voice.

'Hello ... Hi ...' Sam stammered.

Megan almost laughed out loud. Rania's mere presence had put the poor man into a catatonic state.

'Hey.' Lizzie was completely unperturbed, and Megan was reminded why she loved her friend. It didn't matter if she was talking to the queen or a garbo, Lizzie Barrett gave no shits about status, money or looks.

Rania smiled politely at each of them in turn before focusing her gaze squarely on Lizzie. 'I'm Rania.'

As if we didn't friggin' know, Megan thought.

'Sorry to bother you, Lizzie,' she said, 'but one of the

mums said I should talk to you about signing my son up for the morning soccer classes?'

Her accent was feminine and sweet with a touch of Brighton private schoolgirl, and Megan marvelled at the fact that even this woman's voice was enchanting.

'Oh, sure,' Lizzie said. 'Does he want to start this week?'

'That would be wonderful,' Rania exclaimed, clapping her hands. 'Thank you.'

A dazzling smile broke across Rania's face and Megan heard a tiny whimper escape from the back of Sam's throat. She had a strong urge to lean over and whack him.

'No worries.'

'It's very kind of you to offer to coach the kids,' Rania said.

'Oh, Higgsy's the coach,' Lizzie said. 'I'm just the assistant.'

'Higgsy?'

'Mr Higgs. He runs the classes.'

Higgsy was Baytree's very cute – very Energiser Bunny – sports teacher. He'd asked Lizzie if she wanted to be assistant coach for the Baytree soccer team after Dave told him she'd played in the state league as a teenager. She'd also coached Max's team at one point.

'Just fill in a form at the office and they'll pass it on to him,' Lizzie said.

'Thank you!' Rania said, clasping her hands together in a sign of gratitude. 'Tishk will be thrilled.' She swept her dark eyes across all three of them. 'Have a lovely day!'

She turned with a grace that was as captivating as it was effortless and sashayed away. Megan noted that Rania's dress swished about her body as if it had been handmade on a mountain top by a mystical dressmaking guru.

'She's lovely,' Sam said, leaning forward to rest his elbows on his knees.

'She is actually.' Lizzie sounded as surprised as Megan felt.

'Never judge a book by its cover,' Megan said. 'That's what I always say.'

'You've literally never said that in your life.'

Sam pulled out his phone. 'I've gotta text Dave and tell him.'

Megan stood up.

'Where are you going?' Lizzie asked.

'Camp meeting,' she said, swinging her tote bag over her shoulder. 'Nicola has suggested daily meditations. With forty kids. On a school camp. I'm all for mindfulness, but just let the kids do a friggin' rope course.'

Walking away from her friends, Megan wondered if she'd found the cure to a broken heart after all. Playing pretend.

★★★

Sam and the kids arrived just as Megan started chopping the capsicum for her bolognese sauce.

'*I'll get it!*' Oscar abandoned his Death Star drawing and bolted for the door.

Megan followed her excited son as he hurled himself down the hallway, before yanking the door open to Sam, Lola and Tyler.

'Take me to your leader,' Sam demanded in a loud, robotic voice.

Megan clocked Lola rolling her eyes behind his back.

'Hey, gang,' she said. 'Come in.'

Tyler and Oscar immediately scampered towards Oscar's

room, while Sam and Lola entered in a more dignified manner.

'Good afternoon, Megan,' Lola said. 'Would you mind if I sat in your living area to read?'

'Of course,' Megan said. 'What are you reading?'

'*Portrait of a Lady*.' Lola held out the book, a nineteenth-century damsel holding a parasol on the cover. 'Henry James.'

'Can you believe the rubbish kids are reading these days?' Sam said to Megan. 'Amiright?'

Unimpressed yet again by her father's wit, Lola headed into the lounge room.

Sam shrugged. 'She'll love me again in her twenties.'

Sam's eleven-year-old wasn't your average Aussie tween. Lola Hatfield was more likely to be found reading a Brontë sister than *The Hunger Games*, preferred embroidery over TikTok and frequently used words like 'ghastly'. Today she was wearing a light-purple cotton skirt that swished around her ankles and a short-sleeved lacy white shirt, and her hair was tied back into two neat braids. The whole ensemble gave the impression that Lola had walked straight out of the goldrush and into the twenty-first century. Since casting Lola as the Ghost of Christmas Past two years ago, Megan had got to know her quite well and was a huge fan of the sweet, kooky girl.

Leaving Lola to her novel, Megan and Sam headed to the office. Sam sat down behind Megan's pristine, dark wood desk, pulled the mouse towards him and made a few clicks.

'Oh okay, so you've got three different photo libraries,' Sam said, peering at her screen. 'That's not so bad.'

'Um, no,' Megan said, coming to stand beside him.

'That's all I can see here.'

'You might want to have a look in there.' Megan stepped back and gestured to something at his feet.

Sam looked under the desk and frowned before lifting up a large purple plastic tub. 'Good Lord, woman,' he grunted as he hoisted it onto the desk. 'Stockpiling gold, are we?'

Megan grinned, anticipating Sam's reaction when he opened the tub. His expression quickly changed from 'ready and willing' to 'holy shit' as he opened the lid to reveal numerous tangled USB cables, power adapters and external hard drives of various shapes, colours and sizes.

'Right, so, you're actually stockpiling the entire internet under your desk.'

Megan gave him a sheepish 'I warned you' grin.

'So, how many of these have photos or photo libraries on them?'

Megan's lips contorted into an apologetic smile. 'All of them?'

Sam looked back into the deep abyss of the tub with fresh terror as he extracted a large external hard drive wrapped in its own cords. It was a brick of a thing, dusty and – by hard-drive standards – almost decrepit. He stared in muted amazement.

'Still up for the job?' Megan fully expected him to bolt for the front door.

'Absolutely!' Sam's eyes were wide, and he was nodding like a perpetual motion toy. 'I just have to let the kids know they'll have to make their own meals for the next two to three ... weeks. And I'll be needing a caffeine drip, STAT.'

'Coming right up!'

***

After circling the city block for twenty minutes and swearing at the top of her lungs for the duration, Megan finally found a park. She'd left home early, expecting to make it to the city in plenty of time to grab a coffee before class started at 5.30 p.m., but hadn't factored in peak-hour traffic. Now she was speed walking towards the Centre for Adult Education with only five minutes to spare. Thank God Sam had arrived early. Not that he'd managed to get anywhere with her photo libraries.

'I'll feed the kids and then keep going with it, but I reckon you'll need some kind of computer genius to help you,' Sam had finally conceded. 'Someone under the age of fifteen is probably your best bet.'

Megan had been disappointed but completely unsurprised. Eddie had dubbed her purple tub full of cables and hard drives The Unthinkable, and after trying every weekend for a full month to sort it out, had finally admitted defeat. She'd laughed at the look of amazement on his face after he'd taken out and lined up every single external hard drive on her kitchen bench.

Bastard.

Now why did she have to go and think of Eddie just as she was about to embark on a new and exciting chapter of her life? She doubted her ex would even remember that tonight was her first class. *Fuck him*, Megan thought. *This is my night and I'm not going to let him spoil it.*

Megan had been harbouring a secret dream to write a kids' book since running the Baytree school concert two years ago. Charles Dickens's *A Christmas Carol* had initially been considered a ludicrous choice for primary school kids, but Megan had proved them all wrong. Kids, parents, teachers and the community alike had loved the play, almost as much as Megan had enjoyed working on it. And the whole experience ignited a newfound interest in reading.

Megan initially worked her way through books by Dickens, the Brontë sisters, Austen, Hemingway and Virginia Woolf – all borrowed from Lola's collection – before moving on to more contemporary fiction. For a woman who'd previously never read anything more taxing than *Vogue*, it was like discovering a new drug. There were many nights when she stayed up way past a sensible bedtime, engrossed in Stephen King's latest thriller, or Nora Ephron.

'You're a proper addict,' Lizzie said one morning when Megan turned up to drop-off, bleary-eyed, a book in her hand. 'Have you thought about writing something yourself?'

'Yeah, right!'

'You should,' Lizzie said. 'What about that beautiful post you wrote about Henry? You inspired people and got the community's arse in gear with your words.'

Eddie's grandfather, Henry, had been Baytree Primary's beloved lollipop man. When he died and no one at school noticed his absence for a whole week, it caused quite the controversy in their community. Megan couldn't have known then that her response to a nasty tweet about Baytree's uncaring community would set off a chain of events that would result in her running the concert and dating Henry's grandson, Eddie.

'I don't think you can compare a post to actual writing.'

'Why not?' Lizzie shrugged. 'It's still putting words together and making people feel and think.'

Megan had dismissed Lizzie's suggestion at the time. She wasn't a *writer*! Writers were people who got top marks in English at school and Megan had barely scraped through her final exams. But Lizzie's words stayed with her over the following weeks. One night, Eddie was away in Canberra attending a very important-sounding cultural governance conference, and Megan began googling writing courses. For fun, she told herself. Half an hour later, she was clicking 'pay now to confirm your enrolment'.

Megan had briefly considered ditching the writing course after Eddie dumped her, but Lizzie wouldn't hear of it.

'You're doing it!'

'The last thing I feel like doing right now is thinking up cute happy endings for kids' books!' she told Lizzie last week as they sat on the Barretts' back deck cradling a glass of chilled rosé. 'I'm not a writer.'

'So, you'll learn,' Lizzie said. 'If nothing else, it's the perfect opportunity to do something for you. Not Oscar, not the school, not your mum … you.'

Megan knew she was right. Also, it was pointless to disagree with Lizzie when she made up her mind. This was why she was now about to enter her first writing class at the age of thirty-seven.

It was a bland beige room with yellow rectangular tables arranged into a horseshoe configuration. A dozen or so people were already scattered around the tables, waiting for class to start, and there was a silent, strained atmosphere in the room. Everyone stared at their phones or tapped away on their laptops, and Megan suddenly felt like she was back in her first day of Year Seven.

A couple of people glanced up as Megan entered, and tight, polite smiles were exchanged as she scanned the room. She spotted three empty seats in the furthest corner of the horseshoe and made a beeline. Taking a seat on the middle empty chair, Megan began to unpack her brand-new Kikki. K notebook, Lamy fountain pen and her laptop as she discreetly checked out her classmates. She was the youngest by far. It was mostly women in their forties and fifties, plus two men in the same age bracket. But just as she was basking in her youthful superiority, the door opened again to reveal someone much younger.

Her first thought was, *Why the hell is a Calvin Klein model doing a writing course?*

He had giant-sized black headphones draped around his neck and was wearing black jeans and a plain black T-shirt. He couldn't have been older than twenty, and he was beautiful. Actually beautiful. Thick brown hair, olive complexion, a smattering of stubble and dark eyes. Just as Megan was thinking that he could have been cast in a reboot of *Rebel Without a Cause*, the guy scanned the room, locked eyes with her and headed straight for her table.

I guess he figures I'm the only one in this room who knows what Netflix is, Megan thought wryly.

'Hey,' he whispered, slipping into an empty chair and flashing two extremely cute dimples at her. 'I'm Harry.'

'Megan.'

Harry pulled a laptop out of his brown leather shoulder bag and glanced around the room. 'Do you feel like we might be in the special-needs class?' he whispered.

He was leaning so close to Megan that she could smell his woody sea-salt scent. This kid also seemed to have exquisite taste in aftershave.

'Well, I'm definitely in the right place, then,' she whispered back.

He grinned. 'Think you're special, do you?'

'Needy,' Megan responded, then immediately regretted

it. 'I just mean that I've never written anything before so …'

'You're very beautiful.'

The statement came out of nowhere and hung in the air. Many men had told Megan she was beautiful but never in such a matter-of-fact manner. Were all Gen Z kids this confident? More importantly, was this particular Gen Z kid coming onto her? Surely not.

'Wow, that's blunt,' she said. 'But thanks.'

'Sorry.' Harry gave her a sheepish grin. 'I do that.'

'No, it's nice of you. Thanks.'

Harry was far too young for Megan to entertain the notion of even flirting with him, but there was nothing wrong with a bit of eye candy as a regular midweek treat.

Chapter Six
Sam

To: jack_woz_here@hotmail.com
From: samhatfieldchef@bigpond.com
Subject: Babysitting Duty!

Hey dickhead,

Sounds like you're turning into quite the carpenter. Can't wait to see the final result. I might even get you to knock up a fancy-pants waterfall bench seat for me, too. Fair play to you. I would cut my thumb off, for sure.

I envy you and your man cave workshop. I could use one of those right now with an eleven-year-old girl and her raging hormones in the house. Speaking of which, I enrolled Lola in that drama class. Lizzie sent me a link, but I hadn't read it properly, which meant I got the pleasant surprise of discovering there are not just one, but two classes a week! I may have done a little fist pump. Of course, I genuinely hope Lola gets something good out of it, but I sure as shit know that I'll benefit from it greatly. It's like we've reached father–daughter critical mass lately and need some serious decompression.

Now don't freak out, but I'm at Megan's place.

Babysitting.

I'm guessing that's not what you were hoping to hear, but babysitting is still pretty sexy, right?

Yeah, no, it's not. Her son, Oscar, is an easy kid to mind, especially when he has Tyler to keep him occupied. If I'm honest, the iPad is doing most of the heavy lifting. If the iPad could make mac and cheese, there'd be no need for me at all.

I can feel you willing me to talk more about Megan. Eye-roll emoji. Fine.

The reason I'm babysitting is because she's started a writing course. Since she sold her business, she's been a bit … wacky. That's not the right word, but it's the only one I've got. I mean, she pretty much runs Baytree Primary these days, like a mobster with fingers in every school pie. But she hasn't locked onto anything that floats her boat professionally yet. But she's recently decided she might want to write kids' books. She'll probably be the next … I don't know any famous children's authors.

She asked me if I could help sort out the photos on her computer, loads of duplicates and that sort of thing, but it has broken me, and I may never fully recover.

And no, there were no nudes, McPervy. But I only scrolled a few hundred of the approximately fifty thousand digital images she possesses.

Is digital hoarding a thing?

I'm actually really pissed off that I couldn't fix it. I wanted to be able to do this for her, and now she's gonna come back from her writing class and I'll have to be all, 'Oh well, there was a firewall filled with viruses and I'm pretty sure you've been hacked by Russians.' I'd never been in her office before today, and apart from the purple hard-drives tub from hell, it's pretty organised. Exactly what I'd expect, to be honest. There are some really cool photos on the wall, too. I have to remember to ask her about them when she gets back. That's if I haven't been sucked into Megan's computer by then.

I especially wanted to be her knight in shining armour right now because of everything she's going through. She got dumped by a prick who cheated on her. I mean, seriously. Did that fool think he could do better? Was he cheating on Megan with ...?

I can't even think of anyone more beautiful.

And it's not just that. She deserves happiness more than most, I reckon. And that cheating knob clearly paid very little attention to how unbelievably lucky he was.

It always sucks to see your friends hurting and to know there's nothing you can do to help. I just wanted to do a simple thing. But this task is as simple as brain surgery. So, I'll just keep being her friend and telling her bad jokes and getting her coffees and babysitting her kid.

When I say it like that, I sound like a saint!

Go me.

S x

Chapter Seven
Lizzie

'Great, Emma! Now change direction!'

'Good boy, Alfie!'

Higgsy and I side-skipped along the edge of the pitch, yelling encouragement to the prep kids running amok all over the school oval.

'Accelerate with the ball, Jake!'

Then, realising he'd have no idea what that meant …

'Great work, mate! Keep running!'

Jake turned to look at me and I gave him a thumbs up. He beamed.

These five- and six-year-olds could barely find their own toes, so simultaneously running, locating and kicking a ball without face-planting or smashing into each other every few seconds was near impossible. They seemed to have no trouble locating their penises, though. As a mum of two boys, I knew this was standard prep-boy behaviour, but that didn't mean I wanted to be confronted with it first thing in the morning. In fact, part of my role as Higgsy's assistant involved trying to encourage the boys to run with their hands 'away from your body!' But nothing short of amputation would stop their constant fiddling.

Only one girl had signed up for the before-school soccer sessions. Emma had the potential to be a cracking striker, but at this early stage she was still trying to establish better pathways from her brain to her feet. All in all, ten prep kids had shown up for the first training session. They were adorable, but as useless as tits on a bull.

Rania's son, Tishk, was actually the best of the bunch. I'd assumed Rania would stay to watch his first session, as most mums did, but she'd done the old drop and go, instead. I spotted her hurrying back to her sleek black sportscar as I set up the nets at the other end of the oval. I waited for her to drive off, but it seemed she was going to watch Tishk from her air-conditioned vehicle. Smart move. It was one of those brutal summer mornings where it hit thirty degrees before 8 a.m.

The session ended a few minutes before the first bell and ten sweaty little bodies scampered off to hydrate before classes started.

'Hi, Mum!' Max shouted as he ran past at full speed, reminding me of the blurry road runner.

'Hey, where's your hat? If Miss Guthrie ...'

But he was gone. There wasn't a shred of doubt in my mind that my eight-year-old son would be the one to send me to an early grave. The kid approached everything at alarming speed and with zero regard for self-preservation. Whether he was playing football or walking the dog, Max Barrett was full throttle. I was already preparing myself for a future full of broken bones, underage drinking and the occasional crime spree.

I watched Rania lean over the waist-high chain-link fence to hug her son. Even from a distance I could see that her eyes were red and puffy.

She noticed me staring in her direction and instantly popped her glasses back on, gave me a thankyou wave and headed back to her car.

I was intrigued.

★★★

'Are you sure she didn't just have a late night?' Sam asked. 'I've turned up to drop-off looking like a strung-out junkie a thousand times.'

I grabbed the only takeaway cup left in the cardboard tray and sat down. 'She'd definitely been crying. I've been around enough distressed women to know.' I took a sip and cold coffee flooded my mouth. 'Ugh!'

'Yeah, I was gonna warn you.' Sam grimaced. 'It's been there a while.'

'Just pretend you ordered an iced latte,' Dave suggested.

'Good idea. It is three hundred degrees, after all.' I could already feel sweat pooling behind my knees and I'd only been sitting on the bench for a few seconds.

'What's she got to cry about?' Megan asked, returning to the Rania subject. 'Did Daddy only give her one Porsche for her birthday this year?'

'Is the reality star loaded?' Sam leaned forward with interest.

Megan's perfectly manicured eyebrows shot up. 'Have you seen her car? My house costs less.'

'Oh, yeah, the Jalalis are cashed up!' Dave exclaimed.

We all turned our attention towards Baytree's resident Rania expert.

'Her dad's a big-time engineer!' Dave put down his coffee cup, freeing his hands for gesticulation. 'He designed some famous bridge over in the north about ten years ago and made a mint. They moved across the river into a big fancy mansion and sent Rania to Channingford.'

I nudged Megan. 'Didn't you go there?'

She rolled her eyes. 'Hated it.'

Channingford Girls Grammar was the most expensive

private school in our area. Greg and I would have needed to sell Archie just to go on the waiting list.

'Must be a pretty good bridge,' Sam said.

Dave pulled out his phone and typed with impressive dexterity. 'Here it is, The Vida Goldstein Bridge. Says here Rania's dad was a big deal in Pakistan. Built heaps of bridges there, too, but had to start from scratch when they came here.'

'Sasha's been to Pakistan,' Sam said. 'She said it's amazing. She's going back soon for some big arty festival. Siba or Sibi something?'

Smart, sexy Sasha ended up helping us with the Dickens script for the school concert, adapting the ye olde language into something most kids (and adults) could understand. I was glad to hear Sam was still in touch with her.

'Eddie posted about going to a conference somewhere over there in the next couple of weeks,' Megan said, staring vacantly ahead. 'Or maybe it was Qatar?'

'Pakistan and Qatar are nowhere near each other,' Dave said matter-of-factly. 'Pakistan is in South Asia and Qatar is in West Asia.'

'No one likes a geographical smartarse, mate,' Sam said dryly.

Why was Megan torturing herself by scrolling through Eddie's happy travel snaps on social media? Thank God she had the writing course, and the oldies at Applewood, to keep her busy. Not to mention the camp. But still, I wished for Megan to be sixteen and heartbroken; wallowing in the misery of it all while still revelling in the glorious, tragic drama. When relationships end between adults, there's no naivety or twisted romanticism to lean on.

I missed Greg.

'Why are you still following him?'

'I don't follow him!' Megan said. 'Harriet does! She keeps me updated on Eddie's news, but only when Mum isn't around to tell her off for being an "insensitive old cow".'

Bloody hell. Ellie promised not to tell any of the residents about the break-up. I loved Megan's mum, but the woman couldn't keep a secret to save her life.

'Is Harriet the one who suggested the residents wear nappies on day trips, so they don't have to keep stopping for bathroom breaks?' Sam asked.

'The very same,' Megan said.

'Smart lady,' Sam said.

Megan's expression was starting to change with all this talk of Eddie.

'Greg texted this morning saying the weather in Sydney is perfect.'

'Stupid Sydney and its stupid perfect weather,' Megan grumbled.

'That's almost word for word what I texted him back.'

'Listen to all of you talking about your cavorting exes.' Dave chuckled.

I glared at him. 'Um, Greg is very much not my ex, Dave.'

'Yeah, nah, you know what I mean. Just, they're all out there feeding their wanderlust, seeing the world ...'

'Sydney.'

'... while you guys are here, sitting on your bench, y'know ... stagnant.'

We stared at Dave, speechless.

'Thanks, Dave,' Sam said. 'That's a really useful perspective.'

'Oh, nah, nah, don't get me wrong!' Dave began a hasty backpedal, 'being grounded – being *settled* – is the best!'

Megan narrowed her steely green eyes. 'Is it?'

'Sure! Like Dorothy said, "There's no place like home!"' Sensing he was tumbling into dangerous territory, Dave jumped up. 'Gotta bounce, catch yas!'

We watched him lope away, each of us lost in our own self-pity. Dave was right. Everyone else was off having adventures.

'Well, I'm going to Kinglake soon,' Megan said haughtily.

'Yeah!' Sam shouted. 'And I've got that gig at the Frankston Bunnings sausage sizzle coming up in a few months, so who's having adventures now, huh?'

They looked to me, waiting for my contribution to the charade.

'I'm going nowhere. Except work.'

Sam grabbed his bag. 'Speaking of.'

'Hey, maybe we should catch up at pick-up from now on?' Megan said to Sam. 'You're a nine-to-fiver, I do mornings and Lizzie's shifts are all over the shop.'

Sam slung his Crumpler across his chest and nodded. 'Makes sense.'

'Also, afternoon catch-ups have the potential to turn into dinner and wine.'

They looked at me as if I'd just announced a pregnancy.

'Amazing,' Sam said.

'Done,' Megan agreed.

'See?' Sam said, edging towards the gate and snapping his fingers like an upstaging backing singer. 'Who says our lives are boring? We're mixing things up, changing the game, living on the edge!'

'I'm so glad you're all for mixing things up,' Megan said,

as she began to follow him, 'because I need to talk to you and Dave about doing a very "living on the edge" gig.'

Sam froze mid-click. 'Cool, where?'

Megan flashed him her most dazzling suck-up smile. 'Grade Five/Six camp.'

'Yeah, right, wow,' Sam said. 'We are so definitely unavailable.'

'Wait, listen …!'

She gave me a grin and a wink before hurrying after Sam. It made me happy to see her having some fun.

'What happened to me?' Megan had wailed to me after too many chardonnays on my back deck last week. 'I was a strong, successful, happily single businesswoman and mum, then Eddie fucking Paterson comes along and now I'm a miserable, lonely waitress with no prospects.'

'No offence to miserable, lonely waitresses with no prospects.'

Although she'd laughed, in that moment I'd genuinely worried that Megan would never be the same. But it looked like she was now making an effort to get on with things and move forward.

What was the word Dave had used? Stagnant?

Yep, that's how I felt sitting on this bench in the hot morning sun, children running past and squealing in the nearby playground. I felt old. Very old and yes, jealous. Jealous of Sasha and Eddie and their adventures and their youth. Those days were over for me. Once the kids were grown, I might enjoy that kind of freedom, maybe even travel again, but unfortunately you didn't get a second chance at your youth.

From: nmcgintyhamperqueen@gmail.com
Subject: Grade Five/Six Camp

Dear Five/Six parents,

Wow. What an exciting time for your little ones!

All of us on the camp committee are so excited to help your children have the time of their lives on their forthcoming school camp. There will be so many opportunities for personal development, spiritual and emotional growth, and if the children behave as they should, a lot of fun, too. Planning for the camp is a complex affair for the committee and staff, so as per my last email, and Miss Naidu's request over a week ago, could any parent with a child who needs to take medication on the camp PLEASE COMPLETE THE ATTACHED MEDICAL AUTHORITY FORM AND RETURN IT TO THE OFFICE NO LATER THAN FRIDAY THIS WEEK!

Thank you in advance for your prompt attention to this matter.

Very best regards,

Nicola McGinty – President, Five/Six Camp Committee

P.S. Please direct all ongoing camp enquiries to Megan Wylie at meganwylie@me.com.

P.P.S. I am attaching a document I have drawn up that addresses my concerns over the school's dangerous play equipment after a recent spate of broken collarbones. If you could read and sign, I will forward onto Penny Guthrie.

From: naidu.salena.q@eduaddress.vic.gov.au
Subject: Grade Five/Six Camp

Dear Nicola,

Thanks for taking the initiative and sending the above email to all of us Baytree teachers, as well as all of the Five/Six parents. Moving forward, it would be best if we could keep the internal correspondence between staff and camp-committee members until we finalise agenda items. After that time, I will send out appropriate information and requests. The parents find it reassuring to receive this sort of correspondence from education professionals.

Thanks,

Salena Naidu

P.S. I would rather you didn't attach non-camp-related petitions to a camp email.

From: meganwylie@me.com
Subject: Grade Five/Six Camp

Hey everyone,

First off, thanks to Mr Higgs for getting us the extra high-vis vests for camp activities. Although these are daytime activities, I'm sure Nicola is right in that we can't be too careful when it comes to the safety of the kids. Secondly, I talked with my mates Sam O'Connell and Dave Podanski about coming on board as camp helpers. They're keen and also interested in bringing their guitars along for some campfire entertainment. A lot of you know them already from the Mum's Night, and I'm sure you agree they'd be a valuable addition to our camp team. If anyone has any issues let me know, otherwise I'll assume they're in.

Since Nicola's big mail-out last week, I've heard back from some parents about their kids' medication needs. I'll go into more detail at our next meeting but wanted to let you know that we have one child (so far), Dylan, who is anaphylactic, so we'll each need ready access to an EpiPen for the duration of the camp. I've attached a PDF provided by Penny called Preparing for Camp with Food Allergies, which she has encouraged all of us to look through. Also, as many of the staff are already aware, there are at least two kids, Ben Gilbert and Caleb Kotnik, who have existing behavioural disorders. Again, let's discuss further at the meeting. Great work, everyone. This is going to be a lot of fun, hopefully for all of us as well as the kids.

Cheers, Megan

P.S. I believe it was actually only one broken collarbone and one sprained ankle that have occurred on the playground over the past year. Not a 'spate of broken collarbones'. Thanks for your concern, Nicola, but I would rather not sign the petition.

From: nmcgintyhamperqueen@gmail.com
Subject: Grade Five/Six Camp

Thank you, Megan,

Good to see you're keeping track. After contacting each Five/Six parent individually, I've now established a spreadsheet of every child in Five/Six with medical and/or behavioural issues including recommended action plans, necessary medication and medical contingency plans. I have First Aid Certification from St John's Ambulance and will be able to expertly assist.

Nicola McGinty – President, Camp Committee

P.S. The safety of our children should be our primary concern. I'm sure we can all agree that no child can have fun on camp with a shattered collarbone.

From: naidu.salena.q@eduaddress.vic.gov.au
Subject: Grade Five/Six Camp

Dear Nicola,

Every parent and staff member attending the camp has the necessary first-aid qualifications, all of which we confirmed while selecting the members of the camp committee. The school also has detailed records of the specific needs of every student in our care, but I look forward to seeing your spreadsheet regardless.

Your efforts and passion are much appreciated.

Salena Naidu – Grade Five/Six Teacher

P.S. A shattered collarbone sounds extreme, but your point is taken.

From: meganwylie@me.com
Subject: Question ...?

Hi Salena,

I don't want to speak out of turn, but I will anyway. Is Nicola driving you crazy?

Megan

From: naidu.salena.q@eduaddress.vic.gov.au
Subject: Question ...?

Hi Megan,

Completely crazy. But she gets things done for the school, and not a lot of parents get involved as much as the Nicolas (and Megans) of the world. So, we take the help where we can get it.

From: meganwylie@me.com
Subject: Question ...?

Of course. You guys – all the Baytree teachers – do so much. I just wish I'd got involved sooner!

Megan

P.S. If you compare me to Nicola McGinty again, you might be the one coming back from camp with a shattered collarbone.

From: naidu.salena.q@eduaddress.vic.gov.au
Subject: Question ...?

LOL

Chapter Eight
Megan

'A what wedding?'

'Steampunk.'

'What's steampunk?'

'It's a mix of science fiction and the Victorian era,' Bryce said, his eyes shining. 'Nostalgic meets futuristic.'

Megan tried to force an expression of genuine interest as Bryce prattled on about the theme for his upcoming wedding in Tasmania.

'... and Adam and I will be wearing goggles, top hats and red velvet jackets with —'

'Sorry, goggles?'

'Cyber goggles,' Bryce explained. 'Like retro pilot meets welding goggles.'

Jesus Christ, Megan thought. *Can this wedding just be over already!*

In the midst of her feelings of despair about her own love-life, Megan didn't have the capacity to feign joy for her ex-husband. Besides, the lead-up to Bryce and Adam's nuptials felt never-ending.

Megan told Bryce early on not to waste a single handmade, custom- designed, gold-foil-scroll invite on her, making it clear that she would politely decline it. This was why it was only now, two weeks before the event of the century, that she was hearing about their chosen theme. Bryce was a decent guy (even if he had kept his sexuality hidden from Megan for four years) and so had refrained from discussing wedding plans with her. But when he'd arrived to pick up Oscar for a sleepover five minutes ago, Megan had made the monumental error of asking how preparations were coming along.

'So, what will the best man be wearing?'

Their son was playing a major role in his dad's wedding and was slightly nervous about his best-man duties.

'Oh, Oscar's outfit is gorgeous!' Bryce enthused. 'It's a burgundy velvet vest, long black coat with white lace cuffs, leather boots, a burgundy band around his pants and a black velvet top hat with mini-goggles.'

Megan stared at her deluded ex-husband. 'Have you told Oscar?'

Bryce glanced towards Oscar's room and lowered his voice. 'Not yet. Saving it as a surprise for the fitting next weekend.'

'It'll be a surprise all right.'

Megan could already imagine the look of horror on her footy-loving, shorts-and-T-shirt-wearing son's face when he found out he was expected to dress like a character from a lost Guy Ritchie film. Oscar adored his dad and would do anything for him, but this could be a bridge too far.

'So, how are you doing, Megs?' Bryce asked gently.

The look of sympathy on his face made Megan want to slap it.

'Great, actually,' she said in a high voice that immediately gave her away. 'Loving the writing course.'

'Good, I'm glad.' Bryce nodded at her like a funeral director talking to the bereaved. 'And hey, I know it's not my regular night, but I can have Oscie while you go to your classes.'

'Thanks, but Sam already offered,' Megan said. 'Tyler and Oscar are great mates, so it works well. I just need help tonight because Sam had something on, but he's fine for every other week.'

Megan had been annoyed when Sam texted to say he couldn't have Oscar tonight. It was a rambling, apologetic text about his mum not owning a step ladder and needing some light bulbs changed, but promising it was a one-off. Ellie was going out (her mother had a better social life than she did), so she'd had no choice but to call Bryce.

'Come on, Oscie!' Bryce shouted down the hallway.

Oscar bounded out of his room, sleepover bag in one hand and Marvel Helicarrier in the other.

'I packed your book, and don't forget to fill in that worksheet for Miss Goring.'

'Okay, Mum.'

Megan wrapped him in her arms and kissed the top of his golden head. 'Have fun. Love you.'

'Bye!'

Megan felt that familiar sad twinge knowing her son wouldn't be coming back that night. It never felt like home without Oscar there. She watched him bolt towards Bryce's jeep in his Demons footy jumper and scuffed runners and decided there was no way that kid would wear a top hat and burgundy velvet vest without putting up a fight.

The thought cheered her immensely.

★★★

'So, how's your writing going?'

It was break time and Megan had just grabbed herself a coffee at the CAE café and sat down when Hot Young Harry plonked himself down across from her.

'Hello to you, too.'

'Sorry.' Harry grinned. 'Should probably start with "hi".'

It was the first time they'd spoken tonight. Thanks to yet another surprise set of Melbourne CBD roadworks, Megan had arrived ten minutes late to class and slunk into the first available seat closest to the door.

Harry had smiled at her from the other side of the room as she sat down, and she'd smiled back before trying to catch up with the lesson on narrative structure. She spent the whole lesson taking copious notes and barely had time to look at Harry, so she was strangely flattered that he'd sought her out.

Sitting across from him, Megan had a chance to fully appreciate his youthful beauty. With his plunging white V-neck T-shirt, dark hair and square jaw, he resembled a young Jared Leto, but without the God complex.

Harry picked up his flattened chicken wrap. 'You written much?'

'Uh, well … yeah I mean, it's interesting, isn't it?'

Harry took a bite, letting Megan's meaningless question hang in the air. What should she say? That she was a total fraud? As Harry stared at her with his non-judgemental eyes and unlined face, Megan decided to be honest.

'I've written nothing,' she told him. 'In fact, I've never written anything except Instagram posts and copy for kids' fashion websites.'

'Me either.' Harry grinned. 'Apart from English essays at school and the odd misguided love letter. And by letter, I mean text.'

Megan was relieved. Everyone else in class seemed to be a literary aficionado (or claimed to be anyway), but now she had an amateur ally. Her classmates were always banging on about character arcs and story engines, and Megan didn't have the courage to contribute for fear of being marched out of the building for crimes against the written word. Instead, she'd spent the entire time terrified Mrs Berger would ask Megan to share her thoughts on literary tropes or over-use of allegories.

'Well, that makes me feel better,' Megan said. 'When did you finish high school?'

'Last year … but I turned nineteen last month, so …' Then, clearly keen to move on from that subject, 'What sort of stuff do you want to write?'

'A kids' book.' She felt like a fraud saying it out loud. 'My son is eight and I want to write something he'd like, which means it would need to involve a Lego Helicarrier and snowtroopers.'

'Awesome!' Harry said. 'I'd totally read that book. You might have some copyright issues, though.'

'Good point. What about you?'

'Dunno,' Harry said. 'That's why I'm here, I guess. I work for Geek Doc and it's not the most fulfilling job, so I scribble stories at night. Helps keep me sane, y'know?'

An idea sparked in Megan's mind. 'So, you're a tech guy?'

'That's my bag.'

'What about consolidating photo libraries?'

'Sure, why?' Harry asked.

'Houston, we have a problem.'

Harry laughed and Megan was relieved that he got the reference, even if he did only know it as a Tom Hanks GIF.

'I reckon I can get your photos back to earth in one piece,' Harry said after Megan explained her issue.

'Cool,' Megan said. 'So, do I book through the website or …?'

'Nah, nah, it's on me.'

'Um, nah, nah,' Megan teased. 'I'm paying you.'

Harry shrugged. 'Okay, awesome, thanks. Is cash all right?'

'If you can sort out my dense jungle of digital memories,' Megan said, 'I'll not only pay you in cold, hard cash, I'll be your slave for a day. When are you free?'

'Friday night?'

'Really? I would've thought a young guy like you would be hitting the town on a Friday night.'

'Nah, I hate the town,' Harry said. 'Anyway, I'm pretty sure no one has hit the town since the forties.'

★★★

When Megan opened the front door to Harry, it was immediately obvious that he'd dressed up for the occasion. He was still wearing the navy-blue skinny jeans, but now they were rolled back down to shroud his ankles, and he'd donned a pair of well-worn tan brogues. His white shirt (had it been freshly ironed?) was untucked but fit him like a good shirt on a buff young man.

The only thing spoiling the whole effect were the trademark giant headphones around his neck.

Oscar was watching *The Force Awakens*, and as was usually the case when anything *Star Wars* related was on, barely registered the fact that a new person was in the house.

'Oscar, this is my friend from writing class, Harry. He's going to fix my computer.'

'Hello,' Oscar said politely, before turning his attention back to Finn and Rey.

'Kid's got taste,' Harry said as Megan led him towards her office.

'You're a *Star Wars* fan?'

'I work for a company called Geek Doc.' Harry grinned. 'What do you think?'

Harry followed Megan into her office and immediately walked over to study the framed black-and-white photos lining one wall.

'Did you take these?'

'Oh, yeah, years ago.'

They'd been there for so long that Megan didn't even notice them anymore. They were a series of photos she'd taken almost twenty years ago when she travelled to Africa for a modelling job. Megan had bought herself a fancy

Nikon camera (with a little help from Ellie), and had roamed around, taking random shots whenever she wasn't working. Harry was currently examining the top-ten best shots from the trip, including a bunch of kids playing soccer in an African village, a young boy lying beside his dog and a beautiful woman curled up in the foetal position on a mat.

'So, you're a photographer as well as a writer?'

'God, no.' Megan laughed. 'I just enjoy taking photos. I did a lot of it for my business, but those were taken a long time ago.'

Harry pointed to a smaller black-and-white shot of a young woman with short jet-black hair and dark eye makeup in a black singlet scowling into the camera lens. 'What about that one?'

'Oh, that was my Emo phase.'

'That's you?! No way!'

'Yep,' Megan said. 'I was eighteen and rebelling against my "Model Megan" label. Probably same age you are now, yeah?'

'I'm actually nineteen, thanks very much,' Harry said in a mock- offended tone.

'My apologies.'

'These are amazing. There's a real Tracey Moffatt vibe going on.'

Megan was flattered (and made a mental note to google Tracey Moffatt). Harry might have been laying it on to be polite, but it still felt good.

'Thanks, but I think one artistic pursuit at a time is enough for me.'

'Oh right, and you're probably a working mum, too, yeah?'

'Uh, well …'

Just say it, she thought. *It's not like you're trying to impress him.*

'I used to run an online business,' she said, 'but I sold it and now I'm working in a café at my mum's retirement village while I work out what's next.'

'Really? That's awesome.'

Megan cringed a little, as she always did when she heard young folk describe everything as 'awesome'.

'I don't know if I'd call it "awesome".'

'It is. Most people would just sit on their arses after selling a business,' Harry said, almost indignantly. 'And I'm guessing you're not doing it for the money. You wanna give back to your community. Like Picasso said, "The meaning of life is to find your gift. The purpose of life is to give it away."'

Was this kid for real? Quoting Picasso and referencing famous photographers? Were all modern nineteen-year-olds this cultured?

Harry looked embarrassed and Megan realised she'd been staring at him open-mouthed for a good three seconds.

'Wasn't Picasso an arsehole?'

Harry grinned. 'Yeah, but the old prick could paint.'

Megan laughed. 'Anyway, come over here and I'll show you the fun that awaits you.'

Harry turned to survey her desk that was covered in neat piles of paperwork, bills and books. It seemed to Megan that Harry was taking in more than the immediate task at hand.

'Here, let me move this stuff.'

Megan began sweeping notepads, books, bills and magazines into her arms. Harry stuck out his hand, not touching her, but close enough to perform some reiki, if he so desired.

'Man, don't even worry,' he said. 'It's fine. My desk is a "disgrace". That's Mum's word for it.'

Megan pulled the purple tub of digital doom out from under her desk and Harry blanched.

'Whoa!'

'I did warn you.'

'Yeah, nah, I'm pretty sure you didn't,' Harry said, holding up an external hard drive, circa 2002. 'Does this even work?'

'Hey, that thing can hold a hundred gigabytes.'

Harry reached into his pocket and pulled out his keys, locating a USB stick smaller than a lighter. 'This holds a hundred and twenty-eight gig.' He sounded almost sympathetic.

'All right, smartarse.' Megan laughed. 'How about you just get your geek on and sort out my photos instead of tech-shaming me.'

Harry grinned, re-pocketed his keys and settled himself into Megan's black leather desk chair.

'Tea, coffee, water?' Megan offered.

'Got any meth?'

Megan's head jerked around. 'What?'

'Crystal meth,' Harry replied evenly. 'Trying to sort out this mess is gonna induce psychosis, anyway, so I might as well get ahead of the game.'

Megan tried to keep a straight face. 'I'll call my guy,' she said. 'He's often out of meth – mainly due to me – but he's usually well stocked with speed, coke and mushrooms ...'

'Shit no!' Harry baulked. 'If I tried to do this on 'shrooms, I would, like, become these cables.'

'So, I can't offer you anything else?' she said, backing towards the door. 'I mean, until the meth arrives.'

'No thanks, I'm good.' Harry sat in Megan's chair and began to extricate various hard drives from the purple tub, lining them up on the desk behind her monitor.

Megan turned to go.

'Hey, don't forget,' Harry said from behind the monitor. 'If I nail this ... slave for a day.'

'Deal's a deal,' Megan said. 'But don't get ahead of yourself. I'm pretty sure some of that hardware came from Brashes.'

'Where?'

'Exactly. Good luck!'

As Megan left Harry to it, she felt a strange stirring inside her. Was that ...? No. Surely not. She couldn't possibly be attracted to Harry.

And even if she was, there was no way she could seriously think about starting something with him. Technically, he was an adult. *Legally*, he was a grown man. Then again, he was also a hell of a lot closer to her son's age than hers.

That fact alone was enough to stop her going down the *should I, shouldn't I* path.

Nope, she told herself. *You're not going there.*

Chapter Nine
Sam

To: jack_woz_here@hotmail.com
From: samhatfieldchef@bigpond.com
Subject: Camp Gig!

Hola, gilipollas!

I looked that up. It's legit Spanish for 'dickhead'. Say it out loud. *Gilipollas*. How good is that? I'm so happy to have learned that word today, and I'll be sprinkling it into as many conversations as possible with absolutely no explanation whatsoever.

'Did you bring your own bags?'

'Bet your *gilipollas* I did, lanky checkout guy.'

I found this new nickname when I was taking a break from googling 'cheap party supplies'. Lizzie's twins, Zara and Archie, are having a birthday party in a couple of weeks and I told Lizzie I'd research the cheapest dolphin-killing plastic plates, cups, cutlery etc. for her to buy. I'm taking a batch of my famous lime-and-raspberry friands.

Good to hear you've got so much on this weekend. Soon you'll need your own executive assistant to handle your calendar. That boat ride sounds awesome. The photo you sent of the science-fictiony contraption for securing your wheels so you don't roll off the boat mid-journey was even more awesome. I'm jealous enough of your weekend that you can enjoy it just that little bit more. If you catch a snapper, I'm coming over to cook it. Damn the distance, petrol costs, wear on my tyres and the damage it does to my belief in humanity.

Guess what? Megan's asked Dave and me to come on the school camp this year. School camp! She wants us there as the 'musical entertainment' component; play some songs around the campfire and get a good old singalong going. I've been looking up hot young things in the pop world right now, and it looks like I'll have to brush up on my Harry Styles, my Billie Eilish and my Troye Sivan (pronounced 'Suhvahn' in case you want to drop it into your next conversation with a twelve-year-old). Should be fun and it's only two nights. I'll just pull an I've-gotta-work-from-home-for-a-few-days-because-of-a-sick-kid thing. But I smell a rat. There was something in Megan's voice that made me think we'd be roped into helping out with more than singalongs. She was really overemphasising how 'much fun it would be' if we came along, and how 'great we are' with kids and how much she'd 'appreciate it'. It could've been a twitch, but I think she might have even batted her eyelids, which is a very unfair weapon to unleash on men as weak and impressionable as us. Suffice it to say, she got her way. Might be a good chance for some father–daughter bonding time with Lola, too. I'm pretty pumped, to be honest. A mini-getaway! With guitars and campfire jams.

I just have to make sure Bridget can have Tyler. I hate that I have to navigate these requests like a hostage negotiator. Imagine being able to shoot off a quick text: 'Hey Bridg, I'm gonna help out on school camp on dates x, y and z. You cool to have Tyler?' Yeah. Sure.

Megan was also banging on about some young dude from her writing class who was going to come over on Friday night and sort out the ten million digital photos spread over nine thousand different libraries on eight hundred different hard drives. I texted her on our WhatsApp group chat with Lizzie and Dave, and she said he successfully sorted it out. I'm happy for her, but she could've eased off on the lavish praise she was laying on this guy.

'Harry was amazing. Harry seriously changed my life. Harry just did it so quickly.'

I felt like I'd been shown up by the cool kid and nobody cared or even noticed that my feelings were hurt. But why on earth would Megan, or anyone else, think I'd feel stung by the fact that a young hotshot fixed something I couldn't? That's petty and immature. But damn it, I wanted to be the guy who fixed Megan's problem.

Me. Not this Harry dude. I was glad when Lizzie jumped in with, 'Jesus, sounds like you've got a crush.'

Megan was all like, 'Please, he's a teenager.'

Then Dave texted something about age being no barrier to love, and Lizzie wrote back, 'Spoken like a true sugar daddy,' which took out my WhatsApp Comment of the Day Award. In summation, up yours Harry Hotshot for making a grown man feel like the kid sitting on his own under the play equipment at lunchtime.

Soz, dickhead. Didn't realise I was harbouring so much venom for the poor young lad. If I find out his address, could you organise to have him whacked?

Lola loved her drama class. Like, REALLY loved it. This drama teacher is her new guru. Ninety per cent of Lola's sentences now start with, 'Rachel says ...' It's definitely helping her express herself, but I can't say I'm loving what's being expressed.

I finally went deep into the interwebs to understand what Lola has been spouting off at me, and found this: http://whatjaneaustenwordsmean.com/

Turns out she's been spewing some impressive bile my way in the form of some ye olde vernacular. Check out these tasty translations:

Sard off = fuck off.

Maggot Pie = lowest of the low. I had a strong feeling already that Maggot Pie wasn't a term of endearment, but 'lowest of the low'. Jesus.

Nancy Boy = der. I was getting that one in the nineties.

Dafted = dumb.

Berk = the c-bomb.

I didn't know that last one, but it happens to be the word Lola has been bandying around the most. My eleven-year-old is just wandering around the house dropping casual, coded c-bombs. Nice.

I remember seeing the word 'empowered' on the drama school website, and Lola is most definitely feeling that, which is a good thing, right? I just don't think I'm coping with it particularly well. I find myself longing for my baby or even my toddler. I'd gladly take changing nappies over dealing with expert emotional manipulation. I'm all for her growing into a strong young woman; a woman who will take no mess and speak her mind and smash the patriarchy. Just not this patriarch. I'm gonna hang around after the next class and say hi to 'Miss Rachel Says'. I want to suss her out. If she's going to be this new role model for Lola, she needs some patriarchal vetting. Ew. That sounds like a cultish conversion technique.

Send help.

I'm about to waterboard a drama teacher. Speaking of, have fun on the *oceano* (Spanish for ocean if you didn't know), *gilipolla*!

S x

To: codenamedave@gmail.com
From: samhatfieldchef@bigpond.com
Subject: Boys' Night Out

Hey Dave,

Yeah, I'm totally up for going to see a gig or two. What did you have in mind? I always promise myself I'll go see more live music – because I love it every time I do – but then I remember I'm old and that my slippers are hella comfy. I had a look at your proposed setlist for the camp. Couple of thoughts:

1. We aren't playing a set, so we don't need a setlist. Our job is to get the kids singing and having fun.
2. Referring to the latter part of point one, I have my doubts about including 'Nothing Compares 2U', 'Everybody Hurts' or anything by Alice in Chains. No offence to any of the artists, but dude, read the room. It's a group of kids on school camp. Most of 'em love their Top 40, so that's what we should give them. I've chucked a bunch of songs and charts in the Dropbox, so have a squiz and see what appeals.

Now, onto your ongoing obsession with our band name. Your list is as long as it is thoughtful, and I love how invested you are in finding just the right name for an acoustic duo that has finally booked their first school-camp gig. These are my top three:

- The Dave & Sam Jam (with apologies to Paul Weller)
- The Zing Zings

87

- The Greatest Acoustic Duo the World Has Ever Seen Full Stop.

That last one is just ridiculous enough to work. 'Thank you, New York! You've been amazing! And we've been The Greatest Acoustic Duo the World Has Ever Seen Full Stop, GOODNIGHT!'

You choose, mate. You're the one who's given it all the time and effort and thought. I'd be proud to be in any of those bands with you, so have at it, friend. Name this damn band!

See you Wednesday.

Tuned.

Sam

To: samhatfieldchef@bigpond.com
From: codenamedave@gmail.com
Subject: Boys' Night Out

OMFGOMFGOMFGOMFGOMFGOMFGOMFGOMFGOMFGOM FGOMFGOMFG!

DUDE, R U SERIOUS??????

If I can NAME THE BAND, I'll play WHATEVER you want at the camp FULL STOP LOLOLOLOLOL!!!

I didn't think this day could get ANY BETTER THANKS, MAAAAAAAAAAAAAATE!!

I got an email this morning saying that it's CONFIRMED that *CODENAME: CODE* has been optioned as A TV SHOW. AN ACTUAL HOLLYWOOD-PRODUCED TV SHOW!!! OMFGOMF GOMFGOMFGOMFGOMFGOMFGOMFGOMFGOMFG OMFG!!!! BEST DAY EVA!!

FULL STOP LOLOLOLOLOLOLOLOLOLOLOLOLOLOLOLOLO LOLOL.

Stay craycray, dave

To: codenamedave@gmail.com
From: samhatfieldchef@bigpond.com
Subject: Boys' Night Out

Holy shit, Dave! That's incredible news!

I don't see how you can compare my email to the one informing you that your graphic novel is being adapted into a Hollywood TV show, but I'll take it.

Dude, I am absolutely thrilled for you. That is the best news. I'm grinning like a Cheshire cat while I'm typing this. I know how hard you worked on that beast. And for years.

Mate, you have made my day.

I'll put a couple of extra beers in the fridge on Thursday so we can celebrate. And hey, don't eat. Let me cook you up a storm. Got any big food favourites? I know your better half is an exceptional cook, but I've got some moves, too.

Hey, invite Keshini along if you like! We'll make a night of it.

Good on you, Dave. Couldn't happen to a nicer fella.

S

P.S. I demand to get the catering contract for the TV show.

To: jack_woz_here@hotmail.com
From: samhatfieldchef@bigpond.com
Subject: FLASHBACK!!!!

Dickhead!!!

I know you're on a boat in the middle of the ocean somewhere right now and won't read this till at least tomorrow, but I had to tell you straight away that IT'S RACH!!! Lola's drama teacher is Rachel Kleinman from uni days! Yes, THAT Rachel! My Rachel. Well, the Rachel I wanted to be mine but never had the guts to make a move on. I'm still reeling! Here I was, thinking I was gonna be all Mr Powerplay, and I have no doubt I was blushing like a pimply, horny teenager the entire time we were talking. We recognised each other straightaway. She looks just as good as she did then, if not better. She wears her mature age, and her blue jeans and white peasant shirt well. She's fucking gorgeous, actually. Rachel said she had her suspicions that I might have been Lola's dad when she saw her face and surname, but thought it was probably a long shot. She said I looked good (couldn't tell if she was just being nice or genuine) and asked after Bridg and the kids. I told her about the divorce and she made all the right noises. I was trying to get a read on whether my failed marriage was good news to her, but she's as inscrutable as ever.

After our initial, 'Oh my God, it's you!' exchange, she proceeded to wax lyrical about Lola and what an incredible girl she is, and how proud I must be, and what a delight it is to teach such a smart, open-minded, compassionate girl. I was tempted to ask if she could send the girl she was describing home to me, but didn't want to ruin ...

What? The moment? Was it a moment?

I don't know. What's your vibe?

Obviously, you weren't there and only have my one-way ramblings to determine your opinion on the events that just transpired, but I demand you make a thorough assessment and send it to me as soon as you get back from your trip because I'm pretty sure I don't know what the fuck just happened. I know that I was flirting immediately, and I've been getting pretty good at it during my Tinder epoch.

I think she was flirting back ...? Or maybe that's just wishful thinking.

Fuck it, I need to call you and babble into your ear. Brace yourself!

Rachel Kleinman is back in my life. I'm gonna use the word, dickhead. I know you hate it, but I'm gonna use it!

Fate?

S x

Chapter Ten
Lizzie

'But why does it have to be at Abelas? Williamstown is a million miles away!'

'It really isn't,' I sighed. 'It's a twenty-minute drive.'

'That's *ages* away!' Zara slumped in the passenger seat and folded her arms. 'No one will want to come all that way for my party!'

'*Our* party.'

'You're not even part of this conversation!' Zara twisted around to glare at Archie. 'Shut up!'

'Hey!' I said. 'Unnecessary. Say sorry.'

'Sorry,' Zara muttered.

But Archie's attention had already returned to his comic. Nothing much fazed my absent-minded professor of a son. He was firmly entrenched with the Dungeons & Dragons tribe, science and chess clubs, and led a drama-free, very young male existence. Archie chose to spend his Saturday nights playing long-form role-play games or pondering which pawn to lead with, rather than partaking in underage pub crawls and pondering which porn to end the night with (like my brother Lucas when he was a teenager – gross).

I glanced over at my daughter, who was staring out of the car window with a sulky look on her face, and my heart sank. At two-thirty this afternoon I'd made a spur-of-the-moment decision to pick up the twins from school. Max was going to Oscar's for a play date, and Stella to

Lola's. (I had no idea what a play date at Lola's entailed. Needlework?) The twins usually got the bus home, so I thought it would be a nice surprise, and I was looking forward to some quality car time with my two eldest, before picking up the other two and heading over the bridge for my brother's birthday dinner. I pulled up at Baytree Secondary, envisioning a pleasant, chatty drive home.

I was wrong.

All hell broke loose the second Zara climbed into the front seat. As far as I'd been aware, my daughter was happy to have her fifteenth birthday party at the family restaurant. When Greg and I first suggested Abelas as a potential venue – more space, bigger kitchen, huge backyard – she was totally on board.

'Only a loser would have their party at a stupid family restaurant in the stupid western suburbs,' Zara whined now. My hands tightened on the steering wheel. I knew she was in her judgey, self-absorbed teen phase and considered most things in life 'lame' or 'embarrassing', but I didn't have to put up with it.

'You keep speaking like that and there won't be any party,' I snapped. 'You sound like a brat. And since when are you ashamed of your family or Williamstown?'

Zara visibly shrank in her seat. 'I'm not.'

Now I'd done it. I didn't know why I thought screaming at my daughter would make things better. Even Archie – a constant leg jiggler – had gone still in the back seat.

Truth was, I'd had similar feelings about Abelas at her age. I was constantly fantasising about a life where my dad had a big-wig office job and didn't smell like pastizzis. But unlike Zara, I would never have dared say any of this out loud.

Zara stared at the schoolbag at her feet and her fingers

twitched in her lap. Her phone was in there, but I'd banned phones in the car. Not even my strong-willed daughter would dare take it out, so she just stared at the bag instead.

This car ride wasn't going at all as planned. Where was the light-hearted banter? The hilarious stories about teachers trying to slip cool teenage lingo into their lessons? Or a classmate accidentally farting in maths? I wanted some reassurance that Zara's Year Nine was off to a good start. Better than last year at least.

In Year Eight, Zara's friendship group had imploded in full dramatic teenage-girl style, and it took a few months before she found her own tribe after signing up to do work backstage on the school musical. She loved it and subsequently found a new bestie, Ines, along the way. Zara had become more secretive over the summer, which was to be expected, but recently I'd felt a strain between us. I didn't like it.

'So, what day do rehearsals start?' I asked, even though I knew.

'I told you. Next Tuesday.'

'I'm working,' I chirped in what I hoped was my best friendly mum voice, 'but I'll see if Megan or Sam can pick you up.'

'No!'

Even Archie's eyes flicked up from his comic book at Zara's sharp tone.

'I mean, thanks but it's fine,' she said quickly. 'Ines said her mum can drive me.'

Wow. So, even Megan and Sam were embarrassing now? Right. Time to focus on the less-hormonal twin.

'You gonna get involved in the school production this year, Arch?'

My son had said precisely two words since getting in the car. I was determined to drag an actual conversation out of at least one of my kids before we arrived home.

'No.' Archie frowned. 'Why would I?'

'I thought you might want to get in on the production design,' I said. 'You love all that mythical creature stuff.'

'Mum,' Archie sighed. '*The Reluctant Dragon* has nothing to do with D&D.'

Seemed I was wrong. Again.

'We've, like, already got our backstage team sorted,' Zara said. 'We don't need anyone else.'

'I wouldn't wanna do it, anyway.'

'We wouldn't let you even if you did.'

'Well, I wouldn't want to.'

'All right!' I said, cutting short the bickering loop before my head exploded. 'My God, can't you two be civil to each other for one bloody car ride?'

Silence.

'Maybe we could see a movie on Saturday, Zara?' I gave conversation one more try. 'Max has a party, Stella has acting class and you're going to Jasper's aren't you, Arch?'

'Yep.'

An extra word from the son. Excellent progress.

'Whaddya think?'

'Oh, sorry, I can't.'

Aaaaand shutdown.

'Ines and I have to set up the hall for the read-through.'

She did sound genuinely apologetic, so I was going to take that as a win. I was so desperate for a connection that I'd scramble for any breadcrumbs of civility she threw my way.

'No problem,' I said, turning into our driveway.

Zara and Archie were out of the car and inside the

house in five seconds flat. But I was still gripping the wheel, staring ahead at the newly painted side fence.

Greg had painted it last September while listening to a footy final on his beloved transistor radio that was straight out of 1976. Every few minutes he'd shout, 'You beauty!' Or 'Jesus Christ!' or 'Come *on!*'

Greg Barrett was my buddy, my partner, and life felt incomplete without him around. I had no one to exchange glances with every time Archie lost his shoes, or when Max asked loud, inappropriate questions at the dinner table, or when Zara made a sarcastic comment, or when Stella told me off for swearing because the dog rolled in something dead at the park and smelled like death. It was just me and the kids. All the time. And so far, I wasn't convinced I was doing the best job at this single-parenting caper. I loved my children with a ferocity that was overwhelming at times, but I was feeling less and less connected to the twins these days, especially Zara.

Maybe my maternal glory days were behind me? What if I was one of those women who'd totally rocked at the first twelve years of parenting, then began a steady decline? It wasn't as if I had a solid reference point for parenting a teenager since my own mum died of ovarian cancer when I was four, long before she could imprint any sort of parental template onto me.

I've always wondered how Mum had felt, knowing she was going to die, leaving her kids to grow up without her. I couldn't imagine leaving my kids at the ages they were now, let alone when they were little. Aunty Carmen had been the best stand-in a girl could ask for, but it wasn't the same as having your own mum around. Would my mum have been strict or lenient? Would she have sat on my bed at night and asked what was going on with me like I did with Zara when she was younger? Was it best to leave teenagers alone and let them come to you? What if I was screwing everything up because I had no personal experiences to draw on with Zara? What if there were really important mother–teenage daughter secrets that were common knowledge to every woman who hadn't lost her mum before puberty hit that I was clueless about?

I glanced up at the sky. *What do I do, Mum?*

***

'Shut the door! The flies!'

Children scattered in every direction as Aunty Carmen thundered out of the kitchen with a platter of freshly made pastizzis in her hand, headed straight for the open back door and slammed it shut with a panicked expression on her face. Anyone witnessing this display would assume she'd just saved us all from a plague of locusts. Her obsession with keeping flies out of her restaurant was still as solid as when she'd first arrived in this new, fly-infested country.

'Crazy woman,' Dad said, watching her march back into the kitchen.

'You love her,' I said, reaching across him to grab another handful of salt-and-vinegar chips. 'And who are you to talk about crazy when you close your restaurant for a family birthday party?'

'Pah!' Dad waved a wrinkly brown hand at me and stood up. 'Family is more important than money. You should tell your husband that.'

'I'm not getting into this with you again, Dad. It's not like Greg has run off with another woman.'

'Not yet.'

'Nice.'

Dad kissed the top of my head before going outside for a kick with his four grandsons. My youngest brother, Lucas, was turning forty-two, so our whole family had gathered at Abelas to celebrate. Mum and Dad opened the small Maltese restaurant in Williamstown when they first married, and it was now entering its fiftieth year in business. My brothers and I grew up here; folding napkins, doing our homework at the red-and-white checked tables and taking orders from our loyal customers. The white brick walls, white tiled floor and red shutters of Abelas were as familiar to me as my own face, and only slightly older.

Abelas had always seemed huge to me as a kid, but as our family grew bigger over the years, the restaurant grew smaller. There were now twenty of us in total, including wives, husbands and kids, and even with the overhead fans whirring, Abelas felt crowded and stuffy on this warm Tuesday night.

'Those pastizzis were cooked!' Chris groaned. 'Why would she take them back to the kitchen?'

Food was often at the forefront of my fifty-year-old brother's mind. Even more so during family events. Joey smacked our eldest brother across the back of the head. 'Can't you think about anything but your fat gut?'

'Nothing fat about my gut, mate.' Chris proudly patted his flat stomach. 'Two hundred sit-ups a day.'

Joey shook his head. 'Wanker.'

Chris was a fitness fanatic, borne out of necessity considering his voracious appetite. He never missed an opportunity to remind everyone about his daily sit-up count.

'Gotta say, I'm bloody hungry, too,' Lucas said.

'Well, why don't you go help in the kitchen instead of sitting here whingeing?'

I loved Lucas's wife, Shelley. Tough, direct, and she took no mess from my brother.

'It's my birthday,' Lucas said, affronted.

'I'm not allowed in there,' Chris said mournfully, glancing over at his wife, who was helping Aunty Carmen in the kitchen. 'Rosa said I was getting in the way.'

'I offered too,' Joey added, 'but she kicked me out.'

'Me too,' said Shelley.

'Mum!'

Stella stood behind me, staring into the middle distance and mumbling some kind of rhythmic mantra as she moved her arms and body in a way that reminded me of something between tai chi on fast forward and lazy sign language. At one point I was sure she mimed cocking a gun, followed by a move that looked like she was taking a two-handed grip on a broad sword. Over the past few months, my eleven-year-old daughter had morphed into a non-stop dancing machine. At least one part of her body was always moving, swinging, tapping, jerking or dabbing.

Stella's ten-year-old cousin, Poppy, stood behind her, precisely matching my daughter's actions.

'I forgot to tell you!' Stella's face was ablaze with frantic enthusiasm and her hand gestures sped up as she became increasingly excited. 'Miss Mitchell said we have to pick a scene to perform in drama, and Lola and I are gonna do a scene from our acting class!'

My daughter's excitement levels about Lola being in acting class were through the roof.

'Cool,' I said. 'Is it short?' If Lola was involved, there was a good chance they'd end up doing a scene from *Pride and Prejudice*.

Stella shrugged. I couldn't tell if this was in response to my question or a part of her perpetual choreography, but she confirmed it was the former by using actual words again.

'Dunno, we haven't picked one yet. Why should it be short?'

I grabbed both her wrists mid-move (no mean feat) pulled her towards me and planted a kiss on her cheek. 'A short scene is a good scene, sweetie.'

'Dinner!' Rosa emerged from the kitchen holding a huge platter of food.

Dad and the boys barrelled through the back door and rushed to the table, as Shelley looked around, frowning. 'Where are the big girls?'

'Must be out back,' I said. 'I'll get them.'

Dad and Aunty Carmen spent many happy hours tending to the large backyard that connected the restaurant to my family home. Hydrangeas, petunias and pink climbing roses bloomed along the fence and the lawn was green and lush, despite the recent spate of hot weather. I spotted the teenagers sitting cross-legged in the far corner of the garden, their faces illuminated by their phone screens. Zara was only a few months younger than Nessa and Scarlett, and the girls were close. I ducked behind the lemon tree to watch them for a moment as they chatted and laughed together, occasionally leaning in for a selfie.

Zara giggled and pointed at something on her phone. The cousins leaned in for a closer look.

'Oh my God, cute!' Nessa squealed.

My interest was piqued. Who was cute? Did Zara have a

boyfriend? Is that why she'd been so secretive lately?

I suddenly saw myself, hiding behind a lemon tree spying on my teenage daughter. What kind of Mother from Hell was I? Teenagers were supposed to have secrets from their parents and here I was going full psycho stalker on my kid.

'Girls!' I shouted, stepping out from behind the tree. 'Dinner!'

Three startled faces turned towards me and Zara's expression became accusatory.

'Where did you come from?'

'Oh, I've been here for aaaaages!' I said, unable to resist. 'Heard all the juicy gossip.'

She stared at me, horrified.

Scarlett laughed. 'Chill, Zar, she's kidding. And, like, we weren't even saying anything juicy.'

'You got that right,' I said.

'Lizzie, oh my God, Zara said Rania Jalali is at your school!' Nessa said, eyes wide. 'Have you seen her?'

'Yeah, her son is on my soccer team.'

Scarlett and Nessa's mouths fell open.

'You've, like, *spoken* to her?!' Scarlett cried.

'Yeah, a few times.' That was a lie, but the words were out before I could stop them.

Nessa's lower jaw jutted. She thrust out her right hand like a cop stopping traffic. 'Wait, are you like, low-key *friends* with her?'

Zara scoffed, triggering long-forgotten teenage insecurities and more lies.

'Yeah, kind of,' I said. 'I mean, we talk about her son and we're planning a catch-up.'

'Oh. My. God!' Scarlett said.

Nessa started tapping on her phone in a frenzy. 'I'm, like,

telling *everyone* that my Aunt Lizzie is friends with *Rania Friggin' Jalali!*'

'All right, better go in for dinner now.'

I held the door open for the girls to walk through, but Zara didn't move.

'You didn't tell me you and Rania Jalali are friends,' she said, looking dubious.

'I don't tell you everything.' I shrugged.

Zara smiled, shaking her head, then followed her cousins inside.

Stuffed to the gills half an hour later, I couldn't believe my eyes when I saw Chris leaning in for a third helping.

'How can you still be eating?'

'He's a pig!' Rosa looked disgusted.

'You gonna get fat!' Dad thrust his fork at Chris, almost taking out Joey's eye. 'Like your Uncle Angelo!'

'The man was a *walrus!*' Aunty Carmen shouted down the table.

The younger kids always fought over who got to sit next to Aunty Carmen, so she usually ended up at the far end of the table, surrounded by dirty faces and spilled lemonade.

'Better keep an eye on that middle-aged spread, bro,' Lucas said, then turned to me. 'You too, Liz.'

I was outraged. 'Fuck off, I'm forty-four!'

'Mum!'

'Sorry, Stella.' I waved apologetically at my horrified daughter. 'Swear jar when we get home, promise. But your uncle was being rude.'

'I'm way closer to forty than you are,' Lucas teased. 'You're speeding towards *fifty!*'

Lucas ducked as I threw an olive at his head. He piffed

a piquanté pepper back, but his aim was appalling and it hit Chris square in the eyeball. The table cheered before erupting in shouts and flying olives. I ducked and shouted along, but Lucas's comment niggled at me.

Almost fifty, shit. I was already halfway through my life, and ten years older than my mum was when she'd died. A fact recently pointed out by my school friend, Melissa, at our most recent bi-weekly coffee date.

'*Stop wasting food!*' Aunty Carmen shouted now, grabbing a utensil off the table. 'The children down here are better behaved than you lot, for fuck's sake!'

'Aunty Carmen!' Stella cried, aghast.

'You can't hit me!' Lucas cried, as Aunty Carmen began whacking him and Joey around the shoulders with a plastic salad server. 'It's my *birthday*!'

★★★

A few hours later, we were back across the bridge. The kids were all asleep, exhausted from the raucous family gathering. Greg had stayed up late so I could fill him in on the evening's highlights.

'I love it when Aunty Carmen gets slappy with a kitchen utensil.' Greg yawned down the phone.

'Tired?'

'Nah, I'm okay.'

Greg would never complain about his own fatigue. He knew how exhausting it was parenting four kids when *both* of us were here.

'You're working too much,' he said every other day. 'You don't have to. We'll be okay without your full pay for a few months.'

But we wouldn't be okay, and Greg knew it. We needed

the money those extra shifts brought in, but he hated the idea of me doing so much.

'You need some downtime, buddy. Organise a night out with Aileen or Melissa, or Megan and Sam.'

But if I wasn't working at night, the last thing I wanted to do was go out. The only thing I had energy for was flopping down in front of whatever series Max, Stella and I agreed on – usually *Brooklyn Nine-Nine* or *The Office*. Weeknight outings like tonight's were rare.

'I'll let you go,' I said. 'You have to be up in six hours.'

'Christ, don't remind me,' Greg groaned. 'Is that hairy dude in my bed again?'

'Yep, he's keeping your side warm.'

I reached out to stroke our golden labrador, Bailey, stretched out beside me.

'That dog is living his best life.' Greg chuckled.

I scoffed. 'Aren't we all. Love you, buddy.'

'Love you.'

I hung up, turned off the light and settled into my regular sleeping position, cupping my hand under my left breast, and closed my eyes.

But tonight, instead of the smooth underside of my skin, my fingers found a tiny hard lump.

Chapter Eleven
Megan

'Oh, she's so cute!'

'Adorable!'

'Look at her wrinkly little fingers!'

'Divine!'

Every woman in the café was clucking and fawning over the newborn at the corner table. Suzie, the proud great-grandmother, held the swaddled baby in her arms and gazed down at her newest family member with pure love. Every time the tiny creature yawned or opened her eyes, the female Applewood residents swooned.

Megan smiled at the tired new mum beside her grandmother. 'She's beautiful, Rose,' she said as she placed a chocolate-raspberry muffin in front of Suzie.

'And a good girl, too,' Suzie said. 'Already sleeping through the night, aren't you, darling?'

Rose caught Megan's eye. 'If you call 2 to 5 a.m. sleeping through, then sure.'

'Newborn babies are supposed to feed during the night,' Suzie scoffed. 'At least she's not screaming all the time like your father did.'

The older women around the table all murmured and nodded their agreement, each secretly hoping today's Queen of the Village would offer them a cuddle.

'Terrible colic!'

Again, the ladies murmured empathically.

'Malt on the dummy,' Helen said.

'We used caro syrup,' Lucy added.

'I gave your father paregoric,' Suzie said, leaning towards Rose. 'Maybe give that a try if she has any trouble.'

Rose glanced at Megan again, eyes wide. 'They don't really recommend opium for babies anymore.'

Megan chuckled. 'How old is she?'

'Six weeks yesterday.'

'She's gorgeous. What's her name?'

'Amelie.'

'Oh, that's one of my favourite films!'

In fact, Megan had never heard of the movie before Eddie had suggested it one night. She fell in love with the quirky French film, and if she was honest, it was one of the reasons she'd taken the café job. Megan had quite fancied the idea of herself bustling around a busy café, inspiring customers and playing matchmaker.

'Ours too!' Rose said, looking lovingly at her sleeping child. 'As soon as I saw it, I knew that if I ever had a baby girl, I'd name her Amelie.'

Megan was about to say that she too had dreamed of having a baby girl but was surprised to discover a lump in her throat. She swallowed it down and smiled.

'I'll leave you to enjoy your muffin. And the Amelie fan club.'

'Thanks, Megan.'

Megan felt her ovaries contract as she took one more glance at the baby. Walking back to the counter, she tried to ignore the intense yearning she felt the moment she looked down at the tiny creature. Megan had always dreamed of having a baby girl, and when she'd owned Chill, she'd almost wept over some of the adorable girls' stock that came through. She would have loved to dress up a mini-Megan, and style her hair into cute pigtails. She'd almost certainly never have that little girl now.

The lump in her throat returned.

'What's wrong?' Yang asked, standing at the coffee machine.

'Nothing.'

'Liar.'

Megan noticed a bunch of glossy brochures on the counter and pointed at them in an effort to steer the subject away from herself. 'What are they?'

Yang quickly shoved them under the counter and out of sight. 'Nothing.'

'Now who's the liar?'

Megan walked over to pull them out and started flipping through the various brochures advertising 'Luxury Apartments for Sale' and 'Ocean Views'.

'Queensland?'

Yang shrugged. 'Just looking.'

'Hell of a commute.'

'Maybe.'

'You thinking of moving?'

'Maybe.'

'Jesus, it's like pulling teeth!'

'I have no idea what that means, but don't say anything to anyone.' Yang lowered her voice. 'Especially to Ellie. I love your mum, but she got a big mouth.'

'The biggest.' Megan glanced over at her mother, who was gossiping outside in the courtyard with Lucy and Helen. 'Go on, I won't say anything.'

'Okay.' Yang nodded. 'I'm thinking of selling the café and heading north.'

'Where? Queensland is a big place.'

'My friend invited me to stay with her in Coochiemudlo ...'

'I beg your pardon.'

'I looked it up and I'm pretty sure the name is Aboriginal for shithole,'Yang said dryly. 'One Trip Advisor review said, *Kiosk was nice. Could've used more cutlery.* But my friend buy her house for twenty thousand. It came with a car but no electricity.'

'You wanna move there?'

'No!'Yang baulked. 'No way I'm going there. But I start googling Queensland houses, and found these ones. Cheap as chips, too.'

'What about the business?'

'I sell it.' She nudged Megan with her bony elbow. 'Maybe you could buy it? Ellie says you're still cashed up from selling your business.'

'There's that big mouth we know and love.' Megan started rinsing out dirty cups. 'I'm not really the café-owner type.'

'Oh really? And what type is that?'

Megan looked up in time to see a flash of steel cross Yang's face.

'Too smart ... too *important* ... to do something as common as running a café?'

This was exactly what Megan had meant, but she'd never dare say it aloud. 'Of course not.'

'You like people and you're organised,' Yang said.

Megan could see Lucy waving her empty cup in the air and mouthing, 'More tea!'

'Duty calls!' she said, wiping her hands on her apron and scurrying out from behind the counter, grateful for an excuse to escape the Yang Inquisition.

It was a sunny morning and Lucy, Helen and Ellie held prime position in the café courtyard.

'Oh, I'm sorry, sweetheart!' Lucy cried as Megan appeared. 'You were obviously talking about something important!'

'Don't be silly, it's fine.'

'I'll have another flat white please, love,' Helen said.

'How about you, Mum?'

Ellie, who was frowning at her phone, didn't respond.

'Mum? What's wrong?'

Ellie tutted. 'Oh, that bloody folk trio we had booked for Morning Melodies have just cancelled! Bloody bastards!'

A few customers in the vicinity looked over, shaking their heads, but Ellie didn't notice. She was the new head of the Applewood Entertainment Committee. Over the past six months, she'd booked a plethora of acts for the village including an Andrews Sisters tribute act, a politically incorrect comedian who kept referring to the audience as 'old codgers' and 'wrinklies', and a murder-mystery night, which ended early when one of the residents took a turn after finding a severed rubber ear in his soup. The Southside Strummers had been Ellie's safest and most generic booking to date.

Lucy shook her head. 'Devastating.'

'Disaster,' agreed Helen.

'Can't you just book someone else?' Megan asked.

'It's four weeks away!' Ellie cried. 'How am I going to find an act of their calibre at such short notice?'

'Ahem!' Lucy loudly cleared her throat. 'I'm sure The Minor Quays wouldn't mind filling in.'

Megan could almost hear everyone, including herself, inwardly groan. Lucy was a proud founding member of

Applewood's singing group, The Minor Quays, who were as bad as their dreadful name implied.

The incredulous look on Ellie's face made her feelings clear. She gave her friend a condescending pat on the hand. 'I think people might expect more for their twenty dollars, Luce.'

'Oooh, saucer of milk to table nine,' Helen crowed.

'How rude,' Lucy said, pulling her hand away, lips of string. 'We're extremely professional. Last Christmas we performed at the Bayside Carols in the Park!'

'But they put you *riiiiiiight* over the other side of the park on that tiny stage,' Helen said. 'Took me ages to find you.'

Lucy pushed back her chair and threw her napkin on the table. 'Excuse me. I have to go to the ladies,' she said before storming inside as quickly as her eighty-year-old legs would allow.

Megan almost laughed out loud.

Helen sighed. 'Oh dear, I've upset her.'

'The Minor Quays are shit,' Yang said, appearing behind them suddenly. 'I hear them practising. They like a bunch of cats in a blender.'

'I'll have to call the entertainment agency and see if they can find someone,' Ellie moaned, dropping her head into her hands. 'Otherwise, we'll have no choice but to book the Minor bloody Quays.'

'Hey, I know a half-decent acoustic duo who might be able to do it,' Megan said in a stroke of brilliance.

'Who?'

'You know my mates from school, Sam and Dave?'

Ellie perked up. 'Oh, yes! Sam does the music for Oscar's school concerts, doesn't he? Cute too!'

110

'Is he now?' Helen said, nudging Ellie. 'A bit of eye candy wouldn't go astray.'

'*Very* cute. And divorced.' Ellie nodded at Megan. 'I don't know why this one hasn't had a crack at him yet.'

'Ew! Mum!'

'Do you think they'd do it?'

'Don't see why not.'

'We can give them two hundred for the hour, and morning tea is provided.'

'I'll ask them today at pick-up.'

'Excellent!' Ellie clapped her hands. 'And here comes lovely Lucy! Darling, guess what?'

'What?' Lucy muttered, still furious.

'We might have found an act for Morning Melodies,' Ellie chirped, 'but I need someone to MC. Will you do it?'

A smile broke across Lucy's face. 'I'd love to! Thanks, El!'

'No problem, darling!' Ellie crowed. 'Just save any obituaries until after the show.'

***

Megan was scrolling through various job-search apps in the playground a few hours later when Sam and Dave arrived at the bench.

'Where's Lizzie?' Sam asked.

'She had an appointment,' Megan said, sliding over to make room for her friends. 'I'm dropping Max and Stella home.' She turned her most dazzling smile on the two men. 'So, I've got something to ask you both.'

Sam adopted a serious expression. 'No, we will not have a threesome with you. Dave's married and I have a zero-tolerance policy towards ménage à trois.'

'And someone always feels left out,' Dave added, 'which can cause issues afterwards.'

Megan and Sam stared at Dave for a moment, before deciding not to dig any deeper.

'Well, instead,' Megan continued, 'how would you feel about being the entertainment for Applewood's Morning Melodies?'

'Their what?' Sam asked.

'Morning Melodies,' Megan repeated. 'All the oldies gather in the rec room with cakes and tea to watch an act. Last time it was an old guy struggling through the theme song from *The Sting*.'

'"The Entertainer",' Sam and Dave said in unison.

'Have you two fused into one being?'

They nodded. 'Yes.'

'Anyway, some folk trio cancelled,' Megan said, 'so they're desperate for a fill-in act. They'll take anyone at this point.'

'Wow,' Sam said. 'Way to make two old musos feel special.'

'It's Sunday, March twenty-first.'

'The day before camp?' Dave asked.

'Yep.'

'Sure, we could do a couple of sets!'

'We don't have "a couple of sets", Dave.' Sam frowned. 'We have one very short set that we've only ever done once, at the Mum's Night. And I'm not sure a group of senior citizens want to hear our interpretations of "Livin' on a Prayer" and "Shake it Off".'

Dave rolled his eyes and jerked his head towards Sam. 'Glass half empty much?'

'Dave,' Sam said in what Megan recognised as his 'dad

voice', 'we only have about four songs they'd know, or possibly even like.'

'Four songs is a great start!' Megan said. 'Trust me, this lot will just be happy to watch something new.'

'We're in!' Dave cried.

'Hang on, I don't know if —'

'Great!' Megan said, cutting Sam off. 'I'll talk to Mum and find out what time you need to arrive.'

'What's the fee?' Dave asked.

'A hundred bucks each and as many Monte Carlos as you can eat!'

Sam perked up. 'Sold!'

★★★

'Thanks so much again for coming back.'

'Hey, no problem.'

Hot Harry brushed past Megan as he entered the house, and she felt a slight tingle in her tummy. *Stop it!* she told herself sternly. *Act your age.*

Unfortunately, Megan felt anything but her age when Harry was near; however, she needed his IT expertise and hadn't known who else to call. That morning, when she'd tried to create a folder full of photos of Oscar to send to her mum, she couldn't seem to be able to drag and drop them. Nothing she tried worked and she'd wasted a full hour on it before conceding that she was probably undoing Harry's handiwork.

'Fuck it,' she'd said, glancing at her recently organised purple tub and wondering if Harry had locked or encrypted something when he'd sorted out her photos. She didn't want the kid to feel bad but had no choice other than to text him.

This was the last time she'd ask Harry to help her with IT issues. Surely he had better things to do with his evenings.

'Do you want a coffee?'

'Just had one, thanks,' Harry said, following her into the kitchen and dumping his satchel on the floor. 'Water would be cool, though.'

'Sure.'

Harry perched himself on her kitchen stool as Megan grabbed a glass from the cupboard.

'Where's Oscar?' he asked, slouching over the island bench and glancing around the empty room.

'He's at his dad's tonight.'

'Oh, right. So, you two … you're …?'

'Divorced. Yep.'

Megan wasn't sure she wanted to continue this line of chat. If she started talking about Bryce, it could potentially end with Eddie, and the last thing she planned on doing was pouring out her sob story to a teenager.

'So, do you live nearby?' she asked, filling a glass from the filtered water dispenser.

'Ringwood.'

'What?' Megan almost dropped the glass. 'I had no idea you were that far away! How long did it take to drive here?'

'Oh, I don't have a car,' Harry said matter-of-factly. 'I PT'd it.'

Megan frowned.

'Public transport.'

She felt awful. Not just because he'd had to catch a train all the way across town, but also because she hadn't known what PT stood for.

'I'll pay for an Uber home,' she said firmly.

'Nah, PT is awesome.' Harry sat up, looking energised. 'I, like, listen to music and write. It's the best. Way better than sitting in an Uber and dealing with some dude's "I'm not racist *but*" opinions.'

Harry's enthusiasm for public transport was infectious, and Megan couldn't help smiling. 'Actually,' she said. 'I remember reading somewhere that J.K. Rowling came up with the entire story for *Harry Potter* on a long train ride.'

'She did, yeah!' Harry slapped his hand down on the marble island bar for emphasis. 'I love writing on trains. I just, like, head straight to the back corner of the carriage, look out the window and my mind just … y'know … vibes out. It's awesome.'

Megan had never before considered the potential upside to public transport. In fact, she couldn't remember the last time she'd even travelled on a train or bus. But Harry actually made it sound enticing.

'Um, thanks.'

Harry reached out his hand, and Megan realised she'd been standing frozen with the glass of water.

'Oh, sorry,' she said, handing it to him. 'Now, I'm paying you this time, okay? Especially since you crossed the river to get here.'

'Your call. Oh, hey, look.' Harry pulled a crumpled flyer out of his pocket. 'It's for a photo comp,' he said, smoothing it out and placing it on the counter in front of Megan. 'I thought you could, like, submit one of your Africa photos.'

Megan laughed. 'That's very flattering, but I don't think so.'

'Why not?'

'Well, I'm not a photographer, for a start.'

'You inspired me to take some retro-style pics with

my mum's old Minolta,' Harry said. 'I even went out and bought some old-school film.'

'Wow.' Megan felt chuffed. 'I'd love to see them when they're developed.'

'Deal,' Harry said, leaning back and taking a sip of his water. 'So, what's up with the computer?'

'Oh, well, I can't export any photos when I select that hard drive you put everything on as the main library,' Megan explained, snapping back into woman-who-hired-man-for-job mode. 'Does that make sense?'

'Yeah, sort of. Should be easy.' He smirked. 'But y'know, it seemed fine when I left the other day.'

Megan raised one eyebrow and folded her arms. 'Exactly what are you implying?'

'I'm onto you, Megan.'

Megan played along. 'Are you accusing me of something?'

'No, 'course not. Just weird that I had to come back so soon.'

'Who's to say you didn't deliberately sabotage my computer so I'd *have* to invite you back?' She was matching his light-hearted tone but could feel her cheeks heating up.

'You got me,' Harry said, slouching forward on the counter again and resting his chin on the palm of his hand. 'I actually planted a brand-new love-potion virus in your computer.'

'Cunning,' she said. 'And that's why I couldn't help but call you?'

'Worked like a charm.'

'Well, that explains everything. You're an evil genius.'

They smiled at each other and Megan could almost see the electricity buzzing in the space between them. *Okay, that's enough.*

She straightened and grabbed Harry's empty glass. 'Okay, so come on through,' she said, turning to walk towards the office, 'and you can remove your Cupid virus while you're at it, thanks very much.'

Harry laughed behind her, a deep husky chuckle, and she suddenly had a shocking urge to turn around and throw him down on her hall runner.

Chapter Twelve
Sam

To: samhatfieldchef@bigpond.com
From: codenamedave@gmail.com
Subject: Boys' Night Out

SAMMYYYYYYYYYY,

How's your head LOL!

You're probs fine, we were both very responsible
– BOOOORING!!

LOL.

Top night tho srsly cant remember the last time I went to a gig.

Thx for being my hot date.

ha-ha

Dave

To: codenamedave@gmail.com
From: samhatfieldchef@bigpond.com
Subject: Boys' Night Out

Hey Dave,

Yeah, I was fine this morning. I think I only managed four beers, with lots of water in between. Like you said, BORING! Let's promise to get a bit messier next time. Just a little bit. Even though The Nervous Rex used to do a bunch of covers (our ska version of 'The Sign' by Ace of Bass was a crowd favourite), cover bands aren't usually my thing, but those guys were fucking great. That woman on the drums was ferocious, and damn she could lock down a groove.

Thanks for organising it. I wouldn't have gotten off my arse otherwise. I would've just spent the night on the couch watching old UFC bouts on my iPad and regretting never taking up a martial art.

I'll be your hot date any time. Play your cards right and you might get lucky.

Here's to the next gig!

S

To: samhatfieldchef@bigpond.com
From: codenamedave@gmail.com
Subject: Boys' Night Out

ROFL just don't tell my wife.

Soz, you don't have a wife anymore, oops my bad.

We should totes do that Ace of Base song!!!! That drummer was a woman???

I just saw hair and arms and thought it was Animal from *The Muppets* ha-ha.

Next time let's check out peeps who write their own stuff.

I think Paul Kelly's touring soon. I'll google it now.

Sorry for the wife thing.

To: codenamedave@gmail.com
From: samhatfieldchef@bigpond.com
Subject: Boys' Night Out

No harm no foul, Dave. Them's the facts. You have a gorgeous wife who loves you to death (for reasons I will never fully understand) and I am a divorced single dad who has Tinder on his home screen. But we're both happy with our lots.

Not sure 'The Sign' would work acoustically, but happy to give it a whirl at rehearsal. Maybe we could give it a plaintive feel? A 'More Than Words' vibe.

Even though I always assumed Animal was a dude, I don't think his/her gender was ever established on *The Muppets*. Ahead of its time in so many ways, that show.

I would LOVE to go to a Paul Kelly show. In a rare act of benevolence, my mum took me to see him at The Athenaeum in 1992. The night I went was the same night they recorded him for a live album. I've still got the CD. So hell yeah, google the living bejesus out of those dates and let's book our tickets. Wow, 1992. Last night made me feel old enough, but typing '1992' and realising that's nearly thirty years ago … that smarts. Enough of that! But speaking of the nineties, let's remember to add Ace of Base to our rehearsal list.

S

To: samhatfieldchef@bigpond.com
From: codenamedave@gmail.com
Subject: Boys' Night Out

I thought we stacked up pretty good in that crowd last nite. We aren't bald OR fat #WINNING.

Good to hear you're happy, manfriend. I worry sometimes 'cause it must be hard with the kids 'n everything, so yeah glad you're good. I know we aren't besties or anything, but Kesh says I'm a good listener so yeah wotevs. Stick that in your pipe and smoke it LOL!

ha-ha.

Dave

To: codenamedave@gmail.com
From: samhatfieldchef@bigpond.com
Subject: Boys' Night Out

Thanks, Dave.

We may not be besties, but you're a good friend for saying that and I appreciate it. It's weird to think about how we all met; you, me, Megan and Lizzie. Just coincidence. Kids in the same school. Sat on the same bench one day. I won't bang on, but since Bridg left, I think more about this sort of stuff. It's probably symptomatic of a garden-variety midlife crisis, but I find myself feeling these waves of gratitude.

Okay, I'll save the pensive platitudes for after our next shared joint so I can really test those listening skills of yours.

I think you might've finally (accidentally) come up with our band name in that last email, too:

Your Happy Manfriend.

Not even joking, I think it's kind of funny and catchy. What do you reckon?

'Thank you, New York! We've been Your Happy Manfriend, GOODNIGHT!'

To: samhatfieldchef@bigpond.com
From: codenamedave@gmail.com
Subject: Boys' Night Out

GEEEEEEEEEEEEEENIUSSSSSSSSSSSS!!!!!

YES YES YES YES!!!

And the Grammy goes to ... YOUR HAPPY MANFRIEND
LOLOLOLOLOLOLOLOL!

Best name ever for the best band ever.

ha-ha,

Dave

To: samhatfieldchef@bigpond.com
From: codenamedave@gmail.com
Subject: Boys' Night Out

And srsly tho here for ya.

To: codenamedave@gmail.com
From: samhatfieldchef@bigpond.com
Subject: Boys' Night Out

Onya Dave.

See you Thursday.

To: jack_woz_here@hotmail.com
From: samhatfieldchef@bigpond.com
Subject: A Gig and a Show. CULTURE

Hey Dockhead,

Dockhead was a typo, but I like the look of it and maybe it's
your new nickname now.

I'm a bit on the dusty side today. Dave and I attended an actual live music event on the weekend; what we used to refer to as a 'gig' in our wayward youth. Perhaps you remember them. I'd forgotten how fun they are, these crazy gigs, where people turn up to see a band play live music on instruments they've practised and gotten good at. It also reminded me that we were a pretty good band. The purpose of Dave and me attending this gig was (apparently) as research for our own upcoming engagement at the Applewood Retirement Village. Yep, we're playing a retirement village. Next stop, Coachella. There's a chance that we might eclipse the death toll from the infamous Altamont Rock Festival of 1969, just through the sheer power of odds and the passage of time.

By the way, the questions you asked about Dave in your last email made it sound like you were an ex-boyfriend asking about a new partner. Are you jealous of Dave, dickhead? That's SO cute. Don't be. You're forever my one and only and nothing will tear us apart. Not even Dave, with all his manly charms and well-organised widgets.

I just dropped the kids at school. Lola was waxing lyrical about Rachel and her drama class on Saturday. I'm glad she's getting something out of it, but I would've appreciated her expressing her enjoyment with a little less volume this morning. She also passed on a flyer that Rachel had given her for some show that she's doing in the city tomorrow night. It's called 'A Travers L'Enfer', which Lola informed me means 'Through Hell' in French. Rachel wants me to go, apparently. Lola wants to go too, but Rachel told her it's a bit on the MA15+ side. Maybe I'll get to see Rachel's boobs.

Love,

S x

Chapter Thirteen
Lizzie

'Just leave me alone, okay? *Please?*'

The distressed female voice in the quiet street caught my attention. It was still early, and the schoolyard was deserted, apart from the odd kid arriving for soccer training. I looked towards the voice and saw two people standing on the street, a few metres away from the school gate. A chubby middle-aged man in khaki shorts and a dirty white T-shirt, and a woman in plain black leggings and an oversized black singlet. The woman was gesturing wildly towards the massive camera in the chubby guy's hands, and it took me a moment to realise that it was Rania Jalali.

Was that guy a paparazzo? At Baytree Primary?

'Free country, isn't it?' I heard the guy say.

Whoever he was, this guy was clearly an arsehole. I dropped the bag of soccer balls I'd been hauling across the yard and headed in their direction.

'Hey!'

They turned and I was shocked at Rania's haggard appearance. With a makeup-free face and her long, thick hair scraped back into a messy bun, she bore little resemblance to the immaculate beauty queen I'd been glimpsing before and after training over the past few weeks.

'You okay, Rania? Where's Tishk?'

Rania forced a shaky smile. 'He's in the car. I'm fine, thanks, Lizzie.'

The guy smirked. 'Yeah, she's sweet as, love.'

I had an overwhelming urge to punch him. He had food-stain splotches on his T-shirt and looked like he hadn't washed his hair – or any other part of himself – in a month. I could smell him from ten feet away.

'I'm not your "love",' I snapped. 'And unless you have a kid at this school, I suggest you leave now.'

'I'm not on school grounds.'

The urge to punch him was growing stronger by the second.

'True. But you are a middle-aged man holding a large camera with a very long lens, outside a primary school.'

His smirk sank.

'And I reckon that's worth a little photoshoot of my own.' I grabbed my phone from my back pocket and aimed it at his face.

'Relax, lady. I'm going.' He smirked at Rania. 'Got what I came for, anyway.'

Rania crossed her arms. She looked like an echidna trying to fold in on itself for protection. My heart ached for her.

'Get the fuck out of here!'

The guy threw me a mock salute before walking away. That's when Rania covered her face with her hands and began to sob.

***

'You don't need to stay with me, Lizzie.'

'It's fine,' I said. 'Higgsy's more than capable of kid-wrangling for ten minutes.'

Rania and I were sitting far from the oval where the kids, including Tishk, were training. The moment the photographer left, I grabbed Rania's keys, got Tishk out of the car and took him to training. I fed him a story about his mum needing to use the bathroom. 'One too many coffees this morning, I guess.'

I told Higgsy I'd be back soon, then rushed over to Rania, where I'd spent the past five minutes handing her one tissue after another.

'I'm sorry,' Rania sniffed.

'You didn't do anything wrong,' I said. 'He did. It's harassment.'

She shrugged. 'Most people would say I asked for it by going on TV.'

I couldn't respond, especially since I was one of the people who usually would suggest exactly that.

'Thank you so much,' Rania said, for the tenth time in two minutes. 'I am completely useless in those situations.'

'Are you sure you don't want to ask Penny Guthrie to make a complaint?'

Rania shook her head. 'There's no point. Like he said, he's just doing his job. It wouldn't normally get to me, but right now my parents ... we're fighting a lot.'

As Rania blew her nose into the soggy tissue, I felt a rush of affection. Before today, I'd had her pegged as a fame-hungry narcissist. Sitting here now, Rania Jalali seemed more like a scared little girl. I wanted to hug her and tell her it would all be okay.

'Maybe you should have lunch with a friend today?' I suggested. 'That always cheers me up.'

Rania smiled sadly. 'I don't really have any friends.'

I was shocked. I'd assumed a minor celeb would have dozens of mates. According to Megan, she had a multitude of followers on social media. Then again, followers aren't friends.

'Can I ask you something?'

'Sure.'

'Why did you go on *The Rebound*?'

Rania looked surprised, and slightly defensive.

'I'm genuinely curious,' I said. 'I just wondered, what makes someone ... y'know ... go on a national television show to find a boyfriend.'

Rania laughed. 'Sounds ridiculous when you say it like that, doesn't it?'

I grinned. 'No judgement.'

'Like I said, I don't have a lot of friends, so I don't meet a lot of people, and, well ...' Rania took a deep breath. 'When I was thirteen, Dad got a new job and we moved here from the other side of town. We'd never had much money before that, and suddenly we were living in a huge house and they sent me to this posh school where everyone was white except me. It was hard to make friends, and it didn't help having strict parents.'

She gave an embarrassed shrug. 'So, when I met Danny on a rare "non-chaperoned" beach walk one day, I lost my mind a little bit.'

'How old were you?'

'Seventeen,' Rania said. 'I'd never had a boyfriend, so I thought I was being a total rebel running off to marry Danny at eighteen. My family stopped talking to me, of course, so we moved in with his parents.'

'Wow,' I said, completely floored. 'That's the definition of rebellious.'

'Yes, until I had Tishk, and Danny dumped me for a girl he met online.' She laughed ruefully. 'I had to go crawling back to my parents with a baby boy in tow.'

I'd heard similar stories over the years from young girls

who came into the hospital to have their babies with no partner or family member in sight, but it didn't make it any easier to understand.

'My parents took me back,' Rania continued, 'but they never let me forget how I'd shamed them. I was expected to marry a nice Pakistani boy. Instead, I ran off with a white boy, got pregnant out of wedlock and disgraced our family.'

Fresh tears fell down Rania's cheeks. I wanted to lean over and wipe them away.

'Dad was at work a lot, and when he was home, he wouldn't talk to me. Mum spent most of her time crying and watching *Ertuğrul*.'

'What's that?'

'Her favourite Turkish soap opera.' Rania smiled. 'Pakistan is *obsessed* with it. I started watching a lot of TV, too. Like, *a lot*. Especially the morning shows. I'd fantasise about hosting a show like that. When I saw that *The Rebound* was seeking applicants, I thought it would be a way to get my foot in the door.'

'I get that.' I didn't, but I was trying to make her feel better.

'Did you watch it?' Rania asked shyly.

'No, sorry.'

She clasped my hand tightly in hers. 'Oh, don't apologise! You have no idea how good it is to meet someone who hasn't seen it!'

The soggy tissue was still in her hand and I could feel the wetness seeping through onto my fingers, but kept smiling, telling myself I'd dealt with far worse bodily fluids at work.

'My great plan to be a morning TV host didn't quite work out.'

'Is that why you're fighting with your mum and dad?'

'One of many reasons,' Rania said. '*The Rebound* caused a lot of embarrassment for my family. One of their conditions for me coming home was that I'd start a beautician's course when Tishk began school. Also, they want to buy me a salon.'

'I'm guessing you don't want to be a beautician?'

'No, but what else am I going to do?' Rania shook her head. 'I'm a twenty-four-year-old single mum with no money and no qualifications. I didn't even pass my VCE.'

'I wish I could help.' I had no idea why I felt the need to, but her story had hit a nerve.

'Thank you, Lizzie.'

A few parents and kids had started to arrive and glance in our direction.

'You'd better get out of here before your fan club mobs you.' I leaned over to whisper in her ear. 'If you go out the back gate over there, walk around the block and through the alley behind the oval, you can make it back to your car without anyone spotting you.'

'Thanks for the intel,' she said.

'Believe me, when it comes to avoiding Baytree parents, I'm a master.'

Rania put on her sunglasses, stood up and grabbed my hand again. No wet tissue this time. 'Thank you for listening, Lizzie.'

'No problem,' I said. 'My number is on the soccer emails.'

Two of the bolder mums in the group began heading in our direction.

'Better make your getaway,' I muttered.

Rania nodded, pulled out her phone, started a fake conversation about soccer boots and walked straight past the two mums. I was impressed with her technique. Rania and I might have more in common than I thought. We both had rebellious streaks and strict immigrant parents. The difference was that I'd run away from a wedding, instead of into one. Also, Rania's dad seemed to be a whole other level of strict. Dad and Aunty Carmen forgave me when I shamed them, and let me live my life with no guilt-tripping or emotional blackmail. I felt a sudden rush of love and gratitude towards them both. At Rania's age, I was childless, having fun and being free.

On the upside, Rania was only twenty-four. She had time.

I lifted my hand to prod at my breast. The lump was still there. It might be worth getting it checked out. Just in case.

★★★

'This lasagne is simply delectable, Lizzie.'

'Thanks, Lola.' I was chuffed at hearing my basic lasagne recipe complimented so eloquently.

'Simply what?' Max asked, shoving a huge chunk of said lasagne into his mouth.

'*Delectable*. It means delicious.' Stella rolled her eyes at Lola.

'Why doesn't she just say "delicious", then?' Zara muttered.

Lola blushed and Stella glared at her sister across the table. 'Because she chose the word delectable!' she snapped. 'You might have the vocabulary of an eight-year-old, Zara, but intelligent people occasionally use words other than "like" or "literally" in a conversation.'

Zara glowered at Stella, ready to unleash a mouthful of abuse on her sister.

'Hey, Lola's our guest,' I said, 'so let's keep things civil, okay?'

'I'm eight!' Max exclaimed. 'I use lots of words.'

Archie sighed. 'No one said you didn't, Max.'

'*She* did!' Max thrust his finger towards his sister and a gooey glob of pasta sauce flew off his fork and onto Stella's cheek.

'*Ew! Max!*'

Max and Archie burst out laughing, but Lola looked mortified.

'Nice.' Zara grinned.

So much for civil.

'Did you girls get much rehearsing done?' I asked Stella.

Lola had come back to ours after school so she and Stella could work on their scene for this week's acting class.

'Oh yeah, we know all our lines.'

'Great. Are you enjoying the classes, Lola?'

'I absolutely adore them!' Lola gushed. 'The classes are very gratifying!' She was delicately dabbing at the corners of her mouth with a paper serviette. 'And Rachel is a delight.'

I'd met Rachel a bunch of times over the past year and could understand why her students loved her. She was sweet, pretty and a bit of a space cadet. She told me once that she had driven halfway to a job interview before realising that she still had an avocado-and-jojoba face mask on.

'She has been extremely encouraging with her feedback,' Lola continued brightly. 'She said I reminded her of a young Vivien Leigh.'

Everyone apart from Stella and me looked confused.

'Wow, that's very flattering,' I said.

Zara frowned. 'Who?'

'She's just a really old actress from the 1900s.'

'Hey,' I said in mock outrage. '*I'm* from the 1900s. Am I "really old"?'

'Hell yeah!' Max shouted.

I instantly shot Max my ugliest old crony expression and he snorted so hard that lasagne flew out of his mouth and onto the table.

'*Max!* Gross!' Zara yelled.

'She's deceased now, of course,' Lola said, ignoring my son's appalling table manners, 'but Vivien Leigh was a consummate actress.'

Archie and Zara both let out sighs forceful enough to blow out the candles I'd placed on the table for our 'special dinner'.

'I watched Vivien Leigh on YouTube,' Stella said loudly, 'and didn't really rate her.'

I was about to give our offended guest a bit of moral support when my phone chimed from the kitchen. Probably Greg checking in to see if we'd finished dinner. I jumped up, glad for an excuse to escape the fraught, pre-pubescent vibes for a moment.

'I'll just text Dad back.'

But it wasn't Greg.

Hey Lizzy. Taking Tishk to Yo-Chi after school tmw. Do u and kids want to join? Rania. X

I was happy that Rania had taken me up on my offer to get in touch, but suddenly worried that a catch-up might be slightly awkward, especially after this morning's emotional episode. What on earth would we talk about? It wasn't as if we had anything in common. Then again, it might not.

I texted back before I could change my mind.

Sure! Sounds great. x

'Was it Dad?' Max asked when I returned to the table.

Poor Max was missing his dad terribly.

'No, mate,' I said. 'But he'll call soon.'

'I'm finished, Mum,' Archie said.

'Okay, just scrape and wash your bowl, please.'

'Yep.'

My expectations of the kids helping around the house had ramped up since Greg left. I still had to remind them to wash their own dishes (we didn't have a dishwasher) and put their washing in the basket ten times a day, but at least they did it when nagged. Mostly.

'I'm done too.' Zara was already out of her seat.

'And me!' Max cried, jumping up.

'No, you're not!' I pulled him back down.

The phone rang and Max's head swung towards the kitchen.

'Can I ...?'

'Finish your salad, then you can talk to Dad,' I said. 'Archie, will you get it, please?'

Stella and Lola had both finished eating but had their heads down, avoiding eye contact with each other. *What was going on with these two?*

'You girls can rehearse for another half-hour and then I'll drive Lola home, okay?'

'Thank you, Lizzie,' Lola said politely. 'Half an hour should be ample time for another run.'

Stella nodded, but continued staring glumly into her bowl.

I could hear Archie grunting one-syllable responses into the phone and went into the kitchen to put him out of his misery. My son hated talking to people face to face, but speaking on the phone was torture. When I gestured for him to pass me the phone, he said, 'Here's Mum. Bye,

Dad!' and almost flung the handset at me before scampering towards the safety of his bedroom.

'Another in–depth chat?'

'Three "yeps" and two "nups",' Greg said. 'I'm starting a tally. He's up by one "yep" from last night. So, y'know, progress.'

'You wanna talk to Zara first?'

'Nope. I wanna talk to my beautiful wife.'

I took the phone outside into the cool early-evening air and onto the back deck. Our wooden swing bench was my preferred spot for chatting to Greg. It was a meditative end to the day, swinging gently back and forth and staring up at the pink-and-orange sky on beautiful Melbourne nights like this.

'Lola Hatfield is over for dinner.'

'How's Little Miss Brontë?' I could hear the smile in his voice. Greg liked Lola as much as I did.

'Sweet as ever, but I got the sense that there might trouble in tween paradise.'

Greg groaned. 'Not like Zara and Amy? Say it ain't so.'

My poor husband was still recovering from last year's teen bust-up. Greg hated anything resembling a 'scene'. Watching his baby girl in bits every night for weeks on end had broken his heart.

'I don't think it's that extreme,' I said. 'Just sounds as if the acting teacher is favouring Lola.'

'Oh.' Greg sounded relieved. 'She'll be right. So, what are you up to tomorrow?'

'The usual,' I sighed. 'Sleep in, then a few hours on this bench swing with a good book before lunch with Chris Hemsworth. I'll end the day with a three-hour massage.'

'Business as usual, then?'

'Pretty much.' I paused. 'Actually, I do have one social engagement on the calendar.'

'Oh yeah?'

'Max and I have a frozen-yoghurt date with a new school mum, Rania, and her son.'

'Should I know who Rania is?'

'No.'

'Phew.'

With the exception of Megan and Sam, my husband could never remember any school parent's name.

'Hey, why *don't* you lie in the hammock and read all day tomorrow?' Greg said. 'You're not working, are you?'

'Um, yeah. Maybe I will.'

I wasn't working tomorrow, but I would be going into the hospital. I'd finally made an appointment to get my lump checked but didn't want to tell Greg. Not when it was probably nothing.

'Maybe you should,' said Greg.

'Don't tell me what to do,' I quipped.

'As if,' Greg replied.

'Only three more sleeps till Archie and Zara's party. Then you can see for yourself how relaxing my life has been lately.'

Greg chuckled down the phone. 'Do you want me to bring anything?'

'Just yourself, please.'

'You still thinking of bringing everyone here for a visit at Easter?'

'That's the plan!'

'I like the plan,' Greg said. 'Look at us, buddy. Making it work.'

I could hear the effort behind his optimism, and appreciated it all the more, even if it didn't feel true. "Course we are. Chat tomorrow, okay?'

'Love you.'

'Love you, buddy. G'night.'

I didn't go back inside. I stayed on the bench, rocking gently back and forth, thinking about tomorrow.

***

I was trying really hard to read Dr Gina Hutchinson's expression as she looked at the lab results. I liked Gina. She had a friendly, open face, wore funky black-rimmed glasses and had a full head of curly black hair. The breast surgeon and I had shared many friendly chats over the years as we'd waited for our takeaway coffees in the hospital's staff canteen. But her soft blue eyes were giving nothing away behind those funky frames today.

I instinctively tucked my right hand under my left breast and took a deep breath. 'So? What do you think it is? Fatty tissue?'

Gina gave me her best, reassuring doctor smile. 'Nothing conclusive, Liz,' she said, 'but I think we should book you in for a biopsy.'

I swallowed. 'Do you think it's cancer?'

She blinked and her confident smile faltered slightly. 'There's no way of telling yet,' she said gently, 'but yes, there is a chance it's breast cancer.'

Chapter Fourteen
Megan

As she delivered endless cups of tea and engaged in conversations about hip replacements and grandchildren, Megan's thoughts kept straying to Harry. She was glancing up at the clock, feeling like a teenager as she counted down the hours to tonight's class. But she couldn't help it. She had been picturing Harry's blue eyes and smooth, taut chest right at the moment Mrs Wheeler's scone had slid off the plate and straight into her lap first thing this morning.

'Ming!' Yang had shouted at her. 'Where's your head today?!'

If only she knew.

Megan felt certain there was nothing consequential about this kind of daydreaming. Harry was just a welcome distraction from the reality of her recently broken heart. Being around him made her feel ... what? Young? Hopeful? Interesting? Attractive? Like when he'd complimented her photos, photos that no one, not even she, noticed anymore. The way he had looked at them, really looked, and seemed genuinely impressed by something she had done made her feel good. It was a rare feeling to have someone interested in her because of who she was and what she'd done, not just because she was Oscar's mum or Ellie's daughter or Eddie's ex.

Eddie had never shown any interest in her photos. She'd even pointed them out to him once, hoping he'd be impressed.

'Have you ever been to Africa?' she'd asked one day as he sat at her desk.

'Huh?' He'd looked up and followed Megan's eyeline to the photos. 'Uh, yeah, once, for a conference. Sorry, honey, I've gotta send this before six.'

That was the one and only time Eddie had ever (barely) acknowledged her photos. Her ex-boyfriend's constant distractedness had been an issue between them from the beginning. He'd always prioritised his work over everything, including her. *Now he has the best of both worlds*, she thought bitterly. He and his esteemed colleague can shag each other's brains out, then send emails together from their post-coital bed.

As Megan crossed the café with a stack of dirty dishes in her arms, an image of Eddie and his faceless lover in bed together, iPads propped up on pillows, loomed large in her mind. She frowned and shook her head, not noticing that Maggie was standing at the counter smiling quizzically at her.

'Water in your ear, is it, darling?' Maggie said sympathetically. 'I had that last week after aquarobics.'

'Sorry, Maggie?' Megan asked, dumping the dirty dishes in the sink. 'What was that?'

'Nothing, sweetheart. Three flat whites, please.'

'Coming right up, Maggie.'

Harry was uncynical and untainted. He hadn't lived long enough to become jaded, like Eddie, or so many other men Megan had met. Apart from Sam, of course.

Megan had never had any guy friends before Sam and Dave. It might be fun to be mates with someone young and artistic. That was the only troubling word. *Young*. He was so, so young. But he was also mature and easy to talk to.

And kind. Harry would never cheat on his girlfriends. Or maybe he would. Megan admitted to herself that she was most likely creating a fantasy version of Harry in her mind. He probably watched hardcore porn seven nights a week and picked his nose and ate it. He almost certainly didn't have the first clue how to wash a dish or boil an egg. And he'd probably cheated on a litany of women of all ages. But she didn't want to think about that. Her fantasy Harry was the version who made her happy, so she pushed the equally hypothetical truths away. Megan felt entitled to a nice daydream.

★★★

It was just past three and the sun beating down on the hard bitumen of the schoolyard made it feel like the heat was attacking from two directions. A trickle of sweat dripped down Megan's back underneath her light cotton T-shirt as she walked across the schoolyard. She held up one hand to shade her eyes and saw her friends on the bench. Sam and Dave seemed to be in the middle of a robust discussion, but Lizzie was ignoring them and staring ahead. She kept glancing down at her phone to tap the screen, then she'd frown before looking up again into the middle distance. *Poor thing*, Megan thought. She must be missing Greg so much.

'Here she is,' Sam said as Megan approached. 'Our new agent.'

'I'd be an awesome agent, actually,' Megan said, flopping down beside them. 'Ugh. Isn't summer supposed to be over?'

'Melbourne weather has zero respect for the seasons,' Sam said.

'You would, you know,' Dave said, leaning forward and blocking Lizzie from Megan's view. 'Make an awesome agent. Maybe that could be your new career?'

'No thanks!' Megan scoffed. 'I saw what those people had to deal with when I was booking kids for Chill shoots. Back-to-back diva mums.'

'How's the class going?' Dave asked.

'Yeah, it's good.'

'Written anything yet?' Lizzie asked.

'A few pages.'

In actual fact, Megan had stayed up late last night finishing a first draft of her kids' book in anticipation of tonight's class. It was only a thousand words long, but Megan had felt like cracking open a bottle of bubbly when she'd finally finished it at midnight.

I did it, she thought, staring at her computer screen in amazement. *I actually wrote a story.*

She couldn't wait to tell Harry. She might even be brave enough to read some of it out in class.

'That's great, Megs!' Sam looked genuinely thrilled for her. 'Can we read it?'

'Nu-uh!'

'Oh, go on,' Lizzie said. 'We'll be your proofreaders.'

'It's good to show your early stuff to people you trust,' Dave said. 'I got some great feedback before doing the second draft of *Codename: Code.*'

Megan considered the idea. It might be good for her close friends to read the story before testing it on her class.

'Only if you don't mind,' Megan said shyly. 'I can email it to you all today.'

'Great!'

'Can't wait!'

'But I want honest feedback,' Megan said sternly. 'No pussyfooting.'

'Pussyfooting?' Sam said, grinning. 'You've been hanging out with the oldies too much, mate.'

'Or Lola.' Lizzie laughed.

Sam's grin vanished. 'Huh?'

'Pussyfooting is a Lola word, isn't it?' Lizzie sounded defensive. 'I saw it on Stella's list of "Lola words".'

'Stella made a list?' Sam frowned. 'What for?'

'What? Nothing. It's just something she did for fun. Why?'

Sam shrugged. 'I dunno. Just seems like a weird list to make for fun.'

Megan sensed a weird tension between Sam and Lizzie.

Sam turned his body towards Dave. 'What were you saying about that Hall & Oates song for Applewood?'

As the boys began discussing the merits of performing an eighties song to people who were actually in their eighties, Megan leaned over to Lizzie.

'You okay?'

'Yeah, just uh … thinking about the party this weekend.'

Megan and Sam were both invited to the twins' birthday party and she was looking forward to it. She'd heard so much about Lizzie's boisterous Maltese family over the years and she couldn't wait to finally meet them all, especially the famous Aunty Carmen.

'You sure you don't need me to help set up?'

'Thanks, but Aunty Carmen is all over it. It's a miracle that she's letting Greg and me help.'

'When does he get in?'

'Friday night.'

'Oh my God.'

'I know.'

A strange look passed over Lizzie's face and Megan worried that her friend was about to burst into tears. She was just about to suggest a walk around the yard when Lizzie's face lit up and she waved to someone in the distance.

'Sorry, gotta go.' Lizzie stood up. 'Rania and I are going to Yo-Chi with the kids.'

Dave gaped at her. 'You're going out with *Rania*? Can you ask her about Saunagate?'

But Lizzie was already gone. Megan watched as her friend hurried across the yard, fluffing up her hair as she went.

Fluffing up her hair! What the hell? Megan thought as she watched the two women greet each other like long-lost sisters.

She tried to dismiss how irked she felt, but she knew herself well enough to recognise when jealousy was taking hold.

★★★

'Can I read it?'

'Not yet.'

Harry feigned outrage. 'Hey, surely your personal IT consultant should get first dibs?'

'How does that work exactly?'

Harry grinned. 'No idea.'

Writing class had finished half an hour ago and as everyone around them began gathering their things together, Megan pulled out her purse and turned to Harry.

'I need to pay you for the IT work,' she'd said loudly, for the benefit of her eavesdropping classmates, who might assume she was paying her young lothario for any other services rendered.

But Harry had waved the cash away. 'How about you buy me a drink at the bar across the road, instead?'

Her nosy classmates definitely heard that, and Megan noticed a fifty-something woman's eyes widen behind thin purple frames.

You're just jealous because you're going home to your cats instead of being invited to have a drink with a hot young man, Megan thought, enjoying the naughtiness of it all.

'Sure,' she said to Harry, putting the cash away and rewarding her scandalised classmate with a smug grin and slight tilt of the head. She felt like the cat who had got the cream.

She texted Sam.

M: *You okay to stay another hour or so with Oscar? Have to go through notes with the teacher.*

S: *No probs, Girly Swot.*

Megan couldn't tell Sam the truth. He'd rib her endlessly, when in actual fact she was simply being nice to someone who'd helped her out.

You just keep telling yourself that, her inner voice whispered.

Now she and Harry were sitting at a small table in the corner of Paddy's Bar, their bare knees millimetres apart, and Megan had to admit that this felt way more enjoyable than any simple courtesy should.

Harry picked up his bottle of craft beer and tapped it against Megan's glass of rosé. 'To your first story,' he said, leaning across the table.

His face was so close to hers that Megan could smell his malty breath and woody aftershave. The combination of his delicious scent and the feeling of his bare knee bumping against hers had a heady effect. Summoning every inch of willpower she possessed, she withdrew her face and knee and clinked his bottle.

'Cheers.'

Her voice caught in her throat a little, and Harry smiled. He leaned forward again, his elbows bumping against hers on the table.

'My God you're beautiful.'

Megan stared at him with as serious an expression as she could muster. 'Harry, I'm almost two full decades older than you and —'

But Harry cut her off with a kiss.

Chapter Fifteen
Sam

To: jack_woz_here@hotmail.com
From: samhatfieldchef@bigpond.com
Subject: Women!

Hey dickhead,

Have you ever felt a bit giddy after an extended study session? Me neither.

But it seems Megan is being swept away by the romance of literature. When she got home after her writing class last night, she was veritably glowing. It's great to see her happy like this, but I could've sworn she was being a bit cagey. Maybe there is no writing class! Maybe it's all a ruse and she's actually joined a local swingers' group. Or a fight club. If it's the latter, she must be pretty handy with her fists because there wasn't a mark on her.

I will investigate further and report back.

Lola is dialling up her sassy attitude to new heights. Rachel's graduated to being Lola's guru. Or cult leader. Lola's feeling inspired, yes. Great. But hand in hand with that inspiration is the desire to express herself completely and to constantly share her truth. Not so great. Her truth is usually pretty boring. But I need to be available to her for this sort of stuff. I need to be with her and listen and nod and be a good dad. That's when she wants to talk with me, not at me. A lot of the time, she prefers to talk to me like I'm some backward uncle that she has to tolerate. So much sighing and groaning and eye rolling. I confess to feeling like I did with Bridg at times; i.e. I can't win. No matter what I say or do, it always seems to be wrong. I thought drama classes would be a good way to build a bit of confidence. A bit. Not an impenetrable tower of confidence.

This may be exactly what she needs: to dismiss me and grow up and embrace her own thoughts and feelings. I know Rachel's been amazing at shifting the way Lola perceives all her quirks. She's gone from feeling ashamed of her difference to seeing it as a superpower. It's impressive. She looks taller.

I spoke to Bridget yesterday and she's finally agreed to have Tyler so I can go on the camp. Sweet, sweet relief. I tried to give Bridg an update, but she couldn't have been less interested. It made me realise that Lola never got – or gets – any sort of validation from her mum. Someone like Rachel gives Lola licence to be herself. Bridget never did that. Everything she ever said to the kids always sounded like a punishment. Even if she was asking them to just have a shower or pass her the remote. Somehow, she made it sound like they'd already done something wrong.

Rachel is this ball of light in Lola's life, and I love her for it. I'm jealous that she's flown in and done what I haven't been able to do for my own daughter, and I'm struggling with this newly empowered young woman who lives with me, but mostly I'm just grateful that Lola's found a supportive female role model. It's what Lola has always deserved, and I don't want her to lose that once the classes finish up.

I know I've always looked at Rachel as the one that got away, and I've always had her wrapped up messily in my own regrets, but I see her very differently now.

Am I completely insane to think I might have another shot with her? I mean, that's a lot of water under the bridge. Maybe we're both ready for something new. Please tell me if I'm being ridiculous.

Onto other ridiculous things; there's something going on with Lola and Stella. My usual approach after drama class is to ask two things:

1. How was it?
2. How's Stella going?

Recently, the answer to number one is getting more enthusiastic, but the response to question number two is becoming more and more muted, in a way that implies all is not well.

I mentioned it to Lizzie, to see if Stella had said anything, and Lizzie was equally muted. I made some crack about how we shouldn't take on the baggage of our teens and Lizzie said that's our job: to take on their baggage and deal with it. She was talking to me like I'd done something to Stella. I fear this is exactly what I hoped would not happen with my adult friends when our stupid kids develop issues with each other. Parents get all fierce and defensive and irrational when their kids are threatened in any way. It's natural and primal and bonkers, and there's no stopping it. I just have to find a way to readdress the topic with Lizzie in a way that won't make her rip my windpipe out with her teeth.

You've met (and charmed) Lizzie. Come on, Dr Dickhead, gimme some truth. What would you do?

Enlighten me. Teach me. Help me! I like my throat.

Love, S x

To: jack_woz_here@hotmail.com
From: samhatfieldchef@bigpond.com
Subject: Megan's Writing

Hey dickhead,

You know I love you, but could you ease off on sharing the details of your pressure sores? I can't fault your descriptive writing, but once you used the words 'spongy' and 'moist' in the same sentence, I stopped loving you. Sounds awful, Jack. I'd offer advice, but I don't want to be that guy who asks an eczema sufferer if they've tried a good moisturiser. Let me know if there's anything I can do. Online shopping? Medical research? Premium Pornhub subscription? A new wheelchair I definitely can't afford?

While we're on the subject of quality writing, I finally got around to reading the piece Megan did as part of her class (with Hotty McTechGuru). Dickhead, you have always had a way with words, both spoken and written.

Megan also has the gift of the gab, but her writing – oh good Lord – her writing is appalling. Ap. Pall. Ing. This thing was like *The Secret* meets *Twilight* but written by a team of NQR monkeys. And grammar may never recover from Megan's full-blown assault on its fundamentals.

For context, I read it on the toilet. There was a heated Mac versus PC conversation going on in the office and I decided I'd rather enjoy a good BM than sit and listen to competing idolatries. If they could've resurrected Steve Jobs, they would've immediately thrown him into the Colosseum with Bill Gates, forcing them to fight to the death armed only with their respective companies' best-selling tablet. I was gone for an hour. Sixty minutes wasn't necessary for me to do my business, but I couldn't stop reading Megan's thing. I must've read it four or five times, trying to crack its code. I kept thinking there must be some sort of genius buried deep within. But nup. It was just a very, very bad kids' book. Any kid who reads this would be doing their mental development a disservice.

What do I do? Megan's awaiting our honest feedback (she sent it to Lizzie and Dave as well), and I'm not about to copy and paste the above into an email to Megan. My instinct is to lie. If there were any redeeming qualities, maybe I could offer a couple of constructive criticisms, but this piece of writing was D.O.A. And no, I won't send it to you. Mainly out of respect for Megan, but also out of respect for the time you would never get back reading it.

I've got it! I'll contract a rare virus that attacks the vocal cords and makes you lose your voice for at least six months. Then I'll accidentally cut off all my fingers while chopping carrots so I'm unable to type or write. Then I'll suffer a significant head trauma resulting in amnesia. The sort of amnesia that means I can't remember how to read. Maybe just that last one would suffice. What do I do, dickhead? If you tell me to be honest with her, I will reply with an in-depth description of the time I had a papilloma wart burned off the soul of my foot. That spelling of 'soul' is deliberate.

The experience truly burned the soul off my foot.

S x

149

Chapter Sixteen
Lizzie

'Does Dad know?'

'Know what?'

'That the adults have to go outside after the cake?'

'Yes, Zara, I've made it clear that we are social lepers and must be banished to the backyard for the last hour of the party.'

'Good. I just don't want ...'

'You don't want us embarrassing you on the dancefloor.' I paused for effect. 'Although ... it's been a while since I've had a good boogie.'

I executed a perfect hip-and-shoulder shimmy and almost laughed out loud when Zara dropped her schoolbag and clapped one hand across her mouth.

'You wouldn't dare!' she yelled through her fingers.

'Depends on how many drinks I've had.'

'*Mum!*'

'Relax!' I laughed. 'We won't embarrass you. Promise.'

Zara removed her hand. 'Okay, so you, Dad, Nonno, Aunty Carmen, Sam and Megan *all* have to stay outside and not even look into the restaurant after the music goes on, okay?'

'What exactly are you planning on doing in there, for God's sake? Having a pash party?'

'Ew! Gross!'

But a red patch had bloomed on Zara's neck. I

remembered Nessa's *Cute!* when looking at Zara's phone. Maybe Zara was hoping for a bit of dancefloor action? I'd noticed a Reuben on the list. I'd never heard of a Reuben before. Was Reuben Mr Cute?

'I promise we'll stay outside,' I said, feeling a slight thrill that my daughter possibly had embarked on her first courtship.

'Thanks, Mum.' Zara leaned over to give me a peck on the cheek. 'Bye!'

'Enjoy your last day as a fourteen-year-old!' I called after her. 'And tell your brother I said thanks for saying goodbye this morning!'

Archie had been up at the crack of dawn for his Friday-morning philosophy club. I'd been sitting in bed reading Megan's story when I heard the door slam just before seven. I looked out the window and saw my son trudging down the driveway, a comic book in front of his face, completely obscuring his vision. As if I didn't worry enough about the kid's lack of spatial awareness. When Archie was six, he'd almost walked out in front of a bus because he had his head in a Spiderman comic. Remembering this, I'd wanted to throw open the window and shout at him to watch the road, before remembering he was about to turn fifteen and didn't need his mum screaming out the window for him to look both ways. Besides, I would have found it hard to tear myself away from Megan's story.

Sweet mother of God it was bad. Even now, standing at the kitchen bench making Stella and Max's lunches, I couldn't stop thinking about it. What the hell was I going to say to Megan at pick-up today?

From what I could gather, *My Mind's Eye* was about a young, modern-day orphan named Osky – no prizes for guessing who that character was based on – who starts deliberately hurting people with his telekinetic powers until a village full of fairies help him learn to use his powers for good instead of evil. It was a strange mix of Enid Blyton, Dickens and *Star Wars*, and included phrases like 'golly gosh' and 'devil-may-care'. And one character was a blacksmith, which I was pretty sure wasn't a thing in contemporary inner-city Melbourne.

Usually, I'd call Sam so we could get on the same page and plan our reactions to avoid hurting Megan's feelings. But Sam was irritating me lately and I didn't want to collude with him on anything. He'd been so defensive about my 'pussyfooting' comment. It was no secret that Lola was a bit of a nutter. We'd all made jokes about her weird wordplay for years, and Sam was always the first one to take the piss. Now suddenly, he was all sensitive about it? More than that, I was annoyed by his implication that Stella was hatching some evil plan to humiliate his daughter.

'Stella! Max!' I called, zipping up the lunchboxes with more force than necessary. 'Ten minutes!'

''K, Mum!' Max called back.

'Just finishing my hair!'

Oh, Christ. What innovative hairstyle were we in for today? Lately, Stella had been trying out different looks with her long, blonde locks. Yesterday she'd emerged from the bathroom with something called a 'Bun Hawk'; four small buns running from her forehead to the back of her neck. It looked ridiculous, but I accepted it for what it was … an attempt to 'out-weird' her best friend. Lola had always worn her hair in nineteenth-century styles. And Stella obviously wanted to stand out in her own unique way. Fine with me. She'd been feeling insecure and jealous about the attention

Rachel was giving Lola, so if she needed a bun mohawk to feel better, go nuts.

Stella had been furious after this week's class, complaining that Lola was 'showing off for Rachel' and 'banging on about how Emma Thompson's adaptation of *Sense and Sensibility* brings Austen's words so perfectly to the screen'.

'*Then*,' an outraged Stella had continued on the drive home, 'she asks Rachel if she can do Marianne's crying scene for next term's scene study when we've already chosen a scene from *Mean Girls*!'

I made all the right noises as she'd ranted and raved, even though I was secretly impressed with Lola's taste in movies.

'I wish she'd never joined the class!' Stella whined as we pulled into the driveway.

I couldn't tell Sam any of this, of course. You could say whatever you wanted about your own kid, but no one else could criticise them. Same rule applied with family. Greg could (accurately) call his parents racist, right-wing homophobes, but those sorts of observations were off limits to me.

I just hoped Lola and Stella would be okay at tomorrow's party. I felt exhausted just thinking about it. There was so much to do. Apart from finalising the menu with Aunty Carmen, I had to buy soft drinks, sort out the stereo with my brother, pick up fairy lights and two different-coloured sets of cups, plates and serviettes. Zara's favourite colour was red, and Archie's was green, so Abelas would look more like it was hosting a Christmas party than a birthday celebration.

But in just a little over ten hours, my husband would walk through that front door and everything would be fine.

It felt like I'd been holding my breath ever since my appointment with Gina two days ago. I was trying my hardest to push the Big C to the back of my mind until after this weekend, telling myself that I'd address all those thoughts and worries after the party.

But that was harder than it sounded.

Gina had wanted me to book in a biopsy before I left her office, so they could determine how sinister the lump was. If it was cancer and we'd caught it early, it could mean surgery followed by chemotherapy, or chemotherapy followed by surgery depending on lymph nodes and hormone receptors.

I'd nodded throughout Gina's speech, saying that I'd look at my schedule and get back to her next week, but all I could think about was my mum.

Afterwards, I'd immediately pulled out my phone to call Greg, then stopped. I couldn't tell him something like this over the phone. I didn't want to tell him before the party, either. I'd decided to hold off and tell him on Sunday, after the party. He'd insist on coming back for the biopsy, whenever I booked it in, but I wouldn't let him. His boss was already pissed off about Greg missing work tomorrow. We couldn't afford for him to take any more time off.

I'd contemplated asking Aunty Carmen to come to the biopsy with me, but quickly decided that was a terrible idea. She'd be a hysterical mess. Same with Dad. I could ask Melissa, but she'd have to take time off work. Aileen had already left for Ireland to visit her family, which was a blessing since I didn't have to worry about her catching me sneaking in and out of lifts at the hospital. I could ask Megan, but she seemed a bit distracted lately. Also, I didn't fancy being stuck in a car with her right now in case she badgered me for 'honest feedback' on her story. At least Sam and Dave would be at pick-up to act as a buffer this afternoon. Maybe I'd just pretend I couldn't open the attachment. I had enough to deal with this weekend without crushing my friend's dreams.

By the time Stella, Max and I were walking out the door, I'd decided it would be best to go to the biopsy on my own. In my experience, it's the patient who ends up consoling everyone anyway.

***

Megan was humming the tune to 'Let's Talk About Sex' as I approached our bench.

'Are you seriously singing that in a school playground?' I said.

'It's a dedication to you and Greg.' Megan grinned.

'You two are gonna be getting bizzaaaaay!' Sam crowed, tipping his head back and cupping one hand around his mouth.

'Bizzaaaaaaaay!' Dave echoed.

I sat down and flicked each of them on the thigh in turn. 'You know what (*flick*)? I reckon I'd prefer not to discuss how much sex I may (*flick*) or may not have this weekend, if that's okay with you lot (*flick*)?'

'Ow!' Sam whined. 'Oh, but it's totally fine for you to ask me all about my Tinder dates?'

'Correct.'

'Impressive double standards,' Sam said, rubbing his thigh.

'But you're excited to see him, yeah?'

'Yes, Dave. I am excited to see my husband for the first time in two months,' I said. 'Although we're going to be pretty flat out with the party so, you know, it's not really about our sex life this weekend.'

Dave frowned. 'What party?'

Oops. Megan, Sam and I glanced at each other. Dave wasn't invited to the twins' party. He didn't really know them, but Sam and Megan were going so it was a bit awkward nonetheless.

'Uh, Zara and Archie's fifteenth.'

'Oh, cool,' Dave said, then turned to the others. 'You guys going?'

There was a slight pause before Megan leaned forward and clapped her hands together loudly. 'Hey, did you guys get a chance to read my story?'

While I was grateful to Megan for changing the subject, I'd have preferred that she'd chosen a topic that wasn't equally as awkward. Sam and Dave's horrified expressions told me they had similar opinions to mine on Megan's story.

'No, it's weird, I couldn't open the attachment!' I said, adopting my best disappointed expression.

'Yeah, me either,' Sam said, shooting me a grateful look. 'Weird.'

'Well, I ...'

Sam gave Dave a sharp nudge, shutting him up. Thankfully, Megan didn't see this exchange as she was still frowning at me.

'Really? Maybe it was something to do with the new update Harry installed on my computer.'

'The kid from your writing class?' Sam said, sounding strangely put out.

'Um, yeah.'

Did I imagine it, or had Megan blushed at the mere mention of her young tech guru?

'Gee, what a shame that you might have to get him back. Again,' Sam said a bit gruffly.

He was obviously still sensitive about the fact that a guy half his age had fixed something he couldn't. And I could see that Megan got a mild kick out of Sam's misplaced jealousy, although we both knew it had more to do with his ego than anything else.

'Is Rania invited?' Megan asked in an innocent tone.

'No, why?'

'Seeing as you two are hanging out,' Megan said coyly, 'thought she might've made the guest list.'

'Did you see those photos online of Rania outside the school?' said Dave.

'Yeah,' said Sam, grimacing. 'That was cruel. Paparazzi are one rung up from pond scum.'

'I didn't see 'em,' Megan said. 'But Lizzie probably did.'

Megan pretended to be interested in a game of netball going on nearby and I examined her face. Was she *jealous*? That was ridiculous. I was about to say as much when Sam groaned.

'Uuuuunhh! Nicola McGinty!'

Sure enough, Baytree's self-coronated monarch was heading in our direction.

'Oh God, what does she want?' Megan groaned. 'I don't have the energy today.'

Megan picked up her phone to begin one of her fake conversations. 'Yeah ... no ... well, maybe order them from Axil Coffee roasters again, they were good ...'

Nicola approached and stared Megan down.

'Hi, Nicola.'

Nicola ignored me and began tapping on her phone.

'Megan's just on a call,' Sam said, gesturing to our mate. 'Work again. Anything we can help you with?'

Nicola ignored him, too and raised the phone to her ear, just as Megan's loud, effervescent ringtone went off. Megan froze, mortified. She pulled the phone away from her face and looked at it as if she'd never seen it before.

'Hope you don't miss my call!' Nicola said, smiling sweetly.

Sam, Dave and I struggled to keep straight faces as Megan tried her best to look confused.

'I seriously need a new phone,' Megan said.

'This happens to you *all* the time,' I said, coming to her aid.

'I know! So, what can I do for you, Nic?' Megan said, acting like the last twenty seconds had never happened.

Nicola gave Megan a death stare that Zara would applaud, and folded her arms. 'Have you heard from Salena Naidu about the camp safety forms?' she asked in an icy tone. 'She's not returning my emails and I can't find her.'

Hiding from you no doubt, I thought.

'I want to make sure the parents have all filled out the correct information,' Nicola continued.

'I haven't seen her, no,' Megan said. 'But I'm sure she's got it under control. She's been really thorough with all the camp paperwork.'

'Cannot wait!' Dave chirped.

Nicola looked at him like he was dog poo on her boot.

'For the camp,' he said and grinned. 'We're all gonna have a blast together, Nicola!'

Sam and Megan were biting their lips, on the verge of cracking.

'How about you guys go find Miss Naidu and chase up

those forms,' I suggested, providing a much-needed escape route for my mates.

'Yes!' Megan yelped. 'We really need those forms.' She stood, yanking Sam up by the sleeve.

'Can I come?' Dave requested innocently. 'I wanna talk to Salena about storage space on the bus for my amp.'

'Sure.'

Dave jumped up and the three of them walked a bit too quickly towards the school office.

Nicola watched them go, not quite sure what just happened, but definitely not happy about it.

'Text me if you – or any of *that* lot – find her, okay?' she commanded me.

'No worries.'

Nicola marched off towards the gate and I looked back to see Megan clutching at Sam's arm as they ran up the steps of the main building. There was a screech of laughter from Megan just as they disappeared inside, and I was filled with love for my friends.

★★★

'*Lizzie*, where do you want the presents table?'

'*Mum*, I need your charger! My phone died and I have to sync the playlist!'

'*Lizzie*, what do you want to put out first, sausage rolls or mini-quiches?'

'*Mum*, tell Max he can't kick the ball inside!'

The day of Zara and Archie's party had arrived, and while I was being shouted at and accosted at every turn, Greg, Dad and my brothers were transforming Abelas into a sparkly teen haven. Greg's duties for the party, due to start in an hour, included making sure no one snuck outside for a quick grope, smoke or swig. When I'd told him this earlier, Greg reminded me of my own fifteenth birthday party, also held at Abelas.

'Didn't you and your mates spend the whole night drinking scotch out of Coke cans?'

'Yeah. What's your point?'

'So, basically, you're saying *Do as I say, not as I do*?'

'That's right.'

'Copy that,' Greg had said, snuggling up to me on the couch. 'You turned out pretty well for a wayward teen.'

'You reckon?'

'I reckon,' he'd said, leaning in for a kiss.

When Greg had arrived home last night, I'd had to stand back and wait my turn as an avalanche of children descended on him. But when I finally felt Greg's big arms around me for the first time in eight weeks, I almost melted into the floor. I wanted to collapse into him and cry, *I'm scared I've got cancer and I'm going to die!*

It had taken every ounce of willpower I possessed not to. Not then, nor later when we were finally alone and lying in a tangle of sweaty limbs after the best sex I could remember having in a very long time. It was the longest we'd gone without having sex, apart from those late- pregnancy and post-birth weeks. We'd always had a healthy sex life and I was relieved to find that this time apart hadn't changed that. At all.

But this morning I'd noticed something slightly off about him. I didn't know if it was fatigue, or the thought of having to leave us again, but as I watched him stringing up fairy lights with my brothers, intermittently sucking on helium balloons and falling all over the place laughing like five-year-olds, I could see that he was distracted. I'd known the man for seventeen years and something was on his mind.

You and me both, buddy.

After dealing with the multiple requests and demands thrown at me, there were only a few minutes left until party time. I left Zara hovering nervously by the door, and Archie relaxing in the corner with a comic, and headed back into Abelas' kitchen. Every surface was covered with platters of Aunty Carmen's savoury delights and sweet treats, red and green paper plates, red and green serviettes and precarious towers of red and green plastic cups.

'It looks like Santa's elves threw up in here,' I said, starting to unwrap packets of paper plates.

'Here they come!' Aunty Carmen announced as we heard the front door open. 'Punctual little buggers, aren't they?'

I looked out through the serving hatch in time to see a squealing gaggle of girls rush through the door and envelop Zara in a clamour of arms as a cloud of their combined, cheap body spray wafted into the kitchen. Archie's mates sauntered in, cool as cucumbers, and shuffled around each other in a circle, bumping fists and looking awkward.

Aunty Carmen peered over my shoulder. 'You didn't tell me there was a dress code.'

'There isn't.'

'Then why are the girls all wearing the same thing? And why does Archie look like a cat burglar?'

'Because ... teenagers.'

In black jeans, black T-shirt and black hoodie, Archie did indeed look like he was dressed for a nocturnal heist, while Zara's friends were all tall, skinny clones of each other and wore their straight hair long and parted down the middle, a few with bad home jobs of dyed-orange streaks.

Anyone looking out across Abelas' slated floor would be able to tell immediately which guests belonged to which twin. Zara's guests were an even mix of boys and girls, and there was a definite nineties vibe going on. Mum jeans or pleated minis, crop tops and black plastic chokers for the girls, plaid shirts, straight-leg jeans or khaki pants for the boys. The whole lot of them looked like they'd stepped off the set of a teen rom-com.

Archie had managed to rustle up a respectable crew of six, all boys, all dressed in branded T-shirts, dark jeans and runners. But it was their hair I couldn't get past. I never imagined I'd see so many mullets again in my lifetime.

I gave Aunty Carmen a quick peck. 'Thank you again for everything. The food looks amazing!'

'Pah!' she said, waving her hand and heading for the storeroom at the back of the kitchen.

'Sorry I'm late!' Megan appeared with Oscar at her side. She looked as gorgeous as ever in skinny jeans and a blood-red tank top, and although she seemed flustered, there was also a glow about her.

'Am I seeing things or do those boys out there have *mullets*?'

'Mullets are back.'

'What's a mullet?' Oscar asked.

'Go find Max and Tyler,' Megan said, giving her son a gentle shove towards the restaurant.

'Can I have a lemonade?' Oscar asked.

'Sure.'

Oscar looked like Megan had agreed to him snorting a bucket of Wizz Fizz. I was pretty stunned myself. Megan considered soft drink to be right up there with heroin. He bolted from the kitchen before she could change her mind.

'I had to pick up Oscar from Bryce's,' Megan said, putting her bag under the kitchen bench and running her hands through her blonde mane. 'He was banging on about the wedding again. I'm so fucking over it.' She gasped in horror as Aunty Carmen walked in. 'Oh, sorry!'

'Never apologise to this woman for swearing,' I said. 'She's the worst one in our whole family.'

'This is a fact!' Aunty Carmen's face lit up and she pulled Megan to her ample chest. 'You must be Megan! We finally meet!'

'It's so good to meet *the* Aunty Carmen!' Megan said, returning her hug.

'Just as beautiful as Lizzie said.' She stepped back to survey Megan Wylie in all her splendour. 'Like Billy Joel's wife!'

'Well, that's very kind, thank you,' Megan said, who clearly had no idea who that was.

'I bet the old men at the home love you, huh?'

'Well ...'

'Ah, don't be so modest!' Aunty Carmen cried, waving her arms at Megan's figure. 'Those pervy old bastards would all be fantasising about getting down and dirty with you.'

'Aunty *Carmen!*' I cried, as Megan roared with laughter.

'What?' Aunty Carmen said, winking at Megan.

'Told you,' I said to Megan. 'The worst.'

'Okay.' Megan chuckled. 'What can I do?'

'Take those jugs of juice and soft drink out to the table, please.'

'There are more mullets out there than a 1983 Grand Final,' Sam said, making Megan instantly double over again. He held up the platter of his delicious lime-and-raspberry friands in his hands. 'Where should I put these?'

'A man who makes cupcakes!' Aunty Carmen cried. 'I like it!'

Sam visibly shuddered at hearing his friands referred to as cupcakes, but graciously let it go.

'Aunty Carmen, this is Sam,' I said. 'They look amazing, thank you!'

'I'll take them!' Aunty Carmen whipped the tray out of Sam's hand and headed back to the storeroom.

'Might go say g'day to my old mate Greg,' Sam said. 'Good to have him back?'

'So good.'

'Am I allowed to walk across the floor, or will Zara throw a pink fit?'

'Just stay close to the edges of the room and you should be fine.'

'It's okay,' Sam said. 'I'll just disguise myself as an android phone and nobody will notice me.'

We laughed and I felt stupid for giving too much air to any petty grievance between us.

The only adults Zara and Archie had allowed to attend today's shindig were their parents, their grandfather, Aunty Carmen, Sam and Megan.

Rosa, Chris's wife, wasn't happy when she learned her daughter, Scarlett, was invited and she wasn't.

'Maybe I could just come and help out in the kitchen?' she'd suggested over the phone last week. 'You'll need extra hands when you're feeding twenty-plus teenagers.'

'Thanks, Rosa, but we should be fine.'

From what I could see through the serving window, Scarlett and Nessa looked right at home as they chatted and giggled with Zara's friends. Stella, Poppy and Lola stood a little away from the throng, looking less comfortable. I knew Stella would have a harder time with her friends' and cousins' worlds colliding. I'd made her promise to include Lola, but from what I could see there was a lot of standing around going on. I didn't have time to worry about pre-teen dramas today.

An hour later, the party was well underway and the air was thick with teenage sweat. Greg and Joey had set up a makeshift dancefloor in the corner of the room, where Billie Eilish and Harry Styles were pouring from Joey's state-of-the-art stereo. Zara's crew were spread out around the sides of the room, talking, laughing and taking a prolific number of selfies, while Archie and his mates shuffled around in the corner nursing cups of raspberry-and-lemonade punch. Archie's best friend, Xavier, reminded me of a young Emilio Estevez and seemed to spend all his time staring into his cup, not speaking to a single person. When I offered him a party pie, he shook his head and said, 'Thanks, but Mum made me pasta before I came.'

Sam and Megan were being amazing. In the past half hour, we'd cleaned up three spilt drinks and replaced two platters of pastizzis, one platter of mini-quiches and two bowls of potato chips between us.

'Keep 'em coming!' I shouted to Aunty Carmen through the serving hatch.

'Good Lord, it's like feeding a room full of Christophers!' Aunty Carmen yelled back.

'When do you want us to put out the cupcakes?' I asked Sam at one point.

'They're friands, actually.'

'I know,' I said, making a face and scurrying away.

I kept catching Megan checking her phone and

blushing. If I hadn't been so busy mopping up fruit punch and splattered sausage rolls, I'd have demanded to know who was making her smile like a fifteen-year-old scrolling through comments on her casually hot bikini selfie.

Aunty Carmen was chatting to Greg, so I popped another tray of pastizzis in the oven and was just heading out to interrogate Megan when Zara ran in, flushed and happy.

'There you are! So, after the cake, remember ...'

'Oh my *God!*' I cried. 'No adults, I *know*! Mind you, some of the boys are eyeing off Megan. I don't think they'd mind if she had a boogie.'

'Mum!' Zara waved her hands around in a woke rage. 'That's totally inappropriate and, like, illegal! Megan's, like, forty!'

'Relax!' I grabbed her gently by the shoulders. 'We'll leave you to your crumping and your Woahs ... or whatever you do.'

'*Woahs?!*' Zara laughed. Then, to my shock, she threw her arms around my neck and kissed me on the cheek. 'Thank you for tonight, Mum. It's the best party. Everyone is saying so.'

This rare display of affection from my daughter almost brought tears to my eyes. 'You're welcome, darling.' I hugged her tight. 'Now, go ask your dad to restock the soft drinks.'

I was overcome with a crushing fear as Zara ran out: how would she cope if I wasn't around? What about when she needed advice about friends or boys or uni courses? Or when she had her heart broken for the first time? Who would she go to? Aunty Carmen? Megan? Melissa? Definitely not Rosa. The idea of either of my daughters having to go to another woman about their broken hearts was unfathomable. My kids needed *me*, their mum. Nobody else. My nose began to tingle, but I couldn't cry, not now. I poured myself a shot of vodka from the bottle Aunty Carmen kept in the freezer, downed it and went over to Megan to distract myself.

'Are you having sex?'

Megan almost choked on her pastizzi. '*No!* Why?'

'You keep looking at your phone and blushing,' I said, grabbing a lukewarm sausage roll and swirling it in tomato sauce. 'The sure sign of a sexually active woman.'

'It's just my new friend from writing class.' Megan turned away to pick up her drink. 'She's texting me ideas for a raunchy scene she's writing. Trust me, the only one having sex this weekend is you.'

'I won't rub it in,' I said.

'Yeah, please don't,' Megan replied. 'So, which one is Reuben?'

I'd shared my suspicions with Megan, who was as excited as a proud, non-related aunty could be.

'The one next to the sausage rolls,' I said, lowering my voice. 'Green checked shirt. Mullet.'

'He's cute. Apart from the mullet, of course.'

'The girl has good taste, like her mum.'

As if on cue, Greg walked across the floor carrying a full rubbish bag. He stopped right in the middle of the dancefloor and busted out a few MC Hammer moves to a Hilltop Hoods song. Zara was horrified, but Reuben and his mates seemed to appreciate Greg's nineties moves and gave him a round of applause. My husband took a bow before continuing on his way, and I silently gave Reuben a big tick for his reaction. I'd tried to stay cool when Zara introduced me. Reuben seemed like a nice kid, although it was hard to tell with fifteen-year-old boys – all mumbles and lack of eye contact. Her best friend, Ines, on the other hand, was a livewire.

'Hi, Lizzie, it's so nice to meet you and this party is awesome,' she chirped. 'I've never been across the bridge before, but it's actually so cool.'

'Well, it's a Saturday,' I said. 'If you'd come on a Tuesday, we'd all be wearing footy shorts and wife-beaters.'

'Huh?'

'Nothing, darling, lovely to meet you.'

Megan scanned the room now and frowned. 'So, what am I scoping for? Pot? Vaping? Booze? Fingering?'

I almost spat my raspberry punch across the room. 'Jesus!'

'They're fifteen, Lizzie. What were you doing at fifteen?'

'Not that!' I spluttered. 'And definitely not in my grandfather's restaurant!'

'Good point. Okay, so just look out for pashing and groping?'

'Pashing is fine,' I said. 'Groping, drinking, vaping, not fine. Only an hour till it's over. Surely, we can make it through without someone breaking a limb tiktokking.'

Megan nudged me and grinned. 'Do you remember your first pash?'

'Ew, yes.' I shuddered. 'Dancefloor, Altona North Bluelight. Slimy tongue darting in and out of my mouth like a lizard.'

Megan snorted and the two of us stood in the corner giggling. The vodka shot had given me a lovely buzz and I felt good standing here, reminiscing with my bestie about gross first kisses. Megan and I hadn't been in sync for a while and I'd missed this. I promised myself that I'd make more of an effort to spend time with her. Sam too.

'Hey, where's Sam?'

Megan stopped giggling. 'Oh, he had to go.'

'What? Why didn't he say goodbye?'

'I think there was an issue with Stella.'

My heart sank. It had all been going so well. 'What happened?'

'Something about Stella's cousins making fun of Lola's outfit.' Megan paused, looking uncomfortable. 'I don't think Stella stuck up for her. Lola got upset so Sam took her home.'

'Shit.'

Stella was on the dancefloor with Poppy, Scarlett and Nessa, laughing and pulling out some of her best hip-hop moves. My eyes shifted to Nessa. I had no doubt that it was my least favourite niece who'd teased Lola. But why hadn't Stella stood up for her? I'd taught her better than that.

'Don't say anything to her now,' Megan said. 'Leave it till after the party.'

'Okay, but I'm texting Sam.'

As I pulled out my phone, Greg walked over to tell me that Archie and Xavier were throwing up in the backyard.

***

Greg was awake and staring up at the ceiling when I opened my eyes early the next morning. His brow was furrowed, and his hands were clasped behind his head, revealing two thick tufts of blond armpit hair.

I had to tell him. Now. Soon, Stella would be banging on the bedroom door insisting on 'family time' before Greg left for the airport. Also, Greg and I needed to talk to Archie about last night's drunken escapades. But before I dropped the possibility of his wife having cancer, I wanted to know what was causing his brow to furrow like that.

'Hey.'

He instantly adjusted his expression and turned a now smiling face towards me.

'Hey, buddy.'

'You okay?'

He rolled over to fling one arm across me. 'Sweet as. Probably can't say the same for my morning breath.'

I leaned in and took a big whiff. 'Not as bad as you'd think, actually. Mine?'

I exhaled and Greg pretended to pass out.

I rolled onto my back, taking my offending breath with me, and gave his naked torso a nudge. 'So, what's up?'

'Hmm? Oh God, just the whole Archie thing.'

'Greg,' I said. 'I saw your face when I woke up. You're thinking about more than our son getting rat-faced.'

Greg shifted slightly and sighed. 'It's just boring work stuff.'

'Tell me.'

He rubbed his hand back and forth across his stubble. 'There was an accident on the site this week.'

I sat up. 'Shit! Was anyone hurt?'

'Yeah. Badly.' Greg sat up too and leaned back against the headboard. 'And it was on my watch. I mean, I'm a sub-contractor, so technically I'm not the one at fault.'

'Okay.'

'But WorkSafe have been brought in.'

I swallowed. 'What does that mean?'

'Dunno.' He shrugged, vigorously rubbing his hand across his cheek again. 'Bill's on the warpath, looking for a scapegoat. This is his second incident in six months, so he could lose his building licence.'

'But he can't fire you, can he?'

Greg paused. 'Nah, probably not.'

My stomach lurched. If Greg lost this job we'd be screwed. And what if my lump turned out to be cancerous and I needed treatment? I'd have to take time off work, which would mean another financial hit. I was suddenly regretting re-enrolling Stella in another term of acting classes, and Max for another season of soccer. Both sets of fees were almost criminal. Not to mention the money I'd recently spent on the twins' birthdays. Panic began to rise in my chest.

'But I'm definitely not in the good books,' Greg continued. 'Bill didn't want me coming down here.'

'You didn't have to come, you know,' I said gently. 'The kids would have understood.'

'Fuck that!' Greg's face clouded over. 'I'm not gonna miss my kids' birthday. I've had this date on my roster for weeks.'

I could hear the anger and frustration in his voice, and it was disconcerting. My husband was the most placid man I'd ever known. It took a lot to rile him up.

'But would he use this against you?' I asked. 'I mean, does it look bad that you flew off to Melbourne right after it happened?'

'I don't know.'

I was quiet.

Greg reached over and gripped my hand. 'It'll be fine, buddy. Promise,' he said, his face a mask of reassurance. 'I've booked an earlier flight for today and I'll get it all sorted when I'm back. Don't stress, all right?'

'All right.'

But I *was* stressed. There was no way I could tell Greg about the biopsy now. News like that could send him over the edge. He'd quit the job in a second and stay here. And as appealing as that was, I couldn't let it happen. The biopsy could all come to nothing. *But what if it isn't nothing? What if it's stage-four breast cancer and you're not here next year?* These morbid thoughts had been keeping me awake. My mum had died young, so it could happen to me, too. Greg would think the same and insist on being here to hold my hand through every doctor's appointment because that's the kind of man he is. He'd be secretly terrified but would put on a brave face and say we'd get through it together. As wonderful as that sounded right now, I couldn't be that selfish. We needed the money Greg was making, so I'd have to keep it to myself for a bit longer.

'Okay,' I said, squeezing his hand back. 'I won't stress.'

'Good.' He kissed my shoulder and his hand snaked down under the covers to stroke my thigh. 'One for the road?'

I pretended to swoon. 'So romantic. How could I possibly refuse?'

Greg grinned, but as he leaned in for a kiss, I pulled my head away and pointed at the bedroom door.

'Better lock that.'

Zara and Archie wouldn't be joining the land of the living for at least another hour or two, but I could hear our early birds, Max and Stella, bustling around the kitchen. I'd never recovered from the time a three-year-old Stella had walked into the bedroom to find me writhing on top of Greg, holding onto our white wooden headboard for support.

'I play horsey, too, Mummy!' she'd squealed with delight. Mortified.

'Good plan.' Greg jumped out of bed and as he crossed the room, I let out the long, shaky breath I'd been holding. I'd put everything out of my mind for now and focus on my gorgeous husband.

At least for the next ten minutes.

Fifteen max.

Chapter Seventeen
Megan

Megan sat in her car outside Baytree Primary, staring through the windscreen and thinking about Harry. Again. It was something she'd been doing a lot since he'd leaned over and kissed her in Paddy's Bar almost a week ago.

She knew she had to actually get out of this car at some point and attend a camp meeting with Nicola and the teachers, but the second Harry popped into her head, she lost all motivation to do anything other than sit and replay the scene in the pub over and over again, from multiple angles. Megan came to the same conclusion every time. She had definitely kissed him back, for a good thirty seconds. And what a delicious thirty seconds. After that, she'd jumped up – knocking over her stool, almost taking out two women carrying very full pots of Guinness in the process – and run for the door, ignoring Harry's shouts behind her. As soon as she was home, Megan thanked Sam, told him she was busting to use the toilet (knowing he'd show himself out) then bolted to the bathroom, where she found a flurry of texts from Harry on her phone.

H: *R U OK?*

H: *Sorry if that freaked you.*

H: *Can u just let me know you got home okay?*

Megan sat on the toilet and texted back.

Sorry for running out. I'm fine. Just need a minute.

Since then, they'd texted a few more times. Harry had wanted to come over, but Megan didn't trust herself.

M: *Let's just wait until class on Wednesday, okay?*

H: *Okay x*

Now it was Tuesday, and she'd be seeing him in just over twenty-four hours, which was making it very hard to concentrate. It had taken so much self-restraint not to spill the Harry news to Lizzie at the party, but Megan wasn't ready to tell her best friend she was crushing on a teenager. Especially not in an environment where they were surrounded by them.

But there was nothing wrong with having a little crush, was there? Maybe even a fun fling? It wasn't like it would ever turn into anything serious, because of *the age difference.* And surely, Harry would be too embarrassed to be seen dating an old woman. A crowded pub was one thing, but taking her to meet his friends or family was something else entirely. She knew she still looked good for a woman approaching forty – her boobs were in great nick and still upright, so that was a bonus. And even though Harry was only *eleven years older than her son*, what did all these numbers really mean? In the bigger scheme of things, the universe wasn't going to implode because a 37-year-old woman kissed a nineteen-year-old boy. Look at her own mother. Ellie was a decade older than Megan's dad ... although that hadn't exactly turned out for the best.

It's not like I'm hurting anyone, Megan told herself, her hands still in the ten-to-two position on the steering wheel. *I'm not hurting Oscar, who is actually the only person I care about.*

Did a little age difference between two consenting adults in a relationship really matter?

And now we're in a relationship in my fantasy scenario, Megan thought wryly. *Wow. That was fast. But my God, that kiss.* It was sweeter and sexier than anything Megan could have imagined. And the way Harry's hand had gently moved from the side of her face to the back of her head, how he'd threaded his fingers through her hair as his other hand encircled the small of her waist and pulled her towards him. In that moment, all logical arguments for why kissing a nineteen-year-old was a bad idea had vanished.

'*Megan!*'

'Aah!' Megan turned to see Nicola's pointy face staring at her through the window.

'Are. You. Coming. In?' She overemphasised each word, clearly under the assumption that Megan's car windows were triple glazed.

'Yes. I'm. Coming,' Megan overemphasised back.

She sighed, unbuckled her seatbelt and opened the door, reluctant to leave her memories of Harry in the car.

'I've been waving at you from the school gate,' Nicola complained. 'You were in another world. Now, listen, remind me to bring up the vegan and keto requirements, okay? I've been researching keto and it's a nightmare! Although the results are pretty amazing.'

Megan sighed as she followed Nicola inside the school. Passionate kisses with a teenager one week, camp-committee meetings the next. What a world.

***

'You can't cancel!'

'But ...'

'No, Sam!' Megan said, holding up her hand. 'No *but*, you have to play. I've promised Mum!'

Megan swivelled on the bench to address a sheepish Dave. 'How could you not know you had a wedding?'

'Sorry, Megs,' Dave said meekly. 'Kesh said she told me, but I don't remember.'

'Useless!' Megan turned back to Sam. 'You'll just have to do it solo.'

Sam gaped in horror. 'I can't! The set we've been working out is all arranged for *two* guitars and *two* voices.'

'Chill out,' Dave said unhelpfully. 'You can totally rock those songs solo and use the loop pedal for harmonies. Easy.'

Sam leaned forward to glare at him. 'Is it, Dave?'

Megan adopted her most soothing tone. 'Listen, everyone is really looking forward to it, Sam,' she cooed. 'Imagine their poor sad, wrinkly faces if I have to tell them there's no gig.'

'Yeah, old people need things to look forward to, Sammy.'

'Shut up, Dave.'

'Roger that,' Dave said, leaning back.

'Dude, I cannot believe you're doing this to me!' Sam said. 'We've been advertised as an acoustic duo. A *duo*! I'm really not keen on rocking up as a *solo* act. Surely, you have the technological wherewithal to at least send a hologram of yourself. If it's good enough for Tupac, it's good enough for you!'

'RIP,' Dave said mournfully.

'Sam, please,' Megan begged. 'You've got almost two weeks to prepare, and I've already put up a poster.'

Sam looked surprised. 'You made a poster?'

'Yep, Microsoft Word and I made a poster,' Megan said proudly.

'Why didn't you ask me to design it?' Dave asked.

Both Megan and Sam whirled on him. 'Shut *up*, Dave!'

Dave nodded and performed the universal sign for lip-zipping.

'Did you make me look like a rock star?'

'Bowie meets Jagger with a touch of Bon Jovi.'

Sam sighed. 'Okay. I'll do it.'

'Thank you!' Megan gave Sam a hug, followed by a double-handed salute. 'Rock on!'

'Rock on,' Sam echoed.

'Thanks, man,' Dave said. 'And sorry again.'

'You owe me,' Sam said as the bell went and children started to pour into the yard. 'Can either of you see Lola? Oh, there she is.'

A miserable-looking Lola was walking towards them, head down, her polished black shoes scuffing along the bitumen.

'Is she okay?' Megan asked.

'Not really,' Sam said. 'She's still upset about what happened at the party, and Stella's been ignoring her.'

Megan felt sorry for Lola. She'd called Sam on Sunday, and found out that Stella's cousin, Nessa, had asked Lola why she was dressed for Halloween in March. Then the other cousin made some crack about Lola auditioning for a horror film and they'd all laughed. What upset Lola the most was Stella's inaction. She'd just stood there staring at her feet.

'Have you told Lizzie what happened?' she asked Sam.

'No.' Sam shrugged. 'I knew she was with Greg on

Sunday, and she seemed distracted at pick-up yesterday.'

'She'd want to know, man,' Dave said.

'I'd want you to tell me if Oscar was being a little shit.' Megan added, 'Speak of the devil. *Oscar!*'

'At least someone's kid is happy,' Sam said, watching Oscar bounding towards them.

'Until he finds out about his velvet breeches and top hat.'

'His what?' Dave asked.

'Tell you tomorrow.' Megan grinned. 'Bye!'

★★★

'Have fun. Text me goodnight from Dad's phone, okay?'

'Okay.'

Megan gave her son one last squeeze then watched him skip towards Bryce's jeep.

'Have you told him about the goggles and breeches yet?' she asked Bryce, who was rolling Oscar's suitcase down the hallway.

'Not yet. Mum is planning to bribe him with a Kinder Surprise when we get to the hotel.'

Poor Clara, Megan thought. As much as she disliked Bryce's mother, the woman had endured a lot over the past few years. First her son told her he was leaving his wife for a man, then that he was marrying said man, and now she was forced to watch her grandson dress up like a subversive cabaret performer for the occasion.

Her phone beeped the second she closed the front door behind them.

H: *You home? I'm in the city. Wanna show you the photos I took.*

Megan hesitated. If she told Harry she was home and he came over, there was no Oscar buffer. It would just be the two of them in the house. Unsupervised. Then again, it might be the perfect opportunity to make it clear that what happened last week was a mistake and could never happen again.

M: *Sure. Come over.*

I'll offer him a coffee, look at his photos, explain that last week was a one-off and send him on his way, she thought, standing in front of the hallway mirror, tugging at the forest-green jumper that matched her eyes.

But when she opened the door to Harry twenty minutes later, those familiar oversized headphones around his neck, Megan knew she'd been kidding herself. Harry stepped forward, took her face in his hands and began to kiss her. Before her legs completely collapsed beneath her, she pushed him away and closed the door behind them.

'Listen,' she croaked. 'We have to talk ...'

Harry ignored her and started kissing her neck.

'Harry!'

He instantly pulled back. 'Oh shit, is Oscar here?'

'No, he's out, but ... what about these photos.'

'After.'

'After what?'

'After more kissing.'

It took all of her inner strength, but Megan pushed him away again and led him into the lounge room. She stood in front of him, arms folded, and prayed that she looked more determined than she felt. She remembered something Lizzie had once told her.

'Never underestimate the importance of tone when it comes to getting what you want,' Lizzie had said. 'Whether it's the strict-parent-talking-to-a-kid tone, or the firm-owner-talking-to-the-dog tone, or the friendly-talking-to-the-Telstra-guy-who's-kept-you-on-hold-for-forty-minutes tone. It makes all the difference for results.'

'Right,' she said, using her best assertive tone. 'Just to reiterate what we both know, but you, my friendly local IT support guy, are nineteen years old.'

'Correct. And you, my un-tech-savvy client and writing classmate, are thirty-seven years young.'

'Don't be cute.'

'My un-tech-savvy and very *beautiful* client and classmate who I believe may be my destiny,' Harry said, flashing his dimples. 'I mean, we've got the whole Megan-and-Harry thing going on. Like, it's meant to be.'

'What?'

'Y'know ... the royals. The cool young ones.'

Megan tried not to smile. 'Jesus Christ, Harry! I have bras older than you.'

'Show me.'

Megan stared him down, but Harry wasn't budging an inch. She looked into his gorgeous face and felt her resolve melting away.

Chapter Eighteen
Sam

To: jack_woz_here@hotmail.com
From: samhatfieldchef@bigpond.com
Subject: Kids!

Hey dickhead,

What's the timeline etiquette for providing feedback on a piece of writing? Megan only sent us her story a week ago and I feel like, in order to give it the time and attention it deserves before offering my constructive criticism, I will need at least another EIGHT TO TEN YEARS. Jack, how do you tell your friend their writing is a bit shit, to say the least? I know. Just lie.

Speaking of self-expression (radio-worthy segue as always), Stella could've used a bit more of hers at Zara and Archie's party. Intrigued? I don't care, I'm telling you, anyway. Stella's cousins were having a go at Lola about her clothes because kids are mean. Lola was upset, so we left early without telling Lizzie. Lola told me in the car that Stella just looked away while the other girls picked on every element of Lola's outfit. Man, things with Lizzie are already shaky, and I have no idea how to bring this up with her.

Speaking of uncomfortable topics (BOOM – sorry, I'll stop now), last night I watched a grown woman pretend to take a shit in an oversized tray of kitty litter. And I paid for the privilege. Now, if I was paying a sex worker to fulfil my kinkiest, feline-faeces fetish, that would've been all well and good; nothing but a

business transaction. But what I paid to see last night was ART.
The tray of kitty litter – at least three metres by three metres
– was in the centre of a large white room where Melbourne's
most two-dimensional hipsters moved around its perimeter on
invisible hoverboards, staring deep into the kitty litter's soul. If I
thought taking a shit in there myself might've gotten me kicked
out, I would've taken the initiative, but I feel sure I would've
been applauded and lauded as a fresh new voice in the
Australian contemporary art scene.

How did I come to be there? Let me explain. Rachel keeps
texting me about theatre stuff. My re-crush on her is growing
daily, so I write back just to keep the lines of communication
open and flowing. But I'm having to google stuff to be able to
sound like I know what I'm taking about, or more importantly,
that I give a shit. I'm sure there'll be a time when I come clean
about my complete lack of care factor about all things thespian,
but for now, I'm sticking with being deceptive to make myself
more interesting.

So, Rachel invited me to see this 'immersive installation
experience', and of course I said yes. She was transfixed by the
whole thing. In the wall, there was a very large cat flap, through
which a woman dressed in a red-and-white-striped onesie
appeared.

By the time Catwoman made her way into the centre of her kitty
litter tray and brought herself up to a more humanoid squatting
position, I felt like a man about to see something he could never
unsee. Catwoman reached between her legs for the press-
studs of the onesie's bum flap. Then, in a sudden movement
that made the whole room jump, she RELEASED THE FLAP.

A stream of red-and-white glitter spilled from the onesie. She
began moving herself around the tray and made the shape of a

love heart. In the kitty litter. With the glitter. Then she resecured the bum flap and made her way back to her cat flap. The lights came up and there was rapturous applause.

Catwoman reappeared in the main entrance to the room, hand on heart and tears in her eyes. I yelled, 'Brava!' swept up in the moment. I may as well have been cheering for Rachel, because she'd told me at the start of the night that she'd broken up with her boyfriend, Sebastian. (Did I tell you she had a boyfriend?) I should've opened with that, but then you wouldn't have gotten to hear about this incredible art installation. Oh, and do you know what the name of the installation was? The installation, my dear old friend, was called ...

KITTY GLITTER.

You remember how much I was in love with Michelle Pfeiffer's Catwoman. That's been ruined forever.

S x

Chapter Nineteen
Lizzie

I was hugely enjoying something I was expecting to hate.

This afternoon, when Rania first invited me to this fancy fundraiser, I was hesitant for numerous reasons.

1. I didn't have a babysitter.
2. I'd never been to a fancy fundraiser.
3. I'd worked four night shifts last week.
4. My social life mainly consisted of family-movie nights and wine on the back deck with Megan and Sam.

But when I got home from school pick-up, Max was whingeing about wanting to see Greg at Easter, Stella was stomping around the house because I told her off for not standing up for Lola, Archie was giving me the silent treatment because we'd banned video games and grounded him for a month, and Zara was covering her phone screen every time I walked past.

I quickly decided that home was the last place I wanted to be.

'Zara, you and Archie are babysitting for a couple of hours tonight,' I told my daughter as she lay on her bed texting God knows who about God knows what. 'I'll only be gone from six till nine, okay? There's pizza in the freezer.'

Zara looked as happy and relieved to hear that I was going out as I felt.

Ironically enough, tonight's event was a breast-cancer fundraiser. I didn't know this until Rania and I climbed out of the Uber and I saw the pink carpet running towards a nondescript doorway of the city venue.

Was the universe mocking me? I suppressed a head shake as I followed Rania towards the venue. The volume of the pink-carpet press gallery swelled the moment she was spotted. I tried my best to sink into the background, but Rania was having none of it.

'This is my best friend, Lizzie,' she announced to the photographers and journalists.

They didn't seem very interested in me or this piece of questionable information, but Rania snaked her arm through mine, pulled me in close and smiled for the cameras. I fake-smiled along, nervously at first, but soon relaxed until the smile became genuine. A shot of joy went straight to my heart as the two of us posed and laughed. This was fun. No screaming women, no placentas, no grumpy kids. Just superficial, simple fun.

Ever since the sleazy paparazzi incident two weeks ago, I'd discovered that Rania was actually pretty damn great. Whenever we hung out, I forgot about real life. Truth be told, I'd developed a girl crush. Rania was vibrant and sweet, and it was nice to be around a young woman who didn't roll her eyes every time I opened my mouth. Rania and I had taken Max and Tishk on another frozen-yoghurt date and met up for coffee sans kids a few times, and I was learning a lot about the reality-show queen. First and foremost, the woman was smart. She also had the patience of a saint. Every second person we passed requested a selfie.

'Doesn't it drive you mad?' I asked Rania at a café yesterday after the third request in ten minutes.

'No, because I know it won't last,' Rania said. 'And people are a lot nicer in person than they are online.'

She was a great mum, too. The perfect blend of strict and loving, and Tishk was adorable. He was quite possibly the only six-year-old boy I'd ever known, including my own, that I didn't want to throw out of a window at some point.

I'd found out a lot more about Rania's family, too. Her father was, as Dave said, a big-time engineer in Pakistan, but what Dave and the rest of the country didn't know was that Rania's parents had come to Melbourne after years of trying to conceive and having no luck. Rania's mother had finally had enough of the endless badgering from family members and told her husband she wanted a fresh start. Within weeks of settling in Coburg, Rania's father began making a name for himself in the world of engineering, and Rania's mum fell pregnant. They had fussed and delighted over their baby girl for her entire life, which made her elopement even harder for them to bear. Then, when someone from their Pakistani community let slip that Rania was on a reality TV show (after Rania told her parents she was doing a wellbeing course in Sydney), the shit hit the fan again. Her parents decided that buying a high-end beauty salon in Brighton would be the best way for Rania to rebuild her life, and their reputation in the community.

'Gotta keep that façade up, no matter what!' Rania had joked. 'Their next mission is to find me a nice Pakistani boy. One who'll settle for damaged goods.'

'They did not use that phrase!'

'Oh yes.' Rania laughed. 'The best they can hope for is a forty-something widower.'

I'd secretly watched a couple of episodes of *The Rebound* late one night and had to admit that the friendly, down-to-earth girl on screen closely resembled the girl I was coming to know. The only thing she faked were the positive comments about her partner on the show, Robbie.

'He's a bastard,' she told me in the park one afternoon as our boys hurled themselves backwards down the slide. 'He tried to come into my room on our first night in the apartment and I told him to get out or I'd have him charged with rape.' She grinned. 'They didn't put that to air, of course.'

Rania Jalali was a wonderful distraction from the black cloud hanging over my head. Gina said that once I have the biopsy, the results could take anywhere from three days to a week, depending on how busy the labs were. It was hard keeping it all to myself, but I didn't feel right telling anyone when Greg didn't know.

And now here I was, dressed in a blue Decjuba dress I hadn't pulled out of the wardrobe in over ten years (and that actually fit!) and holding a glass of very expensive champagne. The room was wall-to-wall dresses, suits and stilettos, and I was currently watching Rania expertly crop and filter a selfie she took of us on the pink carpet.

'What's your Insta handle?' she said, tapping away on her screen.

'I don't have one.'

Rania looked up in amazement. 'Are you serious? Give me your phone. Now.'

Before I knew what was happening, Instagram was installed on my phone and Rania was grinning at me. 'There! Your first post. Done.'

'Um, thanks?' I took my phone and looked around at

the collection of beauties and bucks. 'Do you get invited to a lot of these?'

'All the time,' Rania said casually. 'But I only go to the ones that actually mean something to me. My aunt in Pakistan had to have a mastectomy a few years ago. How about in your family?'

'No, but my mum died of ovarian cancer when I was four.' *And guess what? I might have breast cancer right now.*

Rania took my hand. 'Oh, Lizzie, that's awful. I'm so sorry.'

I gave her a reassuring smile. 'Thanks. Long time ago now. I don't really remember her, to be honest.'

'Yes, but still, you must —'

'Excuse me. Sorry, are you Rania Jalali?'

Three skinny, immaculately groomed and very orange young women stood in a cluster gazing at Rania, starstruck.

Rania, accommodating as ever, shot them her beatific smile and nodded modestly. 'I am.'

'Oh my God,' squealed one of the women who was sporting a miniskirt the size of most of my headbands. 'Can we *please* get a selfie?'

'Of course.'

The women yelped with delight and huddled around Rania, towering over her in heels that made me fear for their lives. Rania unleashed her well-practised selfie smile, while the younger women put on their best duck faces and snapped off at least twenty shots each.

'Thank you!' the blonde squealed, then turned to me. 'Are you on TV, too?'

I almost choked on my champers. 'Definitely not.'

As the girls trilled their goodbyes and tottered off on their deadly heels, I noticed that Rania was staring wide-eyed at something behind me. 'Oh my God!'

I turned to look only to have her grab my hand.

'Don't look now, but the guy near the door in the pink blazer is Jonathan McMaster. He produces one of the biggest morning shows on TV. I've been trying to get a meeting with him, but he never returns my agent's calls.'

I took a discreet glance behind me at the tall, slim, pink-blazered man with a grey goatee and glasses, who was talking to two other men.

'Why don't we just go say hi?'

'Just go up to him?'

'Why not?' Buoyed by the champagne, I grabbed Rania's hand.

'But that's not how it works,' Rania said nervously as we approached the group of men. 'I have to wait for him to …'

'Hi, I'm Lizzie,' I said, walking straight up to Pink Blazer and sticking out my hand.

The men looked completely thrown for a moment, then Jonathan smiled stiffly and took my hand. 'Jonathan. Hello.'

'And this is my friend, Rania Jalali.' I pushed a nervous Rania forward.

'Hello, lovely to meet you,' Rania said softly, shaking Jonathan's hand.

The men's faces instantly brightened at the sight of my beautiful friend in her metallic-grey, off-the-shoulder mini-dress.

'You did that reality show, *The Reject*, didn't you?' Jonathan said, eyeing her cleavage.

'Uh … *The Rebound*,' Rania stammered. 'Yes.'

'Pretty solid ratings,' Jonathan said.

Rania smiled and nodded.

'All because of her,' I said, quickly filling the silence.

'Yeah well, reality stars are made in the edit.'

Rania shifted slightly but stood her ground. 'It was a good experience overall. I learned a lot.'

'Good for you,' Jonathan replied as the other two men sniggered.

I frowned. I was suddenly wishing I hadn't forced Rania into this guy's orbit.

'I love *Up and at 'Em*,' Rania said. 'Best morning show in the country by a mile.'

'We try,' Jonathan said.

'It's a crime you don't rate better,' Rania continued. 'Stiff competition in that slot.'

Jonathan stopped smiling. 'We were number one for seven years.'

'Rightly so,' Rania replied, holding his gaze. 'But I really liked what you said in *GQ* about not resting on your laurels.'

'Gotta stay relevant,' Jonathan said. 'We'll get 'em back.'

'No doubt,' said Rania.

'Rania's about as relevant as you can get right now.'

'You sure you're not on commission?' Jonathan asked me, causing another chuckle from his lackeys.

'I might just have to put her on the books,' Rania said, giving me a smile.

'Well,' Jonathan said, clapping his hands, 'such a treat to meet you both.'

'You too, Jonathan,' Rania said.

'And best of luck with your next reality show.' Jonathan turned his back on us and muttered something to the other two men. Another patronising chuckle.

Rania turned to me, her face ashen. 'Come on, Lizzie. Let's go.' She was already walking quickly towards the bar. I didn't move.

'Hey,' I said louder than expected. Jonathan and his shadows turned back, surprised but still superior. Jonathan raised his eyebrows expectantly.

'What was your first job?' I asked. 'In TV, I mean.'

Jonathan let out a small, single chuckle as his head tilted skyward. It was always so easy to get men like this to talk, especially about themselves.

'I was a doorstop reporter for a local current affair show in Brisbane,' he said. 'Shoving microphones in people's faces and chasing dodgy tradies down alleyways, that sort of thing.'

Jonathan's companions laughed obligingly. I smiled along.

'Humble beginnings,' he said. 'To say the least.'

'And how did you end up here?' I asked.

He shrugged. 'Someone at the network gave me a chance and I took it.'

'Right,' I said. 'Someone gave you a chance.'

Jonathan frowned slightly. 'That's what I said.'

I took a moment to make eye contact with all three of Jonathan's entourage before looking back at him. 'Way to pay it forward.'

Then I turned and headed off to catch up with Rania.

At the bar, far from Jonathan, I tried to talk Rania down from a ledge.

'Listen,' I said. 'You don't need douchebags like him to validate you.'

Rania chuckled weakly but was clearly fighting back tears.

'It's true!' I said firmly, taking her by the shoulders. 'You're young and smart and gorgeous. You can do whatever you like. Then, when the time is right, go to Santorini and have loads of sex with hot Greek men on the beach.'

That made her properly laugh. 'Is that what you wish you'd done at my age?'

'Maybe not on the beach,' I said with a grin. 'But I definitely wish I hadn't wasted so much time doing stuff I didn't care about because of a guy I wasn't in love with. That's what I don't want for my kids: to waste time doing shit they don't want because of someone else.'

Rania looked thoughtful for a moment. Her phone buzzed. She glanced down and smiled. 'People are loving the post.'

'Really?' I peeked over to take a look.

And that's when I saw the time.

***

'I called you a million times!'

'I'm so sorry! The phone was in the bottom of my bag and the room was noisy.'

After realising I should have been home over an hour ago, I'd rushed outside, jumped in a taxi and rung a near-hysterical Zara. As soon as she'd determined that I wasn't lying in a ditch somewhere, my daughter had slammed down the phone in a rage.

When I walked in the front door fifteen minutes later, I found all four of my children awake, and two of them in floods of tears. Archie, my most pragmatic child, had apparently been reassuring them that Mum wasn't dead or kidnapped by a drug cartel.

'Archie said you were probably drunk and had no idea

what time it was,' Stella sobbed, clutching me around the waist.

Max and Stella were sitting on either side of me on the couch, dripping snot all over my now very creased evening dress. I let them. It was the least I could do.

'I'm sorry I scared you. But look, I'm fine!'

'We were about to call Dad or Aunty Carmen!' Zara glared at me from the other side of the room.

'Oh Jesus, you didn't, did you?' I could just imagine the panic a phone call like that would cause in the Abela household.

'I told them not to,' Archie said proudly.

'Well, what was I supposed to think?' Zara said, furious. 'I thought you were *dead*!'

'Stella woke me up when she came to tell Archie you weren't home,' Max sniffed. 'Zara didn't even notice because she was on her —'

'Shut up, Max!' Zara snapped.

Now I was the one glaring. 'Zara was on what? On her *phone*?'

'No! I mean, I was, but ...'

'We'll talk about it tomorrow,' I said in a steely voice. 'You all need to go to bed.'

It took at least twenty minutes to get everyone settled. Stella still had the post-cry hiccups, so I sat on her bed and rubbed her back until she drifted off. The others fell asleep quickly, exhausted by the night's drama.

When the house was finally quiet, I tiptoed out of Stella and Zara's room and collapsed on the couch. I felt like having a big old cry myself. Was I wrong or had that been a slight overreaction from my offspring? Back in the day, Melissa's parents went out all the time and often left their kids alone until well after midnight. Those children never freaked out. But my twenty-first-century progeny had been brought up with a mum who was always available, for the most part, and always made them a priority.

I'd learned a few things tonight, including the fact that Zara couldn't be trusted to babysit, after all. Too busy snapchatting with Reuben to notice that her mother wasn't home, and that her siblings were melting down. I'd be having a word with her about that tomorrow. Right now, I just needed to soak my feet in warm water and try to work out why the hell high heels exist.

Chapter Twenty
Megan

Megan watched a few parents walking through the school gate for afternoon pick-up and wondered if any of them would be able to tell that she'd spent the past week indulging in a mind-blowing, skin-tingling sex-fest.

A mind-blowing, skin-tingling sex-fest that had come to a screeching halt last night when Bryce, Adam and Oscar arrived back from Tasmania.

'The caves were *awesome*, Mum!' Oscar had shouted as he launched himself into her arms at the front door. 'There was even a *pool* inside!'

Oscar had tried to wriggle out of her embrace, but Megan had held her son tightly, inhaling the sweet, musky scent of him.

'My Helicarrier!' Oscar cried, finally managing to escape, and scampering down the hallway to his room.

Megan turned to Bryce with a rueful grin. 'I think he missed that Helicarrier more than me.'

'Oh, he missed you. A lot.' Bryce smiled. 'Everything we did and saw was instantly followed by, "I can't wait to tell Mum!"'

This made Megan's heart melt a little and she felt a rush of warmth for her newly hitched ex-husband. 'So, the goggles and top hat were a success?'

Oscar had told her over the phone last week that Nana Clara said he looked like a less wrinkly Maz Kanata in his best-man outfit. Maz Kanata was a *Star Wars* character who wore Steampunk-esque goggles. Megan had to admit, it was a stroke of genius.

She was thrilled to have her boy home again, but there was no denying she'd made the most of his absence with a week-long sex- a-thon. Sex with Harry was phenomenal. Actually, it was fucking insane. Megan had never, *never* in her life had sex like it. And when they weren't together, sexy texting was a constant. She'd almost dropped an entire stack of dirty plates into her mother's lap one day when she received a text from Harry that read:

I'm going to spend the whole night worshipping your body.

It hadn't turned out to be the whole night, but it came pretty damn close. Harry had brought a selection of scented oils and kicked off their night in the bedroom with a gentle massage – feathery strokes that went from the back of her neck all the way down to the soles of her feet. That particular session had ended with multiple orgasms that had given Megan blurry vision for a few seconds. *Blurry vision!*

Harry's stamina was incredible – one of the many perks of youth – so when Megan wasn't working, she was having sex. In her bed, on her couch, on her floor, in her bath. The only place off limits was Oscar's room (of course), but almost every other square metre of her house had been wonderfully defiled. And oh, how she had enjoyed defiling it, especially with someone as beautiful and lovely as Harry D'Angelo. Megan had studied his face as he lay sleeping one night and he resembled a dark-haired Apollo. Bare-chested, one arm thrown back behind his head and the other hand resting on her naked thigh. Even sitting in the playground now, she felt a stirring in her loins at the memory, then chastened herself. This was a children's playground, after all.

But it was the way Harry looked at her that overwhelmed Megan. He stared right into her eyes with such a burning intensity. Once he'd even cried a little bit during a particularly fervent lovemaking session, but she put it down to the passion of the moment and the fact that he was sleep-deprived, and probably dehydrated. Another night, Harry took photos of Megan with his old Minolta camera as she lay in bed among the dishevelled sheets. No nudes, of course, Megan wasn't that stupid. They were very tasteful, and Megan kept her bits well covered the whole time. It was quite sexy, actually. She felt like Kate Winslet in *Titanic*, and Harry was enamoured, telling her how exquisitely beautiful she was as he took shot after shot. Knowing Harry adored her as much as he did, only made the sex better. It was addictive.

At various points throughout the week, the age difference between them had been glaringly obvious, like the fact that Harry rarely opened his eyes before ten o'clock. Megan was always wide awake at six-thirty, even after a late night of feathery strokes and multiple orgasms. And when Harry offered to make her dinner one night, she was more than a little surprised when a bowl of two-minute noodles landed on the table in front of her.

'Oh, thanks,' she'd said.

'Sorry,' Harry had said with a rueful grin. 'Not much of a cook. Mum never lets me in the kitchen.'

'That's okay.'

Megan had laughed at the time, but the mention of Harry's mum had been disquieting. For the most part that week, she'd tried not to think too much about the fact that her young lover still lived with Mummy.

Early in the week, she'd returned to the bedroom

with a tub of chocolate ice-cream and two spoons after a particularly vigorous lovemaking session to find Harry texting. He was frowning and shaking his head.

'Everything okay?'

'Oh, yeah,' Harry said, shrugging. 'It's Mum. Told her I'm staying at a friend's tonight and she wants to know what time I'll be home tomorrow.'

'Does she know that your friend is female?'

'Yeah, 'course.' Harry laughed. 'She's a very modern Italian mama.'

They lay in bed for hours. Megan told Harry stories about Lizzie, Sam and Dave, and her favourite Applewood residents, and he seemed genuinely interested and amused. She asked him questions about his family and learned that he was the youngest and that he had three older sisters. She and Harry also shared stories of previous relationships and Megan was unsurprised to hear that the young man had had his fair share of girlfriends.

'They were all just stupid girls,' Harry said, kissing her neck and tracing his finger up and down the inside of her arm. 'I mean seriously, they don't even compare. They were nothings and you're, like, everything. You're like a miracle.'

When she told Harry about her marriage break-up, he had nodded sagely. 'Makes sense,' he said. 'Your kind of beauty can easily transcend sexual preference. I'm not surprised a gay man fell in love with you and convinced himself he was straight.'

Megan had never heard her botched marriage described in such flattering terms before. Her ego decided to claim Harry's perspective as her own personal truth.

'What about Eddie?'

'Basically, I wanted another baby, and he didn't want to be a dad.'

'We'd make a pretty cute kid.'

Megan laughed, but when she looked up, Harry wasn't smiling. 'Yeah right,' she said. 'Because what hot, young nineteen-year-old Franco-Italian boy doesn't want to be a dad?'

'Depends on who the mum is.'

For the briefest millisecond, Megan found herself entertaining the insane idea of having a baby with Harry. *My God, it would be the most adorable baby in the world, especially if it inherited those dimples.* But she shook off the ridiculous notion. She could just imagine that conversation with Lizzie.

'I'm pregnant!'

'Oh wow! AMAZING! Who's the dad?'

'Well, he'll be more of a big brother than a dad ...'

'What?'

'I can't believe he cheated on you,' Harry said, his face clouding over.

Megan shrugged. 'I think he was looking for a way out. At least he didn't steal all my hard drives. Or you would never have become my personal IT guy.'

'I should stalk him online and steal his identity,' he said.

'No,' Megan said. 'You absolutely shouldn't do that because, one: jail, and two: not worth it.'

She wondered what Eddie would say if he could see her now. *Hey, remember how you implied I was just an unimportant single mum and waitress? Well, looky here! This hot, young thing thinks I'm amazing!*

Right now, she'd gladly flaunt Harry up and down Swanston Street, shouting about blurry vision and multiple orgasms, in front of her ex-boyfriend. She was happy in her bubble with Harry. And it felt nice to be happy again. She knew it wasn't a real-life relationship – not by a stretch – but she was going to enjoy it while it lasted. Common sense be damned. And when their bubble finally burst, she'd have the memories of this incredibly romantic week forever.

The night before Oscar arrived back, Harry had presented Megan with a gift.

'What's this?'

'Open it and find out.'

She unwrapped the small rectangular-shaped gift and recognised the distinctive light blue of Tiffany & Co.

'Harry, what the …?'

'Open it!' Harry was like an excited child on Christmas morning.

When Megan saw the gold bean pendant lying on black velvet lining, she'd stared up at Harry in disbelief. 'This is too much.' In more ways than one.

'Please,' Harry said, taking it out and starting to unclip it. 'I want you to have it.'

Megan tried to argue for a bit longer, but he was having none of it, moving behind her and clasping the necklace on, then removing all her clothes and making love to her on the living-room floor.

Yesterday, an hour before Oscar's plane was due to land, Harry had stood inside her front door, away from the prying eyes of her elderly neighbour, and kissed her goodbye.

'I'll see you in class?' he'd said, tucking her hair behind her ear.

'Yep,' Megan had replied, suddenly realising that she still hadn't heard back from Sam, Lizzie or Dave about her story.

Part of her was dying to tell Lizzie all about her

marathon shag-fest, but another, more sensible part knew that would be a bad idea. As open-minded as her best friend was, Megan wasn't sure she'd approve of her great romance with a teenager, especially when she was the mother of two herself. Luckily, Lizzie had been working a lot last week, so Megan hadn't seen her. And with no child to pick up from school, she'd also managed to avoid having to hide her coital glow from Sam and Dave.

'We should go for a drink after class,' Harry had said. 'It's only right to pay tribute to the Irish on their special day.'

'Maybe. I'll ask Sam if Oscar can stay at his for a bit longer.'

'Awesome. And maybe I can come over later?'

'Oscar's home,' Megan said firmly. 'But don't worry. We'll find a time.'

Harry stared at her with that intense green-eyed gaze and frowned. 'How am I going to survive three days without you when you go on this camp?'

Megan felt an uneasy stirring. Harry was crushing pretty hard on her, as evidenced by the fifty-something texts he'd sent her during the week, saying he missed her and describing in graphic detail what he'd do when they were together again. But that was just young men, Megan told herself. Especially young, sensitive, romantic men like Harry. He'd forget about Megan in a hot second when a more youthful model presented herself, with her taut body and complete lack of responsibilities.

Megan waved now as she spotted Sam and Dave walking across the yard.

'Hey, Megan!' Dave called out when they were still at least ten metres away. 'Do you reckon the kids would like a bit of Leonard Cohen on the camp?'

Megan smiled. 'Sure!' She was on such a post-sex high that she was even prepared to approve Dave's terrible music choices. 'Great idea.'

Sam frowned suspiciously. 'You're chipper today.'

'Am I?'

'What's going on?'

'Nothing! Isn't a girl allowed to be happy on a beautiful Tuesday afternoon?'

'It's seventeen degrees and cloudy,' Dave pointed out.

Lizzie appeared in front of them, yawning.

'You work last night?' Megan asked.

Lizzie shook her head. 'No, just ... stayed up a bit later than usual.'

'Did you get on it?' Dave asked, leaning forward. 'I do that sometimes on Monday nights. LOL.'

'No, Dave, I just didn't sleep much.'

'Why?' Megan asked, sensing potential gossip. 'Come on, spill. Something happened. You look like shit.'

'Thanks,' Lizzie said, then sighed. 'I just ... I had a massive fight with Zara.'

'Was it about Instagram?' Sam asked.

Lizzie frowned. 'How do you know about that?'

'Stella told Lola that Zara's been hassling you about it.'

Megan could see this irked Lizzie. 'So, was it that?' she asked.

'That was part of it,' Lizzie said. 'She's just been so selfish lately, and spending way too much time on her phone and not doing things she's supposed to be doing.'

Megan scoffed. 'She's fifteen! She's meant to be selfish and not do what she's supposed to. I bet you weren't exactly a golden child at her age.'

'Of course I wasn't,' Lizzie said defensively. 'But I got my arse kicked if I did the wrong thing.'

Dave gasped. 'Your father hit you?'

'No, Dave! I meant that figuratively!'

'Thank God.'

'Once when I was Zara's age,' Lizzie said, 'Melissa and I drank all the vodka in Dad's bar and replaced it with water. They came home to find us passed out on the bed and vomit all around the toilet. I was grounded for a month.'

'Classy,' Sam said. He turned to Megan. 'I bet you were a perfect little miss at your fancy-pants private school.'

Megan frowned. It rattled her that Sam might perceive her as a prissy little private schoolgirl. 'Actually,' she said hotly, 'the rich girls at my school were way worse than the local high school kids. They got up to all kinds of shit with their no-limit credit cards while Mummy and Daddy were hitting the slopes at Thredbo.'

Megan neglected to mention that she herself hadn't actually got up to much of anything at all when she was a teenager. Mainly because she didn't have any friends to get up to anything with. The closest she had come to bad teen behaviour was witnessing models do coke before fashion shows.

'I got stoned and burned down my bedroom when I was seventeen,' Sam said proudly. 'Left a candle burning a bit too close to my Jeff Buckley poster.'

'That sentence has given me more insight into you than any other thing you've said in the past four years,' said Megan.

She could actually picture teenage Sam – sitting on the edge of his messy bed, strumming his guitar and singing softly to nobody while precariously placed candles flickered around the room.

'Once,' Dave said, 'Sheryl, the tuckshop lady, gave me two nut chews when I'd only paid for one.'

Megan and Sam looked at him, waiting for the good part of the story.

'And I kept them both,' Dave finished, agog at his own juvenile delinquency.

'Anyway,' Megan said, moving on, 'this just proves that you've gotta let Zara have some independence.'

'You don't get it, Megs. You don't have girls,' Lizzie said.

Megan's good humour disappeared. She felt her hackles rise. But before she could respond, Sam jumped in.

'And remind me again why Instagram is bad for her?'

Lizzie ticked the reasons off her fingers one by one. 'Time-wasting, distracting, pointless, creates FOMO and encourages narcissism and a toxic habit of comparing herself to impossible ideals.'

'Wow, you've put a lot of thought into this,' marvelled Dave.

'What will you say when Lola wants social media?' Megan asked Sam, turning away from Lizzie.

'Lola will probably prefer a *Jane Austen Regency Magazine* subscription.'

'Don't be so sure.'

Sam frowned at Lizzie. 'What do you mean?'

'Things change when they get older,' Lizzie explained. 'Teenagers are all about their peers. Just because she's into Jane Austen and embroidery now, doesn't mean she won't be into selfies and YouTube later.'

'Thanks for the tip.' There was an edge to Sam's voice.

'Megs, didn't you say the other day that it's natural

for girls that age to be jealous of each other?' Dave was oblivious to the escalating tension between his mates. 'Like Stella is with Lola in that acting class?'

There was a horrified silence. Lizzie turned to Megan, a stunned look on her face. 'Who said Stella was jealous?' She turned back to Sam. 'The way Stella is jealous of Lola with her teacher?'

'Well, no, she …'

'And you were all talking about this?'

Megan tried to laugh it off, but it caught in her throat. 'No, we … I mean … we didn't mean …'

'Because she's not,' Lizzie said sharply. 'Jealous.'

The schoolyard was starting to fill up with parents, all chatting in small groups and happily killing time before the bell rang. But the four friends on the bench were silent and as still as statues. Megan couldn't stand it. This wasn't like them. They were mates. *Real* mates. She was determined not to let everyone's kids' dramas infiltrate their precious pick-up time. Actually, maybe that was the problem. Their environment was a constant reminder of their kids. Maybe if they were somewhere else …

'Hey, I've got an awesome idea!' she said suddenly.

'*Awesome?* I thought you hated that word.'

Megan ignored Lizzie's comment. 'Why don't I call my mum and ask her to watch the kids for a couple of hours and we can all go have a drink at Bar 404?'

Lizzie baulked. 'We can't ask Ellie to watch nine children!'

'She wouldn't mind.' But even as she said it, Megan wasn't so sure.

'I've got a better idea,' Sam said. 'Why don't you all come to mine for homemade pizzas?'

'I've got a curry in the slow cooker.' Lizzie's tone was starting to thaw.

'Freeze it!' Megan said. 'Come on, you've all been bitching and moaning about never doing anything spontaneous. The kids would love an impromptu pizza night.'

Megan also liked the idea of spending an evening with grown-ups. And it would provide the perfect opportunity to pin them all down for feedback on her story.

'Keshini has book club,' Dave said, as the school bell rang. 'But the kids and I are in for sure.'

'Okay,' Lizzie agreed, half smiling. 'Zara and Archie probably won't come, but I'll bring Stella and Max.'

'Great!' Sam threw Megan a wink that said, *Nice one, Megs*. 'Five-thirty at mine. BYO bevvies.'

They all stood up to find their respective offspring. Megan was feeling so pleased with herself that she briefly considered telling them about her shag-fest. Although, if Sam reacted so scornfully to Harry fixing her tech issues when he couldn't, how would he feel knowing she'd slept with the guy?

Maybe she'd keep it to herself, after all.

***

Sam lived a ten-minute walk from Baytree Primary, in a lovely, single-storey Victorian house that was all high ceilings, wooden floorboards and fireplaces. When his ex-wife, Bridget, had lived there, the house had a minimalist feel with its white walls, sharp edges and abstract art. But over the past couple of years, Sam had created a much cosier home. It exploded with colour, warmth and rustic charm, and Megan was impressed with Sam's interior-design skills.

A deep red, Turkish rug covered the floor and brightly patterned cushions lined two comfy couches in the open-plan living area. There was a long wooden table in front of bifold doors, which opened out to an expansive deck and backyard. Seven kids were currently out there chasing each other with plastic lightsabers (Max, Tyler, Oscar and Jack) or sitting on the deck playing the Rat-A-Tat-Cat card game (Stella, Lola and Ella). The Hatfield kitchen was decked out with Miele appliances and stone benchtops, and a large breakfast bar, where Sam was now kneading pizza dough.

Megan sipped her wine at the breakfast bar and marvelled at how tidy the house was. Most men living on their own with two kids might let the housework slide a bit, or just be outright slobs. Not Sam. He cooked like Jamie Oliver and kept house like Marie Kondo. Freak.

The gang's impromptu catch-up had started well. Excruciatingly punctual, they'd all arrived with their excited kids in tow and quickly settled into their designated areas, kids outside and adults around the kitchen bench. Lizzie and Sam occasionally glanced towards the back deck, but if they were worried about their daughters' issues with each other they weren't saying so.

All offers of help were politely refused, and his friends watched in awe as Sam zipped around the kitchen, expertly chopping ingredients for toppings. Megan had seen the talented ex-chef in action before, but tonight she was particularly impressed.

'I feel like I'm watching *MasterChef*,' Lizzie said, tipping her beer at Sam.

'I'll chop the ham,' Dave said, jumping off his stool and ignoring Sam's protests.

Megan and Lizzie kept the kitchen stools warm while the two boys chopped and kneaded, and the four friends chatted happily about TV shows they were bingeing on, and which federal politician they'd have sex with if they had to. Megan was pleased to note that all talk of their children seemed to be well and truly off the table.

'You ever think about going back to working in a restaurant?' Megan asked, watching Sam flatten out a dough ball.

'Not many chefs are full-time single dads,' Sam said. 'For good reason.'

'So, start your own business,' Lizzie suggested. 'Like a Hello Fresh or Youfoodz type of thing.'

'Nah,' Sam said. 'Anyway, I find the food-processing-equipment industry deeply fulfilling.'

Megan snorted, almost losing her mouthful of wine.

'You could start small,' Dave said excitedly, 'like, sell your food wares out of an Esky in the Baytree schoolyard!'

'That's actually a really good idea,' Megan said.

Dave furrowed his brow. 'Don't "actually" sound so surprised.'

'It is, Sam,' Lizzie added. 'I'd totally buy a few ready-made meals off you every week. Especially with Greg away. The last thing I feel like doing before going to work is making dinner.'

'I dunno.'

But it sounded to Megan like Sam might be seriously considering the idea, which she really hoped he was. Sam's talents were wasted in an office job. He loved cooking, and Megan wanted her friend to spend his days doing something that made him happy.

When the kids' pizzas were ready, Lizzie and Megan

delivered them to the back deck, where they were received with much excitement.

'Dad's pizzas are *the best*!' Tyler crowed proudly.

'*Yum!*' Dave's daughter, Ella, cried, her glasses almost flying off her face as she threw her head back with exalted glee.

The adults had decided to eat their pizzas at the bench because no one could be arsed setting the table. Everyone was in high spirits and the afternoon's minor altercations were a distant memory.

Sam raised his glass and tipped it towards Dave. 'I'd like to make a toast to Dave's graphic novel being made into an actual TV show!'

'Hear, hear!' they all cried, clinking their glasses and beer bottles.

'Aw, thanks guys,' Dave said, beaming.

'You can shout us all dinner at Donovan's with your big advance next time.' Lizzie grinned.

'You've even started dressing the part,' Sam said, nodding at Dave's feet. 'Are those original Air Jordans?'

'Indeed they are.'

Megan was thrilled. Dave's novel was the perfect segue into her own creative pursuits. 'So, now that you're officially a proper writer, Dave,' she said, 'maybe you could give me your professional feedback?' She nodded at Lizzie and Sam. 'You too, of course. I assume you've all read it by now?'

Everyone suddenly found their drinks extremely fascinating.

Megan frowned. 'You still haven't read it?' She was pissed off. 'You're the ones who wanted me to send it and you didn't even —'

Lizzie cut her off. 'We've read it.'

'You have? Then why ...?' Megan's gut lurched as the penny dropped. 'You didn't like it.'

Sam's expression was pained. 'We didn't say that ...'

Lizzie began peeling the label off her beer bottle and avoided Megan's eye. 'It's just —'

'I *love* the freaky-hands thing,' Dave interrupted.

Megan turned to Dave, feeling a surge of gratitude.

'But structurally, it was all over the place.'

Gratitude turned to annoyance. 'What do you mean?'

'Well, the perspective kept shifting with no explanation,' Dave continued. 'And that bit about the serpent was just weird. It was totally out of line with the protagonist's character. I mean, he wasn't set up as a Sage, he's more of a Magician or Innocent.'

An icy chill ran across Megan's chest. 'Anything else?'

'Ummmmmm.' Dave tapped his beer bottle against his teeth, searching his mind for more constructive criticism. 'Well, the grammar was ... erratic.'

'Mmmhmm ...' Megan's lips seemed to be glued together.

'And ...'

'I reckon you've had your turn, Dave.' Sam gave Dave a meaningful look.

Megan turned to Sam and Lizzie. 'How about you two? And you swore you wouldn't lie.'

'It's not really my genre.' Sam looked like he'd rather be doing push-ups on a bed of nails than having this conversation. 'I'm more of a music-bio guy.'

'Yeah, and what the hell would I know about writing?' Lizzie added. 'The only thing I can write is a labour-ward register.'

'You've both read a million books to your kids.' Megan

was trying desperately to keep her tone light. 'You'd know if it was good or not.'

'Well ...'

'Yeah, um, but ...'

No one knew what to say, but their silence said it all.

Her writing was bad. Really bad, it seemed. Megan stared at the glass in her hand, while Lizzie and Sam stared at the floor. The only sound in the room was Dave's bottle clinking off his front teeth.

'Well, clearly I'm not a writer and that's fine,' Megan said, forcing a laugh. 'Thank you for your honesty. I mean it. Really.'

'Megs,' Sam said. 'Nobody's good at anything straightaway.'

'Exactly,' Lizzie agreed. 'Like, you must've cooked some God-awful food before you became a chef.'

Sam paused and stared up at the ceiling for a moment. 'Nah, I was pretty good at it straightaway.'

'*Sam!*'

They all laughed, and Megan laughed along, in part because Sam was a funny bastard, but mostly for appearances. As bad as she felt, it wasn't worth taking her friends down with her.

Chapter Twenty-One
Sam

To: codenamedave@gmail.com
From: samhatfieldchef@bigpond.com
Subject: AWKS

Hey Dave,

That was awkward, but at least it's done. We didn't exactly rip the bandaid off for Megs, though, did we? Hope she's okay. What do you reckon? She laughed it off, yeah?

Regardless of badly managed bandaid rippage, it was great to have everyone around and cook up a storm and hang out. And I must confess to some selfish pride that Lizzie and Megs got to see me in all my domestic glory. Megs in particular was very impressed with my kitchen skills. When I was sharpening my knife (with all the theatricality I could muster), she even gave me a cheer and a round of applause. Wish I could've done the same for her writing.

When it comes to the school camp, can you please stop referring to our 'set list'? We just need to make sure we have access to a bunch of Top 40, offline charts on the iPad and we'll be apples. We will not dress as Wham! Let it go. No men our age should wear shorts that short. But I do like your idea of Hall & Oates. Pop duo, typical eighties fashion. Easy. Let's lock it in. And I've been googling kids' music games, too, so I have a couple of those to run through with you tomorrow. We need to engage with the kids, not just entertain them with our rockstarness.

To: samhatfieldchef@bigpond.com
From: codenamedave@gmail.com
Subject: AWKS AS

Sammy, don't ever leave me III stalk you and hunt you down ha-ha-ha.

Megs came out of the kitchen at one point and said there was nothing sexier than a man in an apron – LOL – so yeah I think your mad skills paid off.

Can we pretend the writing stuff didn't happen or just build a time machine and go back and stop it ever happening??? I think she was pretty upset tbh. Kesh just got back from her book club and I told her what happened. She said we should've lied to encourage her and we're all idiots and bad friends so I'm in the doghouse LOL.

I'm gonna print out a bunch of charts for camp too, I'll laminate and put 'em in a folder so rain can't mess 'em up, clever huh?? So we should be good for material. Can you send links to some of those games so I can have a look before we catch up.

ta very much,

dave

Chapter Twenty-Two
Lizzie

'Since when are you on Instagram?'

'What?'

Megan shoved her phone in my face, and I was confronted with the image of Rania and me on the pink carpet.

Dave leaned over. 'Three thousand likes!'

'You've been tagged!' Megan cried. 'You are now someone people *tag*!'

I felt like a teenager who'd been caught with a pack of ciggies in her schoolbag. 'What's the big deal? Rania invited me to a thing.'

'And obviously set you up with an account,' Megan said, sitting beside me on the bench, 'because I know you wouldn't have a clue how to do that, and now you have ...' She tapped on the screen and her eyes widened. 'One thousand followers!'

'Wowzer!' Dave said.

'So what?'

Secretly, I was chuffed. I had nothing to compare it to, being a social media novice, but one thousand followers sounded impressive even to my luddite ears. I knew Melissa only had two hundred on Facebook. My life may have been coming apart at the seams, but at least I was Insta relevant.

Megan narrowed her eyes, not buying my nonchalant act. 'Who are you and what have you done with my best friend? Or is Rania your bestie now?'

Her tone was light and breezy, but I wasn't buying it. She was jealous.

'Yah,' I said in my best Valley Girl voice. 'We've been having sleepovers and doing each other's nails and talking about boys!'

'Hilarious.'

'And pillow fights?' Dave asked. 'You having pillow fights?'

'You'd like that, wouldn't you, Dave,' I asked.

Dave nodded vigorously.

'Where's Sam?'

'He had to stay back at work.' Megan poked me. 'And don't change the subject. I wanna know when you started going to red-carpet events ...'

'It looked like a pink carpet, actually.'

Megan glared at Dave. '... *pink*-carpet events, with a vacuous D- grade celebrity.'

I bristled. 'She's not, you know.'

Megan frowned. 'Not what?'

'Vacuous,' I said. 'She's actually very smart and lovely.'

'Ha! Knew it!' Dave slapped his thigh for emphasis.

Megan stared at me as if my eyebrows were on fire. 'We're talking about the same person, right?' she said slowly. 'The girl who went on a TV show to find love?'

'You can't judge if you don't know the full story.'

Megan laughed sharply. 'Says Queen Judgey herself!'

'Gee, thanks.'

Dave didn't know where to look.

A tense silence hung in the air, broken only by the sound of a few mums laughing and talking in Snack Shack, where they were baking green cookies and leprechaun doughnuts for after-school treats. Every few seconds the delicious scent

216

would waft across the netball courts. I had no idea exactly when St Patrick's Day had become something that Baytree Primary celebrated (probably Nicola's idea), but the kids seemed to get a kick out of it. When Max asked if he had anything green to wear this morning, I found the top half of an elf costume Zara had worn as part of the Christmas concert last year and told him he was a leprechaun.

But not even the yummy smells in the air could improve the strained mood on the bench. Our banter had taken a turn and I wasn't in the mood for it. Not today. My biopsy was booked in for tomorrow morning and I was a bag of nerves. Not only because of the whole needle-in-my-boob thing, but because I would be one step closer to finding out if my life was about to be flipped upside down.

Maybe Megan was right. Maybe I was Queen Judgey, but that didn't mean I wanted to hear it today. I certainly wasn't up for an argument about a stupid social media photo. But I was also feeling guilty about our less-than-enthusiastic feedback session last night, so decided to steer the subject away from all Rania-related topics and make peace. Judging by the look on poor Dave's face, he would be eternally grateful to me if I did.

'How's camp prep going? Is Nicola doing your head in yet?'

'God, yes.' Megan sounded slightly petulant, but a fraction of the tension abated at the mention of our common enemy. 'She's sent out a million emails about keeping kids safe on camp, as if that wouldn't be our main priority.'

Irish folk music suddenly blared out of the school PA system, making all three of us jump. We watched as a sea of green-haired children, carrying an array of green art projects, swarmed out of the building and into the yard.

'Nicola asked if we were going to play age-appropriate music on camp,' Dave said. 'She wanted to make sure there were no songs containing inappropriate content.'

'What did you tell her?'

'I promised we'd only play songs by Mötley Crüe and Eminem.'

Megan and I both laughed. But separately.

★★★

'You have Instagram?'

'Why does everyone care so much about me having an Instagram report?'

'It's an account, Mum, not a report!' Zara spluttered. 'So, why have you got one?'

I unzipped Max's lunchbox and was greeted by a half-eaten banana and a crusty white yoghurt tub. 'Because I do, that's why.'

'Since when?'

This felt like déjà vu. The mood in the house was already volatile, but Zara's recent discovery had brought a whole new level of tension.

Archie was still grounded after his drink-spiking and subsequent spew-fest with Xavier and had been walking around with a face like a smacked arse. He was furious about missing this month's D&D sessions and had barely spoken five words to me since Greg left. In fairness, this wasn't much different from his usual two words per day, but the silences were now laden with venom.

Stella was still upset about the incident with Lola at the party. She'd broken down in tears the next day, saying Lola ran off before she could defend her, and had been sullen and weepy ever since, insisting that she wanted to quit acting class. She and Lola were officially on non-speaking terms, which was going to make sharing a cabin on camp next week tricky. Max had only just learned that we wouldn't be going to Sydney at Easter because it was too expensive and was equal parts furious and miserable. Meanwhile, Zara was in a strop because I said she couldn't go to a St Patrick's party after rehearsals tonight.

'You're not going to a party on a school night,' I'd told her. 'Aunty Carmen will drop you at rehearsals and then Ines's mum can bring you home when they finish at ten-thirty, okay?'

It hadn't been okay, of course.

All I wanted to do was go into my bedroom, close the door and blast Faith No More and 4 Non Blondes like I did when I was a teenager and Dad and Aunty Carmen were giving me the shits. Unfortunately, I wasn't allowed to do that kind of thing anymore, because out of the five of us, I was supposed to be the mature one. It didn't always feel that way.

I stared at my incensed daughter and something occurred to me.

'Hang on,' I said, the half-eaten banana in my hand. 'How do you know I have Instagram?'

'Uh ... Ines told me. She saw it.'

I dropped the banana and held out my hand. 'Give me your phone.'

'No.'

'Give. Me. Your. Phone.'

'It's in my room.'

She turned to leave, but I pointed to her bulging school-dress pocket. 'It's there. Hand it to me right now.'

Zara's eyes filled with angry tears as she unzipped her pocket. 'I have no rights! I'm *fifteen*!'

I opened it – knowing her passcode was the first rule of buying her a phone – and swiped all the way across the multiple screens until I saw the pink square icon hidden on the last screen. Zarbar21's profile pic showed Zara and Ines's smiling faces squished together.

'How long have you had it?'

'Not long,' Zara muttered. 'Anyway, what's the problem? Everyone in Year Nine has Insta!'

'It's about you doing this behind our backs. You've just lost your phone for a week.'

Red blotches appeared on Zara's pale neck. 'I *hate* you!'

'Wanna make it two?'

Zara balled her hands into fists, her face a mask of fury. 'You're making a fool of yourself, you know!'

'What?'

'Running around with Rania Jalali.'

'Zara, I'm warning you ...'

'I'm telling you the truth,' she barked. 'Isn't that what you want? The truth?' She ran out of the kitchen, just as Max ran in.

'And I wanna see Dad at Easter! This is *bullshit*!'

Before I could respond to this latest verbal attack, the doorbell rang.

'Hello, my beauties!' Aunty Carmen bellowed, entering the house in all her colourful and joyous glory. 'How is my favourite family?'

I'd never been so happy to go to work in my life.

Chapter Twenty-Three
Megan

'Tonight will be my last class.'

'What? Why?'

Megan raised one eyebrow. 'Why do you think?'

She watched Sam scramble to think of something to say. He was watching Oscar for her so she could go to her final writing class.

She'd been thinking about it a lot since last night and had decided that she wasn't a writer and never would be. Writing had never come naturally to her, and she couldn't handle the criticism, so she was done. But she was glad she'd given it a go. She may not have learned much about writing, but she'd sure as hell learned a few new tricks from her classmate Harry.

'Just think,' Megan said, giving Sam a sly grin. 'Your Wednesday nights will be yours again for more Tinder action.'

'Nah, I'm done with Tinder,' Sam said. 'I've met someone in the real world.'

'Really?' Megan said, trying to keep her tone light. 'And who is the lucky lady?'

'Nope. You're not getting anything out of me, Wylie. I'm not saying a word until something actually happens.'

'Well, I wish you all the best,' she said.

'Thank you, ma'am,' said Sam, matching Megan's

teacherly tone. 'I appreciate your good wishes for my love-life.'

'I've packed his lunch in there for tomorrow, too,' Megan said, handing Sam Oscar's sleepover bag.

'You didn't have to do that,' Sam scolded.

'I thought a vegemite sandwich would probably be too much for you to handle.'

'Fair enough,' Sam replied. 'Vegemite can be a fickle mistress.'

'Did you just call vegemite your mistress?'

'Don't judge.' Sam scowled. 'Hey, have fun tonight.'

'Thanks.'

'From the way you've described your matronly classmates, you'll be doing flaming shots and dancing on the bar by eight-thirty.'

'Oh, for sure,' Megan said. 'It'll be off the hook.'

Megan had told Sam that her classmates were taking her out for a drink after her last class, which was why Oscar was staying over at his. This was, of course, a lie. She'd arranged to go for a drink with Harry, and possibly back to her place afterwards. Actually, there was no possibly about it. They absolutely would end up back at her house.

Megan knew the relationship wouldn't continue now that she wouldn't be seeing him every week, and that was for the best. She would miss the sex, though, which was why she was looking forward to a healthy last hurrah tonight.

★★★

'I'm in love with you.'

The city bar was packed with noisy office workers wearing oversized felt leprechaun hats and green plastic novelty glasses, so Megan's first thought was that she had misheard.

'What did you say?' she asked, leaning across the booth table.

'I'm in love with you,' Harry repeated, louder this time.

Megan laughed. 'Yeah, okay.'

His face fell. 'Don't do that.'

'Do what?'

'Laugh at me like that.'

'Sorry.' Then, gently, 'Harry, we've only known each other for a month. You don't even really know me.'

Harry clutched Megan's hand. 'I know you,' he said fiercely. 'I know you better than you think.'

Megan again tried to suppress her smile, worried it would send him into a rage. 'Is that so?'

'Yes. And I know that I love you. I do.'

He said it with such conviction, his intensity was unnerving. This wasn't the plan. Megan felt as if she was losing control of the situation; like none of the pedals in her car were doing what they should.

Harry was a sweet kid, but other than the fact that he was a demon between the sheets, loved books and writing and was a whiz on the computer, what else did she really know about this boy? And actually, Megan didn't even know if Harry *could* write. He'd never offered to show her any of his work and she'd never asked. She hadn't let Harry read her writing, either, much to his chagrin. Thank God, since it was apparently shit.

'I thought you wanted feedback,' Harry had said when she'd told him she wouldn't be workshopping her writing in class. 'You could at least let me read it, yeah?'

'No,' Megan had said firmly. 'It's not ready for you to see.' *And never will be,* she'd thought.

Megan hadn't planned on her young lover becoming so involved. Today alone, Harry had sent her seventeen texts. And she'd arrived home from Sam's last night to find flowers on her doorstep.

Megan had assumed that Harry saw her as a novelty. She'd assumed he would quickly tire of his cougar and move on to younger pastures. But right now, here in the pub, he was gazing at her with complete adoration.

'Harry, listen ...' Megan began, then noticed that Harry's attention was suddenly elsewhere.

'What's his problem?'

She followed Harry's eye line to three businessmen in green ties drinking pints of Guinness at the bar. One of them was staring brazenly at Megan.

Eddie.

Megan wrenched her hand out of Harry's and began sliding along the leather seat. 'We've gotta go.'

'What? Why?'

'Please, Harry, now!'

As Megan stepped out of the booth, Harry reached out to grab her hand. 'What's going on?'

'I'll tell you outside, just —'

'Megan?'

Eddie had somehow managed to make it across the crowded bar in seconds, and was now swaying before them, glassy-eyed and drunk. His mouth was doing the lopsided thing Megan used to find cute. She felt Harry stiffen beside her.

Eddie gave Harry the drunk once-over and smirked. 'Who's the kid?'

'Why don't you ask the kid?' Harry shot back.

Megan squeezed Harry's hand, trying to reassure and calm him. 'Eddie, Harry. Harry, Eddie,' she said.

Harry's head jerked back. 'Oh, this is the douche who cheated on you? He's even uglier than his LinkedIn profile pic.'

Megan glanced at Harry in surprise. *He had stalked Eddie online.*

Eddie's face twisted into an ugly scowl. 'The fuck ...?'

'Okay, we're going.' Megan began to move, but Eddie put up his hands.

'Sorry, sorry!' he cried. 'Megs, can we talk? Just for a second?'

Eddie didn't deserve a second, but Megan didn't want a scene. She knew from experience that a drunk Eddie was a tenacious Eddie. If she acquiesced, he'd let her leave peacefully and this would be over. As Eddie tipped dangerously to one side, she turned to Harry. 'Can I have a minute?'

'Megs, I don't ...'

'I'm fine, really. One minute.'

Harry looked from Megan to Eddie and frowned. 'I'll be right outside,' he said gruffly.

'Here.' Eddie clumsily reached into his pocket and pulled out some loose change. 'Get yourself some lollies.'

Harry stepped forward, but Megan laid a hand on his arm. 'He's drunk,' she whispered. 'Please go. I'll be okay.'

Harry glared at Eddie for another moment before turning and pushing his way through the rowdy crowd.

'Right, you've got your minute.'

Eddie raised his hands again, as if about to break into the YMCA dance routine. 'Hey, whoa, chill, babe!'

'Not your babe. Fifty-five seconds.'

''Kay, 'kay … I just wanna … I just … we never … I didn't …' His expression suddenly changed to outrage. 'Who the fuck is that *child*? What're you doing, Megs? Is he even legal?'

Megan fought the impulse to storm out. 'Fuck you and it's none of your business.'

'Come on, Megs,' Eddie slurred. 'You're making a fool of yourself and I'm only telling you because I still love —'

'Time's up. Bye, Eddie.' Megan swivelled to leave, then turned back. 'Just so you know, that "child" is more emotionally mature, sensitive, caring and sure as shit a better listener than you'll ever be. And he's hung like a stallion, so I'd avoid getting into a dick-swinging contest, figuratively or literally. You'd lose.'

Eddie's bottom jaw moved up and down as Megan's eyes bored into his, but no words came.

Stepping into the street, Megan took in a deep lungful of fresh city air. Despite her parting salvo, she was shaken. She doubted Eddie would remember much of their interaction, except for the fact that she was dating a guy half her age. A guy who was now leaning against a bollard staring at his phone, the light from his screen illuminating his perfect, and oh-so-young, features.

Harry spotted her and jogged over. 'You okay?'

'I'm fine,' she said. 'I just … I want to go home. On my own.'

Harry was clearly disappointed, but Megan hoped he wouldn't push it.

'Where's your car? I'll walk you.'

'Just opposite the cathedral.'

'I'm coming,' Harry insisted.

They walked down Flinders Lane in silence. Harry was upset at having his proclamation of love overshadowed by the appearance of Megan's ex-boyfriend, but tellingly, she didn't really care. All she wanted was to go home, crawl into bed and forget this night entirely.

As they approached Swanston Street, Megan spotted a small group of teenagers sitting on the grass outside St Paul's Cathedral. She envied the simplicity of their experience. One of them suddenly let out a loud, very familiar shriek of laughter.

Zara?

It couldn't be. Lizzie wouldn't let her go into the city at nine-thirty on a school night. But when the girl sat up to take her turn swigging from what appeared to be a bottle of booze, Megan was in no doubt. It was Zara Barrett. She also recognised the other kids from Zara and Archie's party, including Ines, and Reuben; the boy whose lap Zara was lying in.

Harry declared his love ... Eddie crashed in ... now this. Had some sort of dark Celtic magic descended on the world on this St Patrick's Day?

'Hang on a sec,' Megan told Harry, before she began walking towards the teens.

'Zara?'

At the sound of her name, Zara's head whipped around. Even in the darkness, Megan saw her face blanch. She immediately stood up and dropped the bottle behind her back, almost taking out Reuben's eye in the process.

'Megan, oh my God, hi.'

'Hey, what's up?'

Zara hurried over. 'Please don't tell Mum!' she begged in a low voice and on the verge of tears. 'Please?'

'Where does she think you are?'

'Rehearsals.' Zara glanced back at her friends, who were watching the exchange with horrified glee. 'But we wagged. We'll be back at school by ten-thirty, then Ines's mum is driving me home,' Zara said. 'We're just hanging out.'

'And drinking,' Megan said, nodding at the pink Vodka Cruisers and beer bottles scattered on the grass.

'Yeah, but ...'

'Don't worry, dude. Megan won't rat.'

Megan turned to Harry. *What the fuck?* 'Harry,' she said, not knowing what to say next.

'Who's this?' Zara's panic was momentarily forgotten as she stared at Megan's cute companion.

'This is Harry.' Megan hoped Zara couldn't see the blush rising up in her own cheeks. 'He's a writing-class friend.'

'Boyfriend, actually,' Harry said, putting his arm around her waist.

Zara stared in amazement, a sly smile playing at the corner of her mouth. A look of understanding passed between them.

You keep my secret and I'll keep yours.

Chapter Twenty-Four
Sam

To: jack_woz_here@hotmail.com
From: samhatfieldchef@bigpond.com
Subject: Rach and Bridg and Camp OH MY

Hey dickhead,

Just got a typically brusque text from Bridg: 'not sure camp can happen', suggesting that she won't be able to have Tyler while I'm away at camp. She just gives and gives.

I noticed that the text I'd received most recently before Bridget's was from Rachel. I tapped it and reread it. It was gentle and kind and thoughtful. Rachel wasn't making an effort to be any of those things, I don't think. Just how she is.

I imagined my alternate existence, married to Rachel. Bad idea. In Bridget's defence, she did accidentally end up being the sandwich between two of my favourite people at the mo. Megan and I have graduated to something verging on best friends, and you know how I feel about Rachel. Rachel, who is a part of my regret-filled history and now back in my messed-up present.

Do you think if I'd had the courage to sweep her off her feet back in the day that we'd still be together? Impossible question, I know. But you're my guy for impossible questions. Who's to say we wouldn't have hooked up, gotten married, had kids, ended up hating each other's guts with a burning passion and gone through a bitter divorce? Then I'd still be here filled with regret and shame that I was foolish enough to think that a uni crush could be The One. Do they have time machines on eBay yet? *Sam & Jack's Excellent Adventure*. I know what you're gonna say, but I have to entertain all these ideas at the moment. I'm still at sea and I can't pick the direction of the wind, so it's useful to look away from the horizon and try to figure out how I got here.

I can feel you patting my head and telling me to chill. I'm lucky, dickhead. I know it. I have Megan and Lizzie and you and Dave (aka Dickhead 2.0 – no offence). But you're the only one with whom I have serious history. And I play the what-if game with you in my head a lot. You get to an age when you can't help but look back and recognise the ripple effects of so much of what you've done. Memories and actions and choices all lay themselves out like a map of the London Tube, and you can see where things intersected and collided, and when things passed each other by. Lost chances. I'm going to sign off now, because I've polished off most of an Oyster Bay Sav Blanc and it's starting to show.

Love you, dickhead.

S x

To: codenamedave@gmail.com
From: samhatfieldchef@bigpond.com
Subject: Sorry Stevie

Hey Dave,

No, I can't watch a five-minute video of Stevie Nicks singing 'Wild Heart' backstage in 1981 right now.

Bridget just called to say she has to go on an emergency, damage-control meeting in Sydney and hopefully she'll be back in time to take Tyler but probably not so best for me to make other plans. So now I have to make alternate arrangements for someone to babysit my son for two nights.

I never thought I'd say this, but Stevie Nicks will have to wait.

Sam

P.S. Don't forget your sunscreen. The weather's looking good.

Chapter Twenty-Five
Lizzie

'They hate me.'

'They don't.'

'Yeah, I'm pretty sure they do.'

I'd texted Rania from work last night to see if she could meet for coffee straight after drop-off and before I headed to the hospital. I needed to see a young, friendly face who didn't believe I was the devil incarnate. Normally I would have texted Megan, but yesterday's 'judgey' comment still stung, as well as the way she'd confronted me about my friendship with Rania. Then I'd arrived home to the Barrett family shitstorm, followed by a shift where a particularly vocal labouring woman had called me an 'evil fucking ice queen'. In a nutshell, I was feeling pretty sorry for myself. I was sick of being the bad guy and felt like I'd lost any sense of who I was outside of a cranky dictator.

My nerves about this afternoon's biopsy weren't helping, either. All I wanted to do was call Greg and pour out every single fear and worry, but I couldn't do that. When we'd spoken yesterday, Greg had spent the first five minutes telling me how Bill was giving him shit about coming down to Melbourne for the twins' party and had started dropping hints about the trip going against him in the investigation.

'Jesus, listen to me,' he'd eventually said. 'I'm not the one singlehandedly wrangling four kids. Sorry, buddy. You okay?'

'Yeah, I'm good, buddy.'

What else could I say to my overwrought, faraway husband? I'd promised to love, honour and cherish, not burden, worry and trouble. But it was getting harder to keep the creeping dread of a potentially scary diagnosis to myself.

Rania's lovely face stared at me from across the table in our local café now, and I wondered what her reaction would be if I just came right out and said, *Hey, guess what? Apart from being a shit mum, I might have cancer!*

'They don't hate you,' Rania repeated. 'You're an amazing mum. I know I don't have older kids, but from what I've heard, this is standard behaviour. Kids always push. Tishk told me yesterday he hates cheese sandwiches and if I put another one in his lunchbox it'll end up in my slippers.'

I laughed and picked at my peanut-butter toast. 'I guess so.'

'It's a lot, being on your own with four kids,' Rania said. 'You're one of the strongest, most capable mums I know, Lizzie, but you're still human. You can't hold everyone up all the time or your back will break.'

'You're probably right.' I felt better already. 'I just needed a mini-vent.'

'Anytime,' Rania said, taking a sip of her soy chai latte. 'Anyway, it gave me the perfect excuse to avoid the talk my mother wanted to have after drop-off. I told her my friend was having a nervous breakdown and I had to meet her.'

'You weren't far off.'

Rania laughed. 'I've been thinking a lot about what you said at the fundraiser.'

'Oh shit, what did I say? Remember it was my first night out in a while.'

'You said you wished you hadn't wasted so much time when you were younger doing stuff you didn't want to do,' Rania said. 'It made me think about telling my parents I don't want to be a beautician.'

'Good for you!'

'Can you give me some advice on what to say to them?'

'Just be honest,' I said. 'Tell them you haven't figured out what you want to do yet, but you know this isn't right for you.'

'I'm not sure,' Rania said, looking pained. 'You don't know my parents. They're very old-fashioned and would see it as a sign of huge disrespect and ingratitude.'

I smiled reassuringly at her. 'Trust me, they'll understand. They're your parents. They love you. Just tell them that you'll figure things out eventually, but that you need more time. You have to talk to them and be honest.'

'Okay.' Rania took a deep breath, as though preparing to talk with her parents in the next five seconds. 'Thank you, Lizzie.'

She unleashed her full radiant smile, and it was like being thrust into a sudden burst of warm sunlight. Rania was so lovely, and I felt a need to protect her from the world, which reminded me ...

'Can I ask a question?'

'Sure!'

'What's Saunagate?'

Chapter Twenty-Six
Megan

'Are you sick?'

Megan frowned as she placed two cups of tea down in front of Ellie and Helen. 'No, why?'

'Tired?' Helen asked.

'Um ... a little.'

'Got the painters in?'

'Mum!'

Megan glanced over at Bert, Jim and Reg at the next table.

'Don't worry, love,' Bert said with a wink. 'We lads are all too familiar with Aunty Flow. Why do you think we started the Activities Shed?'

Ellie and Helen exploded with indignance.

'Rubbish!' Ellie scolded. 'No woman at Applewood has heard boo from Aunty Flow in thirty years!'

'The only reason you lot started that shed was to get away from us at *all* times of the month,' Helen added.

They all cackled with laughter and Megan felt jealous of these seniors and their distinct lack of middle-aged problems. Problems like how to tell your best friend that her teenager was sneaking into the city and drinking with her boyfriend on a school night.

'Now listen, Megs. I don't know why I can't have Oscar while you're away next week,' Ellie complained. 'His father just had a full week with him. Surely it's my turn.'

'Yes, that would be nice for your poor mum,' Helen agreed.

Megan sighed. 'I told you, Mum. It's easier if Bryce and Adam have him during the week when Oscar has stuff on. Anyway, you're always busy! But maybe he could stay with you Wednesday night?'

Ellie frowned. 'Hmm ... I've got bridge that night, so I'm not sure that would work. Let me check my calendar.'

'Yep, right. You do that, Mum.'

Honestly, Megan thought, *the woman was impossible.*

'So, what's up, then?' Ellie asked. 'You're very distracted. Isn't she, Helen?'

'Just a lot on my mind with the camp.'

Megan walked back to the counter, feeling confident the camp excuse would satisfy her nosy mother. There was simply no way she could tell Ellie Wylie about any of the troubling issues that were occupying her mind this morning.

Troubling Issue #1 was the fact that Eddie had sprung her feeling up her young lover in a public place two nights ago. Viewing Harry through the Eddie lens had been embarrassing to say the least. Even though Eddie had texted Megan the following morning, apologising for his 'drunken and boorish behaviour', he'd ended the message with, *And please apologise to your young friend for me, too.*

Yes, okay, Eddie, she'd thought. *You've made it perfectly clear that you consider my rebound shag to be a foetus.* Megan hadn't replied. But she was finding it hard to get their brief conversation off her mind. Eddie's slurred, 'I love you', had been especially memorable.

When she got home that night, she'd lain awake for hours, wondering if Eddie was still seeing his co-worker. And at 3 a.m., she had finally got up, grabbed her laptop and started scrolling Eddie's socials. Unfortunately, Eddie was as useless on the socials as Lizzie. As useless as she used to be, anyway.

That was Troubling Issue #2. Lizzie's new friendship with Rania. Megan didn't want to admit that she was jealous, but she was. However, there was a more pressing problem where Lizzie was concerned right now, and this was Troubling Issue #3.

Zara.

If Megan told Ellie she'd sprung Zara in the city, her mother would most likely tell Megan to 'stay out of it' and 'let the child have some fun'. But the guilt Megan felt at not telling Lizzie clawed at her throat. She'd want to know if it was Oscar. But Lizzie herself said that she had got up to much worse when she was Zara's age, so who was Megan to stick her nose in?

Also, Zara has some pretty damning info on you, too, a tiny voice in Megan's head whispered.

But Megan still wasn't convinced she was doing the right thing by keeping the truth from her best friend. Even if she would feel like a total 'rat', as Harry had so succinctly put it.

She'd felt annoyed with Harry at the time. It was like watching a kid siding with another kid. Zara was only four years his junior, after all. This fun fact had kept Megan awake until the wee hours last night.

'Psst!'

Megan turned to find Ellie leaning across the counter and gesturing to her to come closer.

'I didn't want Helen to hear,' Ellie whispered, glancing over Megan's shoulder into the kitchen, 'but Yang told me you might be interested in buying the café.'

'Okay, firstly, that's totally untrue, and secondly, how do you know she's selling it?'

'She told me.'

'Another lie.'

'Okay, I heard her on the phone to the bank yesterday.'

'Mum!'

'What? I can't help it if these old ears of mine are bionic!'

Megan looked over her shoulder to see Yang stirring today's soup special in the kitchen. The radio in there was blaring so she wouldn't be able to hear them, but Megan lowered her voice, anyway.

'I think it would be an excellent business opportunity for you, darling.'

'Yang mentioned it,' Megan said softly, 'and I told her I wasn't interested.'

In actual fact, Yang had mentioned it at least five times a day for the past few weeks, telling Megan she was 'the stupidest shithead giraffe in the world' if she didn't consider it. But Megan refused to be drawn into Yang's aggressive negotiation style.

'But why?' Ellie cried now. 'I can help you out with finance if you need, not that you do with your Chill money ...'

'Yeah, thanks for spreading that information around, by the way.'

'You could run the café during the day and write your kids' book at night. It's perfect!'

'I'm not writing a book anymore.'

'Since when?'

'Since I discovered that I'm a shithouse writer.'

'Who told you that?'

Failure, fatigue and frustration suddenly reached boiling

point. 'It doesn't matter how I know I'm a shit writer, I just am, okay?' she hissed. 'And I don't want to own and run a café in a retirement village, Mum.'

She watched as her mother's face arranged itself into what Megan called her 'cat's arse expression'.

'I see,' Ellie said. 'It would be an embarrassment, hanging around old farts like us all day, would it?'

'That is *exactly* what I do now!'

'You're obviously too important for a business like this,' Ellie continued. 'Most people would view running a successful café as something to aspire to, something to *strive* for and be proud of, but not my daughter. She's too smart for that.'

'Oh my God, that's not ...'

'I think I'll head back to my quarters now.' Ellie spun on her rubber heel and strode past the Activities Shed brigade. 'Good day, gentlemen.'

Her *quarters*? *Gentlemen*? Oh Christ. Things were dire when her mother started reverting to her upper-middle-class vocabulary.

'She's right pissed off,' Jim observed.

'What's up her bum?' Bert asked.

Megan was about to make something up when she noticed an email notification from Nicola flash up on her phone screen on the counter.

She swiped it open. As she began to read, her face clouded over.

'Mother *fucker*!'

★★★

'*Please*, Lizzie!'

Megan's hands were clasped together in front of her chest, her expression a mask of desperation.

'I can't!' Lizzie said, as parents and children swarmed around the two women. 'I've got the kids and ...'

'Aunty Carmen said she was *gagging* to have them!' Megan cried. 'She told me to talk you into going to a spa for a few days.'

Lizzie raised one eyebrow. 'Are you seriously comparing school camp with forty kids to a relaxing day spa?'

Megan clutched at Lizzie's arm. 'I will do *literally* anything you want for the next *year*!'

'Megan ...'

'Think how much fun we'll have!' A manic smile seemed to be frozen on her face. 'It's almost a blessing that Nicola can't go!'

Three nights before camp, on a Friday afternoon, Nicola McGinty had emailed Megan to say she'd been offered a once-in-a-lifetime opportunity for her therapeutic kitchen-hamper business and couldn't come to camp. Over the past hour, Megan had alternated between calling Nicola every name under the sun and begging Lizzie to take her place.

'The kids won't be able to do half the planned activities if we don't have the right adult-to-student ratio,' Megan said. 'It'll be fun! We'll have walks and games and campfires and ...'

'... supervise forty kids who don't belong to us,' Lizzie finished.

Megan racked her brain. It was time for a new tact.

'Think how happy it would make Stella if you came,'

she said. 'Especially when she's going through all this shit with Lola.'

Lizzie shook her head in admiration. 'Using my child for emotional blackmail. Nice.'

But Lizzie's will was crumbling and Megan knew her friend was on the verge of agreeing. She didn't dare say another word in case she frightened the 'yes' away.

'Okay.'

Megan screamed so loudly that a prep girl nearby started to cry. The girl's mother glared at Megan.

'Sorry,' Megan called to the mum, looking anything but sorry. 'Right, let's go to the staff room and I'll talk you through everything!' she said, grabbing Lizzie's arm and dragging her friend into the school.

★★★

'Harry!' Oscar shouted.

Megan nearly crashed the car into the gutter. She stared at her son in the rear-view mirror.

'What?'

Oscar pointed out the car window. 'Your friend from writing class.'

Megan looked to her left and there he was, standing on her front doorstep and looking for all the world like he belonged there. Like it wasn't at all out of the ordinary for him to show up unannounced at 4.15 p.m. on a Friday afternoon.

What the hell?

'Oh, hey, Harry!' she said, in what she hoped was a casual voice, as she stepped out of the car.

'Hi, Megan,' Harry said, matching her tone. He grinned at a confused Oscar. 'Hey, mate, how's it going?'

'You here to fix the computer again?' Oscar asked, walking up to the door.

'Yeah, I need to upload some new software.'

'Oh, right.'

Megan opened the front door and as soon as her son disappeared inside, she turned to Harry.

'What are you doing?' she whispered.

'I missed you,' Harry said, reaching out a hand to touch her arm.

'You should have texted,' Megan said, taking a step back and glancing around to make sure Oscar was gone. 'I don't want Oscar to get suspicious.'

Harry shrugged. 'So, why don't we tell him?'

'Tell him what?'

'That I'm your boyfriend,' Harry said matter-of-factly.

'Harry, listen,' Megan said calmly. 'You have to go. I promised Oscar that we'd hang out and order pizza.'

'I love pizza.'

'Harry.' Megan's tone became stern and she had the unnerving sensation that she was talking to one of Oscar's friends. 'You have to go. It's going to be weird if my IT guy joins us for movie night.'

'But ...'

'No buts.'

Harry looked annoyed. 'Well, when can I see you? I miss you.'

He went to put his arms around her waist, but Megan took another step back. 'Bryce is picking him up tomorrow afternoon to take him for the next few days. How about you come over after that?'

'What time?'

'Um ... I don't know ... maybe seven?'

'Seven it is!' Harry's face instantly brightened. He leaned in and his lips brushed her ear. 'I love you.'

No, you don't! Megan wanted to scream, but instead she smiled and gently pushed him away. 'Tomorrow, okay? Bye.'

The bubble had officially burst. She couldn't have Harry turning up on her doorstep and trying to wriggle his way into her life with Oscar. As soon as Harry came round tomorrow night, she'd tell him it was over.

Well, maybe not as *soon* as he got there.

Chapter Twenty-Seven
Sam

To: jack_woz_here@hotmail.com
From: samhatfieldchef@bigpond.com
Subject: ART!

Hey dickhead,

So, here's one for the books. Bridget was just nice to me on the phone. She was apologetic about bailing on babysitting Tyler for school camp. And she meant it. And then she said, 'You're a great dad, Sam.'

I looked around, waiting for the world to unfold and collapse inwards like a scene out of *Inception*, but nothing happened. I thanked her. I couldn't bring myself to say the same about her – i.e. that the kids were lucky to have her as a mum – but I felt no real compulsion to. It wasn't up to me to reciprocate. It was up to me to show gratitude for a nice thing said, and I did.

It might've been the first time I've gotten off the phone with Bridg and haven't felt like I wanted to punch a wall. And that's progress, dickhead! Pathetic progress tangled up in my own residual feelings of emasculation and resentment, but progress goddammit!

I'll take it where it comes. And in whatever twisted form it comes in.

Rachel told Lola about an exhibition at the national gallery that explores how artists respond to gender identity and experiences. So, when I picked up Lola from drama last week, I asked Rachel if she'd come with us so Lola could have at least one intelligent adult to guide her through the exhibition. Rachel agreed and we met her outside the gallery Sunday morning, where we all touched the water wall, and Rachel and I reminisced about childhood memories of doing the same.

Lola was bouncing around like a little kid once we were inside, which made me realise that I don't take her out as much as I should. We headed up to the gender-thingy exhibition, and I deliberately hung back, letting Lola and Rachel move through together. Lola pointed at paintings and tilted her head at them knowingly, while Rachel pointed out small specifics in the artworks, describing techniques used and decisions made. Lola was loving it and Rachel knew her stuff. I had no idea she was so cluey when it came to art; or at least art beyond theatre. But she was like a proper gallery guide. She moved through the rooms like she lived in them, encouraging Lola to stay for a bit longer, or to sit on one of those central couches and take more time to absorb the art.

I heard her ask Lola if she ever re-watched TV shows for fun and Lola listed about five or six of her go-to binges. I was actually surprised to learn that my little Miss Brontë is a big Buffy fan. Rachel told her that great artworks can give just as much joy, revealing more of themselves every time you revisit them. If I'd tried to tell Lola anything remotely close to that she would've been gone before I'd reached the midpoint of the thought. But when Rachel said it, Lola looked at her like she was revealing the secrets of the universe. It was sweet. I thought maybe she'd slipped beyond the point of childlike wonder. I felt so grateful to Rachel.

We went to Chinatown for lunch afterwards and I shouted us a feast of way too many dumplings and Chinese broccoli with oyster sauce, and Lola's obligatory special fried rice. Our waitress brought us some complimentary lychee ice-cream and said we were a nice family. None of us corrected her; we just said thanks and quietly ate our ice-cream, looking at each other and giggling a bit. Rachel didn't talk about her ex, Sebastian, at all and I didn't bring up Bridget. Lola was the third wheel, but a necessary one for the flow of the day. And you know what was weird? I felt more honest and open with Rachel than I have with Megan and Lizzie recently. That's a bit shit, isn't it? Not to mention the fact that I made the poor decision to talk to Dave and Megan about Lola's issues with Stella. So not only is there ongoing dishonesty around Megan's writing skills, now there are more secrets to keep (or at least conversations to keep to ourselves). And that way lies the breakdown of friendships. But it's like we've never really acknowledged our friendship, y'know? Megan and me. We were plonked together by fate and got along well, but it's not like we've ever taken a moment to look each other in the eye and say that we're important parts of each other's lives. Maybe if we had, we wouldn't have let these sorts of petty intrusions affect us the way they are now. And maybe now it's too late to remedy an already precarious situation.

Maybe it's finally time for you and me to run away together and embark on a fruitful career as cruise-ship entertainers.

I get top bunk.

Love, S x

To: codenamedave@gmail.com
From: samhatfieldchef@bigpond.com
Subject: Babysitting

Hey Dave,

Thanks for the offer, but the last thing your household needs while you're away is yet another chaotic male presence. But please pass on a massive thanks to your most excellent wife for even considering having Tyler.

Bridget was actually the one who called my mum and sorted it all out. Then she called me to tell me that she'd drop Tyler to Mum herself. It was weird. But good.

SCHOOL CAAAAAAMMMP!!

S x

P.S. I watched the Stevie Nicks vid. That goddess. Thanks for forwarding. Your emails that just have a YouTube URL in the subject heading are always a welcome lucky-dip musical surprise in my inbox.

To: jack_woz_here@hotmail.com
From: samhatfieldchef@bigpond.com
Subject: Drunk Texting? Nailed it.

Hey dickhead,

So, as you know, Bridget picked up Tyler this afternoon to take him to Mum's. And Lola has gone to bed early after a mid-afternoon adrenaline rush about all things school camp. I treated myself to a couple of Lagavulins. And after Lagavulin number two, I texted Rachel.

ME: *Hey after this camp, I may be craving adult company. Wanna grab a bite at Yu Chu on Wed? We're due back around three, so loads of time.*

RACH: *Won't you be shattered??*

ME: *Nah. Be good to see you.*

RACH: *Okay cool. I'll book for seven?*

ME: *Perfect. Now I just have to make it back alive.*

RACH: *Watch out for those drop bears!*

Then we exchanged a hilarious string of emojis and GIFs.

I'm going to tell her, dickhead. I don't even care if she completely rejects me. I'm going to tell her everything I've ever felt, from uni to now. Crush, love, fear, regret, crush again, possible love again. The whole enchilada.

I've spent a lot of my adult life being some level of scared. And I'm bored of myself. I want to surprise myself. Which may just lead to me surprising other people, too.

S x

Chapter Twenty-Eight
Lizzie

My phone pinged. I turned away from the frying pan where tonight's dinner was sizzling away to see multiple notifications popping up on my screen.

@mad4realz98 started following you

@disdatandtheother started following you

@hellajezzabella started following you

@ajmac_2004 started following you

@thechrissychronicles started following you

What the ...?

I was staring at my phone in confusion, when hot oil flicked up from the pan and spattered my arm.

'*Shit!*'

'Swear jar!' Stella called from the next room, where she was watching a *Brooklyn Nine-Nine* episode for the tenth time.

'Whatever,' I muttered, taking a quick glance around the kitchen as I swiped my phone open.

I didn't know why I felt like I was doing something wrong by looking at Insta while cooking dinner on a Saturday night. Luckily, there was no one to witness my criminal act. Zara was at rehearsals, Max was playing Minecraft in the office and Archie was in his room. The only one keeping me company was Bailey, who was lying at my feet, hoping for a sausage to roll out of the frying pan and into his mouth.

I had 1387 followers? I frowned. Why the new flurry of activity? I hadn't posted a single photo and my page remained blank. Then I noticed a new notification.

Rania Jalali has tagged you in a post.

The notification took me to Rania's feed, where there was a photo of the two of us at the breast-cancer event. The photo was cropped at our waists, which may or may not have been a thoughtful gesture, but either way I was grateful. We were laughing and clutching each other's arms as if we were in danger of toppling over with mirth. I racked my brain to remember what we'd been giggling about, but we'd actually laughed a lot that night. Rania had only posted this thirty-eight minutes ago, but it already had over one thousand comments and endless likes.

The thought of all those strangers looking at this photo, studying my flaws and imperfections, brought on a rush of panic. I began to scrutinise my features as if seeing myself for the first time:

1. Clean medium-length brown hair (thank God I'd washed it that day), presentably but not professionally blow-waved.
2. No trace of lipstick or eyeliner.
3. Light foundation holding up.
4. Flattering scoop neckline.
5. Good colour dress – the blue looked good against my olive skin (no need for a spray tan with my Maltese genes).
6. Laugh lines on full display.

Rania looked radiant and as if she should be laughing it up with Kendall Jenner rather than a woman who looked like her nice, middle-aged aunt.

The caption underneath read, "*The great thing about new friends is that they bring new energy to your soul – Shanna Rodriguez.*"

A warm feeling spread through my body. What a sweetheart.

As notifications continued to pop up, I made a mental note to ask Megan how to turn the bloody things off. I was now up to 1428 followers! Maybe I should post my first picture?

But of what?

I glanced around the kitchen for inspiration. The sausages? *Can't wait to serve these bad boys up to the fam tonight! #sausagesaturdays*

The half-drunk glass of red wine on the counter? *Going down a treat! #mamaloveswine*

A shot of Stella lolling on the couch with Jake Peralta and Amy Santiago on the screen in the background? *Stella getting her daily dose of the Nine-Nine! #nine-nine #TV #chillin*

No. Pathetic.

How did people do this multiple times a day? I wasn't cut out for this kind of pressure. Also, my daughters would tease me mercilessly if I posted anything as lame as sausages or wine. And I could just imagine Aileen, Melissa or Megan's reactions.

'*Sausages?* Ya fecking eejit!' Aileen would roar.

'You didn't think to put up a nice pic of you and Greg?' Melissa would ask.

'Worst dick pic ever,' Megan would snort.

Maybe I should just post a photo of my left boob with the caption, *Cannot WAIT to find out if this tit has cancer in it!! #goodtimes #whoknows #cancervibes*

Reality came crashing in and my good humour melted away. I'd been trying so hard to pretend that I wasn't awaiting results that could potentially change my life, and my family's lives, forever, but it was like trying to ignore the sky.

I put my phone face down on the bench and took a deep breath. The waiting was excruciating. It was also why I'd agreed to go on camp. In some irrational part of my brain, I thought running away from home might somehow make me forget. It was the perfect distraction; forty kids who didn't belong to me would undoubtedly be easier to handle than my own daughter. Zara had been cold and distant since I took her phone, and I couldn't see the ice thawing anytime soon.

'Mum! The saucepan!'

Max had appeared from nowhere.

'Fuck!' I said, whipping the lid off the boiling saucepan.

He gasped.

'Sorry.'

Max glanced towards the lounge room, where Stella was still sprawled on the couch, glued to the TV. 'I won't tell Stella,' he whispered. 'Promise.'

'Thanks, mate.'

'When's dinner? I'm *staaaaarving*!'

'I just have to do the mash,' I said, grabbing the colander out of the cupboard with one hand and turning down the heat on the sausages with the other. 'Can you set the table, please? Stella! Get the drinks, please, and tell Archie to feed Bailey.'

At the sound of his name, Bailey leapt up from the kitchen floor and ran for the laundry.

'Okay,' Stella said, getting up. 'And I heard you swear, but I'll cut you some slack because you're coming on camp.'

'So generous,' I muttered.

Ten minutes later, the four of us were settled at the dining table and happily tucking into our meat and three veg, when I was overcome with emotion. All around me, the kids were arguing and shit-stirring, yet all I could think about was the possibility of me not being here one day. Greg was an amazing father of course, but Archie's absent-mindedness drove him mad, and he lost patience with Zara too easily. And who would talk Stella through how to use a tampon when the swimming carnival came around? Greg knew nothing about soccer, so Max would have to ask Dad about that. Then there was the issue of helping Zara select her formal dress. Maybe Megan could take her shopping. Or Melissa. I'd have to start a list of specific people for specific jobs. Tears stung my eyes as I wiped mash onto my sausage and reached for a serviette to blow my nose.

'You okay?' my annoyingly observant daughter asked.

'Hay fever.'

'In March?'

Damn that child and her seasonal knowledge.

'Listen, if you ever need an honest opinion on shoes or clothes, you can always ask Aunty Carmen or Megan. Just not Aunt Rosa, okay?' I blurted out. 'And make sure you always wear undies under pantyhose, or you'll get a yeast infection.'

'Um ... okay,' Stella said, frowning.

'And Archie, always ask people how they are and actually

listen when they tell you, okay? In fact, that goes for all of you.'

'Mum, why are you …?'

'None of you should say, "that happened to me" when someone is telling a story,' I continued, sounding slightly manic now, 'it's their story so let them tell it. And say thank you when someone gives you a compliment … and if you're the smartest person in your group of friends, it's probably time for some new friends.'

I stopped when I noticed my children staring at me like I was insane.

'Um, random,' Archie said.

Max screwed his face up. 'Yeah, Mum, why are you telling us all this stuff?'

I pushed my peas around on the plate and shrugged. 'I was just thinking out loud.'

'Why don't I just ask you about clothes?' Stella said. 'You're the queen of honest opinions.'

'You can ask me! I'm just saying … if I'm away …'

'Like when you're away on camp?' Max asked.

'Exactly!' *Phew.*

'You're being weird,' Max said.

'Sorry,' I said, reaching out to squeeze his hand. 'I'm just getting my period.'

Max immediately pulled his hand away. 'Gross!'

'Unnecessary information,' Archie mumbled into his glass of soda water.

'You sound like Zara, Max,' Stella snapped. 'Periods are totally natural!'

'Where *is* Zara?' Archie asked.

'Rehearsals,' I said, picking up my glass of red. 'Ines's mum is dropping her home at ten.'

'Tonight?' Archie asked. 'That's weird. They never rehearse on Saturday nights until the week before the show.'

I froze, the glass halfway to my mouth.

★★★

Three hours later, and half an hour past the time Zara said she'd be home, there was still no sign or word from my eldest daughter. In that time, I'd texted a Baytree Secondary mum only to learn that there were, in fact, no rehearsals tonight. But I had no way of getting in touch with Zara because I'd confiscated her phone.

'I'm sure she's fine, Mum,' Stella reassured me. 'Probably just at Ines's house.'

I had no idea where Ines lived, or who her parents were. It was becoming clearer with every passing moment that I wasn't exactly Mother of the Year. I knew nothing about my daughter's new friends and cursed myself for dropping the ball. I headed into Zara and Stella's bedroom to do some investigating. The first thing I found was a notebook in Zara's dresser drawer. Words full of teen angst and emotion jumped out at me as I flicked through.

This is true love … feels so right … can't tell … Mum wouldn't understand … hate her … held hands and kissed all night …

My phone rang and I guiltily dropped the journal into the drawer.

'Hello? Zara?'

'Oh, no, this is Chloe, Ines's mum,' a cautious voice said in my ear. 'You're Lizzie, Zara's mum?'

'Yes, is Zara okay?' I had a sudden and terrifying vision of my girl lying in the back of a speeding ambulance, siren blaring.

'She's fine, but I think you need to come and get her,' Chloe said, sounding haughty now. 'She and Ines haven't exactly been honest about their whereabouts tonight. I've just picked them up from a party.'

'*What?*' My mind was racing.

'They're okay,' Chloe said. 'They're back at my house and safe.'

I closed my eyes and allowed myself a sigh of relief.

'But they're very drunk.'

My eyes shot open.

'And stoned.'

I closed them again.

★★★

In bed the next morning, I lay staring at my sleeping eldest daughter, whom I'd hardly recognised when I walked into Ines's house last night. The girl sitting in Chloe's kitchen was a mess. White-faced and red-eyed, Zara had wet hair and vomit stains on her singlet top and was swaying gently back and forth on Chloe's kitchen stool. As soon as she saw me, Zara jumped up, stumbled, then fell into my arms, telling me how much she loved me and how sorry she was. Then she turned to Chloe and apologised to her at least ten times before falling back against me with another string of apologies.

On the way home, she'd gazed out the car window, humming tunelessly along with the songs on the radio and asking me questions like, 'Why does the moon *look* like that?'

By the time we got home, Zara's blinks were lasting four seconds each, and I deposited her straight into my room. I'd already texted Archie, telling him to make sure Stella and Max were in bed when we got back so they wouldn't have to see their sister in her current state. I hoped this was the peak of my twins' bad behaviour. Or rock bottom. Whichever analogy meant this was the worst of it.

When Chloe told me that Ines had confessed that she and Zara had been doing this kind of thing for a while now – saying they were at rehearsals then sneaking off elsewhere – I was shocked and angry, but more than anything I was just so relieved to see my girl safe and alive. Those few hours of not knowing where she was, and imagining the worst, had been the longest and most stressful I could remember. I'd been so busy worrying about not being here for them, but the idea of losing one of them was unfathomable. All I wanted was to have my girl back in my arms and hold her tight.

After Zara finally passed out, I'd done exactly that. I'd lain down next to her, wrapped my arms around her and held her all night. I only let go when light began to filter through the blinds.

Looking at my daughter now, I had to resist the urge to reach out and push a strand of blonde hair back off her face. I didn't want to wake her yet. I needed to think some more about what I was going to say. It wasn't the kind of scenario I'd envisioned having to deal with on my own. When Greg and I first had kids, we'd joked about the dreaded teen years, always assuming we'd both be there to tag team in times like this. The old good cop, bad cop. Now I had to be both, and I had no idea where to start.

I glanced at the clock and saw that it was almost nine. After all the excitement of last night, I doubted any of the kids would be up early, except maybe Max, so I had a bit of time up my sleeve to work out my strategy.

My phone buzzed with a text from Rania. When I opened her message, I was greeted with a mini-essay.

Lizzie, I did what you said. Last nite I told my parents I don't want to b a beautician and need 2 live my own life and stop doing what they want me 2 do. They were so angry. They said I am ungrateful and have shamed them again and if I want their ongoing financial support I am not 2 leave the house for any reason except for beautician's course.

I wish I never told them now. I told you they wouldn't understand.

An icy chill crept around the back of my neck.

Chapter Twenty-Nine
Megan

'Welcome, everyone, to this most exciting and splendid occasion at Applewood Retirement Village! It is going to be a marvellous morning ...'

As Lucy continued with her introduction that seemed more befitting of a royal visit, Megan stood at the back of the Applewood rec room watching Sam fidget with parts of his guitar that she was sure didn't need that much attention. He eventually looked up over the heads of the one hundred or so assembled residents and caught Megan's eye. The two friends shared a bemused expression at Lucy's waffling.

'... so without further ado ...'

'*Ado' is right*, Megan thought as she noticed her mother giving Lucy the wind-up.

'... here is our wonderful, amazing and hugely talented act for this morning, Sam Hatfield!'

'Thank you. Thank you so much for that enthusiastic intro, and good morning, folks,' he said, hushing the low buzz of chatter in the room. 'I'll be playing a couple of songs for you before tea and scones are served.'

'Scones?' exclaimed a feisty old dame in the front row.

Sam looked to Lucy, who shook her head. 'No, my apologies. No scones today.'

'There are never scones!'

Megan didn't know who had shouted this but hoped she wouldn't have to step in.

'Right. Well, I'm sure there will be … biscuits?' Sam looked again to Lucy, who this time gave him an effusive nod.

'Yes indeed,' Sam said, looking relieved. 'Tea and bickies it is. So, I thought I'd start with …'

'But we want scones,' a woman barked.

'I hate bickies!' a man rasped.

The scent of revolution filled the rec room as other residents started voicing their hatred of digestives and their longing for better-quality baked goods.

Before Lucy could make her way back to the microphone and call for order, Ellie stood up and glared around the room.

'Shut up and let the boy sing, will you?' she shouted.

Sam raised an eyebrow at Megan, and she grinned back. He gave her an ironic rock salute, which she returned, sticking out her tongue for extra effect. She was enjoying the morning already and Sam hadn't sung a note yet.

'Um … okay,' Sam said into the mic. 'I'll, uh, get started, shall I?'

He cleared his throat and Megan could see his hands shaking as he began to strum the guitar. It was odd to see her laconic friend so nervous, and she found it endearing.

At first, she couldn't pick the song Sam was playing until he began to sing. The room had fallen completely silent. And as Sam continued his rendition of Sinatra's 'The Way You Look Tonight', one of the great jazz standards, Megan noticed hands moving to rest over hearts, and heads lolling gently to the side in the audience. She smiled.

Sam played six more songs and each choice was pitch perfect for the Applewood crowd. As he crooned his way through 'Someone to Watch Over Me', Ellie slipped out of her chair and very conspicuously started making her way to the back of the room. Megan hoped her mother wasn't going to start on at her again about buying The Cozy Corner. She was enjoying the serenity of listening to Sam perform. It felt like a long time since she'd taken a pause like this.

She'd left Harry in her bed to come to Applewood this morning. That had never been the plan, but any plans she may have had to tell him it was over between them had gone out the window the moment she opened the door last night and Harry had handed her another Tiffany's box.

'Harry, I can't ...'

'Yes, you can,' Harry had said, stepping inside and closing the door. 'I wanted to get it for you.'

It had been yet another understated, and undoubtedly expensive, bracelet. A gift that Megan would normally have been ecstatic to receive. But it was too much, and she knew she couldn't possibly keep it. Not when their relationship was approaching its inevitable end, in her mind, anyway.

Also, Harry's constant requests to read her writing had moved from playful to just plain annoying. No matter how many times she told him she didn't want him to read it, he continued to badger her. Their lovemaking last night had been as good as ever, but good sex wasn't enough anymore. Megan knew she needed to end it.

But how? she thought, watching Sam sing sweetly into the crackly microphone. *And when? Maybe if Harry is still there when I get home, I'll suggest he stay for dinner tonight so we can talk about things, calmly and rationally, like two mature adults.*

'So,' Ellie's whisper brought Megan's mind back to the rec room. 'He's cute, he can cook and he sings like an angel.'

261

'He's also a divorced single dad with a few fresh notches on his bedpost.'

'Oh, that's right.' Ellie's good-humoured tone vanished. 'I forgot about your impossibly high standards.' She walked back to her seat, muttering angrily to herself, earning some indignant shushing from several members of the audience.

Megan saw Sam looking at her quizzically as he finished the song. During the ensuing applause, he mouthed a quick, 'You okay?' having witnessed the brief altercation with her mum. Megan nodded and joined in the applause.

After closing his set with a toe-tapping version of 'Splish Splash', Sam was instantly surrounded by a throng of ageing groupies, who spat biscuit crumbs all over him as they waxed lyrical about his performance. Megan considered saving him, but it was way too much fun watching him try to cope with his adoring fans. Instead, she grabbed her handbag and snuck out to her car, keen to avoid another run-in with her mother. She was also eager to get home to talk to Harry. She was determined not to put off the inevitable any longer.

As soon as she got in her car, she texted Sam.

You were AMAZING! Thank you so much again. I owe you!

Her phone pinged almost instantly.

WHERE ARE YOU?? HELP ME!!

Megan selected the rock-salute emoji, smiling as she hit 'send'.

★★★

Megan stood in the doorway to her office, staring in confusion at Harry's mop of dark hair sprouting from the top of her monitor.

'What are you doing?'

'This is really good,' Harry said, grinning at her over the computer. He stood up and stepped out from behind the desk in nothing but boxer shorts and socks, which made him look even younger than he was. 'I love the title, too. *My Mind's Eye*. The plot needs a bit of work, but —'

'You read it?'

'I did.' Harry smiled like a naughty child who'd been caught with his hand in the biscuit tin.

'Harry,' Megan said calmly. 'Please get dressed and go.'

Harry's cocky expression wavered, but only slightly. 'Megs,' he said, taking a step towards her with his arms out.

'Harry,' Megan raised her voice along with her right index finger. 'I mean it, get dressed and get out of my house.'

Harry's face fell. His pained expression was difficult to look at, but he had gone too far.

'I told you,' Megan said gently. 'I told you not to read it. I didn't want you to read it.'

'Okay, look,' Harry said, a slight quiver in his voice. 'I'm really sorry. I am. I'll go and we can talk later.'

He scurried past Megan and mounted the stairs two by two, as he always did. In a matter of seconds, he reappeared with his jeans and T-shirt on, holding his shoes, flashing his most charming, apologetic smile.

'I really am sorry, Megan,' he said. 'But I just had to read it. I think if you just get your structure sorted, it could be so good. I'd be happy to edit it with you if you like?'

Megan shook her head in amazement as Harry dropped his shoes on the floor and stuffed his feet into them. He wasn't even close to understanding what was going on. The kid was oblivious.

'Harry, listen to me ...'

'I'll call you later and we can work out how I can say sorry.'

'No,' Megan said. 'You won't call me later. You won't call me at all. I'm sorry, but this is over.'

'What?'

'We both know this relationship isn't going to work, Harry. We've had a wonderful, very special few weeks together, but we don't belong in each other's worlds. Also, I have Oscar to think of and —'

'I'm not like Eddie,' Harry cried. 'I want to be a father to Oscar!'

The absurdity of this statement almost made Megan laugh out loud, but she didn't want to hurt Harry any more than she already was.

'Harry, I'm far too old for you,' Megan said. 'Our lives are just too different, and you don't want an old woman like me. You'll meet someone your own age and then —'

'I don't *want* someone my age.' Harry sounded angry and petulant now. 'I love *you*!'

'You don't. Please hear what I'm saying, Harry. This is over. I'm sorry.'

Harry's lips began to tremble. He dropped his head, slid his hands into his jeans' back pockets and walked towards the front door.

Megan couldn't help noticing that from behind he looked like a child.

Chapter Thirty
Sam

To: codenamedave@gmail.com
From: samhatfieldchef@bigpond.com
Subject: ROCK STAR

Hey mate,

Turns out I don't need you at all. If we are Take That, I am Robbie. If we are NSYNC, I am Justin. If we get world famous as a duo then have a messy, public break-up, your future solo work will be relegated to the bargain bin of JB Hi-Fi. I jest. I missed you and was very scared performing without you. I never thought I'd be so grateful to compete with loud snoring during a gig. I'd like to think that it was my dulcet tones that lulled the old gent off to a sweet slumber, but he was asleep before I'd sung a note. There was enthusiastic applause from frail hands between every song, and Megan seemed to have a great time watching me sweat and squirm and strum and sing.

In answer to your question, we don't need to bring amps to camp. Which means we also don't need twenty-metre extension leads and/or a portable generator to power the amps. It is not Coachella. Just bring your guitar and your boundless enthusiasm. This is gonna be fun! Our first tour. Rock on!

Sam

To: samhatfieldchef@bigpond.com
From: codenamedave@gmail.com
Subject: ROCK STAR

Megan's never happier than when you're squirming ha-ha weirdo.

You're right no amps just me getting carried away ha-ha.

Coachella LOL.

IT'S CAMPCHELLA BABY!

What goes on tour stays on tour amiright LOL.

Chapter Thirty-One
Megan

Megan stood outside her house next to an absurd collection of suitcases, looking every bit the Hollywood star awaiting her limousine. Lizzie's car turned into the street and Megan grinned at her friend as she pulled up beside her and got out.

'Where's Stella?'

'She wanted to walk,' Lizzie said, staring in horror at the luggage at Megan's feet, which consisted of two large suitcases, one large backpack and one tote bag (that alone could hold enough for a long weekend away). Lizzie circled her forefinger in the direction of the baggage collection. 'You, um ... planning on jetting off to Europe for a few months after camp?'

'Too much?'

'We're going on school camp, not relocating to another country.'

'Okay, *fine*!' Megan yelled dramatically. She pretended not to notice her friend's bewildered expression as she picked up the suitcases and effortlessly lifted them off the ground. Megan winked at Lizzie then walked back towards her front door, taking the empty suitcases with her.

'You're not funny,' Lizzie called as Megan opened her front door and flung the cases inside. 'And we're gonna be late!'

Megan skipped to Lizzie, slung her backpack over her

shoulder and picked up her tote bag. 'Totally worth it!'

Megan had delighted in plotting her little trick of pretending to pack like a Kardashian for a three-day camp, knowing that it was as much for her own distraction as it was for Lizzie's amusement.

She'd made the right decision, ending things with Harry, but the anguish in his face had stayed with her all day and night. Harry hadn't made any attempt to get in touch since walking out of her house yesterday, which was for the best. Theirs was a relationship destined to fail. Megan would like to think it wasn't just about his age, but his youth had become more and more apparent at every step, and she had no interest in having a partner who looked to her as a teacher of emotional intelligence. She'd done her time with Bryce.

But she couldn't help feeling a pang of sadness at the way things had turned out. In the shower this morning, she promised herself she'd say yes if Harry asked to meet for coffee when she got home. At the very least, she owed him a proper goodbye. Also, she needed to give him back the two very expensive pieces of jewellery he'd bought her. Jewellery she never should have accepted in the first place. Megan would miss having fun with Harry – more than that, she'd miss the sex – but they couldn't keep it going for a second longer.

Harry needed to find someone age-appropriate, and she needed to stop making a fool of herself. Megan now clearly saw her fling with Harry for what it was – the rebound to end all rebounds. He was also the perfect distraction from her vacant career and complete lack of direction. At least none of her family or friends had found out about her momentary lapse of sanity.

'Come on, funny girl!' Lizzie said, sounding slightly terse. 'Chuck your stuff in the back seat and let's go before we miss the bus.'

'We're fine,' Megan said, getting a whiff of her friend's annoyance.

'That was a lot of effort for a pretty average prank.'

'But oh, how we'll laugh about it one day,' Megan said. 'We'll say, "Remember when I pretended to bring all my worldly possessions to school camp? Good times."'

'You're an idiot.'

'Agreed. So, how're you feeling? We're going on camp! Woo hoo!'

'It's good timing,' Lizzie said, as she pulled the car away from Megan's house.

'Yeah?' Megan asked.

'Yeah.' Lizzie sighed. 'There was a bit of a shitstorm with Zara on Saturday night.'

Megan shifted uncomfortably in her seat as a fresh wave of guilt washed over her. 'What happened?'

'It was a build-up of stuff,' Lizzie said. 'The screaming match we had to have.'

Megan felt her face heat up, so she began rummaging through her handbag for some lip balm. 'Zara's a good girl. She'll be fine.'

Lizzie exhaled loudly. 'It's not like she's six, Megs.'

'You know what I mean.'

'Not really,' Lizzie said sharply. 'I can't exactly drop a Tonka truck at her feet and tell her to go play.'

Megan turned to examine Lizzie's face. Her friend looked angry. Angrier than this conversation warranted. *What was going on with her?*

'Oscar has his moments, too, Lizzie.'

'He's not a teenage girl,' Lizzie shot back.

Megan turned to stare out the window at the passing suburban houses. 'Well observed,' she said coolly.

'I'm just saying —'

'I get it, Lizzie,' Megan cut her off. 'It's complicated for you. Zara is older and more female than my son, so I couldn't understand.'

Megan's initial bonhomie was gone. Lizzie's consistent implication that raising a boy was a walk in the park compared to girls was insulting and just plain wrong. And it was starting to piss Megan off.

'Well, yeah,' Lizzie said, in a less tetchy tone. 'But that's not a criticism.'

'Maybe if you cut her some slack, she wouldn't push back so hard.'

'If I cut her some slack?'

Lizzie kept her eyes on the road, but Megan could feel that her attention was well and truly on her.

'Yes,' Megan said, feeling like she couldn't back down now. 'You're a self-confessed control freak and Zara is fifteen. Are you surprised that she's acting up and lashing out at you?'

'I'm more surprised that you are, actually.'

That stung. 'I'm not lashing out,' Megan said. 'I'm just being honest.'

'Thanks, but I'm not sure I feel like hearing your brand of honesty right now.'

'Oh, sorry, would you rather hear bullshit honesty from your new best friend, Reality Rania?' The words were out of Megan's mouth before she could stop them.

Lizzie turned to stare at Megan in amazement. 'Are you serious right now?'

'You've got to admit.' Megan softened her tone, hoping she didn't sound as childish as she felt. 'You've been acting differently since you've been hanging out with a woman swallowed by her own celebrity. Does it make you feel cooler? Younger? What? I genuinely want to know.'

'Neither.'

There was a long, loaded pause as the two women stared at the road ahead, and Megan tried to justify her interrogation to herself. Lizzie had admitted to acting out as a teenager, so how could she not recognise standard teen behaviour in her own daughter? Lizzie wasn't wrong about the differences between having a young son and a teenage daughter – Megan got that – but that didn't mean Megan wasn't allowed an opinion.

The fact that she still hadn't told her best friend that she'd run into her slightly drunk daughter in a city park late at night continued to niggle. Especially when Lizzie was having issues with Zara at the moment. Information like that would probably go a long way to helping Lizzie understand what was going on and try to work things out.

I have to tell her, Megan thought suddenly. *Lizzie has a right to know and I shouldn't have kept it from her for so long. She'll be pissed at me, but I'll just have to wear it.* The moment they get home from camp, she'd tell her, Megan decided. There was no way she could tell Lizzie before that, and especially not today. It would be no way to kick off their school-camp adventure.

She turned to Lizzie and grinned. 'Hey, remember that time I pretended to bring all my worldly possessions to school camp?'

Lizzie's face remained impassive as she continued staring ahead and replied in a monotone, 'Good times.'

★★★

The Baytree playground was teeming with activity. Kids and parents were flapping all over the place as they dealt with all manner of luggage, nervous tension and excitement. Megan and Lizzie walked along the footpath outside the school and instantly spotted Sam, sitting on their bench with Lola.

Lola was sitting on her duffle bag, arms folded and leaning against her dad's leg. *She looks exhausted already*, Megan thought. For her first day of camp, she'd chosen a more suitable ensemble than her usual day wear. Khaki pants, a light-blue lace-trimmed top and a long dark-green scallop-edged jacket. She looked like a cleaner version of one of Fagin's boys from *Oliver Twist*.

The two women wheeled their bags past the large bus dominating the narrow streetscape, into the busy yard and headed straight for Sam and Lola. As they approached, Lola stood up and walked over to the netball courts to join the rest of her class. Dave was heading towards the bench from the opposite direction, looking more excited than any kid in the playground. A large backpack bounced around his shoulders and his guitar case grazed the ground.

All three of them arrived in front of Sam at the same time and plonked their bags down.

'Morning, campers!' Megan chirped.

Sam narrowed his eyes. 'You abandoned me yesterday.'

'Oh please,' Megan replied. 'Who am I to come between you and your rasping fans?'

Higgsy materialised from among the throng of Grade Five/Six kids, clipboard in hand.

'Hey, guys,' he said brightly. 'We're still missing quite a few and Jonah's mum forgot to bring his medication, so she's had to go home. Reckons she'll be back in plenty of time, but we might have to find a pharmacy on the way.'

Megan couldn't remember ever hearing Higgsy say so many words at any one time.

'Copy that,' Dave said. 'Jonah medication. Possible pharmacy stop.'

Megan and Sam rolled their eyes at each other.

'And we're gonna need to keep a close eye on Logan,' Higgsy said. 'He's like an evil little Pied Piper.'

'Copy that,' Dave repeated. 'Bring the Logan smackdown.'

Higgsy frowned. 'Well, no. Just be aware of him,' he said, clearly concerned by Dave's choice of words. 'Caleb's our other focus,' he went on, nodding his head at the small dark-haired boy sitting on the steps of the school's main building, fiddling nervously with the straps of his backpack.

'He's asthmatic,' Megan explained to the others.

'And there are two others,' Higgsy said. 'But Caleb's going to need the most support.' He lowered his voice. 'His dad was in the army, back and forth to Afghanistan for years and was killed by a landmine last year.'

'Jesus,' Sam said.

Dave's brow furrowed suitably. 'Care for Caleb, smackdown for Logan.'

'Yep, okay, sure,' Higgsy said, realising he was fighting a losing battle.

As Higgsy continued to bombard them with information and instructions, Megan took the opportunity to try to get back on the right foot with Lizzie, shooting her friend an almost imperceptible glance as if to say, *Higgsy needs a drink.* She was relieved when Lizzie smiled. It was a small one, but a smile, nonetheless. Megan hoped that meant they could put their morning spat down to first-day camp jitters and put it behind them from here on.

Higgsy finally finished his spiel, leaving them all with their instructions, then scampered away to his next urgent task. The four friends exchanged wide-eyed stares.

'Right!' Megan announced to her shell-shocked mates. 'Let's do this!'

Over the next twenty minutes, they, along with the teachers, Higgsy, Salena and Kylie Fitz – new this year and looking to score brownie points by volunteering for camp duty – managed to corral the Five/Six kids onto the bus. They also helped their bus driver, Evan, load every backpack, pillow, sleeping bag and oversized wheely suitcase into the bus's baggage compartment.

Finally, every child was safely aboard, while their parents had secured prime waving positions on the footpath.

Higgsy tapped a pen to his clipboard, which looked to Megan as if it had fused to his left hand, and turned to his fellow supervisors. 'All right, let's get this show on the road!'

Dave rushed forward, mounting the bus steps two by two, giving Higgsy a congratulatory whack on the arm on his way up. Lizzie went next, then Sam. As Megan climbed up behind them, she noticed that the bus already smelled like forty over-excited kids.

Dave had claimed a spot at the very front and was eagerly patting the seat next to him for Sam, but Lizzie was making her way down the aisle towards the back.

'Hey, Lizzie? You gonna sit up here with us?' Megan called out, pointing to the empty front seats.

Lizzie turned and gave Megan a half-hearted grin. 'Nah, I'd rather sit back here, thanks.'

'Oh, okay.' *Shit*, Megan thought. *She's still shirty with me.* She considered following Lizzie to ask if she was okay, then decided it might be better to leave her alone until everyone had woken up a bit more. She'd be fine by the time they got to Kinglake.

Megan plonked herself down in the seat, right behind Evan and across the aisle from Sam. Salena and Kylie both seated themselves strategically so as to have visual access to all goings-on at each end of the bus. Higgsy was the last to board. He raised one hand above his head and silence slowly spread through the noisy bus as every kid mimicked his action.

'Okay,' Higgsy announced loudly. 'Final roll call, then we're off.'

As he and the kids went through their well-rehearsed call and response, Sam reached over and poked Megan's shoulder. 'You kill her dog or something?' he asked.

'What?'

Sam jerked his head towards the back of the bus. 'Lizzie. What's up?'

'We're fine.'

Megan had no intention of giving anyone, not even Sam, an inkling that anything was wrong today. Not before they'd even left Baytree. But she could see that Sam wanted to dig deeper, so she raised a finger to her lips and gestured towards Higgsy. Sam rolled his eyes and leaned back in his seat.

As Evan turned on the ignition and pulled away from Baytree Primary, Megan looked out the window at the parents all waving and blowing kisses. One mum was actually holding a handkerchief to her mouth as she waved with her other hand, reminding Megan of a wife farewelling her husband who was being sent off to war. Glancing over her shoulder at Lizzie, Megan hoped there would be as few battles as possible on this trip.

Chapter Thirty-Two
Lizzie

Children chatted and squealed all around me, including Stella, who was sitting next to her friend, Lily. But I couldn't tear my eyes away from the back of Megan's blonde head at the front of the bus. A head that stuck up a good fifteen centimetres above Higgsy's headrest beside her. I was silently willing my friend to look around, just so I could pretend I didn't care that she had.

It was schoolgirl behaviour, but I couldn't help myself. I was the only adult sitting the back of the bus, which was bringing up all sorts of memories of the kinds of kids who always used to monopolise the long bench seat below the school bus's rear window. I was never one of back-of-the-bus brigade, and even now I was regretting my decision to distance myself from Megan.

Why did I have to get so defensive with her in the car this morning? The Tonka-truck comment was completely unnecessary. Megan was trying to be diplomatic for Zara's sake. But the Rania stuff had pissed me off. Just remembering it now, I frowned and any idea that was beginning to form about apologising to Megan vanished. She had definitely crossed a line there.

I stared out the window, breathing in the wonderful feeling of driving away; away from the city, from my day-to-day and the streets I knew too well, relishing the gentle lull of the moving bus. I took a deep breath and exhaled, then opened my bag on the empty seat beside me to get my phone and text Greg. Higgsy had asked us to keep any phone usage to a bare minimum on the bus, so as not to spark the kids' separation anxiety about their own devices, but I figured this was enough of an emergency to risk triggering a few screen-addicted tweens.

On the bus now. Stella buzzing like a speed freak. Love you. x

There were no other notifications. My phone was eerily muted this morning. No message from Greg (he had an early start today) no call from Gina (the biopsy results still hadn't come through), no texts from Aunty Carmen (I had left her cooking a bacon-and-eggs feast for the kids this morning – a rare treat for a school day) and no Instagram notifications (understandable since I'd now deleted it).

Crickets on all fronts.

After I received Rania's text yesterday morning, I'd checked her Instagram only to find that she'd deleted the post with the photo of the two of us and the caption about 'new friends energising one's soul'. Did a deleted Instagram post equal a deleted friendship?

I'd texted Rania a few times over the past twenty-four hours, but had received no response. Late last night, I'd finally decided to leave her alone until I was back from camp.

A more pressing issue was how to deal with Zara's secret expedition on Saturday night. In the end, Greg and I had conferred privately yesterday morning, before he jumped on FaceTime so we could talk to our daughter together. She was grounded for a month (non-negotiable) and Aunty Carmen would be driving her to and from rehearsal tomorrow night. Once I was back, I would be doing the same. There would be no more lifts home with Ines, and I had printed out the production schedule and put it on the fridge so we could all see exactly when rehearsals started and finished. Zara was as contrite and miserable as a hungover fifteen-year-old could be all day yesterday and had barely uttered a word besides 'I'm sorry' and 'Okay'. There would be more conversations to be had when I got home, but at least I knew she was in Aunty Carmen's firm and loving hands while I was away.

The biopsy results could come through at any moment over the next couple of days. Usual protocol involved a face-to-face appointment to hear the results, but I had convinced Gina to bend the rules and call me if they came in while I was on camp. Chances were the results wouldn't come in until I was back on Wednesday, anyway, but I wanted to make sure I found out the second they did.

'Just don't tell anyone,' Gina had said. 'I can't have it getting around that I'm doing favours for staff. Not even one of my favourites.'

I'd smiled at that. 'Thanks, love.'

Gina and I were both keeping secrets.

I knew she would never betray doctor–patient confidence but had still made a point of asking her not to say anything about our appointment in front of my colleagues. The hospital was a hotbed of gossip – the one thing *Grey's Anatomy* definitely got right.

I turned to look out the window, taking in the passing view of power lines, trees and suburban rooftops, willing myself to leave behind the actualities of my life for a couple of days and enjoy the camp.

Chapter Thirty-Three
Sam

Dear dickhead,

Challenge accepted. I am writing to you – with an actual pen on actual paper – to catalogue my experiences of the school camp. A diary of sorts, hence the more formal greeting at the top of the page.

Guess where I am? On a bus with forty stinky pre-pubescent children. This trip's already rife with drama and excitement. I should double-check that Sandra Bullock isn't driving the bus.

Oh, looky here. Bridget just texted asking which drawer the takeaway menus are in. How very nineties of her. Let me just quickly reply … there we go. I texted her 'third drawer down to the left of the sink' and nearly added, 'where they've always been' but chickened out. The unsent portion of text messages is many a modern adult's version of cheap therapy.

Megan just leaned over and asked who I'm writing to. I told her it was you and she said, 'Say hi from me.'

Now you can die happy.

I think something weird is going on with Megan and Lizzie, but more on that as news comes to hand.

But first, roadkill! What's an Aussie road trip without it?

We were only about half an hour into the trip, cruising down the highway when I heard the dreaded thunk and the bus lurched slightly.

Lord Evan of Bus Manor pulled into the emergency lane, quite shaken, and Dave was up and out of his seat in no time, insisting that he check if the animal was dead and/or needed to be cleared from the road. Evan couldn't have been more pleased that Dave had volunteered. He looked like he could've used a cup of tea.

The kids were all starting to buzz when we pulled over, asking why we'd stopped and where we were, and Higgsy, Salena and Kylie were doing their best to calm them, but Dave took it upon himself to commandeer Evan's headset and announce over the speaker system that he would be 'getting off the bus for a sec to check on the wallaby, confirm that it's dead, check its pouch for a joey, check if the joey's dead, then remove it safely from the road'.

As soon as Dave grabbed the headset, I grabbed my notebook, because I knew it was gonna be good, so that's word for word what he said, followed by, 'I wouldn't recommend trying to look at the wallaby. The bus has made a bit of a mess out of it.' That's when every little face on the bus jammed itself up against the roadside windows to try to get a glimpse of the poor animal. Classic Dave. He'd be the one to say to kids, 'Whatever you do, don't push the big red button.'

So, Evan opened the door, Dave exited the bus and jogged back down the emergency lane towards the carcass (I think in bus versus wallaby, one can safely assume the bus won). Kids were going mental and shouting about Dave getting hit by a car or getting rabies from a wallaby bite. I hadn't considered the latter, but the traffic on the freeway was hardly light. Most of the Five-Sixers, along with Megan and I had now pushed our way to the back of the bus to watch the show out of the rear window. Lizzie didn't seem particularly interested in the hullabaloo, shifting forward a few seats to get out of everyone's way and staring out the window.

Like I said, weird.

Dave was on the roadside, looking left and right like he was watching a very tense tennis match, waiting for a lull in traffic, then he scuttled out onto the road and inspected the wallaby for a few seconds before grabbing it by its hind legs and dragging it off the road. The kids were screaming with gleeful horror. Higgsy and Co. were trying to placate or distract them, but this was probably the most captivating thing these kids had seen since TikTok. Megan and I shared a look of disbelief as Dave jogged back to the bus. He re-entered with loud applause and cheers and a volley of shouted questions from the Five-Sixers, who now flooded towards the front of the bus.

'Is it dead?'

'Was it heavy?'

'Are you a crocodile hunter?'

'Is that blood?' (That one caused Salena to drop back into her seat.)

'Can I go and look?'

Dave reached his hand towards Evan, who obligingly handed him the headset again.

Dave held the microphone part to his mouth and announced, 'Yes, the poor fella has gone to wallaby heaven, but they get hit by cars all the time, so he'll get to see all his mates up there.'

So glad I had this notebook.

A couple of kids started crying and Kylie quickly made her way to them to offer support (and possibly a sneaky valium), but for the most part, the Five/Six cohort took the news pretty well.

Higgsy ordered the kids back to their seats so we could drive on.

We're about half an hour away from camp now, and things have settled. Some kids are sleeping, all slack-jawed and jelly-necked, some are playing games with their hands that I don't recognise (whatever happened to a good old game of Slaps?) and some are staring out the window, thinking kid thoughts.

It's nostalgic and strangely pleasing.

So, there you have it; day one, hour one of my school-camp experience.

Chances are this could be the most entertaining and action-packed entry in 'Dear dickhead'. I'd be fine with that. I'm already exhausted.

And I didn't even pull a dead wallaby off the freeway.

Now where the hell do I get postage stamps out here?

Yours sincerely,
S.J. Hatfield, Esquire

Chapter Thirty-Four
Megan

Megan stepped off the bus and took a bracing breath of fresh country air. It was almost midday, but they'd finally arrived at Crestburn Recreational Camp.

Megan thought the kids looked like toy soldiers being tipped out of their tub. The teachers patted them on their backs as they exited, congratulating them on surviving the journey, and asking them to retrieve their belongings.

Megan and Lizzie hadn't spoken a single word to each other on the bus. It wasn't at all the start to camp she'd imagined. The two of them should have been sitting up front together, spending the whole journey taking the piss out of Sam, and giggling about Dave's unexpected knowledge of macropod death statistics. She now regretted all she'd said in the car about Rania and Zara. That didn't mean she thought she'd said anything wrong, however.

It was true that she'd struggled watching Lizzie and Rania build a friendship. She'd never thought of her and Lizzie's relationship as exclusive, but she had to admit that part of her wished Rania had never appeared at Baytree Primary. It wasn't Rania's fault, but she was the only one Megan could blame. Irrational as it was, it made her feel better. But Megan knew that both Rania and Zara were currently touchy subjects with Lizzie, and that she had chosen the worst possible time to pour salt on Lizzie's wounds.

Megan was so lost in these melancholy thoughts, that she didn't see Lizzie get off the bus until she was almost directly on top of her and leaning over to whisper in her ear.

'Nothing like a dead marsupial to kick-start a camp.' Lizzie grinned.

Megan grinned back. 'Roadkill: bringing kids together for generations.'

Lizzie laughed and pointed to the back of the bus. 'I'm gonna get my stuff.'

Megan breathed a sigh of relief as she watched her friend go. It was going to be okay. Now, Megan could just focus on making the next few days as enjoyable as possible for her friends and her, especially Lizzie.

'All right, Five-Sixers,' Higgsy announced, in his most enthusiastic sports-coach voice, 'let's bring our gear over here and form six lines in front of the grown-ups.'

He started reeling off ten names at a time, instructing each group where to stand (with minimal, hand-flapping help from Salena and Kylie).

Evan stepped up into the bus and turned back to face them all. 'I wish you the very best for a cracking camp,' he said, before climbing into his cab and almost triumphantly pushing the button to close the bus door.

Higgsy turned to the assembled kids. 'How about a big thankyou to Evan the bus driver?'

But Evan had started the engine and the bus was already rumbling its way back down the gravel drive.

'Wait, my stuff!' Sam shouted in a panic.

'It's okay,' Lizzie said. 'I got all our things.' She pointed to a collection of luggage, including two guitar cases.

'Thanks, Lizzie,' Sam said.

'No probs. I don't want to smell any of you after a couple of days without clean undies.'

'Smart,' said Sam.

'I don't get BO,' Dave chimed in.

'Not even downstairs?' Megan inquired. 'No C and BO?'

Dave looked to Megan for clarification, but she didn't have a chance to explain her acronym because a loud voice suddenly bellowed through the crisp clean air.

'*Campers!*'

The loud female voice was enough to give the Baytree kids a much-needed jolt. All eyes shifted to a short woman and a tall man, wearing matching khaki shorts and shirts, thick, knee-length brown socks and well-worn hiking boots. They reminded Megan of the rangers from the TV show *Skippy*. The robust woman looked like she could comfortably punch a hole in the side of the bus and the sinewy man had a calm, furry face.

'Welcome to Crestburn Recreational Camp,' the woman continued at a slightly lower volume. 'We're glad you finally made it.'

'Thought you might've all been dead on the side of the road somewhere,' the man added happily, drawing a severe look from his counterpart. He adjusted his stance and pointed his face to the ground.

'We're going to have a great few days. My camp name is Crouching Tiger.'

Megan heard a muffled squeak from Lizzie beside her.

'And this is Hidden Dragon,' she said with a dismissive gesture to her partner.

Megan felt a giggle rise up in her chest but pursed her

lips to suppress it. She couldn't bring herself to look at her friends, fearing she'd lose all self-control.

'You can refer to us as Tiger and Dragon respectively for the duration of the camp.'

Dave jabbed his hand into the air. 'Do we all get camp names?'

'No. It takes many years of service at Crestburn to earn your camp name.' Crouching Tiger cast a critical eye across the motley lot in front of her. 'This is a place where friendships are forged, and lifelong bonds are made.'

It sounded to Megan like this woman was paying penance. The words coming out of her mouth were encouraging, but her tone had the enthusiasm of a bored priest.

'Now, let's get you all settled in your cabins, then you can make your way to the mess hall for lunch!'

Not fifteen minutes later, the kids had been divided into their cabins, six by six, and the teachers and parents were shown to the five smaller cabins that were dotted around the larger kids' ones.

The adult cabins contained two single beds each. Megan hadn't slept in a single bed since she was Oscar's age. Higgsy, Kylie and Salena scored one each, and the two remaining cabins were divided up by gender. Dave and Sam were sharing one, and Megan and Lizzie would be bunking in the other together.

'You hungry?' Megan asked Lizzie as they dumped their bags in the small log cabin.

'Starving,' said Lizzie, flashing Megan what seemed to be a genuine grin.

'Let's go see what Tiger and Dragon have in store for us, shall we?'

Lizzie snorted. 'Don't!' she cried, holding up her hand. 'I seriously nearly lost it. Can you please never say those names out loud?'

Dave poked his head in the door. 'Hey, guys, Tiger and Dragon want a pow-wow with the grown-ups outside before tucker time.'

Hearing the camp leaders' nicknames again along with Dave's cross-cultural selection of slang sent the women over the edge and they both let out the laughs they'd denied themselves earlier.

Yep, we are gonna be fine, Megan thought happily.

Chapter Thirty-Five
Lizzie

'These are to be used overnight, in case of an emergency,' Tiger said, as Dragon distributed walkie-talkies to each of the adults assembled.

'Breaker, breaker,' Sam said into his walkie-talkie.

Dave scowled at him and shook his head.

I grinned and nudged Megan.

'And *only* in case of an emergency,' Tiger reiterated for Sam's benefit. 'The students are your sole responsibility until sunrise, as per the Crestburn agreement. On/off and volume top right,' Tiger continued. 'Channel selector next door; we're always on channel two. And PTT on the side.'

We all looked down, frantically examining our two-way radios. The only one of us who seemed to be confident with theirs was Dave, who had already clipped his walkie to the back of his belt.

I glanced at Megan and we exchanged a *What's up with Ranger Dave?* expression.

We'd only just arrived at the campsite, but already I was feeling like a different person. There was definitely something in this whole fresh air, trees and sunshine thing. The biopsy, Rania's text, my wayward teens, this morning's spat with Megan … they all felt very far away right now. Almost dreamlike. I felt grateful to my friend for providing me with this much-needed escape from real life. Out here, in this gorgeous setting, I was filled with optimism and hope. It would all be okay. I was suddenly sure of it.

'Breaker, breaker,' Sam said again. This time, his voice echoed through the walkie-talkies attached to Tiger and Dragon's matching brown belts.

Tiger snatched hers up quickly. 'Emergencies only,' she snapped, her order hissing back through Sam's two-way. Megan was suddenly overcome with a coughing fit.

'Sam, please,' Dave said, leaning over. 'Respect the kit.'

'Sorry.'

'Where's *your* cabin?' I asked Tiger, trying to distract myself from Megan, who seemed to be turning purple. 'In case we need to find you.'

Tiger shook her head. 'No need for you to know our location,' she said stiffly. 'You have your two-ways.' She turned and walked away, with her trusty sidekick, Dragon, following close behind.

'Wow,' said Sam.

Megan finally recovered enough to whisper, 'Oh my God.'

'*Deliverance*, anyone?' I asked.

'We were late,' Higgsy said. 'I'm not surprised they're a bit pissed off.'

Ah, Higgsy. Always the diplomat.

'A bit pissed off?' Sam repeated. 'She's homicidal and he's ...' he trailed off, lost for the word.

'*Deliverance*,' I repeated. 'He's pure *Deliverance*.'

'What's *Deliverance*?' asked Salena, surprising us all with her newfound powers of speech. The woman had hardly said two words since leaving school this morning and I'd noticed that she wore a perpetually worried expression.

'Y'know, "*Squeal like a pig*"?' Dave said a bit too loudly.

Kylie burst out laughing, but Salena just stared strangely at him.

'Let's not explain the plot of *Deliverance* right now,' I suggested, thinking a school camp out in the bush was neither the time nor place to discuss said movie. I received supportive noises from the group.

'I'll tell you over breakfast,' Dave reassured Salena. 'Hey, you guys heard the one about the sound of the banging on the car roof?' Dave asked in his spookiest campfire-story voice.

Higgsy clapped his hands together. 'Right, I think that's lunch!'

★★★

Higgsy and the teachers led the way to the mess hall, followed by a winding, haphazard line of Grade Five/Six kids, with the four of us bringing up the rear. One by one, the smells emanating from the main building hit the kids' nostrils and the pace was picked up. There were some very, very good smells coming from inside this building. Some kids even overtook Higgsy, forcing him to run ahead and block the front door.

'Five-Sixers,' Salena called out. 'We know you're hungry. But let's please all take our time and be courteous and show Crouching Tiger and Hidden Dragon our best manners, okay?'

'Okay!' Dave called out.

'Not a Five-Sixer, mate,' Sam said. Megan and I chuckled.

'We will enter in our cabin groups and line up quietly along the service area,' Salena continued, 'which is immediately to your left after you go in. No running. No pushing. No shouting.'

'Okay, Five-Sixers,' Higgsy called. 'You heard Miss Naidu.'

Higgsy opened the door and the glorious food smells spilled out into the midday air. I was sure I could smell freshly baked bread and my mouth watered. When the four of us finally made it into the ground-floor mess hall after the last of the kids had tottered in eagerly, we couldn't believe our eyes.

'Whoa!' Dave said, echoing my thoughts.

As Miss Naidu had indicated, there was a long service bench stretching along the left wall, and the kitchen was situated behind the main wall, slightly visible through its tall saloon doors. The service bench itself looked like something that had been conjured up by Peter Pan's Lost Boys. There were pastries, loaves of bread (that definitely looked freshly baked), platters of fresh fruit, and a selection of different pastas, including gluten-free options, with a variety of different sauces on offer. There was also an impressive selection of condiments and spreads.

Most four-star hotels wouldn't be able to compete with this spread.

'Was not expecting this,' Megan said.

I nodded. 'This is way better than any camp food I've ever seen.'

'I have nothing to compare it to, so I'll just take your word for it,' Megan said, almost running to join the long line in front of us. We quickly followed her, and as we all began to grab at the stack of sturdy plastic bowls and plates, a man wearing a white chef's hat and apron backed his way through the saloon doors, carrying another tray of aromatic goodness. Was it Anzac biscuits? The chef turned to confirm that he was indeed carrying a tray of Anzac biscuits that would impress the most ardent *Women's Weekly* devotee. He laid the tray of biscuits in a small remaining space on the long, interconnected service tables.

'Attention, kids!' Dragon said loudly.

Everyone stopped.

'We don't control your portions here, okay?' he announced. 'That's up to you guys. The most important thing is to make sure that all your classmates get well fed. Taking care of each other is what camp's all about.'

He turned and went back into his kitchen, and I was left struggling to compute that the loud, friendly chef was the same silent, submissive man we'd met earlier.

I glanced around the room, searching for my daughter. Stella was sitting with Lily and a few of the girls from her class, and they were all giggling and munching away happily at their food. She looked up and gave me a wave and I waved back. I couldn't see Lola anywhere, but when I glanced at Sam, standing on the other side of the table, flapping his empty plastic bowl back and forth, he looked worried. I followed his eyeline to see a miserable-looking Lola sitting at the end of another table, far from Stella's. There were kids sitting near her, but none of them were talking to her. I briefly considered going over to Stella to ask her to invite Lola to sit with her, but decided it wasn't my place. Yet, my heart ached for the two girls and their fragile friendship. Camp was supposed to be fun with your friends; making memories that last a lifetime. I noticed that Sam was watching me watching Lola, and I quickly glanced back down at the delicious array of pastas. The last thing I needed was a lunchtime confrontation about our daughters' issues.

Our plates loaded up with excellent camp feast, we turned to find a spot to sit.

'Over here,' Megan said, jerking her head towards a half-empty table at the far end of the room.

A few kids, including Logan – the kid Higgsy had described as the 'evil little Pied Piper' – sat at one end of the table, while Caleb sat alone at the opposite end. We sat in the middle and I plonked down next to Caleb, eager to tuck into my delicious-looking carbonara.

'How's it going, Caleb?'

'Good, thanks, Lizzie.' He smiled, but he was pale and had a thin sheen of sweat across his brow.

'Hey, mate, you okay? Want me to get you some water?'

Caleb shook his head.

'Water's pretty good,' I cajoled. 'Just a little sip?'

'I'm fine, thanks,' Caleb said.

'You sure …?'

But I was interrupted when Higgsy stood up and clapped his hands loudly.

'Five-Sixers, just to let you know that this afternoon's activities will run concurrently. Half of you will commence with kayaking …'

This was met with murmurings of approval.

'While the other half will engage the rope course.'

I noted that mention of a rope course was also met with a positive buzz. *Winning so far, Higgsy*, I thought affectionately.

Seemingly out of nowhere, Tiger appeared behind Higgsy and made her own announcement.

'The rope course is an excellent chance for you all to build confidence with your peers,' she explained, 'by engaging in exercises of trust and teamwork.'

All positive buzz fizzled out.

'We will meet at the north gate at precisely fourteen hundred hours,' Tiger ordered. 'Then divide into our groups and proceed to the aforementioned activities.' She stood for a moment, looking like she might have more to say, but then turned to leave.

Dave began rhythmically tapping the bottom of his cutlery on the table, quietly chanting, 'Rope course! Rope course!'

I turned to give Caleb a gentle nudge and make a scary monster face. He giggled and I was hit with a sharp pang of missing my other three kids. I was about to ask Caleb if he'd ever kayaked before when he looked over my shoulder and his expression switched from happy to hurt in a split second.

I turned around just in time to see Logan making faces at Caleb, and leaning over to whisper to some other boys, who were all sniggering.

I frowned and turned back to Caleb, lowering my voice. 'Did something happen with the other kids?'

Caleb looked panicked. 'Don't be mad at anyone, okay?'

'What do you mean?'

'They don't like me,' Caleb answered. 'But don't say anything. It doesn't matter.'

I wondered what these kids had said to make him look so terrified at the idea of me confronting them. 'That's not true,' I said. 'Kids can be arseholes sometimes and it *does* matter if they say something.'

Caleb's lips curled into an involuntary smile.

'But you'll be fine,' I said, glancing over at my mates. 'You'll find your tribe, I promise.'

Chapter Thirty-Six
Sam

Dear dickhead,

Welcome to the end of day one!

I wasn't planning on updating you any further, assuming the bus ride would be the day's highlight.

Not so.

Where to begin?

The camp leaders call themselves Crouching Tiger and Hidden Dragon. I'm just going to leave that there for you.

Hidden Dragon (the Sonny to Crouching Tiger's Cher) is also the resident cook, and based on the lunch he served, used to be a personal chef to the Queen of Sheba. The food was preposterously good.

After lunch, we were divvied up to help with different activities. Higgsy, Dave and I were allocated to a ropes course, with Sheba's chef leading the way. (I've told you about Higgsy, yeah? Sports teacher? Cute as a button? Well now you know.)

The kids were gagging to get into it, but our fearless leader had to give a very detailed safety briefing first, which seemed a tad over the top; the highest rope on the course was barely a metre off the ground. There was a lot of laughter once the kids were allowed to start the course. Kids wobbled and swayed their way through, buoyed by constant encouragement from Higgsy, who has a contagious enthusiasm. It didn't take long for Dave and me to join in, yelling all sorts of inspirational one-liners. I thought Higgsy was telling us off when he yelled, 'Stop!' but it wasn't our string of sporting clichés that had upset him. He'd actually just done another head count (Higgsy loves a head count) and had discovered that we were down one kid.

Dave had been the first to pick it. Logan was missing. In brief, Logan is the sort of kid I'd happily lose, but the stakes were a bit higher from a teacher's perspective. Everyone started yelling his name in every direction, which went on for a good minute. I wasn't sure it was the most effective approach to a search and rescue, but I was scared that if I ran off into the bush to find the kid that it would be my remains discovered weeks later. You know what my sense of direction's like. It was while I was cursing my human compass that the little shit came sauntering out of the bush and back into the clearing with the rope course.

You could tell he was very happy with all the attention and commotion. He was so unfazed by the stress he'd caused, in the most unlikable way. And his excuse for wandering off? He saw a lizard and thought it'd make a great pet.

Logan was winning big points. Not only did he do exactly what he was told not to do (i.e. piss off on his own without telling anyone), he also wanted to kidnap a wild lizard and keep it captive for his own amusement. What a guy.

Higgsy was doing his best to stay calm and reprimand him properly at the same time, but Logan kept telling him to 'chill'.

HooooWEE, I wanted to hit him. For Higgsy. And me.

Higgsy continued his multi-pronged explanation of why Logan's behaviour was not okay.

When Higgsy finished, Logan shrugged and said, 'It was just a fucking lizard.'

I had to think of rainbows and unicorns and fairy floss to force my fists to unclench. This kid. I hope he spots a deadly snake he'd like to try to befriend.

Yours in murderous thoughts directed at intolerable youths,
Headmaster Samuel J. Hatfield, M.Ed.

Chapter Thirty-Seven
Megan

Megan returned to the campsite with Lizzie and the rest of her group to discover that Dragon had set up afternoon tea outside the main building. While Megan, Lizzie and the rest of their group had been kayaking around the small lake on the edge of the campsite, Dragon had evidently been setting up trestle tables in the sunshine, laden with frittata, fresh fruit, crudités and a selection of sandwiches fit for a high tea. The kids happily descended on the food. Once again, Dragon's surprising culinary prowess had blown everyone away.

Megan had built up quite the appetite, paddling through the still, clear water, and was ready to indulge in a bit of frittata and fruit, before that night's scheduled hot dog and marshmallow dinner around the campfire.

Although they'd been in different kayaks during the activity, Megan and Lizzie had had a lot of fun splashing each other with their paddles and shouting out across the water to one another over the past couple of hours. Megan felt almost giddy with the fun of it all, and like a schoolgirl herself as she and Lizzie approached the trestle table where Logan and a couple of other boys were hotly debating who would win in a fight between various mythical creatures and Marvel superheroes.

The two women listened as they pondered Thor versus a werewolf (the consensus was Thor would win that one easily), Hulk versus a kraken (that was a split decision, two to one in favour of the kraken because the ocean offers a home-ground advantage) and Ironman versus a vampire (a much trickier proposition for the trio of boys; Logan argued the vampire wouldn't be able to bite Ironman through his suit, but was countered with the idea that, depending on the vampire's age and strength, Ironman wouldn't stand a chance).

Megan was suddenly struck with inspiration and a vivid memory from her own childhood. She nudged Lizzie, then turned to address the boys.

'What about Aussie creatures?'

The boys gave Megan the look kids often gave adults when they try to join their conversations.

'What, like a bunyip or something?' Logan scoffed.

'Good guess,' said Megan. 'But bunyips are pretty harmless if you know what you're doing.'

The other two boys racked their brains for another Australian beast, but Megan wasn't waiting.

'Around these parts,' she said quietly, 'it's the drop bears you wanna watch out for.'

'Oh yeah, true,' Lizzie said with a sombre nod.

'What the hell's a drop bear?' Logan asked, unconvinced.

'They're like koalas,' explained Megan, 'but a lot less cuddly.'

Logan's two lackeys leaned in.

'Drop bears are twice the size of a normal koala,' Lizzie continued, 'with claws and fangs that can rip a fully grown crocodile apart.'

'Where do they live?' Logan asked sceptically.

'Here,' Megan said, casting her eyes up and around. 'This is their natural habitat.'

'So why didn't those weirdos tell us about them?' Logan asked.

Lizzie chuckled. 'If everyone knew about drop bears there'd be no more school camps.'

'Do they only attack crocodiles?' one of the other boys asked.

'No,' Megan said. 'They kill crocs for sport. But their favourite food is human flesh.'

Megan felt like maybe she and Lizzie were pushing the boundaries of responsible adulting, but she also felt like Logan needed a scare. She'd seen the faces he'd been pulling at Caleb at lunch today. He was a bully and a ringleader. A dangerous combo.

'The weird thing is,' Megan said, leaning down to the three boys and resting her hands on her knees, 'they seem to prefer eating kids.'

Lizzie shrugged. 'I guess you guys are just tastier.'

'Yeah, well, nobody likes old meat,' Logan said to Lizzie.

Megan's fingers twitched with the temptation to smack him across the face.

'What a crock,' Logan said. 'Attacking crocs, eating kids. It's *all* a crock.'

Megan looked intently into each boy's face. 'Sometimes it's good to know when someone's telling the truth.'

Logan's confidence faltered as he stared into Megan's trustworthy adult face.

'Why would I lie?' she asked, furrowing her brow. 'Come on, Lizzie.'

The silence left behind them gave Megan a wicked satisfaction. The two friends had to stifle their giggles as they walked away, their plates piled high with frittata, and only allowed themselves a discreet high-five as they sat down to enjoy their afternoon tea.

Chapter Thirty-Eight
Sam

Dear dickhead,

Jumping forward from young Logan's near-punch experience (this camp really is back-to-back action, so I'm grabbing time to write to you when I can).

Afternoon tea went a long way to appeasing us all. Dragon must've been up well before dawn to have all of that food prepped and ready to go. Either that or he has an army of Paul Bocuse–trained Oompa Loompas. I took some discreet photos on my phone, not just so I can show you proof of this amazing food, but so I can analyse it and try to replicate it!

This chapter of 'Dear dickhead' isn't really camp-related, but still worth a correspondence.

Out of nowhere, while all the kids were banging on about the disco and their costumes and Logan running off, Dave asked if I liked Megan. That way.

I know, right?!

I told him what I've always told you: she's one of my best friends. Then I reminded him about my designs on Rachel, of which he's well aware. And he just looked at me and nodded and said 'okay' over and over again, driving me nuts with his sanguine acceptance.

You know I've allowed myself the odd Megan-and-me fantasy, but that was way back when, when I only really saw her as a hottie. I didn't know her properly. But now I do, and her hotness is way down the list of her greatest attributes. Which is not to undermine her physical beauty, as if either of us ever would, but there are just heaps more things that I value so much about Megs now. It makes me despair for idiotic straight dudes (both of us included) who waste vast swathes of time objectifying women. I make no claim to being enlightened on this front, just observing my own idiotic straight maleness.

Although a couple of those early fantasies had developed well beyond your typical sexual scenario. Totes enlightened.

Have you ever thought I – y'know – wanted Megan? Because Dave obviously thinks that's the case. I just don't want to be inadvertently sending weird signals to Megan. I don't think I am. But refer to straight male idiocy.

It feels like 4 a.m. and the sun's still up. I'm already reminiscing about simpler times on the bus all those thousands of seconds ago.

Yours idiotically,
Prof. Sam J. Hatfield, PhD

Chapter Thirty-Nine
Lizzie

Sam and Dave took their performance positions on the other side of the fire, guitars at the ready. Megan grinned and nudged me.

'Play "Jessie's Girl"!' she shouted.

'Play "Khe Sanh"!' I called.

Megan and I chortled into our hot dogs as Sam and Dave shook their heads at us. We felt our age as teachers and students alike stared blankly at us, their knowledge of late-seventies and early-eighties chart toppers clearly limited.

It was dusk and we were all sitting on logs around the large campfire, chomping on delicious homemade hot dogs – courtesy of our camp-chef extraordinaire, Dragon – throwing bush detritus into the fire and looking forward to some musical stylings. Actually, I couldn't be sure the kids were as excited as the adults, but at this point I didn't really care. I was happy. For a brief moment in time, everything felt good.

I'd spoken to Greg when we got back from kayaking and also checked in with Aunty Carmen and the kids. Well, Archie and Max, anyway. Zara had 'too much homework' to come to the phone. I would be confronted with a very salty teenager when I got home, who would beg and plead to have her grounding punishment overturned. I would refuse, she would get even saltier and it would all escalate, with voices raised and doors slammed. But right now, I didn't want to think about any of that, so I pushed all thoughts of teen confrontations from my mind and focused on the flickering fire.

Fire would forever be the most magnetic and entertaining element for humans of all ages, evidenced by the sound of happy nattering Five-Sixers all around me, and the feeling of calm in my body right now. Overlapping, primary school conversations formed a strangely soothing cacophony, and marshmallows impaled on the longest sticks available were dangling in the fire, being toasted with varying levels of success. Most were extracted from the flames looking like, well, burnt marshmallows, but not a one went to waste. No matter the extent of a marshmallow's char, they were all consumed by their toasters with pride.

I looked across the fire at Stella and my heart filled. I was so glad that my baby girl was here to share this night with me. Stella looked at me, smiled and jerked her head towards Sam and Dave. I grinned back. She was quite possibly the only child here who was looking forward to their performance. Lola had her head down and was staring into her lap, looking like she'd rather be anywhere else.

'Okay, bit of shush everyone!' Higgsy announced. He turned to Megan and me. 'That includes you two,' he said with a wink.

'Copy that,' Megan said, giving him a mock salute.

'Best behaviour,' I said, crossing my heart.

'Good evening, Baytree Fives and Sixes!' Dave announced grandly. 'We are Your Happy Manfriend!'

As the kids and teachers all burst into applause, I turned to Megan. 'They're what now?'

'Best not to ask,' Megan said.

Higgsy shot us a look.

Sorry, I mouthed.

'Thank you, thank you,' Dave said, offering multiple mini-bows. 'You're too kind.'

'Tonight, ladies and gentlemen, boys and girls,' Sam continued, 'is but a teaser before the main event at tomorrow night's disco to end all discoes!'

The kids and teachers cheered.

'But before we force you to get up and dance tomorrow night,' Dave said, 'we are here tonight to provide some mood music. Some soothing sounds. Some acoustic stylings suitable to the setting at hand.'

'So, without any further ado …' Sam said to Dave in a low voice.

'So, without any further ado,' Dave echoed, 'please enjoy these sweet, sweet tunes.'

The duo began strumming a tune, and when Sam sang the opening line of the Bruno Mars classic 'Count on Me', I felt a warm rush, and knew that I was going to tell Megan about the biopsy before this camp was over. It wasn't fair for her to know before Greg, but I needed to share the load with someone who truly cared. Someone who was here, now. It felt ridiculous to carry a potential cancer diagnosis alone when I was with a friend like Megan. I'd tell her tomorrow night after the disco. Greg would understand.

I slipped my arm through Megan's and lay my head on her shoulder. She rested her head on mine and the two of us relaxed into each other as the boys filled the still, cool air with their music.

The children had hushed. Some had put their arms around each other, swaying out of time and unaware that, in an innocent way, they were doing the song's bidding.

I glanced up at Megan, wanting to share the observation,

when I noticed the way she was looking at Sam. And it wasn't just a look of admiration and respect for her talented mate. There was more going on in her look than that.

I looked back into the fire, my mind racing.

Sam? Was Sam the one Megan had been secretly texting and blushing over at the twins' birthday party? I knew Megan had been keeping something from me, but *Sam*? I couldn't wrap my head around it. Had I been that distracted by everything going on that I hadn't seen the signs?

I gave my friend a gentle nudge. 'I'd be happy for you,' I said, staring ahead at Sam and Dave.

'Happy if …?'

'If there was something going on. If you were in love.'

Megan frowned. 'I'm not.'

'Megan, if there's someone special, then they're special to me, too.'

'I know that.'

'So, you can tell me.'

'I know. But there's seriously nothing going on.'

But I could hear the nervousness in her voice. I didn't understand why, but I knew she was lying to me. She was seeing someone. Maybe it was Sam, maybe not. But for whatever reason, she didn't want to tell her best friend. And it hurt. Especially when I'd been there for her after Eddie.

I sat up straighter on the log, and ever so slightly, pulled away.

Chapter Forty
Megan

Did Lizzie somehow find out about Harry? Megan thought, as Lizzie sat up and pulled away from her.

She didn't understand where Lizzie's questions had come from, but she didn't want to worry about that. Right now, she wanted to enjoy the campfire performance. Sam looked different in the firelight. The flickering glow changed his features. Dave looked the same as always, but there was definitely something different about Sam tonight.

It was the second time in two days that Megan had watched Sam performing, but tonight it seemed as if she was hearing him sing for the first time. His voice was so pure and fragile, like he was scared to make too much noise, but somehow that made it more captivating. He was lost in the chorus and Dave was harmonising beautifully, and feelings began to stir in Megan that she wasn't ready to confess to anyone, least of all herself. And she didn't even know if these feelings could be trusted. It was *Sam*, for fuck's sake! He was singing so very beautifully, just like he had at Applewood. She pushed these thoughts to the side and reached forward to toast a marshmallow.

The song ended and Sam's eyes fluttered open, bringing him back to the present. 'That,' Sam said dramatically, 'was our last tune, folks.'

Everyone booed, including Megan.

'I know,' Dave added, 'it's devastating for everyone.'

'But all good things must come to an end,' Sam said.

'And all good Baytree kids,' Dave said, 'must get a good night's sleep.'

This was met by more friendly booing from the student body.

Sam lifted one arm in the air. 'We've been Your Happy Manfriend! Goodnight!'

Megan and Lizzie cheered along with everyone else, and then, peppered with pleas and protests, the teachers started wrangling the students back to their cabins.

Megan stood up and turned to Lizzie. 'I'm going to go wash the campfire smell off me,' she said. 'See you back at the cabin.'

'Okay,' Lizzie said, and Megan noted that the slightly steely tone had returned to her voice.

★★★

Megan was leaving the women's block, fresh from a shower and wrapped in her knee-length, pale-blue dressing gown, just as Sam was heading towards the male toilet block next door.

As soon as she spotted him, she burst into applause. 'Bravo!' she cried. 'Brilliant performance!'

Sam bowed low and tipped an invisible hat to her. 'Thank you, m'lady!'

They both laughed, before Megan felt a shift in the air between them. She didn't think she could ever remember a time in all the years she'd known Sam when she felt awkward with him, but in this moment, standing outside a toilet block, wrapped in a flimsy gown, she was struggling to find words and feeling embarrassed. She could tell Sam was in the same boat.

'So ... how's the water pressure?' Sam said, breaking the silence.

'Shit, but the water's hot enough.'

'Well that's something.'

'It is indeed.'

This was excruciating. Megan couldn't stand it for a second longer. 'Okay, I'm knackered. See you tomorrow.'

'Yep, bye.'

What was that? Megan thought as she walked back to the cabin. Whatever it was, she wasn't sure she was keen on finding the answer.

Chapter Forty-One
Sam

Dear dickhead,

It may have only felt like 4 a.m. earlier, but now it is actually pretty damn close to 4 a.m.

Dave is asleep, sleeping the sleep of a hero. And I am literally writing to you by the silvery moonlight.

An hour ago, when I stepped outside our cabin after being woken by the blood-curdling screams of many children, I felt like I'd walked into the middle of a jailbreak. There were torches flashing everywhere and bodies running in random patterns. I was grateful for the lack of gunfire that usually accompanies a jailbreak (in my experience). Then I spotted Dave, fully dressed and wearing a head torch, marching towards me through the chaos. He vaulted the steps to our cabin and took a place next to me on the small landing. He must've seen the look on my face, but the words he spoke didn't help. He clapped a hand on my shoulder and said, 'Don't worry, Sam. It's just a snake in one of the kids' cabins.'

Lizzie and Megan had emerged by now as well and were helping to herd the children towards the front of our cabin. It looked like forty Jurassic fireflies approaching. Higgsy suddenly appeared on my other side, clipboard in shaky hand, and started calling out the role, and the monotonous familiarity of it seemed to settle the kids a bit.

Everyone was accounted for, even Logan. (An image of a Logan-shaped bulge in an anaconda's belly flashed through my mind and I let it linger for a moment.)

I suggested that I grab one of our two-way radios and called Tiger and Dragon. Dave reminded me gently that they were only to be contacted in case of an emergency. I gently reminded Dave that there was a fucking snake in one of the kids' cabins. Higgsy insisted we should leave the camp leaders to deal with the situation, but Dave insisted he could take care of it. He tried to reassure the adults present that we were overreacting by asking the kids very loudly if anyone had been bitten, which sent the camp back into pandemonium. Kids started screaming again and grabbing at their pyjamas like someone had just tipped a bucket of spiders (or indeed snakes) all over them.

By the way Dave rolled his eyes, he apparently believed this to be a gross overreaction.

Then he walked down the steps of our landing, leaving me and Higgsy trying to reduce the panic with help from Megan and Lizzie, who were making their way from child to child, placing hands on cheeks and shoulders like evangelists with bad aim.

I shone my torch in Dave's direction and watched as he found a large, thick stick, held it in front of his face and gave it a 'this'll do' nod. Higgsy had noticed too and called to him, but Dave ignored him and marched deliberately towards the empty cabin. Empty but for the snake, that is.

A hush fell over the assembled kids as they watched Dave approach the serpent's den. He arrived at the door to the cabin, briefly turning back to his captive audience to give them a quick wink, then stepped inside. Everyone was silent. Waiting. Higgsy, Lizzie, Megan and I took a couple of tentative steps towards the cabin, craning our necks to hear any hint of noise coming from within. Megan looped her arm through mine and clutched my wrist, which was painful, but I was grateful to share my fear.

We heard Dave's voice from inside the cabin moments later, sounding positively ebullient. 'Wow! She's beautiful.'

Lizzie, Megan and I looked at each other, frozen in the face of Dave's imminent demise. The light from Dave's headtorch flickered through the doorway and onto the ground outside, suggesting that he was about to come out. And he did. Everyone took a collective step backwards as Dave made quite the grand entrance back into the night. His stick of choice was tucked under his left arm and his smile was as big as I had ever seen it. In his right hand, he held the tail end of a very large snake. Not kidding, dickhead. This was a snake large enough to be left well enough alone by the most daring of daredevils. The kids gasped, yelped and clutched at each other. I'm pretty sure I got a whiff of wee.

Megan's nails were digging into my wrist and I had to tell her to loosen her grip lest she leave puncture wounds. She apologised, but her nails remained firmly dug into my skin.

As if we were all on a fun-filled wilderness safari, Dave happily informed the group that 'this sweetheart' was 'just a harmless little python'.

We all shuffled backwards as one while Dave slowly lowered his sweetheart onto the ground and watched with pride as she slithered away into the darkness of the bush behind the cabins.

Dave made sure the snake was out of sight before walking — casual as you please — back over to us.

Megan shook her head and said, 'Dark Horse Dave' as she finally relaxed her talons.

It took at least another hour to settle everyone down, especially after Higgsy asked Dave to do a sweep of every cabin before being able to coax the kids back to their beds.

All's quiet now. Dave's snoring a bit, but I'll forgive him, because I'm sharing a cabin with Indiana Jones.

Yours dripping in leftover terror,
Master Sam J. Hatfield, Order of the Phoenix

Chapter Forty-Two
Lizzie

I woke from one of those horrible anxiety dreams where everything was going wrong. We were late to Max's soccer game, and I couldn't find a park. Then when I finally found a spot a woman in uniform told me I couldn't park there, and pointed to a spot that was miles away and told me to move it. I pulled out my phone to call one of the other parents, but I couldn't make my fingers press any of the buttons. I was so frustrated I started to cry. That's when I woke up.

I lay completely still for a moment, trying to get my bearings, as I waited for the anxiety to subside. After last night's snake encounter, it was no wonder I was a hot mess.

It wasn't even 6 a.m. I couldn't have been asleep for much more than an hour. I still smelled like last night's campfire, the smoke having infused into every follicle of hair, so I decided to have a shower before the rest of the Baytree cohort descended on the toilet block. Megan was still asleep, so I threw on my dressing gown, grabbed my toiletries bag and crept out as quietly as I could.

As I approached the cinder-block showers, I heard a small whimper. I walked around the corner of the building to investigate and saw a pyjama-clad Lola sitting at a picnic table, her face wet and red.

'Lola, what's up, sweetie?'

She started to cry harder, so I rushed over and sat down beside her.

'Hey, honey, what's the matter?' I said, putting my arm around her. 'Are you still freaked out about the snake last night?'

Lola shook her head and sniffed. 'No, it's not that.' She took a deep breath. 'It's just … my mum doesn't even know where I am.'

I believed her. From what I knew about Sam's ex-wife, Bridget wouldn't have the foggiest idea about the location of her daughter's camp.

'Oh, sweetie,' I said, 'if I didn't have those stalking apps on my phone, I wouldn't know where my kids were half the time.' This was a lie (for the most part), but I wasn't going to tell Lola that.

'Rachel knows,' Lola continued. 'Before leaving, she informed me that I might glimpse a real flying fox.'

'Wow,' I said. 'That'd be cool.'

Lola started crying again and her words fell out in bursts. 'Rachel's a far superior mum than mine in every way and … I desperately want her to be my *real* mum, but … I … I've been showing off because I … want her to like me and want … her to be my mum, but … now Stella …'

Lola took a long, shaky breath, looking to me for permission to go on. I stroked her hair out of her face and smiled reassuringly. 'It's okay.'

'Now Stella positively hates me,' Lola said with a fresh sob.

'No, sweetie.'

'She does, she … I … Stella was Rachel's student first, and her favourite, but now I … I think I've replaced Stella in that regard and … I did that … on purpose.'

'Lola,' I said, cupping her face in my hands. 'Stella doesn't hate you, okay? She's just feeling a bit ... overlooked right now. But I know my kid and I know she loves you.'

Lola seemed unconvinced but mumbled something that sounded vaguely affirmative. I felt that familiar pang of affection for someone in pain. For as long as I'd been a parent, I felt like I'd been flying blind, without any memory of my own mother's wisdom and care. But the one thing I'd always been good at was offering care where it was needed most. And Lola needed care.

'You're both good kids,' I said gently. 'Good people.'

'Do you really think Stella loves me?'

'I know she does. Friends go through all sorts of things together, and not always good things. But it's when you get through these times that you become better friends.'

Lola looked like she might be giving that some thought. I could feel my own tears rising as thoughts of Megan, my mum and my own family started to fill my head. I gave Lola a hug and smiled.

'Come on, sweetie. I'll take you back to your cabin and you can get a bit more sleep. I think we all need it after last night.'

★★★

A few hours later, the camp's morning activities were in full swing. Salena, Megan and I were put in charge of supervising a group of ten kids at the ring toss, and although there was residual friction between Megan and me, we were having fun. It was the perfect low-key activity after a night of interrupted sleep and impromptu snake wrangling.

'Nice work, mate!' I said, when Caleb landed five rings in a row on the wooden stick. 'You're a natural!'

A beaming Caleb sat back down on the log with the other kids. Megan gave me a wink of approval. We both knew this kid needed all the encouragement he could get. I was happy to note that Logan was in Sam and Dave's group.

Halfway through the game, amid cheers and jeers from the opposing teams, conversation between some of the kids turned to the disco. Megan and I sat at either end of the log, close enough to be within earshot of the kids' chatter.

One of the boys said something about kissing, receiving a chorus of 'Eeeww' from the girls.

'We can kiss whoever we want, anyway,' Stella said loudly, standing up to have her go. 'And it doesn't have to be a stupid boy.'

It was the boys' turn to react with noises of disgust and delight and I felt proud of my girl.

'All right, Five-Sixers,' Salena said. 'That's enough of that.'

'Zara's in love with a girl,' Stella continued, landing a ring to the left of its target.

I frowned and stared at my daughter. 'What?'

'Ines. The one she does all the theatre stuff with,' Stella said, keeping her focus on the game. 'They've hooked up and everything. Nessa says it's all over Snapchat.'

Zara was gay and I didn't know? I was reeling. This couldn't be right. But if it was, I didn't know my daughter. Not at all. I was officially the worst parent on earth.

Stella threw her last ring and it landed perfectly on the stake, spinning to a stop as her team cheered, all talk of burgeoning teenage homosexuality forgotten in an instant of sporting glory. I cheered along, but inside I was dying of shame. I needed to get away from here.

'Lizzie?'

Megan was looking at me. Her expression was the catalyst I needed to snap me out of the temporary paralysis that had taken hold. I needed to call Greg. Now.

I walked quickly towards the lake and pulled out my phone, just as Megan caught up. I appreciated my friend's concern, but I needed a moment, a few moments, actually.

'Megs,' I said, turning to show Megan the mobile phone in my hand, 'can just I have a minute?'

'Jesus, don't call Zara now.'

'I'm calling Greg.'

'Okay, but before you do I think you need to calm down and —'

'Megan, I just found out that Zara's "hooked up" with another girl,' I snapped, 'and I didn't even know! Her own mum! What kind of mother does that make me?' I dropped my head and pressed the tips of my fingers hard into my forehead.

'Lizzie,' Megan said gently. 'There's no way you could have known. I mean, when I saw her lying in Reuben's lap, I definitely thought ...'

Megan stopped, making me look up. 'What?' I asked. 'When did you see her?'

Megan swallowed nervously and let out a deep sigh. 'Last Wednesday night,' she said. 'Zara was in the city with Reuben and Ines and some other kids. She made me promise not to tell you.'

I felt unstable on my feet. 'You're telling me this now?'

'Teenagers keep secrets,' Megan said. 'It doesn't mean Zara's a bad kid. It's no different from you keeping secrets when you were her age.'

I wasn't going to let Megan derail this conversation. This was Zara we were talking about, and I was going to stay

317

on topic. I thought of the car ride when Megan had also offered me unsolicited advice on parenting teens, but this time it was too much to bear.

'Thanks, Megs,' I said in a shaky voice. 'I feel heaps better now, knowing that I don't have the first fucking clue what's going on in my daughter's life, that she's lying to me and that she'd rather confide in *you*. But as long as you know Zara isn't a bad kid, I'll be able to sleep at night.'

'Lizzie, please, I'm sorry I didn't tell you, but I —'

'*Megan!*'

We both turned at the sound of Salena's voice. She was running towards us, a look of alarm on her face.

'Someone is here looking for you,' she said, puffed from her quick sprint. 'And she's really angry.'

Chapter Forty-Three
Megan

When Megan arrived back at the campfire, with Lizzie close behind, Dragon was talking to a slim, middle-aged woman Megan had never seen before. The woman was dressed in grey linen pants and a soft-pink cashmere coat, and a grey-blue scarf was wrapped around her neck. She had long, brown, wavy hair and was holding a pair of large sunglasses as she waved her arms around, seemingly berating Dragon. Whoever this woman was, she had style. And money.

Dragon's hands were held up in surrender, and as Megan got closer, she began to decipher the woman's words.

'... and I am not trespassing! I just want to talk to the woman!'

A few of the Baytree kids had formed a circle around the two adults and Megan half expected them to start chanting, '*Fight! Fight! Fight!*'

'Excuse me, madam,' Salena interjected. 'This is Megan Wylie.'

The woman spun on her pumps and Dragon took the opportunity to back away slowly, his hands still in a halfway stick-'em-up position. The children parted to make way as the woman approached Megan at pace. After her recent confrontation with Lizzie, Megan felt warmed up and ready for whatever the hell this was.

She was wrong.

The woman stopped a couple of feet away and looked Megan up and down. There was something familiar about her striking features.

'Hello,' Megan said. 'Can I help you?'

'*Puttana!*' the woman spat.

'All right, everyone!' Megan heard Salena say as she shooed the students away from the escalating situation. 'Let's go and see how the other group is going.'

Despite a few protests, she successfully managed to usher the goggling group away, but Megan saw that Lizzie had stayed, and that Dave was now standing beside her, looking as worried and confused as Megan felt right now.

'Excuse me, but who are you?' she asked the woman.

The woman took another step towards Megan, who didn't budge an inch.

'I'm Francesca D'Angelo,' she said in an icy tone. 'Harry's mother.'

Megan drew in a sharp breath. She had been doling out advice to Lizzie about secrets, when she hadn't told her best friend about Harry because she thought Lizzie would judge her harshly. But whatever judgement she might've received from Lizzie about dating a very young man, would now pale in comparison to keeping it a secret from her.

Francesca was staring at Megan, her perfectly shaped eyebrows arched, awaiting an explanation. *Harry has your eyes*, she thought.

'Is Harry all right?'

'No, Harry is not all right,' Francesca snapped. 'Harry has been taking money out of my account to buy you expensive jewellery. Harry has quit his job and is talking about moving to the other side of town. Harry had his heart broken by a *much* older, divorced woman who decided to use and discard him like a plaything.'

Lizzie stepped forward. 'Wait, the guy from your writing class?'

Megan turned to look at her friend, but all she could do was nod in answer.

Sam and Higgsy, who had presumably been brought up to speed by Salena, ran over and stopped a few feet behind Francesca. Megan wanted to sink through the ground.

'Do you like seducing boys?' Francesca asked.

'He's nineteen,' Megan said, not helping her case.

'He's a *boy*!' Francesca shouted.

'Excuse me,' Higgsy said, stepping forward. 'My name's Mr Higgs. I work at Baytree Primary.'

Francesca turned and smiled coolly. 'Hello, Mr Higgs.'

'This is a private school camp,' Higgsy said calmly.

'I am aware of where I am,' Francesca answered just as calmly. 'My son told me the name of this camping ground, which is how I found you.'

Harry told her? Megan thought in disbelief. *He knew she was coming here to attack me?*

'Maybe this is a conversation for another time,' Higgsy suggested.

'No,' Francesca said. 'I have driven fifty minutes to get here, so this is a conversation for right now.'

'Mrs D'Angelo,' Megan said. 'I've already told Harry that I have absolutely no intention of keeping the jewellery and will be giving it back to him. Also, I think you should know that our relationship was entirely mutual.'

'I'm sure that's what you tell yourself,' Francesca said. 'Paedophiles use the same logic to justify their actions.'

'Hey, hey, hang on.' Sam walked around to stand beside Megan.

Francesca was becoming increasingly frustrated with the interruptions. 'Is this awful woman your friend?'

'Yes, she is,' Sam said. 'And she's not awful.'

'That's a matter of opinion,' Francesca said.

'You don't know her,' Sam said.

'I know enough,' Francesca countered. 'My son is a mess. He is devastated. Why do you think I've come here? She should know! She should know how she has hurt my boy and hurt me! Not to mention the fact that he has stolen five thousand dollars from my account! My boy is not a thief.' The woman thrust out her hand, pointing her finger in Megan's face. '*She* is the one who is responsible for my beautiful boy's behaviour!'

'It's not her fault that your son did that to you,' Sam said.

'Is it not?' Francesca asked. 'You have children, I'm guessing.'

'I do,' Sam said. 'One of them is here on this camp.'

'And how old is your child?'

'She's eleven,' Sam answered.

'Ah!' Francesca nodded. 'And can you imagine your daughter, at the age of nineteen, informing you that she was in a sexual relationship with a man twice her age, and that she spent five thousand dollars on him? Five thousand dollars of *your* savings?'

Megan could tell straightaway that Sam couldn't imagine it. She knew he was the kind of father who would put a stop to it at all costs. She also knew in her heart that Sam would never say this to a complete stranger about his friend.

'It's nobody's business but Megan and Harry's,' Sam argued.

'I'm his mother,' Francesca said.

'Harry isn't a child,' Sam said. 'He's responsible for his choices.'

'What sort of woman seduces a boy?' Francesca said, turning her attention back to Megan. 'My Harry is a good boy! You've ruined him!'

But Megan had had enough of this public degradation. 'Mrs D'Angelo, I'm sorry that Harry is upset, but I won't be told off by his mum for our consensual relationship.'

Francesca glared at Megan, her eyes burning with hatred.

'Mrs D'Angelo,' Higgsy said. 'This is a children's camp.'

'Yeah, it's really not appropriate,' Dave added.

Francesca turned and surveyed the group of adults with a look of pure scorn. 'Absolutely disgraceful,' she said, then marched off in the direction of the carpark.

Sam put his arm around Megan's shoulders and she immediately slumped against him, feeling all the bravado drain out of her.

'You okay?' he asked.

Megan didn't answer, she just let Sam embrace her, fearing she might fall.

'Have you got any more advice for me?' Lizzie said. 'Or is it more of a do-as-you-say-not-as-you-do thing?'

'Lizzie!' Sam snapped.

'No, Sam,' Lizzie bit back, 'she told me I've been making a fool of myself, while she's been screwing a teenager.'

'Lizzie,' Dave began.

But she was already walking away, leaving Megan with her arms still around Sam, wishing she could disappear.

Chapter Forty-Four
Sam

Dear dickhead,

From wallabies, to lizards, to snakes, to soap operas.

We had a visitor today. More of an invader, really.

Take your mind back to when I was irrationally jealous about that young tech whiz fixing Megan's IT issues.

His mum stormed the camp today to confront Megan. Because Megan's been sleeping with her son.

I know. Take a moment.

Reread the above as many times as you need to. Okay? Good.

Now I'll remind you that he's nineteen years old.

Just breathe.

His mum — who was pretty fearsome — drove to camp to confront Megan about the relationship, and because apparently since they split up, he's a broken man (child).

It was sands through the hourglass. It was bold and beautiful. It was a shitshow.

Megan's mortified and Lizzie's furious with her. I'm experiencing mild shock, but ultimately feel for Megs and want to be there for her. She's dealing with enough judgement.

And now we're getting ready for a fun-filled disco night!

Woo. Hoo.

I fear an actual disco inferno.

Speaking of unlikely romances, while we were setting up the mess hall for the disco tonight, I had a chat with Dragon about the cooking crush I have on him. He's completely self-taught! All he read when he was a kid were cookbooks. He loved the pictures and learning about the ingredients. I asked why he didn't pursue food as a career and he just gestured around himself, smiling and scoffing like, 'What and give up all this?' This camp is his happy place, and he loves it.

Made me think about what my happy place is. And apart from home with the kids, I think it's the Baytree playground. Is that sad?

I couldn't think of another place that I feel so connected to. Then I started wondering how I could become the Dragon of Baytree. I guess I could overthrow Snack Shack, but the only kids I want to cook for are my own. Anyway, food for thought and thought for food.

Righto. Off to get my eighties on.

Here's hoping Megan and Lizzie don't commit murder on the dancefloor.

Yours with shell-shocked optimism for a glorious night ahead,
Sam 'Oates' Hatfield, of Hall & Oates

Chapter Forty-Five
Lizzie

I wasn't sure that an underage eighties disco was top of my list for 'ways to spend the night after discovering your daughter has been hiding her sexuality from you', but that was exactly where I'd soon be headed.

Megan and I had decided on Friday night to go as Annie Lennox and Dave Stewart respectively. I had immediately put my hand up to be Mr Stewart, insisting I'd make a better man. So I had just spent the past twenty minutes standing in front of the mirror on the bathroom wall, fixing a false beard to my face and transforming into the male half of eighties pop sensation the Eurythmics.

It felt good to look like someone else right now.

Megan had moved into Sam and Dave's cabin, so I had ours to myself, and it was unnervingly quiet.

I watched in silence as she shoved her belongings into her backpack after lunch. Part of me wanted to hug her and tell her how sorry I was that that awful woman had laid her private life bare like that in front of everyone. But a larger part of me was still feeling hurt and betrayed. Megan had lied to me about Zara and her own relationship with this Harry kid, and I needed a bit of time out to process that. Also, Stella's blurt about Zara's sexuality was still making my stomach churn. Not at the thought that Zara could be gay, or even that Zara could possibly be having sex, but at the thought that I had no idea. I felt ashamed.

326

Megan picked up her pack and walked past me, our shoulders brushing. She stopped and turned to look at me. 'I'm sorry I didn't tell you about Zara,' she said with tears in her eyes, 'or Harry. But you've been keeping things from me, too, Lizzie. I know you have. I'm sure you have your reasons and they're probably better than mine ... I'm being a hypocrite. But I really wish you'd tell me.'

Then she left.

***

I had mixed feelings about a twelve-year-old girl dressing as Madonna circa 'Like A Virgin', but I couldn't fault her costume. As I walked into the hall, I was surprised to see which of the kids had gone above and beyond for the eighties disco theme. Some of the more introverted of the Five-Sixers had definitely taken the opportunity to unleash their inner extrovert. The hall was awash with brightly coloured scrunchies and neon T-shirts, as well as a few tie-dye T-shirts and even a couple of pairs of flares. I assumed that the seventies and eighties were pretty interchangeable to twenty-first-century kids.

The kids were milling around, giggling and fawning over each other's costumes. Dragon had laid out a feast of vol-au-vents, cocktail frankfurts, party pies, sausage rolls and fairy bread. Some party foods never went out of fashion.

A few of us, with the notable exception of Megan, had spent the afternoon transforming the giant mess hall into a disco, with nothing but a handful of balloons and a disco light that looked like it had been around since the dawn of disco itself.

Tiger was walking the kids through 'The Macarena', even though that was definitely a nineties song. Stella, of course, was right down the front, waving her arms around and spinning on her Converse sneakers. My hip-hop queen had decided to dress as Grandmaster Flash for this evening's event and was in her element as she waved her arms around and threw in a few Running Man moves to mix things up a bit.

I was just about to grab a Coke and sample one of Dragon's sausage rolls when I spotted Megan laughing with Sam and Dave on the other side of the hall. Megan looked amazing and seemed to be having a good time, which, given the day's events, was surprising. But there Annie Lennox stood, dressed in a man's suit and tie with slicked-back hair and black Zorro mask, chatting and laughing with Hall & Oates.

The only evidence that Sam and Dave had dressed up as one of pop rock's most successful proponents was their white T-shirts with the appropriate surnames printed on them in black letters. Sam was Oates and Dave was Hall. Dave looked very proud of his long, blond wig, and Sam had teased up his thinning hair as best he could, but I couldn't help thinking that their costuming effort was pretty pissweak.

'So, who are you?'

I turned at the sound of the familiar voice and burst out laughing at the sight of Higgsy dressed like Mel and Kim, from their 'Respectable' video. He looked adorable.

'Dave Stewart from the Eurythmics,' I said. 'You look fantastic!'

'Thanks.' Higgsy grinned. 'No idea which one I am, though. I'm definitely either Mel or Kim.'

'You're Kim,' I clarified. 'Mel calls your name at the start of the video.'

'You sure know your Mel and Kim, Mr Stewart.'

'You bet I do,' I said. 'It's weird that the eighties have retro appeal. We're old.'

'I was born in eighty-nine,' Higgsy said apologetically.

'Gross.'

Higgsy laughed and I was about to ask him where the other teachers were when my phone vibrated in the pocket of the black leather jacket I'd borrowed from Megan.

'Sorry,' I said, reaching for it. 'I'll just be a sec.'

I was instantly buoyed at the idea of hearing Greg's voice, or even Zara's, after today's revelations, but when I looked down it wasn't either of their names on the screen.

It was Gina's.

Chapter Forty-Six
Megan

'It's sixteen years old and distilled in a castle in the Scottish Highlands,' Annie Lennox told Daryl Hall proudly. 'A castle, Dave.'

Megan, Sam and Dave were standing in the corner of the brightly lit hall, nursing their plastic cups of ginger ale and discussing the risks of ducking out to their cabin and adding a few shots of whisky.

Dave was dubious. 'I don't know, Megs,' he said, looking at the kids dancing up a storm, still just young enough to avoid self-consciousness. 'It doesn't seem right to drink on a school camp. We're supposed to be supervising.'

'There are five other adults in here, Dave,' Megan said. 'That's more than the one-staff-to-ten-kids ratio, as per the Education Department's minimum supervision requirements.'

Dave and Sam stared at her.

'What?' Megan said defensively. 'Nicola drilled it into me. I know my Education Department protocols.'

Sam nodded. 'Impressive.'

'So come on, what do you say, boys?'

Megan was feeling reckless, which may have had something to do with the fact that she was dressed as a strong, trailblazing female pop icon. Whatever it was, she wanted a drink and she wanted it now. Having your ex-boyfriend's mother call you a *puttana* in public will do that to a girl.

Megan didn't resent Francesca D'Angelo for the scene she'd made today. Harry was her son, and she was being the fierce protective lioness all mothers were. It was no less than Megan would have done if it were Oscar.

But even as she thought this, another voice in her mind questioned, *Really? Even if Oscar was nineteen?* Okay, maybe not. But at the very least Megan was sure she'd want to rip the head off any woman who broke her boy's heart. She'd never had deep feelings for Harry, and knowing that made her feel even worse about how she'd behaved, and how ruthlessly she'd cut him loose. He was a kid and she, Megan, was supposed to be the adult. So, yes, maybe she had deserved Francesca's spray. She just wished it hadn't happened in such a public forum.

Megan knew that part of what she'd been seeking from Harry was escapism; from her failed relationship and her endless indecision on what she was going to do with her life. She'd been trying to avoid real life and all the questions and uncertainties that went with it, because it had become hectic and fractured over the past couple of months.

She'd spent the afternoon racked with guilt. But with Lizzie not speaking to her, and the other teachers now knowing her private business, Megan was feeling shaken and exposed. Sam and Dave had done their best to cheer her up in the cabin, but now that she was here with some of the people who had witnessed her embarrassing smackdown, ginger ale just wasn't cutting it.

'Do you think Lizzie will come?' Sam asked.

Megan shrugged. It had been a snap decision to move out of the cabin. Sam and Dave had been more than a little surprised when she'd turned up on their doorstep with her pack, but she just couldn't sleep in the same room as Lizzie tonight. There was too much friction between them right now, and they needed space. So tonight, she wanted to have fun with her mates and try to forget about all of it. A few shots of whisky would help.

'Listen,' she said, 'we'll just go and have a couple of drinks then come back. No one will even notice.'

Dave shook his head firmly. 'You two go, but I'm not leaving. What if there's a power outage and the only available source of music is Your Happy Manfriend?'

'Okay, we'll stay,' Sam said, quickly receiving a smack on the arm from Megan.

'I'm kidding,' Dave scoffed. 'Go be naughty, it's fine.'

'You're a good man, Dave,' Sam said.

'The best,' Megan agreed, tugging at Sam's jacket sleeve. 'Let's go.'

★★★

The warmth of the whisky had started spreading through Megan's chest as she and Sam sat facing each other, cross-legged at either end of Sam's single bed.

'I snore,' Sam said.

'Not tonight you don't, roomie,' Megan replied, taking another sip.

'My room, my rules,' said Sam.

'My booze,' Megan shot back.

'Fair enough,' replied Sam, reaching for the flask.

'I fart quite a lot in my sleep,' Megan informed him. 'And I sleep in the nude, so they're extra loud.'

'Then I too will sleep starkers in solidarity.'

'Lizzie usually sleeps starkers,' Megan said.

'Really? Interesting.' Sam nodded his approval.

'Yep, but she wore a singlet and undies last night,' Megan said. 'Out of respect for my eyes, she said.'

Sam laughed, but tears sprang to Megan's eyes. Sam reached across to put his hand on hers.

'Hey, you two will be okay,' he said gently. 'It's *you two*!'

Megan shook her head. 'I don't know, Sam. Lizzie's been keeping her distance and ... well, I haven't exactly been honest with her.'

'You mean about the fact that you're a dirty cradle snatcher?'

Megan glared.

'Too soon?'

She laughed and whacked his arm. 'Let's just put the whole thing down to temporary insanity, okay? It didn't mean anything.'

'But it did to him, yeah?'

Megan dropped her head into her hands. 'Yeah, it did,' she said. 'God, I feel terrible.'

'His mother is terrifying.'

'Right?'

They laughed.

'I can't talk,' Sam said, taking back the flask for another top-up. 'I once shagged a Tinder date who wouldn't shut up about cannibalism.'

'Oh, yeah, I remember her. You said she was the only woman you'd ever actively prevented from going down on you.'

Megan was surprised by the blush that suddenly rose up in Sam's cheeks.

'I've really been oversharing about my sex life recently, haven't I?' he said, looking abashed.

'Nah,' Megan said. 'You've just been excited to have a sex life post-Bridget.'

'True.'

'Do you miss her?'

Sam looked amazed at the idea. 'Bridget? No. Not at all.' He paused and looked down at his drink. 'I miss me.' Sam's head shot up and he looked at Megan, horrified. 'Wow, that sounded much less wanky in my head.'

'Don't be stupid,' Megan said. 'What do you mean?'

'You just get,' Sam began, 'I dunno … swallowed by definitions; single dad, divorcee.'

'Man-whore?' Megan chipped in playfully, bringing a rueful smile to Sam's face.

'I'll take that,' he said. 'Anything with connotations of shame and failure fits the bill.'

'Jesus, Sam!' Megan laughed. 'Is that seriously what you think?'

'A bit,' Sam confessed. 'I mean, it's only since we've been here that I've sort of felt like I have a real place back home.'

'I know what you mean,' Megan sighed. 'I miss the Applewood gang.'

It was true. Over the past couple of days, Megan's mind had kept circling back to the café and her wrinkly regulars. She felt safe there. It had become a haven and she missed the place and the people. Yang, Maggie, Franny, Jim … even pervy old Bert.

Sam nodded. 'I get that.'

'Really?'

'They're good folks,' he said matter-of-factly. 'They care about you and you care about them. From what I saw, you're happy there.'

'You know, Yang has offered me a chance to buy the business.'

'No shit?' Sam beamed. 'You should do it!'

Megan shook her head. 'Nah.'

'Why not?'

'Me? Owning a café in a retirement home?'

Sam frowned. 'So?'

Megan looked into Sam's face. His open, puzzled face. Of course her hesitation made no sense to him. She'd just admitted that she missed the people who made her happy. Who wouldn't want to make that a permanent part of their life; to be happy and surrounded by people who made you feel good? She smiled. 'I don't know. Maybe.'

Sam took another sip from the flask.

'Hey, hey, hey.' Megan made repeated grabbing motions with her hand.

He grinned and passed it back, nodding at her mask, which she was still wearing.

'I thought you were going to do the whole spiky-orange-wig thing, too,' Sam said, referencing the Eurythmics album cover from which Megan took her inspiration.

'I tried a couple,' Megan said, 'but I looked like Prince Harry about to rob a bank.' She put a hand to her face, touching the mask. 'I forgot it was on.'

'Don't take it off,' Sam said as she began to untie it. 'I feel like I'm drinking with Annie Lennox.'

She giggled. 'Does that mean I'm drinking with Oates?'

'Good point,' he conceded. 'Not quite as appealing.'

'You're way better looking than the real thing,' she reassured him.

'Gee thanks,' Sam replied.

Their giggles instantly dissipated, and they sat quietly, nodding at nothing.

'Megs.'

'Yeah?'

'I really want to kiss you right now.'

Chapter Forty-Seven
Sam

Dearest dickhead,

A bottle of whisky somehow ended up on camp (some people!), so Megan and I snuck out of the disco to have a tipple. We were talking and drinking and drinking and talking and somewhere along the line, the air began to feel charged.

Personally, I was suddenly acutely aware of our aloneness in this cabin and felt worried that Megan thought I'd orchestrated the situation. Had I subconsciously done exactly that?

I hope you're sitting down (classic wheelchair humour).

I told her I wanted to kiss her. I didn't know it was true until I'd said it out loud. I heard the words come out and I sounded almost contrite. Megan looked stunned silent, like all her communicative faculties had gone into meltdown. I took her silence as a mute form of rejection and immediately started apologising, certain that I'd just irrevocably damaged a treasured friendship.

Then she kissed me.

Megan kissed me.

Chapter Forty-Eight
Megan

Megan was still shocked by her spontaneous decision to kiss Sam. She had an awful moment of thinking Sam wasn't kissing her back, but once they'd established a stable position, the kissing most definitely became a mutual endeavour.

I'm kissing Sam Hatfield! she thought in astonishment. And then, an even louder inner voice piped up with another startling observation. *And it's really, really good.*

Sam suddenly pulled his mouth away from hers. She couldn't read his face but felt certain he was about to put an end to this. So she decided to hedge her bets.

'This is weird, yeah?' she asked, oh so rhetorically.

'Very,' Sam replied, leaning forward to kiss her again.

'Good weird?' she asked as she pulled back, not at all rhetorically.

'Best good weird ever,' Sam agreed, holding her gaze. 'But can you lose the mask now? I'm still not sure it's really you.'

Megan reached behind her head, undid the mask and dropped it to the floor.

Chapter Forty-Nine
Sam

Soz for the cliché, dickhead, but it felt so right.

Any thoughts of jeopardising my friendship with Megs evaporated once we were kissing.

I know that's often the case when friends cross the line, and the cold light of day can bring a watershed of regrets. I'll be curious to see what tomorrow brings. For now, I feel better than I have in years, and I'm happy to hold onto that.

And don't even get me started on the Annie Lennox outfit.

Chapter Fifty
Lizzie

There was an urgent knocking on the door.

'*Mum! Are you in there?*'

'Just a sec!' Dammit. Why wasn't Stella doing the Bus Stop or at least joining a conga line?

I jumped off the bed, took a quick check in the mirror to make sure my Dave Stewart eye makeup wasn't streaked all down my face and opened the door.

Grandmaster Flash (Stella) and The Cure's Robert Smith (Lola) stood on the doorstep wearing two very freaked-out expressions behind all their makeup and accessories.

'What is it?' I said, hoping my daughter would assume the red puffy eyes were part of my costume. 'Are you guys okay?'

They looked to each other before Stella started speaking at breakneck speed.

'Logan was telling some of the kids at the disco that you and Megan were lying about drop bears and Caleb got really upset and said that you're not a liar —'

'I think Caleb may have formed somewhat of an affection for you, Lizzie,' Lola interrupted.

Stella screwed up her face. 'Yeah, and gross, by the way.' She shuddered. 'Anyway, Caleb said adults don't lie about stuff like that and then Logan said he was going to prove that there were no such things as drop bears and that if Caleb really believed in them he should go and find some evidence and ...'

'And now they've gone to search for drop bears!' Lola finished.

'In the bush!' Stella cried. 'And it's dark and they didn't tell the teachers and we're scared they'll get lost and ...'

'Okay, calm down,' I said, even though I was feeling anything but calm myself.

I knew Caleb would be no match for Logan's powers of persuasion. Logan understood how to leverage peer pressure better than most adults, the little turd. But it was dark out there, and although there wouldn't be any drop bears, there were definitely other equally unfriendly, non-fictional creatures.

'We've conducted a search of the entire camp and they're nowhere to be found!' Lola said, looking more panicked by the second.

'Let's go get Higgsy and ...'

'No!' Stella cried. 'We can't tell the teachers! You'd both get in so much trouble! We have to try to find them ourselves!'

She was right. If kids were missing because of something we told them – no matter how innocent our intentions – we'd be in big trouble.

'Mum?!' Stella said with a tone of dire urgency.

'Right,' I said, attempting to engage my professional capacity for working under pressure, 'you two go tell Dave to meet us at his cabin. And tell him to leave discreetly.'

Over the past couple of days, we'd all discovered that Dave was basically a cross between Grizzly Adams and Pocahontas. Hopefully, he was also part bloodhound and could help us locate the boys and get them back before the teachers noticed.

The girls nodded their understanding, and I had an

oddly timed feeling of relief seeing them voluntarily sharing the same space.

'And don't let the teachers see you, okay?'

More vigorous nodding.

'Then you both stay at the disco,' I went on, 'and try to have fun. I'll sort this out, okay? I promise.'

I leaned down to kiss Stella's forehead, tasting a combination of cheap makeup and sweat. 'Girls, it's going to be fine,' I said, with more confidence than I was feeling. 'Off you go.'

***

As I hurried towards Sam's cabin, I noticed that the inside light was on. Sam must already be in there. Good.

I knocked once then pushed the door open. 'Sam are you —'

If it had taken me a few seconds to process what Stella and Lola told me, it took at least double that to comprehend the sight of Megan and Sam sitting cross-legged on the bed with their lips locked.

'Oh my God,' I gasped.

The two of them instantly pulled apart and stared at me in horror, their mouths smeared in Lennox-coloured lipstick.

I felt like I was coming into a movie halfway through and couldn't keep up with the plot. As Megan and Sam scrambled to their feet, I stood mutely, staring at them in complete shock.

'Lizzie, listen —'

But he was cut off by Dave, who was bellowing as he ran up the steps and into the room. 'What's going on, Lizzie, I ...?' He stopped when he saw Megan and Sam's faces covered in lipstick. 'Whoa, were you two …?' He beamed, looking like a man who had just walked into his house to see the Christmas tree up for the first time.

I decided to ignore whatever the hell this was for now and focus on the bigger problem at hand. I couldn't bring myself to look at Sam and Megan, so I spoke directly to Dave. 'Logan and Caleb have gone missing.'

'What?' Sam replied.

'They've gone to look for drop bears,' I said, still just to Dave, then quickly explained the situation.

'Are you sure they aren't just in another cabin?' Sam asked.

'No, they're gone.'

Megan stared, uncomprehending. 'Wait, what?'

'I said, they're gone!'

'They can't be *gone*. Where would they go?' Megan looked panicked. 'Maybe they're just hiding somewhere?'

'The girls searched the whole camp.' My voice sounded shaky. 'They … have … gone.'

I was trying desperately to stay on point, but another part of my brain was still reeling over my second shock of the night.

'Shit!' All the colour drained out of Sam's face as he ran his hands through his hair.

Megan took a step forward. 'Are you sure? They're probably just —'

'I told you!' I roared. 'Are you listening to me, or are you still too wrapped up in …?'

'Hey, hey, come on, guys,' Dave said, stepping forward. 'We're not going to get anywhere by attacking each other.'

'Shut up, Dave!' I snapped. 'You don't know what I saw when —'

'Don't!' Megan glared at me before her face crumpled. 'Jesus, this is all my fault.'

'It's *our* fault!' I hissed. 'I'm to blame, too!'

'Come on!' Sam stood up. 'We have to find them.'

Dave nodded, then looked back at me. 'And we have to tell the others,' he said.

A strange feeling of calm washed over me. 'No. We're not telling anyone. Not yet.' I looked to Dave. 'Dave, tell us what to do.'

Dave exhaled through his nose and pursed his lips. 'Get your boots and your torches,' he said, snapping into Ranger Dave mode. 'Lizzie, grab a walkie-talkie and I'll grab mine, too. Then meet me behind my cabin in thirty seconds STAT!'

'Thirty seconds or STAT, Dave?' Sam asked. 'They're different things.'

'This is no time for sass, Sam,' Dave snapped. 'Get your shit together and get moving.'

★★★

Twenty-three seconds later, we were all kitted out and standing behind the cabin listening as Dave issued our instructions.

'Megs and Lizzie, you head towards the stables and the horse trail. Sammy, you and I will head to the rope course.'

'Roger that.'

'Stay on Channel Four,' Dave instructed me, holding up his two-way. 'We don't want Tiger and Dragon getting involved.'

I adjusted my walkie-talkie to the right channel.

'Good luck,' Dave said. 'Keep in touch.'

He turned to jog into the darkness, watched by all of us,

until Sam realised he better get a wriggle on if he was to keep up and ran after him.

Megan took a breath, but before she could say a word I turned to head for the stables. 'Let's go.'

Chapter Fifty-One
Megan

Megan couldn't believe how this night was unfolding. Her head was still reeling after what had taken place in the cabin with Sam, and now here she was, racing through the dark searching for a couple of kids who were missing, because of something she had said.

She desperately wanted to talk to Lizzie about it all, but knew her friend's expressions well enough to understand that now was definitely not the time. She'd have to wait until this Twilight Zone night was over and the kids were safely back at the disco.

They reached the stables, but there was no sign of the boys.

'Should we keep going?'

Lizzie didn't answer, she just spoke into the walkie-talkie. 'Dave? Any sign where you are? Dave?'

When no response came, Lizzie looked down to examine her device.

Megan noticed that the little red light wasn't flashing. 'Did you turn it on?'

Lizzie frowned. 'Fuck,' she whispered.

As soon as she turned it on, Dave's voice came through loud and clear.

'Lizzie! We found Logan! Can you read me?'

Lizzie pressed the 'talk' button. 'I read you, Dave. That's great. Is Caleb with you?'

Megan could hear a child crying in the background and assumed it was Caleb.

'No, just Logan.'

That meant Logan must be crying. *So you should, you little shit*, Megan thought.

'He says Caleb is near the rope course. And he's hurt.'

'We'll meet you there!'

Megan and Lizzie ran.

Chapter Fifty-Two
Lizzie

'*Stop!*' Dave yelled, just as Megan and I came into view on the other side of the ravine.

Megan was ahead of me, so I reached out, grabbed her by the scruff of her puffer collar and flung her to the ground.

She stared up at me, startled. 'What the ...?'

'Look!' I shone my torch just beyond her feet to reveal the precipice of the ravine she'd almost fallen into.

'Jesus.'

'You okay?'

'Yep.' She gave me a shaky smile. 'Thanks.'

She crawled cautiously to the edge for a look and I stared across the ravine to where Dave, Sam and Logan were standing. I glowered at Logan. That kid was lucky he and I were on opposite sides of a very big ditch right now.

'Lizzie,' Megan said quietly, from her position near the edge of the very big ditch. 'Come look.'

I didn't like the expression on her face. She'd gone even paler, and her lips were open and quivering. I edged forward, following the light of Sam's torch, and saw Caleb lying at the bottom, curled in a ball with blood on his face.

Shit!

I estimated the ravine was at least three metres deep and was too wide for Dave to find a way around for us all to join forces. Also, Caleb was much closer to our side of the ravine than the men's. There was no way they'd be able to reach him from there.

'Hey there, buddy,' I heard Dave say in his chirpiest voice. 'You take a bit of a spill?'

Caleb remained silent and still, but Lizzie could hear Logan loud and clear in the quiet bush as he wailed to Sam and Dave across the ravine.

'I was,' Logan sobbed, 'running ... ahead ... to scare ... to scare him ... and ... and then I ... then I couldn't ... couldn't see him anymore.'

A switch flicked inside me. I called across to the others, 'I have to get down there.'

'I should go,' Sam called back. 'I'm tallest.'

'But how's your first aid?'

'Non-existent,' he said miserably.

'It will take too long for us to run around and help, anyway,' Dave said.

We all stopped as we heard a noise coming from the bottom of the ravine. I got down on my hands and knees. 'Caleb?'

The boy had turned his face slightly towards the sky and I could just make out a nasty gash above his left eye.

'Ow,' Caleb squeaked.

I was instantly flooded with relief at the sound of his voice. He was alive. That was a good start.

'Hi, Caleb,' I said through a forced, practised smile. 'How're you going down there?'

'It hurts,' he said in a small, scared voice.

'Where does it hurt, mate?' Sam called.

'My arm ... and my head.'

That wasn't good.

I turned to Megan, who looked like she was about to cry. 'Megs, can you see anything we could use to lower me down?'

'I'll look!' she said, looking relieved to be given a job to do, just as Dave called across the ravine.

'Human chain!'

I stared down. It was a steep decline, but not steep enough to cause a straight fall. The human-chain idea was much better suited to flat surfaces, not steep-edged ravines, but it was the best idea anyone had had so far. And we had to get him out of there.

I quickly placed my walkie-talkie on the ground and shoved the torch into my belt. 'Grab my ankles,' I told Megan. 'Lower me in slowly and I'll reach down and get him.'

Megan looked down at my ankles, then straight at me. 'I won't be able to hold you,' she said.

'Thanks heaps.'

'For fuck's sake, Lizzie,' she said, then called down into the ravine. 'Sorry, Caleb.'

'S'okay,' he called back. 'My mum says it, too.'

Megan turned back to me. 'I'm saying I'm weak,' she said. 'You're stronger than me and I'm lighter than you. Grab *my* ankles,' she ordered. 'And if you give me any shit about my first-aid skills, I'll drop you in.'

I couldn't help but be impressed. Also, it felt like the first time in a while that Megan had spoken to me like my friend.

'Okay,' I said, leaning in to whisper in her ear. 'But be careful with him, Megs. We don't know what state he's in.'

Megan nodded and got down on all fours. I dug my feet into the dirt, just back from the edge of the ravine and sat up straight, holding her ankles between my own legs. She crept towards the ravine with me moving behind her like an attached mechanism. She let her hands feel beyond the edge then looked over her shoulder at me.

'Don't you let go.'

I gave her ankles a reassuring squeeze. 'I won't.'

Megan started lowering her body all the way over the edge and I was relieved to find that I was managing her weight well.

'Can you reach him?' I called.

'She's nearly there,' Dave responded from the other side.

Chapter Fifty-Three
Megan

Megan reached out one arm and gently touched Caleb's cheek. The top half of his face was covered in blood, making his bright eyes pop out like beacons.

'Hey, mister,' Megan said, steadying herself on an outcropped tree root with her other hand. 'No offence, but worst cubby ever.'

Caleb smiled. Some of the blood on his cheeks had dried enough for the smile to crack it slightly. 'Logan ran off,' he whispered.

'It's okay,' Megan soothed.

'He said he saw a drop bear and then he ran off,' Caleb continued. 'As if they're real.'

'As if,' Megan replied, feeling horrendously guilty.

'I scratched my eye and fell down trying to catch up to him. Is it bad?' Caleb asked, almost hopefully.

'Nah,' Megan scoffed, 'it's not terrible.'

'Megan,' Lizzie called from above, a reminder to hurry.

'Righto, then,' Megan said cheerily, 'let's get you out of here. Grab my wrist, okay?'

Caleb reached out his left arm and latched onto Megan's wrist with a healthy grip. But when he shifted his body to try to reach out his right arm he screamed in pain, releasing his grip and slumping back into the dirt.

'You okay?' Dave called.

'What happened?' Sam shouted, sounding panicked.

'It's okay, Caleb's arm is just a bit sore,' Megan called back.

'What colour is it?' Lizzie asked in a calm voice.

'Totes normal,' Megan said. 'Just a bit sore.'

'Okay.' Lizzie's voice was strained with effort. 'Time to go!'

'Hey, Caleb,' Megan said. 'What if we link arms? You know, like at the Baytree Bush Dance every year. We're in the bush. May as well dance like it.'

'Time to go,' Lizzie repeated, sounding more breathless by the second.

'Come on, Megs,' Sam called.

'You've got this, Lizzie,' Dave shouted.

Logan continued to sniff and sob.

Caleb moaned as he looped his left arm into Megan's left arm, his right arm flopping by his side.

'Feel those muscles?' Megan asked him, flexing for effect. 'I've gotcha.'

Caleb closed his eyes.

'Lizzie, go!' Megan called.

Lizzie pulled. It wasn't much, but it was enough to bring Caleb to more of a seated position.

'I can stand up if you like,' he said, eyes still closed.

'That'd be awesome, mate,' Lizzie yelled from above them.

Caleb gingerly made his way to his feet, arm still linked through Megan's for support.

'Pull me up a bit more,' Megan said.

'Push back with one leg at a time while you pull Megan's legs towards you!' Dave instructed Lizzie.

'Got it!' she called back, pulling Megan a bit higher.

Megan was now face to face with Caleb, who looked more and more like a character out of *Braveheart*, with his blood-stained face and oversized shorts.

'Okay, here we go again,' Megan said. 'Let's dance.' She pointed her elbow towards Caleb. He reached up his good arm and linked it into hers once more.

'Let's go,' Megan called out.

'Go, Lizzie!' Sam yelled.

'Come on, Lizzie!' Dave joined.

Between the encouragement of the cheer squad, Megan's free hand, Lizzie's strength and Caleb's scrambling legs doing all they could, Megan was now able to clutch at the earth over the safe edge of the ravine.

Lizzie immediately lunged forward, grabbed the waistband of Megan's leather pants and gave a final heave, revealing Caleb, who was still clinging onto Megan.

'We're coming!' Dave yelled. He and Sam disappeared into the darkness as Megan, Caleb and Lizzie lay face up, gasping for air and staring into the night sky.

'Thank you,' Caleb said.

'It was nothing,' Lizzie panted.

'You okay, mate?' Megan asked. 'How's the arm?'

'It's okay,' Caleb said, but Megan could see how much pain he was in.

'You were so brave, mate.'

'Really? You think?'

'Totally.'

An unexpected look of joy passed over Caleb's features. 'Do you think my dad would be proud of me?'

Megan's heart gave a wrench. 'One hundred per cent,' she said.

'The others will be here in a sec,' Lizzie told him, still gulping air. 'Then we'll all get you back to camp, don't worry.'

'Okay.'

Megan suddenly turned and wrapped her arms around Lizzie, burying her head in her friend's chest.

'I'm sorry ... for everything,' she whispered.

Lizzie threw her arms around Megan and squeezed tight. 'Me too.'

The two friends hugged in silence for a moment, until Megan whispered softly in Lizzie's ear, 'I think you've given me a permanent camel toe.'

'Well, I've got cancer,' Lizzie whispered back. 'So I win.'

From: nmcgintyhamperqueen@gmail.com
Subject: Regrettable Incident

Dear Baytree Council Committee Members,

I hope this email is the final piece of correspondence that needs to address the dreadful events that transpired during the school camp. I would also like to reiterate my wish that I had attended the camp. I firmly believe that had I been in attendance, we could've avoided this whole sorry mess. Unfortunately, we cannot change the past, so let us look to the future.

Firstly, it is a relief to inform you that Caleb continues to rest and recuperate at home. There will be no ongoing complications from his injuries, and he is expected to make a full and speedy recovery.

All relevant incident reports have been filled in and filed, and no fault has been found, neither in the actions of any of the teachers nor any of the parents who attended the camp. The staff at Crestburn Recreational Camp have also been absolved of any wrongdoing. Although it seems odd to me that not one adult present on the camp is being made to accept any responsibility for this most unfortunate and terrifying event, at least we can now attempt to put all of this behind us, while at the same time learning the hard lessons that we must learn.

Yours sincerely,

Nicola McGinty

Chapter Fifty-Four
Sam

To: jack_woz_here@hotmail.com
From: samhatfieldchef@bigpond.com
Subject: Rachel Who?

Dickhead, I'm in love.

I'm in love with Megan.

All the things I know about Megan, all of the different ways I know Megan, just all bonded together in an instant to form this all-consuming love. The kiss was also mind-blowingly good.

And now we're on our way back to the real world and I'm realising this is a disaster. I've fallen in love with my friend and I don't think she knows it. Megan will probably joke about it at drop-off tomorrow and that'll be the end of it. Because as far as she's concerned, it was just an in-the-moment, whisky-fuelled pash on a school camp.

So, there you have it. I've fallen in love and now I'm going to get my heart broken by the woman I'm in love with. And in case you missed it, she doesn't even know I love her.

Yours deflatedly,

The Right Honourable Sam J. Hatfield, Minister for the Unrequited

Chapter Fifty-Five
Megan

On the day she returned from school camp, Megan called Yang to tell her she wouldn't be in. Oscar was still with Bryce, so she had spent the night at Lizzie's, and the two of them stayed up talking, crying and laughing until the wee hours. The next morning, Megan insisted Lizzie sleep in while she got the kids off to school. Now, with the four Barrett children safely deposited at their respective institutions, Megan was back in her own house, sitting at her kitchen bench and wondering what the hell had happened over the past few days.

Lizzie had cancer. Megan didn't know what to do with that information. It seemed unbelievable that her vibrant, funny, full-of-life best friend could have such an ugly illness growing inside her.

Her initial reaction after hearing Lizzie say, *I have cancer*, was to laugh. Lying there on the cold, hard ground, their adrenaline surging, Megan had assumed Lizzie was making one of her typical one-upmanship gags. But when she pulled back to look at Lizzie's face, there was no doubt she was serious. Before she could scream, cry or rail against the world, Dave and Sam had appeared, sweaty and panting, and Caleb was the priority again.

The five of them had stumbled back through the bush, Megan and Sam avoiding eye contact the whole time, only to find Higgsy and the other teachers waiting for them.

There was an ambulance and parents to call and incident reports to fill out and children to comfort, so Lizzie's shock news was lost in all the commotion. It wasn't until Caleb had been loaded into the ambulance and taken away and all the other kids were safely back in their cabins that Megan and Lizzie were alone in their cabin.

They didn't talk much that night. Just hugged and cried a lot.

'I don't remember Mum dying,' Lizzie had sobbed. 'But my brothers do, and it was horrible for them. I don't want my kids to go through that. They'll be messed-up adults because I had to go and die of stupid cancer!'

'You're not going to die!' Megan had said, stroking Lizzie's head as they lay together in the single bed. 'The oldies at Applewood are always saying how amazing the latest cancer treatments are. And you don't even know if it's spread.'

'I don't want my kids to grow up motherless.'

'They won't!' Megan had told her firmly.

But Megan couldn't know that for sure. There was only one thing she had felt certain about in that moment.

'You have to tell Greg, first thing tomorrow.'

'I know.'

On the journey home the next morning, it was Lizzie and Megan who sat at the back of the bus. Together this time. Megan couldn't even look at Sam, and although Dave tried his best to make jokes about 'what goes on camp stays on camp', no one was in the mood.

Megan had received an email overnight from Harry's mum, warning her to stay away from her son. She'd replied with a simple, *I'm sorry for any distress I've caused. If you send me a postal address, I'll return the jewellery as soon as possible. Megan.*

Francesca replied instantly with the address and nothing else.

Megan also found a flurry of missed texts from Harry, warning her that his mother was on her way and apologising for the scene she was undoubtedly going to make. Twenty-seven texts in all. In the last five, there was a definite shift in tone.

H: *U could at least reply.*

H: *Hello?*

H: *Wow so just nothing.*

H: *So fucking cold.*

H: *Went home with a 25-year-old last nite.*

Megan couldn't help smiling a little at that.
She sent Harry one final text.

I'm sorry I hurt you, Harry. We had a wonderful couple of weeks and I'll never forget our time together. You are a talented, smart and kind man, and I know you're going to do amazing things with your life.

A series of texts immediately started popping up on Megan's screen, one after another.

H: *okay*

H: *sorry about my mum*

H: *and sorry for reading your work*

H: *you'll never find an IT dude as good as me*

H: *take care Megs x*

Then there was Sam. Anyone would think that what had happened between them would have paled in comparison to Lizzie's diagnosis, and of course in one way it did. But in another way, it brought the situation into sharper focus for Megan.

They were Lizzie's friends, and she needed them now more than ever. She and Sam couldn't let their momentary lapse in self-control get in the way of being there for their mate.

Lizzie, however, saw it differently and had told Megan as much last night as they lay on the couch, her feet in Megan's lap.

'You know, it's not as much of a shock as it probably should be,' Lizzie said, as the two of them polished off a tub of cookies and cream ice-cream they found at the bottom of Lizzie's freezer.

'What do you mean?'

Lizzie shrugged. 'I can totally see it.'

'What?'

'You and Sam.'

Megan snorted. 'Yeah, right.'

'I'm serious,' Lizzie said, giving Megan a gentle nudge with her foot. 'You've spent so long looking for your true love, and maybe he's been in front of you all along.'

Megan scoffed. 'Thanks, Richard Curtis.'

Lizzie was wrong. What happened in Sam's cabin had been a moment of madness that could never happen again. She'd been feeling rattled by Harry's mum and had made a huge error, mistaking genuine, deep friendship for something more. She and Sam had been great friends for four years and she loved him dearly, but they would never work as a couple. The kissing was really good, and Megan was fairly certain they'd be sexually compatible, but so were she and Harry and look how that had turned out.

She didn't want to lose Sam, so she was determined to find a way for them to get past this without any lingering weirdness. His friendship was too important.

She picked up her phone and opened a new message to Sam.

Hi Sam, can we meet? Tomorrow at the park with the boys? 10 a.m.?

She had to tell him all of this in person. They would address what happened, agree it was a one-off camp romance and put the situation to bed, so to speak, once and for all.

Chapter Fifty-Six
Lizzie

'The biopsy results show that the lump is malignant. Now we will need to run further investigations. We'll look at your lymph nodes, a PET scan or a sentinel node biopsy to see if it's spread, but in the meantime, we can plan your chemotherapy regime.'

These were the words Gina had said to me over the phone two nights ago. The same words I now repeated to my stunned husband.

'I'm coming home.'

'Greg, listen …'

'I'm coming home.'

On the one hand, I'd never heard him sound so assertive, but I could also hear the slight tremor in his voice.

'This is not up for discussion, buddy,' Greg said, his tone less sharp now. 'I need to be there with you at your appointment. And I'm going to be there for every single moment of this, until you're better.'

It felt like someone had finally popped the balloon that had been slowly expanding inside my chest. I burst into tears. 'I'm going to be bald!'

'It's going to be okay.' Greg's soothing tone calmed me. 'We're going to get through this, you hear me? I'm getting off the phone now to book the first flight I can get. Call you back in a minute. I love you.'

The second thing on my to-do list this morning was to talk to Zara. We hadn't had the chance when I got back from camp with all the kids around, but I had spent a lot of the bus ride thinking about what I was going to say to her.

I waited to hear back from Greg, who told me he was booked on a 6.30 a.m. flight tomorrow morning, then drove straight to Baytree Secondary.

'Where are we going?' Zara said, panicked after being pulled out of her science class. 'Is someone dead?'

'No, everyone's fine,' I said, leading her out of the front office and outside. It was a lie, but that was a conversation for another time. 'I just want to talk to you, and I didn't want to wait,' I said. 'Come on, sit over here.'

We walked to the park next to the school and sat on a bench. Zara stood staring at me for a moment, until I patted the seat beside me. Reluctantly she sat down, and I immediately clasped her hands in mine.

'I love you.'

Zara smiled uncertainly. 'Um, I love you, too?'

'I want you to know that, first and foremost,' I said. 'I love you. More than anything in this whole world.'

'More than Archie?'

I laughed. 'Look, this year has been a total shitfight for you and me ...'

Zara gasped. 'Mum!'

'... and that's okay, because mums and daughters fight,' I said, holding back the tears. 'But no matter how much we argue, or disagree, I'm always here for you when you need me, okay? Always. And you can talk to me about anything. I'm not going to judge you, or criticise you, or make you feel bad.'

'Okaaaay ...' Zara was looking more freaked out by the second. 'Is this about last Saturday night?'

'A bit,' I said. 'I wish you hadn't lied to me about where

you've been going, and what you've been doing, but I also understand that maybe you've felt like you couldn't be honest with me. About what's going on in your life … and your heart.'

Zara blushed and pulled her hands away.

'Zara, honey, I know about you and Ines,' I said gently. 'I just wish you'd told me. I'm sorry you didn't feel like you could. If you had, I could have told you how happy I am for you.'

Zara's head jerked up. 'You are?'

I grinned. 'Of course, I am! It's your first relationship!' I put my hands on either side of her face. 'It's exciting and wonderful, and I want to hear all about the girl who's stolen my daughter's heart!'

Zara blinked, still uncomprehending. 'So, you know that I'm … that I …'

'That you're gay? Yes, darling.'

'But how did you …?'

I lowered my hands. 'That doesn't matter,' I said. 'But I know, and I think it's wonderful and that any girl would be lucky to have you.'

Zara's eyes filled with tears and she lunged forward to hug me. 'I was so scared you'd be … that you wouldn't …'

I squeezed her tight. It was so good to feel her in my arms again. 'I love you.'

***

Rania finally replied to my text messages. It turned out that while we were away on camp, she'd been offered a job co-hosting a new reality TV show called *Date Your Mate*, where long-term friends were encouraged to push the boundaries of their relationship.

Ha! Sam and Megs could be on the poster!

A quick internet search revealed that one of the producers was Jonathan McMaster – the douchebag from the fundraiser. I couldn't quite bring myself to believe that my drunken lecture about paying it forward might have had an impact. But I liked entertaining the idea.

I'm sorry for my text before you left, Rania wrote. *I was angry. You were right about being honest with my parents. They're not happy about Tishk and me moving to Sydney, but they've accepted my decision. Maybe you can visit us when you come to see Greg?*

I didn't tell her Greg had quit his job and was coming home to nurse his wife. I wrote back wishing her luck and saying how lovely it was getting to know her. I meant it, too. Rania had made me feel valued at a time when I needed it. I'd learned a lot from her in the short time I'd got to know her. I was happy for her and where she was in her life right now, but a life like hers wasn't for me.

I was a middle-aged midwife, with four beautiful kids, an amazing husband, good friends and a big, noisy family. And I was loved. It had been fun getting dolled up and having the tiniest taste of fame, but it wasn't for me. I was happier on the couch, in my Uggs, with my family around me. I wasn't young anymore, and that was okay. Becoming friends with Rania had also made it clear to me that I needed to let my kids make their own mistakes. If I tried to control them the way Rania's parents had, I'd end up losing them.

Chapter Fifty-Seven
Sam

To: jack_woz_here@hotmail.com
From: samhatfieldchef@bigpond.com
Subject: SAVE THE DATE!

Dear Jack,

I'm maintaining the formal tone of 'dear dickhead', because I have news worthy of hoity-toity wordage.

Save the date! April 22nd, 7 p.m. at the Elwood Lounge. Dave and I have a gig and you're coming. We've been writing together and I want you to hear our originals. Then you can tell us everything that's wrong with them. Other, less musically literate, people have been liking our stuff, and we're getting better. Amazing how playing gigs and practising can actually make you better. I know. Mind blown. You better come to this gig, too, because very soon after it, Dave's nicking off to Sydney for a month to workshop the TV adaptation of his graphic novel. There are big wigs flying in from LA to attend. And they're paying for Kesh and the kids to go with him! He'll probably come back with a tan, pointy shoes and perfect teeth.

And I hate to tell you, but there's a cover charge. Oh yeah! We're getting paid! To play music!!

In unconnected – but kind of connected – news, I gave notice at work yesterday. Not because I believe for a second that Dave and I could make a living from our timeless tunes, but because it was time. I'm thinking of getting back into the cooking game. At a slightly boozy catch-up with the gang, Dave had the idea of me making a bunch of precooked family meals and selling 'em out of Eskies in the Baytree playground. And after being inspired by my friend and yours, Hidden Dragon, on the camp (I have no interest in ever learning his real name), I've decided to give it a crack. And if it goes well, I might've found a way to make some coin, and to feed the folk who occupy my happy place. Dragon would be proud.

Megan called an official one-on-one meeting at the park the other day. I opted for heart on sleeve and told her I loved her as soon as I sat down. I didn't exactly read the room. She told me she doesn't feel the same, but would be crushed if we couldn't stay friends. It was a very gentle and affectionate relegation to the friend zone. It'll take a few weeks, but we'll be fine. Time heals all foot-in-mouth-unrequited-love-declaration wounds.

Hey, I like that. I'm gonna grab my guitar and write The Foot in Mouth Unrequited Love Declaration Blues.

Chapter Fifty-Eight
Megan

'And don't let that milk-delivery guy take any more free muffins!'

'Gotcha.'

Megan was stationed at the coffee machine, while Yang paced back and forth behind her, reading from a small notebook. A notebook that contained a list of information Yang felt it was crucial for Megan to know before she handed over the reins of The Cozy Corner.

'And remember that on Tuesdays the fruit guy is supposed to be here by nine but ...'

'... doesn't arrive until at least ten,' Megan finished for her. 'I know!' Megan threw Yang a cheeky smile. 'You sure you don't want to stick around and work for me? You've got potential. And I'll be a good boss, promise.'

Yang stopped pacing. 'Work for you?' she scoffed. 'I'd quit, first day.'

'Probably.'

Yang shot her a rare smile, before walking back into the kitchen.

It had been a revelation to Megan how much she'd missed this place and its snail-paced inhabitants while she was away. For all the chaos and drama of the camp, her mind had kept returning to the café, wondering if any of the ladies had accidentally spouted any more social gaffs entirely on purpose or if Maggie had shifted to taking her tea white with one after three weeks of herbal tea on doctor's orders.

On her first day back, Megan decided to trust her gut and make Yang an offer on the café. And after successfully squeezing another couple of grand out of her, Yang had accepted. Megan couldn't have been more excited.

Yang had made Megan promise not to tell any of the residents until after she'd left. 'I don't want any slobbery goodbye kisses from the old cronies.'

Helen raised her hand from a nearby table to get Megan's attention.

'Another iced coffee, Helen?'

'Yes, thanks, love,' Helen said. 'And pop an extra scoop of ice-cream in there for me. Life's too short.'

'Too true,' Megan replied, grabbing a tall glass from the shelf.

'I was never allowed ice-cream, you see,' Helen went on, 'because it was bad for me.'

Megan nodded, only half listening, as she fetched the ice-cream from the freezer behind her.

'Couldn't care less now,' Helen continued. 'It's what I want so I'll bloody well have it, thank you very much.'

'So you should,' Megan affirmed as she dug the scoop deep into the tub, determined to give Helen an impressive extra hunk of vanilla.

'If you love something,' Helen said, 'it can't be that bad for you, can it?'

Megan shrugged, contemplating heroin addicts, smokers, alcoholics and problem gamblers. But she understood Helen's meaning.

She froze, the scoop halfway between the tub and the glass, as that simple understanding made way for another. It was suddenly as clear as day to her, and she felt a fizz wrap itself around her face from the back of her neck, strong and sudden enough to make her gasp.

She was in love with Sam.

She looked down at Helen's iced coffee and squeezed the ice-cream scoop, placing the extra serve perfectly on top of the first. Then she grabbed the chocolate shaker, sprinkled the final touch and stood very still, staring at nothing.

After a few long seconds, she looked back to her bewildered-looking customer.

'Helen, you're the best,' she said, untying her apron and dropping it on the counter. 'Yang!' she yelled. 'Service!'

Then Megan ran.

★★★

Megan spotted Sam before he saw her. He was leaning against the wall of his office building eating a wrap of some type and she immediately smiled at the sight of him.

Swinging her car into an angle park across the road at an unsafe speed, she cranked the handbrake, killed the engine and adjusted her rear-view mirror to watch him for a moment.

Sam was leaning forward off the wall, trying to avoid wearing the wrap's fillings as they splattered to the ground below him. Megan found herself suddenly laughing through tears as she watched him trying to deal with his disintegrating, dripping lunch.

When he looked up and around, checking to see if anybody was witnessing his food struggles, Megan saw his expression change as he recognised her car. She opened her driver-side door and stepped out onto the street, turning to face him. His hands were already quizzically held out to his sides, with one still holding his lunch, and he rushed to finish his mouthful as Megan crossed the street.

By the time she reached the footpath, Sam's mouth was finally free of food, and as she approached him, she wiped away a tear that had made its way to her jawline.

'Megs, what's wrong?' Sam asked her, visibly trying to figure out how to get rid of his wrap, which continued to drip and droop.

Megan laughed again. 'Nothing,' she said. 'Nothing's wrong.'

Sam looked baffled and Megan imagined how she must appear to him right now. Wet-faced and probably looking a tad crazed. The thought made her laugh again.

'How're you going there?' she asked, pointing to his wrap.

'Really badly,' Sam replied. 'This thing lost all structural integrity after one bite.'

She took a breath and smiled at Sam, who retained an expression of startled concern.

'Megs, what is it?' he pressed. 'If you came here because you're worried about me being weird with you now, it's okay. I won't be. I know how you feel.'

'No, you don't,' Megan said. 'You don't know. So I'm going to tell you.'

Sam's expression shifted to fear, and Megan realised she must be sounding downright threatening.

She shook her head and exhaled quickly, trying to pull it together. She managed to achieve a satisfactory level of stillness and calm as she looked into Sam's eyes.

'I love you.'

Sam's wrap hit the pavement with a wet *thwack*, but he remained perfectly still, his eyes fixed on hers.

'You're my scoop of ice-cream,' Megan continued, not caring if she was making sense. 'You're the thing I think I shouldn't have but I want all the time.'

Sam's face flushed and he began blinking quite rapidly.

'And you're not even bad for me.' She laughed. 'So why shouldn't I love you?'

Sam's arms had slowly come to rest at his sides. 'I don't know,' he said. 'No good reason?'

'No good reason,' Megan said. 'And I do. I do love you. I know that now. With every fibre of my being I know that. And even if you don't love me back, that's okay. I just needed to tell you that I ... like I said ...'

Megan couldn't read his face. He'd stopped blinking and was staring at her like she was covered in pig's blood.

'I love you, Sam,' she said, feeling her euphoria giving way to despair.

'Megs ...'

His tone was steady and low, and Megan realised how unreasonable and unfair this was. Sam had already said these exact words to her and she'd rejected him. She'd said no to love but pleaded for friendship, and now she was being a flip-flopping psycho who could clearly never be trusted in matters of the heart. Megan felt sure he was about to remind her of all of this, triggering a minimum three months' worth of heavy drinking, self-pity and aggressive burger eating. Her nose tingled as tears sprang to her eyes.

'Who wouldn't want to be ice-cream?' Sam said, taking a step towards her. 'Especially yours.'

He stepped closer still, reaching out to touch her cheek and letting a tear roll from her skin to his. Megan closed her eyes as Sam's other hand took her other cheek. She opened them again to see Sam looking at her with the wonder and delight of a child watching a shooting star.

'I love you, Megs,' he said softly. So softly she didn't believe she'd heard him at first.

'Still?' she spluttered, desperate.

Sam planted his feet firmly in front of her and pressed his hands gently into her cheeks, his right thumb drifting across her cheekbone. Her arms instinctively circled around his waist.

'Always,' Sam said. 'I love you so much it makes me literally swoon. I feel it in my stomach and my throat. My legs wobble when I know I'm going to see you. That's proper swooning.'

Megan laughed and moved her face towards his. Sam recoiled.

'Full disclosure. That wrap was seriously overloaded with garlic.'

Megan grinned as they stared at each other in a way they'd never allowed themselves to; not even when they'd kissed on camp. They stayed like that for an elastic moment, staring, grinning, discovering each other's faces as if for the first time.

'Garlic ice-cream,' Megan whispered. 'Ew.'

The elastic snapped back, and they kissed like they might never get the chance again.

Chapter Fifty-Nine
Lizzie

I'd always loved the Abela Easter Sunday lunch. It was the only family gathering where Aunty Carmen allowed the rest of us to take over the kitchen, so she could paint hard-boiled eggs and make Easter bonnets with the kids. It was an Abela tradition. Once the array of brightly coloured eggs were dried, the kids were herded into the storeroom while the adults hid the eggs around the backyard. Wearing their newly crafted Easter bonnets, no matter how hideous they might be, was mandatory for the Easter-egg hunt.

Dad always loved hiding the eggs in the most impossible places to find, like right under the bottom step of the outside deck, but somehow the Abela kids always managed to sniff them out. The real reward, and the only thing the kids cared about, came at the end of the hunt when the eggs were all found. Then, the hard-boiled eggs were replaced with chocolate ones and the kids were allowed to eat as many as they wanted ... *before* lunch!

But this Easter Sunday was more special than ever. This year, I got to share the day with both my family and my dearest friends.

When Megan brought some books into the hospital for me last week, Aunty Carmen was there, and she insisted on Megan and Sam and their kids all coming to Easter Sunday lunch. Megan happily accepted.

I wasn't the only one with special guests at today's family event. Ines was here, too.

Zara almost fell off her chair at dinner a few nights ago when I asked if she wanted to invite her girlfriend to Easter lunch. Max thought it was hilarious for about five seconds, until his two older, more evolved, siblings informed him that there was nothing wrong with Zara liking girls. Stella took it a step further by threatening to shove his face in his mashed potato if he ever laughed about it again.

Ines accepted the invitation and the two of them were now sitting with Zara's three older cousins at the end of the table, squealing and giggling as they painted eggs, and fashioned bonnets out of tissue paper, cotton balls and pipe cleaners. Seemed that even the cool teens still loved a bit of craft.

Stella and Lola were loving it, too. I watched as Stella proudly lifted up her impressive bunny-rabbit bonnet, complete with eyes, nose, whiskers and cute bunny ears. Lola squealed with delight and gave her a clap. Meanwhile, her floral-inspired bonnet looked like something straight out of an Audrey Hepburn movie. The child was in her element.

Sam offered to help in the kitchen as soon as he and Megan arrived, but Aunty Carmen wouldn't hear of it.

'Aunty Carmen,' Sam whined dramatically. 'You know I'm handy in the kitchen.'

'Are you an Abela?' Aunty Carmen asked, jabbing her forefinger at his face.

'Honorary?' Sam pleaded.

'Out, out, out,' Aunty Carmen barked, ushering Sam out of the kitchen like he was a wayward chook.

So now, Sam and Megan were sitting beside me, painting eggs, drinking beers and trash-talking.

The school camp was only two weeks ago, but so much had happened since then, it felt like months ago. A lot of what had transpired since camp had been bad, but some of it was good.

Really good.

Megan and Sam's relationship definitely fell into the 'really good' basket. I was still trying to get my head around seeing the two of them together – mooning over each other, holding hands and doing all that other lovey-dovey stuff that new couples did. I wouldn't want it any other way. They were perfect for each other.

'How did I not see it before?' Megan asked me in the hospital.

'You both had to be ready for it,' I said.

'Yeah, I think you're right.'

'And it's tricky to recognise the love of your life when you're rolling around in the hay with a teenage sexual dynamo twenty-four seven.'

'Right again.'

Megan met up with Harry for a coffee a week after camp. She felt she owed him that. She said it was awkward as hell, and that Harry spent the whole time alternating between being tearful, then indignant, then overly affectionate, then back to tearful, but at least they'd achieved closure.

'He told me he's started dating a twenty-eight-year-old,' Megan said afterwards.

'Good,' I said. 'Hopefully, he'll knock another ten years off again for his next squeeze and will finally be in his own dating demographic.'

Megan told me Sam had been supportive of her meeting up with Harry, as long as it was in a public place and they both remained fully dressed at all times. Sam might well have some residual jealousy issues to work through, but he and Megan were solid. Anyone could see it. Dave called them Dwayne, because they were 'as solid as The Rock'. Then again, Dave also called them MegaSam. It was the closest thing to Brangelina he could come up with.

The three of them had been absolute champions about helping Greg and me with the kids. Greg had been a constant at my side since he got back, and between my husband, Megan, Sam and Dave, they'd all been doing school drop-offs, pick-ups and running the Barrett kids around to their various extra-curricular activities. And I'd been more than happy to let them help. If I'd learned anything over the past few weeks, it was that I needed my friends. It was called a support network for a reason. In the first week he was back, Greg made me say, 'I can't do everything all the time' about twenty times. After a while, it actually sank in.

Aileen and Melissa both cried when I told them about the cancer over the phone, but since then they'd been the strong, brilliant women I'd always known. Melissa had been popping in to see me as often as she could, usually with a warm covered dish of some sort, and when I was in hospital having the lumpectomy, Aileen kept sneaking upstairs to visit me during her shifts.

'Shouldn't you be on the ward?' I'd asked her when she walked into my room for the fifth time that day.

'Kate's all over it,' Aileen had replied. 'The girl's turning into a fine young midwife. Still shits me to tears, but she's getting the job done.'

As expected, my family freaked out. I might have triggered some Mum-related post-traumatic stress in my brothers, and poor Dad broke down and wept, causing

Aunty Carmen to turn on him in fury.

'No tears!' she cried. 'Lizzie is strong and she's going to kick this fucking cancer right in the nuts!'

As fierce as Aunty Carmen sounded, I could hear the tremor in her voice. And when she hugged me to her, her heart was racing.

But having to tell the kids was the hardest thing Greg and I have ever had to do. I'd go through all four labours again in a heartbeat, rather than witness the expressions on my kids' faces when we told them I had cancer. There were a lot of tears and hugs, then many reassuring words about treatments and the miracles of modern medicine, but it was so difficult to allay fears when cancer was such a terrifying beast.

Greg and I finally accepted financial help from Dad and Aunty Carmen. It was going to make a big difference, and we (and they) knew we'd pay back every cent. It was a huge relief. Greg's workplace investigation was ongoing, but as far as Greg was concerned, it was the lowest of low priorities.

'I couldn't give two shits about it, buddy,' he said when I asked him how he was feeling. 'Money doesn't mean a thing. *You* mean everything.'

On the Monday after camp, Greg and I went into Gina's office, holding hands as Gina talked us through the next steps.

The first surgery I had last week went well, but they discovered that the cancer had spread to some nearby lymph nodes, so I was starting a new course of chemo. We were all trying to stay positive, but I could feel an undercurrent of dread and sadness in the restaurant today that seemed to be manifesting itself as a kind of manic merriment.

I'd been told I wasn't to lift a finger. I'd been placed at the head of the egg-painting table in Dad's comfy armchair, while everyone waited on me hand and foot. It was quite nice, actually. Although, I would have loved to be in the kitchen right now. I could hear Rosa berating Chris and Joey for not properly greasing a baking tray and they could definitely use my support.

'Here, Mum,' Zara said, walking towards me, carrying a huge colourful bonnet with 'Queen' spelled out in crepe paper across the front. 'Made this for you.'

'Thanks!'

She stood behind my chair and crowned me, as the whole table cheered with delight at how ridiculous I looked. Then, Zara leaned down, wrapped her arms around my neck and kissed me on the cheek.

'Love you, Mum.'

I reached my hands up to put them over hers on my chest. 'Love you, too, darling.'

Greg looked up from where he was helping Max paint eggs blue and purple (his favourite colours) at the other end of the table and smiled at me.

I knew then, in that moment, that if the worst happened – if I died – my kids would be fine. Every person in this room would make sure of that. I was their mum, and that was a mantle that couldn't be taken by any other creature on the planet, but having family was different. Family was a big, broad, ever-changing thing. It didn't just exist through bloodlines; it existed where love was unconditional and where kindred spirits met.

My despair about what might happen to my kids if they had to grow up motherless actually had nothing to do with fearing for their future without me. That despair was a simple and selfish heartbreak that came from knowing I might not be there to see it. And looking around this room, I knew – I had not a single doubt – that their future would be as bright as Aunty Carmen's wardrobe.

Epilogue

Eighteen months later...

'I thought you were doing the risotto,' Megan said, topping up Sam's wineglass sitting next to the stove.

Sam shook his head. 'Megs, I've told you. Risotto is the ultimate stovetop ball and chain. It's high maintenance.'

I nodded at Megan. 'Like you,' I said, bouncing gently on her kitchen stool, rocking the sleeping baby.

'Exactly,' Sam agreed. 'Lizzie gets it.'

'Then maybe you two should've hooked up.'

I fake-retched.

'Don't be like that,' Greg said after a good swig of his pale ale. 'You and Sam would make a cute couple.'

'Exactly,' Sam said, still facing the stove. 'Greg gets it, too. Never say never.'

Megan and I shared a look of abject disgust.

'Guess who's sleeping on the couch?' Megan shot back.

Sam turned to face us, his eyebrows high and mighty. 'I'm already sleeping on the couch,' he said, then pointed at the baby in my arms. 'That evil kid took my side of the bed weeks ago.'

'Don't call her that!' I leaned down close to her angelic face and whispered into her perfect ear. 'Don't you listen to your mean daddy.'

'Well, the evil kid doesn't have restless leg syndrome,'

Megan said. 'Or snore. So, she gets to share the bed.'

'The kids always win, mate,' Greg said to Sam without the hint of a joke.

When Ruby Wylie-Hatfield entered the world a year after her parents first kissed on a school camp, Oscar's class at Baytree Primary teamed up to make her a blanket. I immediately complained that I deserved it more than the baby, since I was the one who delivered her, after all. Also, my hair was then back to a length where the blanket would've made a perfect headscarf.

Ruby was almost six months old now, and we all adored her. Her parents were obviously besotted, but her three half-siblings were completely in love with her, too. I almost had to wrestle Lola to the floor today, just so I could take Ruby for a cuddle.

I'd never forget the first morning Sam turned up to drop-off with an Esky in one hand and Megan's hand in the other, a few weeks after they started going out. The looks on the scandalised Baytree parents' faces were priceless – Nicola gave them 'a month, tops' – but the school community soon adjusted to the sight of Sam and Megan as a couple at functions, or when they occasionally witnessed inappropriate public displays of affection in the schoolyard.

Within a few short months, and with their kids' blessings, Megan had rented out her terrace and she and Oscar moved in with Sam, Lola and Tyler.

'When you know, you know!' Megan had said. 'Why wait? Life is short.'

'Thanks for the reminder,' I'd said.

Sam had rolled his eyes. 'Lizzie, you'll outlive us all.'

'Jesus,' I'd moaned. 'That's nearly as depressing as cancer.'

'Easy there, buddy,' Greg had said. 'Nothing wrong with a long life.'

With their new living arrangement, Oscar and Tyler thought all their Christmases had come at once. Endless hours of PlayStation and *Star Wars* movie marathons lay before them. Aunty Carmen loved pointing out to Megan and Sam, at every given opportunity, that they were living in sin. And Megan and Sam loved pointing out to Aunty Carmen that she didn't know the half of it, which of course, she loved.

The Cozy Corner was doing well. Since taking over, Megan had given the place a total makeover, complete with quirky second-hand furniture, a variety of pot plants and she even stripped back the plaster to reveal the original red-brick walls. The oldies loved the new look. They considered themselves the funkiest seniors in the south these days. Megan had also set up a few different initiatives with local community groups for the café, including poetry slams, open-mic nights (Sam had a regular gig there; Ellie and Helen were his number-one fans) and local art and photography exhibitions. A month before Ruby was born, Megan even included a couple of her own shots in one of the exhibitions.

'I didn't know you were into photography!' Dave had said when he saw Megan's name at the bottom of a series of African photos.

'You're not the only Dark Horse around here, Dave,' Megan had teased.

Dave had beamed. 'Maybe I'll teach you how to wrangle a snake one day!'

'No thanks.'

We all went along to the exhibition. Even Lola and

Stella's acting teacher, Rachel, came. She and Megan got along really well. At one point I overheard Rachel suggesting to Megan that the café would be a great space for a visual art installation ... and something about glitter on a cat.

The café walls were now adorned with Megan's photographs, some old, some new. She'd even started a wall of fame where she displayed an ever-growing collection of photos entitled *Customer of the Month*. It had become quite the Applewood honour to have Megan hang your picture in The Cozy Corner.

Apart from his thriving takeaway food business at Baytree Primary, Sam was also doing the odd Sunday-arvo gig around the corner at Bar 404. Megan and Ruby were always first on the dancefloor, which meant that Sam had to play at least one Wiggles song.

Since the investigation at his Sydney workplace, which absolved my husband of any wrongdoing, Greg had gone all entrepreneurial, too, starting his own small construction business. He said he never wanted to be put in the position of having to leave his family, or be at the whim of an arsehole boss, ever again.

After my annual check-up this year, when I was given the all clear, I allowed myself to feel happy and relieved for a few days, but I'd learned to live with the constant expectation that I'd find another lump. That would never go away, and it hung like a pall over every goddamn waking moment. But I'd had to choose between spending my days dreading a recurrence or living.

It sounded like an easy choice, but it wasn't. It took focus and persistence and fortitude to keep making that choice every day. And it was a fragile state. The dread could kick down the door at any moment, and then I had to stare it down until it retreated again. People fought worse every day, so I couldn't and wouldn't complain. I was alive.

Stella ran into the kitchen. 'It's starting!'

Sam, Megan and I immediately scrambled for prime position in front of the TV in the lounge room. Seeing as I had a sleeping baby in my arms, I scrambled a little more carefully than the others.

There, on the TV, was Rania Jalali, looking as effortlessly gorgeous as ever.

Megan sighed beside me on the couch. 'Why is it that only the most beautiful women get access to a hair and makeup department to help them look *even better*?'

'Life's unfair,' Sam said.

Megan shot him a death stare.

'I mean, there's no hair and makeup department in the world that could improve your beauty, my love.'

Greg leaned over and whispered in Sam's ear, 'Abort, abort!' He didn't.

'No, you know what I mean, it's because I think ...'

'Do you want the couch to be permanent?'

The kids turned from their cross-legged positions on the floor and scowled at us. '*Shush!*'

Rania looked into the camera and began to speak in her perfect TV hostess voice. '*Welcome back,*' she said. '*Three years ago, in a comic bookstore in downtown Los Angeles, an Australian-made graphic novel caught the eye of an American teenager, who became so obsessed with* Codename: Code *that he started reading it at the dinner table every night. His mother became so frustrated that she confiscated the book, hiding it in her bedside drawer, until one fateful night weeks later, she found it in there and decided to read it for herself. That mother's name was*

Laura Vallanté, a Hollywood power player who's produced some of the most successful TV shows of the last decade. And after reading Codename: Code, *she knew she'd found her next big hit. Please welcome the creator of* Codename: Code, *via satellite from his temporary home in LA, Dave Podanski.'*

A huge cheer went up around the room. There he was, our mate, on TV!

He was wearing the same glasses he'd had for the entire time we'd known him, and a typical Dave T-shirt (this one with an image of the Hulk holding an avocado with the word SMASH under it), but he'd been kitted out in a slick charcoal blazer and the hair and makeup department had given his thinning locks a decent spruce.

'*Dave Podanski, welcome,*' Rania continued. '*How's La La Land?*'

Dave beamed into the camera, his eyes a bit too wide. '*Hi, Rania, ha ha, yeah really awesome, thank you. Thanks for having me.*'

'*It's our pleasure, Dave. Now, this is an amazing sto—*'

'*You know, Rania,*' Dave interrupted, '*we actually had kids at the same school for a bit. You probably don't remember, but yeah, we met.*'

Rania smiled. '*Actually, I do, Dave. My son was only there for a short time, but I remember you very well.*'

No amount of TV makeup could hide Dave's blush. '*Really?*'

'*Of course!*' Rania said, throwing up her hands. '*You and your friends were so great and made me feel really welcome ...*'

'That's us!' Sam yelled, sloshing wine onto his jeans and not caring. 'She's talking about us!'

'*... especially Lizzie,*' Rania continued. '*Hi, Lizzie, if you're watching!*'

Everyone turned to look at me and screamed. Zara looked like her head was about to explode. Greg squeezed my knee.

'Hi, Rania.' I saluted the TV.

'*Oh, they're watching all right!*' Dave shouted. '*They're making a night of it back there in Melbourne. Hi, guys! I'll be home soon.*'

As everyone in the room cheered and waved back at Dave, I leaned down and gently pressed the tip of my nose to Ruby's.

'Aunty Lizzie's your favourite, isn't she?' I whispered. 'Yes, she is. Yes, she *is*.'

Acknowledgements

In Lin Manuel Miranda's musical *Hamilton*, the eponymous character sings about his ability to write his way out – out of poverty and out of strife, and subsequently into the history books. But during Melbourne's strict lockdown due to the Virus That Shall Not Be Named, we found ourselves having to write our way *in* – into sanity, into a sense of stability and, if all went well, eventually out of our tracksuit pants. The result of all that writing was *The Pick-up*.

Along with our amazing families, our dear friends have always occupied an important space in our lives. We're blessed to have many special, long-term friendships. We keep in touch with each other, check in on each other, support and champion each other. Lockdown brought an even more intense sense of connection with our nearest and dearest. Checking in took on more import; being there for each other became more crucial. New connections were made too. We sent out so many advance copies of *The Drop-off* (our prequel to *The Pick-up*) that we're now on a first-name basis with the woman at our local post office.

We weren't always so community-minded. In truth, we initially felt the same way about volunteering at our kids' school as Lizzie does about going on school camp in *The Pick-up*. When our eldest daughter first donned a school uniform, we had no interest in making new friends. We were in our thirties, for God's sake; surely our friend-making days were done and dusted. And we were *way* too busy with our *very* busy lives to volunteer at our daughters' primary school. We were struggling artists! We couldn't afford to be doing work *for free*!

Then someone at school got wind of the fact that we were artsy types and asked if we could help out with an upcoming school production. For the next seven years we found ourselves writing, directing and stage managing the bi-annual school productions, as well as co-ordinating all of the stage events at the school fetes. And we loved every second of it. Not only that, but our experiences inspired our web series, *The Drop-off*, which led to the novel of the same name, and now here we are a couple of years down the track with *The Pick-up*. Dipping our toes into that school community has informed and enriched our professional and personal lives beyond measure. Today, we can't imagine what our lives might be if we'd stayed true to our selfish ways!

But throughout 2020, all of that felt like ancient history. The rehearsals, the gatherings, the mums' nights, the working bees, congregating at the school drop-off … it all felt like a lost world. Heading into the halfway point of 2021, there's a growing realisation about the importance of one's neighbourhood, one's community. Community spirit seems to be reforming and galvanising in entirely new and different ways. Let's hope it continues to evolve and take hold.

The Pick-up was only possible because of friends and colleagues who have become our extended and beloved community. We want to say a huge thank you to all of them here.

To the truly awesome team of women at Echo Publishing. Tegan Morrison, we can't express how much it means to us to know that you always have our back. Thank you for motivating us to keep going when the Melbourne winter lockdown was particularly depressing and we felt like we couldn't possibly write one more word. Your beautiful spirit, kindness, encouraging words and passion kept us going in the dark times. Benny Agius, your smiling face and ebullience came right through those Zoom calls and gave us so much joy. We couldn't ask for a more enthusiastic, supportive or joyous general manager. Thank you too to Echo's marketing guru, Rosie Outred, for all of your excellent work in getting *The Pick-up* out into the world, and to Emily Baynard, for being the sort of publicist who deserves more publicity than the authors she champions.

To our brilliant editor, Alexandra Nahlous, and proofreader, Rod Morrison, for keeping our word count in check and reining us in when we went too far or not far enough. Thank you for helping us shape our book into something much better than it would have been without the benefit of your sharp minds.

To our dear, trusted peers and friends who either took the time to read the book at various stages of (in) completion, talk through characters and storylines with us through our masks on long walks along the foreshore. Your feedback, comments and expertise were invaluable. Thank you in particular to Kylie Jeffares, Zarmeen Hassan, Rose Jost, Judi McCrossin, Irma McCrossin, Mark Stracey, Dr Jane Isaac and Sammy J. Also, a huge thank you to Fiona's most excellent myotherapist, Maddie Bellis, and physiotherapists, Adam Joffe and Bernie Simai, for keeping her arm, neck and back in working order throughout the marathon writing months!

Finally, to Finn and Abbie. Thank you both for indulging our boring 'work' conversations at the dinner table and for reminding us when to switch off after hours. Thanks also for always making time to read the kid- and teen-related excerpts in the book and giving us your brutally honest and much-appreciated opinions, and apologies for the times we heard you giggling and ran into the room screaming, *'Which bit is that?!'*

We love you both so much. It's all for you.

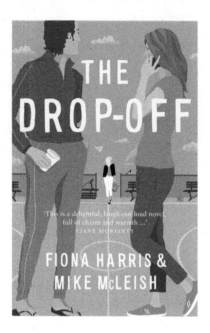

THE DROP-OFF

At Baytree Primary, it's the adults who are behaving like children.

Lizzie, Megan and Sam don't play by the rules. Lizzie is a part-time midwife with four kids and a secret past. Sam is a stay-at-home dad whose marriage is on the brink. Megan is a former model with a son, a thriving business and no time for loneliness. None of them are very interested in the world of school concerts and working bees . . . until the day the lollipop man dies and ruins everything . . .

> 'A cross between Kitty Flanagan and Liane Moriarty, *The Drop-off* will make you laugh and cry while reminding us all of the redemptive power of friendship, community and good coffee.'
> – *Herald Sun*